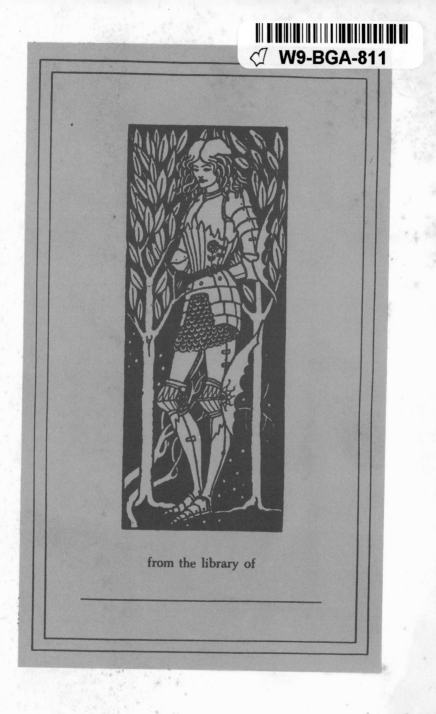

from the library of

_____

THE LADY FROM BOSTON

The Lady from Boston

Tom McHale

Doubleday & Company, Inc., Garden City, New York
1978

Library of Congress Cataloging in Publication Data

McHale, Tom.
  The lady from Boston.

  I. Title.
PZ4.Ml492Lad   [PS3563.A3115]   813'.5'4
ISBN: 0-385-01865-7
Library of Congress Catalog Card Number 76–42370
Copyright © 1978 by Tom McHale

For Sara and for Gerrity

PART ONE

Aldrich–1975

CHAPTER 1

Aldrich at North Hollow

Poor Dwight David Aldrich: inevitable victim of the sad clash of his really shameless posturings for universal moral reform and just plain low-down greed. All told he had thought that for people like himself America was really quite a manageable Republic from sea to shining sea, until all sorts of unforeseens ganged up on him and harshly smote him down.

He sat out the winter of '74 (comforting Bourbon whiskey at hand even though he was widely overheard calling this his penitential season) in the Northeast Kingdom of Vermont in the near-ruined monument to his short-lived entrepreneurial dream that had turned into a veritable chimera of implacable investors, stung environmentalists, warring lawyers, heedless creditors, heartless utilities and poker-faced auditors of the IRS who were determined to get a cut of the rubble for their Uncle. The rubble was what remained of North Hollow—a four-season family-oriented condominium vacation village—that was systematically being burned, dynamited and otherwise toppled down around Aldrich with a genuinely admirable precision.

Dwight David Aldrich had enemies who unhappily were not ethereal and spooky Green Mountain out-of-stater-hating spirits. They were for real, and entered the island of brigand lawlessness that North Hollow had become on snowshoes or cross-country skies, horseback, and once even a Caterpillar tractor stolen from the Vermont State Highway Department

3

to send up their offerings of destruction to whatever punitive little godling it was that had it in for Aldrich.

The State Police had no idea of the destroyers' identity keen enough to call for the actual issuance of an arrest warrant, and of late their science had degenerated to a low-stakes barracks' lottery on when and how those very destroyers would strike again. In short there seemed to be not a single person on a long list of possible suspects without a reasonable alibi, even if it were as invidious as the assertion of need to repress the memory of any dealings whatever with Dwight David Aldrich.

They were not local folk either; he was convinced of that. North Hollow lay aside the shambling little Vermont village of Inglenook that ancestors of Dwight David Aldrich had founded on the run from creditors in England a bicentennial's time ago. The animosity of the village was real enough (the righteous certainty that generations of Aldrich genes since the Revolution had spawned an uncommon number of idiots and misfits in Inglenook and the rest of the Northeast Kingdom as well), but it had a more muted expression: the hell-raising kids out for beer parties and early pregnancies of a midsummer's night on the North Hollow golf course fairway that Aldrich feared to run off; or the snowmobilers that roamed the land unchecked during winter for whatever witless pleasure a snowmobiler derived from snowmobiling; or the tacit Vermonter's unseeing snub when he occasioned to pass one on the street that somehow hurt more than a sledgehammer blow full in the face. But it was none of these people. Burning, dynamiting and pulling down another man's buildings was simply not their style.

Whoever they were, the destroyers of North Hollow lacked any reasonable compassion in Aldrich's opinion. After they had done two condominium clusters and it became evident they did not intend stopping at the remaining seven, he had printed up five hundred pleading handbills and

posted them all about the buildings and in the forest sur-
rounding North Hollow.

Dear Sirs:
I am currently undergoing a penitential season for all the
wrongs against Man and Nature I have committed in the
past. Might not my estrangement from the community of
Man and intense scrutiny of conscience I am undertaking
serve to indicate my heartfelt repentance for whatever
abuses you consider I have perpetrated against you?
                                        Contritely,
                                        D. D. Aldrich

Their response came after the handbills had fluttered and
weathered on the trees for more than three weeks and
Aldrich dared to think their rampage was ended. He returned
from a brief foray to Montreal for servicing by a prostitute
to find that the rampage was on again, another building was
gone, and that a wide cloth banner was tied up between two
trees proclaiming in large block letters for all the world to see:
YOU ARE NOT NEARLY PENITENT ENOUGH!

Now in the bitter cold depths of late February, his
memory exhausted, his winter penitential season more than
half done, part of Aldrich was affected with a curious calm
and resignation: Many things had bottomed out. They had
done six buildings already, they would doubtless do the three
more left to go. If they kept at their schedule, the destruction
of North Hollow would be complete by early April, and
Aldrich was certain that spring, besides bringing thaw and
rebirth, would bring him the names of his enemies as well.
There was a keen telepathy between them already; he sensed
a fierce and determined pride in their prowess and cunning
that would not ever be satisfied until they let him know who
they were and why they had done him so much wrong. Then
they would try to kill him. He was certain of that also: just
as they had assassinated his ex-wife, Liddy, with a high-
powered rifle on the steps of an Episcopal church in Boston

on the day, short weeks before, of her remarriage to another. They would tell him why they had done that one, too. Aldrich was especially curious about that.

Every day now, Aldrich's heart quickened more with anticipation at all the news the spring thaw would bring.

CHAPTER 2

Resignation Day

Aldrich's penitential season began at roughly the same moment in summer 1974 as his hero, Richard M. Nixon, resigned the presidency of the United States. Up until then, North Hollow still had a fighting chance for survival because Dwight David Aldrich was still there fighting with his usual blind and blunt resolve that he liked to think was uniquely akin to his President's own. Unfortunately for Aldrich, that same resolve gave way on an August day with a loud and shuddering crack forty floors up in a Manhattan tower in the office of an original North Hollow investor named Augustus Raabe, whom Aldrich was trying to dun for more money.

Before him, across the wide expanse of a smooth-grained leather-topped desk, a gray and sickly Raabe spoke distractedly of the foolishness of throwing good money after bad, his eyes traveling the line of sunburst haze above the long hedge of trees on the crest of the Jersey Palisades across the Hudson. He popped into his mouth two or three of the tiny pellets of breath freshener that he chewed interminably and fresh waves of cinnamon and clove wafted over the desk toward Aldrich. Aldrich searched the rheumy eyes that would not look at him and decided that if Raabe did not black out and altogether collapse out of his chair in a defense maneuver, he would yet find a way to cull a token number of bucks out of the man this day. It only meant finding a means. Aldrich was good at that. He turned a shrewd eye on the face that had begun sweating despite the loud hum of air conditioning, wondering if he should offer to supply the girl he bunked with currently for a couple of nights' trysting in some quaint old Vermont inn, or himself even, if Raabe had any homosexual inclinations and was not overly discriminating about apprentice methods.

"Mr. Raabe . . . ?"

"Call me Augustus, Aldrich. All my friends call me Augustus. Don't you find it amazing how beautiful tree-studded New Jersey conspires to look from the right distance and with the proper density of smog cover? It's a symbolic promise for the future, I tell you. Men can reverse the cycle of nature-rape, reprogram that old lady computer for a second whirl that will be gentle lovemaking generations long. Of course Metropolitan New York will never be that lovely state of mind called Vermont that you live in. But there is hope for us. Just last week someone fished a salmon out of New York Harbor. It was dead, of course, but it died trying, and that means it had a pretty good notion that the way to the upper Hudson was passable, that the degree of pollution that has kept salmon out of here for more than fifty years is abating. There's hope, Aldrich."

"I don't doubt it, Augustus. I don't doubt it at all. But it's a damn sight safer return on your money to participate now in the current rape of Vermont than the proposed reclamation of Metropolitan New York, if you see my meaning."

Aldrich laughed his best practical businessman's conspiratorial laugh, slapping his arms across his chest in easy camaraderie with himself, and Augustus Raabe turned a hardened glance on him, stared him straight in the eye for the first time.

"I do, Aldrich. I do indeed. And that's why I couldn't permit myself to invest any more money in North Hollow. It's against my principles. My conscience couldn't live with it . . ."

"Your fucking conscience wasn't anywhere in sight when I made the original North Hollow proposal to you, friend Augustus."

8

"Why should it have been? Do you think I keep it handy like the revolver I keep in my desk for self-defense? I thought I was dealing with an honest gentleman, not a goddam landscape rapist. They should have banished you from Vermont by legislative fiat for putting up that tumbledown Disneyland you call North Hollow. It absolutely defies every law of man and nature, to say nothing of aesthetics into the bargain."

"You've never even seen the place, Raabe!" Aldrich hurled at him, rising dramatically from his chair to pound a calculatedly enraged fist into the leather covering of the desk. Such intensity was not lost on Augustus Raabe: He snapped open a desk drawer and whipped out a pearl-handled revolver that he pointed right between Aldrich's eyes: "Sit down, Dwight David, or I'll blow your ass off."

Aldrich sat down, less terrified by the gun than fascinated by the harsh western twang of Raabe's words, the steely glint of the normally suffering eyes that told the act of getting the drop on his adversary had been much practiced. Leather fetish? Aldrich wondered. A touch of S and M? Anyhow, some sort of little cowboy lived in a secret place in Augustus Raabe who commuted home to Westchester in a chauffeured Cadillac limousine. Aldrich might easily have carried the day if he had known enough to wear the Stetson hat and Frye boots legacy of his native Kansas into Raabe's paneled offices. Across the desk the gunslinger lay down his iron with the business end pointed at Aldrich. His eyes cast downward at the burnished leather covering, seeking his own reflection. Narcissistically appeased evidently, he even smiled somewhat indulgently at Aldrich.

"Now I'm just gonna keep this little peacemaker on top here, Dwight David. You're a big strong boy with a mean-ass temper 'n I don't need any trouble from you, friend, if you understand my meanin' . . ."

"Aw, shit, Augustus . . . Ah'm truly sorry," Aldrich drawled in Kansan vowels even wider than the ones he had been trying to leave behind in the four years since he had

9

moved East to New England. "It's just that you haven't even seen North Hollow one time, 'n you're makin' such uncharitable statements about the place."

"Ah've seen it, Dwight David. Ah flew over it one time in a airplane. Ah'll tell you the sight just caused palpitations in my poor heart. Ah might've dropped a bomb if Ah'd had one with me. For me to have landed would've meant a surefire coronary. From one thousand feet up North Hollow is a mean-lookin' mining camp, Ah can tell you."

"Then that speaks well of mah original idea, Augustus. Complete rusticity was the ideal in the plannin' of North Hollow. A new departure, if you see my meanin'. There's been too much shlock 'n imitation cutsie-pie Tyrolean Swiss second-home development in Vermont already. It degrades the New England aesthetic to look down from a low-flyin' plane 'n suddenly see a clustered little village that ought to be sittin' below the Matterhorn."

"It degrades it even worse, Dwight David, to look down 'n find a gen-u-ine instant slum, if you see mah meanin'. It's too bad that Mr. Robert Altman has already produced his marvelous film *McCabe and Mrs. Miller*. Otherwise, we might be able to get back about ten cents on the dollar by sellin' North Hollow to Mr. Altman to use as his minin' camp set. Course he'd have to dub in the mountains since there ain't any anywhere near North Hollow. . . . Tell me, Dwight David, what part of Kansas do you hail from?"

"Abilene."

"Never been there. Been up to Dodge City, though. Know the Marshal, Mr. Dillon. Fine gentleman."

"Ah know him, too," Aldrich twanged desperately, willing to go a loonie's limit if it brought in the bucks. Outside in the twentieth century a helicopter whumped past, lower down than the height of the fortieth floor where two grown men played *Gunsmoke* in the middle of a business day. On the river tugs nudged a cruise ship out of its berth, ready for the swing downstream. The sun played brilliantly over the roofs of cars rushing both ways on the West Side Highway. Aldrich prepared to surge on, but Millie, the investor's secretary, marched in unannounced and, wildly ebullient at that moment, went up to her boss and whispered something in his ear, her face a great wreath of a smile that Raabe instantly matched with his own. She picked up the revolver, pointed it at a horrified Aldrich and squeezed the trigger. The gun went off with the clap! of a cap pistol while she laughed delightedly at the joke and flipped the smoking weapon into Aldrich's lap. Raabe hopped up and did a little jig for joy beside his desk. Aldrich was absolutely astounded to realize he had not been shot.

"Well, what do you know! That son of a bitch Nixon resigned! Now maybe we can get this fuckin' country back on the track. No, Aldrich, I can't lend you any more money. Come on, Millie, let's go out and get liquid for lunch. There may even be street dancing this afternoon. Goodbye, Aldrich. Good luck. I'm already hard at work on my North Hollow tax write-off . . . You should be, too, pardner . . ."

Nixon resigned: Something snapped, then collapsed in Aldrich, the sinewy interior bands perhaps that until now held the Nixon-like gut-fighter part of him taut and suspicious and ever opportunistic. He resisted the urge to hurl an imprecation after the investor and his playful Millie, instead hissed downcountry toward Washington at the resignee: Thou traitor! Why didn't you tough it out yourself like you're always telling the rest of us to do?

He stood a long moment before the great expanse of window that gave out on the West Side towers that declined away toward the river, staring down at the files of insects who marched along the canyon streets, curious as to whether they would all come together like New Year's revelers in Times Square to celebrate the resignation. North Hollow was a dead duck: The final admission came to him in a single rush, overwhelming him, blanketing the torrid energy of his mind that might normally have produced three fund-raising alterna-

tives to the rejection by Augustus Raabe, even if the alternatives were only comfortable illusion for the time being. Nothing so overextended as North Hollow could survive, even in
America. For the first time in his life Aldrich thought of suicide. He tapped the heavy glass before him loudly, deciding
its thickness would require a full running lunge across the
room to make it to the freer air of his death place outside.
Forty floors down, between the pedestrian files, a solid carpet
of cars negotiated Sixth Avenue. He saw himself falling atop
one of them, then bouncing to other roofs with elastic intensity until he flipped ingloriously and pretty much unrecog-
nizable off a last roof and onto the sidewalk. Then he would
become but a worn cliché in the *Daily News* since he carried
only his alternate set of Kansas ID cards with him these days.
YOUNG MAN FROM THE PROVINCES ACKNOWL-
EDGES HIS FAILURE TO SUCCEED IN GOTHAM.

Behind Aldrich the investor's accountant may have sur-
mised the death wish.

"The last one that went out that window was Gus's
brother, Richard. I went down to identify him. He looked like
a pizza pie, but he was smiling. Yes, he was a smiling pizza
pie."

"Why did he do it? Bad investments?"

"No, a woman. This family knows all about money. It's a
woman they don't understand."

Aldrich caught sight of himself smiling disdainfully in the
window reflection at the notion of anyone leaping forty stories
because of a woman.

"Of course, you couldn't get through that glass anyhow,
Aldrich. A truck couldn't. It's the strongest stuff there is. Gus
ordered it himself and saw to the installation."

"Why so impenetrable?"

"Gus's melancholia. He's felt like it so many times that
he's afraid it's in the blood. He guards against it everywhere.
You should see his house out in Westchester. Enormous. A palace. But only a one-story palace."

"Western ranch?" Aldrich inquired.

"Close. Adobe hacienda. Very Spanish. Heavy timbers."

"What a waste of good views," the architect in Aldrich judged. "Besides, life is so cheap anyhow. You could die trying to get the cork out of a wine bottle. Your heart could go from the strain."

"You're right. But then it's a heart attack. Not suicide. There isn't any stigma. A heart attack doesn't imply the death wish. Doesn't raise the eyebrows and cause that clucking of tongues that's only a kind of self-congratulations anyhow. See what I mean?"

"I see," Aldrich agreed. In that instant he decided he would only commit suicide if Nixon did; and Nixon never would, even if there were a Mishima down there in his heart of hearts. So nobody was going to go a-clucking over Aldrich's stigma, especially considering the number of people for whom that clucking might turn out to be self-congratulations in the delirious extreme. Aldrich shored himself up for the leave-taking. He shook hands with the informant accountant with condescending politeness, hinting at the man's untrustworthiness, then left the investor's offices for the street, where the people were not dancing for joy over the resignation, but simply looked as preoccupied as New Yorkers always did to Aldrich with successfully negotiating the next step . . .

Aldrich could not think of another thing to do but return to Vermont. The day was a dismal failure, except for cheating Death. He walked west through the theater district on Forty-fifth Street, obligingly shaking hands with a bum with a bottle tucked under his arm who did a shambling Resignation Day soft-shoe in the middle of Eighth Avenue while traffic-bound cab drivers looked on and actually laughed.

"It's a great day for a drink, isn't it, pal?" the bum delighted. "It's so rare you get a chance to celebrate anything but your own birthday nowadays. And I won't feel a twit of guilt over it either. Today's the day for a national binge by a guiltless public."

"Was Nixon a personal enemy of yours?" Aldrich quizzed. A cab slid by them and a florid-faced woman hung out the window fanning herself with a filthy handkerchief and screaming at the dancing bum: "Here's a dollar, cutie! Dance some more for me!" Aldrich took the dollar and handed it to the man, resisting the urge to clobber the woman with his briefcase because he could not think of a way to call it an accident. The bum made an elaborate curtsy, then started his dance again, staring all the while at Aldrich.

"To answer your question, sir, yes, he was a personal enemy of mine. Richard Milhous Nixon and I are the same age but for four days and you can't imagine how embarrassing it was of late to realize that the man my own mother proposed as my chief competitor in life was toasting Chairman Mao in Peking while I was falling down drunk and getting rolled in Chinatown, New York. And all this because my heart was too pure, and for no other reason."

"Fuck your pure heart! Look at the man's roots! Look at how far Nixon had come to the office of the presidency. Doesn't that at least impress you, that kind of determination and resolve?"

"No, it only frightened me. And I don't label it determination and resolve or anything laudable. I call it a winning streak of the kind that reflects damagingly on the country in which it occurs. America is redeemed today in the eyes of this poor drunk you see dancing for joy before you. Otherwise, before too long I should have had to go into exile and unhappily renounce my citizenship. Leaving my fucking mother behind, I might add . . ."

"We Nixonites are going to have to tuck in our wings for a while after today," Aldrich said gravely to the world at large. He thought of Nixon's hero De Gaulle returning to Paris from the Colombey exile to reorder the chaos of France: "We'll let the crazies have the running of the country until it's evident there's a dire need for him to return from San Clemente."

14

Then a private car with Jersey plates and full of kids
stopped right beside him and began energetically boiling over
in the heat. The kids started a furious crescendo of cursing to
a background clamor of angry horns and Aldrich remembered
suddenly that he meant to return to the quiet of Vermont. He
bade goodbye to the heedless dancing bum, who was trying to
hoist himself to the trunk lid of another stopped taxi, for
greater exposure perhaps, and snatched the florid lady's dollar
bill from the man's hand as he walked briskly past.

"Buy a drink on me with that buck you just stole, pal,"
the bum called after him, then fell from the trunk lid onto the
street, where his bottle shattered on the pavement. Aldrich
looked back, curious to know if the man was about to be run
over. But a truck halted in time with a loud screech of brakes
and Nixon's joyous rival still lived to celebrate.

On Tenth Avenue Aldrich bought a case of cold beer for
the trip home that he carried on his shoulder to his pickup in
a lot on Forty-third Street. He put the case on the seat beside
him and began negotiating the truck out of the city, cracking
his first brew as he ascended the ramp to the northbound
lanes of the West Side Highway. Before him, cresting the top
of the ramp, was a swaying busload of black kids who were
hanging out the window jubilantly chanting: "Nixon is dead!
Nixon is dead!"

Aldrich raged within: Good riddance to all that Ken-
nedyesque potato love of my undergraduate days that so determined to integrate a nation that one Dwight David Aldrich
of Abilene, Kansas, actually got his skull creased a couple of
times in places like Kansas City and Hannibal, Missouri, for
his egalitarian ardor. And where was that marvelous idealism
that had seemed to him a buoyant and exhilarating certainty
that America was about to make a racial about-face as soon as
doubtless shining and well-intended young men like Dwight
David Aldrich completed the conversion of the red necks?
Spent and gone, thank God!

In retrospect, what a waste of time it had all been. He

had believed in the U.S. role in Vietnam, become chary of blacks even before King's assassination, annoyed by either the endless whining petulance over their deprivation or the polemical abuse they heaped upon him merely for being white, trying to reverse the onetime black slavery of bondage into a new American white slavery of guilt. They had been in the forefront of the antiwar movement, too. But Aldrich had seen through them, he congratulated himself, seen their master plan soon enough to become smoldering livid when those black demands for financial reparations or a separate U.S. state began pouring in. Militancy everywhere, campus blacks started turning inward and scorning whites at a time when Aldrich found it quite convenient to be scorned. In 1968, in his third year of graduate training in architecture, when Martin Luther King was shot, Aldrich enjoyed a quite pleasant catharsis, and went out the very next day and joined the Young Americans for Freedom. In the bristling company of stung young midwestern conservatives from the Goldwater campaign and embittered veterans of Vietnam, Aldrich was home to stay.

"You fucking rat warren of little overbreeders," he screamed at the busload of black kids, who were already sure they had his goat about something and capitalized on fanning his anger with slurs and obscene gestures. Bastards! Was it the conversion of the red necks he had once proposed? What presumption! Thank God they had resisted the tinselly new faith of liberal pipe smokers in Bass Weejuns: If anything, it was Aldrich himself who had been converted and like any new convert he was strong in the faith. His most fervent wish now was that all the kids were somehow packed together in the confines of a tiny Volkswagen that he might harass repeatedly with the high bumpers of the pickup. Ahead of him, seeing his license plates no doubt, the kids had penciled out a sign on cardboard and pressed it to the rear window of the bus: Vermont Sucks.

Nearly apoplectic at that insult, Aldrich popped open another beer after dropping the first can out the window, then grew suddenly calm with cunning: You could not attack a bus with a pickup truck, obviously, but what if all those kids were on their way to Fresh Air Camp for a couple of weeks in Vermont, of all places? Aldrich fell behind the bus about a hundred feet, watchful as a fox, checking the tight superior smile of his lips in the rearview mirror, thinking delightedly of the punishment for their impudence he might wreak with a few well-placed phone calls to the capitol at Montpelier if he determined those kids were meant to clear their lungs in the unpolluted blades of the Green Mountains. But in minutes more the bus swung off the West Side Highway into Harlem, the Vermont Sucks sign thrown contemptuously out a window at him, and Aldrich was left again with only the frustration of his massive anger against blacks in general.

In time he crossed the George Washington Bridge and gained the Palisades Parkway, heading north for the New York State Thruway. He stopped at the first roadside rest and got out to finish his third beer, standing on the precipice of the Hudson, staring downriver at the smogged-in towers of Manhattan. When he had drained the beer, he flung the can furiously against a rock, to his own mind a symbolic throwing down of the gauntlet against the enemies of Mr. Nixon and himself.

But his thoughts grew graver as he turned about to furtively pee, considering that for the life of him he just did not know where to start.

CHAPTER 3

Three Wayfarers
at an Inn

Three hours and twenty cans of beer later, Aldrich crossed the state line from New York to Vermont at the little village of Arlington, then headed north up U.S. 7 to Manchester, where he thought to stop before darkness for a moderating sandwich at a favorite small inn, to avoid falling asleep at the wheel trying to make the last leg home to North Hollow.

Inside the bar he spied the Abbé Gaston out for an evening in civilian dress, seated before the bar mirror, looking slightly drunk, smiling fondly at his own image, and adjusting his battered old trademark of a beret for effect. A newly penciled sign taped to the mirror just to the left of the priest's reflection promised a free Resignation Day drink after the first purchase. The Abbé frowned sourly at the sight of Aldrich.

"*Monsieur l'Abbé, bon soir!* Nice summer day, hasn't it been?"

"It was, Aldrich. It was a lovely day until now. If you turn around and go away it will be a wonderful day all over again until darkness. Then it will be a wonderful night, I promise you. Just go away."

The Abbé Gaston was a French-speaking Swiss from Lausanne who had left his monastery in Switzerland in the late fifties and because of a spiritual crisis had come to Vermont to teach skiing. The crisis done, he had stayed to found a monastery near Stratton Mountain. It was built of stone and timber atop a craggy peak someone had given him that was negotiable only halfway by vehicle. This left a hard climb up to the feathering edge of the timberline. After winter storms it was sometimes impassable for days. Aldrich and Liddy, his ex-wife, had been marooned there for eight days the previous December. Aldrich reached for the Abbé's hand, intending to kiss it with a Kansas parody of Old World reverence. The Abbé snatched the hand away: "Don't touch me, Aldrich, or a chancre will grow on that hand!"

"Aren't you holding a grudge just a bit overly long, Abbé? You Catholic clergy are required to be forgiving, aren't you? I didn't know the State Police were going to raid the monastery."

"Ah, you never told me you had kidnapped your wife when you brought her there last December. You said you were in spiritual crisis, that you'd come together to try to save your marriage. When she seemed incoherent, I assumed she was distraught. I didn't know she was drugged. You lied to me, Aldrich," the Abbé snarled, plunking down his martini glass with a quick nod to the bartender. "You have lied, I think, at least once to everyone in New England. You should return to Kan-sas where you came from. You have no more credibility here."

"A beer, please." Aldrich smiled through his hurt dignity at the bartender, who had overheard the exchange with Gaston and looked momentarily uncertain as to whether or not to serve him. Aldrich paid for his beer, then caught and held the Abbé's eye as he slid beside him onto a bar stool: "Have you heard any word from Mildred, Monsieur l'Abbé?" he inquired softly.

The anger in the cleric's face dimmed to instant pain, and inwardly Aldrich congratulated himself on having found the mark. Ah, the wicked ease of it all, the deft certainty over which dangling a carrot brought the horse forward.

"I heard from her not two months ago," Gaston whispered. "She wrote me from France that she still loved me very much.

"Do you think you two will ever get together, Roland?"

"It is certain later, when her youngest finishes the university. She feels her responsibility too greatly now, though. She has told her eldest daughter Marie about us, and Marie was *très sympathique* for us."

"A great sadness," Aldrich judged, barely able to keep from snickering. He loved the weakness of other hearts. When Gaston taught skiing at Stratton Mountain during his spiritual crisis, he fell determinedly in love with a rich man's bored wife named Mildred. When Mildred would not leave her husband for Roland Gaston, he took up with the Faith again and founded his monastery, L'Abbaye des Neiges. Somehow, perfectly, it looked down across a valley on the Stratton slopes and on clear days the Abbé hungered for the sight of his star pupil Mildred bombing the mountain through a high-powered telescope.

Two winters before, Aldrich had driven with the Abbé to Stratton to visit with Mildred and her husband Jason. They lived in a palatial ski house with an indoor swimming pool. Two winter-white Rolls-Royces stood in the parking area. They wore reflective snow chains all around that achieved the look of rubies and sapphires on gilded gold necklaces. Their real home was a waterside palazzo in Westport, Connecticut. Gaston sighed beside the swimming pool for the tragedy of love. Mildred, who swam the waters naked, played at sighing for the tragedy of love, drew (for warmth, not modesty) a sable coat about her shoulders to warm the chill when she emerged from the pool. Aldrich and Jason the husband smiled with identical bemusement at the scene. Mildred was never going to leave Jason for L'Abbaye des Neiges.

Remembering that day, something occurred to Aldrich that he had never thought of before.

"Roland, *mon ami*, who was it that made you a gift of that mountain where you built the monastery? I don't know if I ever asked you."

"But didn't I ever tell you this, Aldrich? It was Mildred and Jason, of course."

"How good of them," Aldrich gurgled, biting hard on the glass lip of the beer schooner to keep from laughing out loud.

"Yes, they are very kind people. It makes me so guilty, so hard to think of hurting Jason the way we are going to have to hurt him . . ."

"She was one of the most beautiful women I'd ever met," Aldrich crooned softly. "You deserve each other like no two people have ever deserved each other."

"It will be a celestial marriage. I pray to God every day that it will happen soon. You know, Aldrich, you are not a bad person. You are a sensitive person even. But misdirected one should say."

"It appears so." Aldrich sighed deeply, feigning sadness. Seeing that they appeared to be getting on, the bartender gave them each their free Resignation Day drink. They touched glasses and drank and Aldrich suddenly wondered why in the past he had never thought to put the tap on the Abbé Gaston for funds. He had already, on the Abbé's behalf, gotten fifteen hundred dollars from Jason and Mildred for the proud and indigent priest's cornea transplant, despite the fact that Gaston had no idea he needed a cornea transplant and still had vision like a hawk with his original issue . . .

"*Tu sais,* Dwight David, I don't question your business acumen as much as I question the veracity of your research as a developer. I mean, North Hollow is practically in Canada and at least sixty miles from the nearest skiing. The advertising brochures you circulated were quite imaginative, it has to be said, but less than totally factual—though I hasten to add, probably through no fault of your own . . ."

The Abbé, consumed by the joke, began a kind of unmasculine and shuddering giggle that the bartender and two other men at the nether end of the bar joined in on. "One must admit, Dwight David, that North Hollow does not lie in an area of quaint towns and prosperous farms and thriving cottage industries in quilts and woodworking. Nor is there a viable industry in cheese and maple syrup . . ."

The bartender and the two other patrons, who had moved in close beside the Abbé at the bar, were laughing openly now, and Aldrich, not unwisely, decided to laugh good-naturedly along at himself. In truth North Hollow lay in a country of scrawny dirt farms and sagging pickup trucks, and people with chiseled suspicious faces. The sun seemed hardly ever to shine. To hedge the lie a bit, though, all Aldrich promised might arrive to the Northeast Kingdom in fifty years perhaps if the cities died outright, the birthrate soared, and there was no land left anywhere else.

"Well, I guess I did exaggerate things a little bit at the time," Aldrich admitted. He now ordered drinks for four people and wondered if he had enough money to pay for them. "But the day isn't far off when all that I promised will come true. It has to. They aren't making any more land in Vermont . . . People are getting out of the cities every day . . . Who needs all that crime and political corruption when we've got law and order and basic town-meeting democracy here in Vermont . . . ?"

Aldrich stifled himself in mid-pitch at the sound of his own voice and stared into the bar mirror. He saw three pairs of glazed eyes staring myopically back at him. The Abbé shook his head dismally. The heavyset man beside the Abbé said stonily: "Your forgot the part about clear spring water and clean air versus urban pollution. And what about concern for your children's lungs?"

He handed Aldrich his card; predictably enough, he was a realtor.

"You forgot the part about the niggers and Puerto Ricans, too," the Abbé chimed in.

"I never did use that except with Italian or Irish people," the realtor said. "Wasps and Jews don't like that sort of thing. I mean hearing it, that is. It's all right to think it, but you just don't say it."

"I never sold to any black people," Aldrich asserted. "I never would, either. There are just some places they don't be-long."

"That's a lie, Aldrich!" the Abbé charged. "You sold one unit to a black family from Albany. You cost them money they had saved for years. Your tried selling all of North Hollow, liens included, to a black foundation from Boston to use as a camp for black city kids. Liddy told me these things last December when you kidnapped her. My God, how did you ever expect to get her back? A girl like that especially needs a man whose honesty she can respect. Every time she turned around you were screwing somebody else out of something. Do you know why she ran away from you and went back to Massachusetts to her family last fall? No? Well, it was because some drunk slapped her face at a reception in Montpelier when he heard she was your wife. Once before someone spit on her . . ."

"Are you a Vermonter?" the realtor growled. Florid-faced and jowly, he suddenly looked as if he were spoiling for a fight.

"I'm proud to say I am a Vermonter now," Aldrich rejoined, "though I was born and raised in Kansas. My name is Dwight David, after the General, who came from Abilene."

"Aldrich?" the man to the right of the realtor queried in a wide country twang. "Is this here North Hollow rip-off you're talkin' about up there in Northeast Kingdom?"

"Yes it is, sir. Town called Inglenook. My family first settled it from England before the glorious Revolution . . ."

"Thought it might be the same family," the man announced to the world at large. "I worked for ten years as an orderly in the nut house up there in Caledonia County. There was always Aldriches comin' and goin'. Zebidiah Aldrich kin of yours?"

"Yes," Aldrich acknowledged weakly, knowing that it was useless to lie, that the Abbé Gaston knew her and would not protect him. "She's my great-aunt."

"She's a gen-u-ine witch." The ex-orderly pounded an emphatic fist on the bar. "They say she can change the weather accordin' to her whim. First time I ever lay eyes on her they brought her in for tryin' to seduce a Baptist minister in Plainfield. She stood stark naked in the snow in front of the minister's house on a twenty-below night, holdin' a candle in a thirty-mile wind for more 'n two hours before the troopers come 'n took her away. They say that candle never did flicker once, 'n when she come in, there wasn't a spot of frost on her. Not on her feet or anywhere! Can you imagine that?"

"Jesus Christ!" Surprisingly it was Aldrich's own voice. Somehow Great-aunt Zebidiah's escapade had escaped him. Sexual aberration among the Aldriches was not condoned: The severe and withering hereditary gaze that Aldrich always had turned on lusters after the flesh was now burning because Zebidiah's madness had violated a sexual province—she had gone chasing after a clergyman of all things . . .

"They brought her in three or four times more when I was there," the ex-orderly went on. "You should've seen the place. The other loonies just went crazy whenever she showed up. It was like their queen was comin' home from a goddam Royal Tour or somethin' like that. Some of 'em even kissed her hand, I remember."

"I didn't know . . . I mean, I didn't even consider that Aunt Zebidiah thought about men, about sex, that is," Aldrich said, flustered.

"She did. She did all the time," the man avowed. "It's all she ever did talk about. She once put a curse on a brother orderly of mine. Told him—excuse me, Reverend—told him his pecker had just died on him for good. He was but fifty years old, twice married 'n fathered fifteen kids, so you know he was a good horse. And you know what?" He leaned forward into the silence where you could hear dust drop. "It happened! He'd come in every mornin' and we'd all say 'Well?' and he'd just give the saddest shake of his head. He died shortly thereafter. About two years later I guess it was. He lost the equiva-

lent weight of his pecker every day just like that witch
Zebidiah promised he would. It pained me, I'll tell you, to see
a virile man go like that. It just seemed like he had no more
reason to live after his pecker didn't . . ."

"Aldrich, all of your kind should be run out of the goddam state," the realtor said vehemently. "It gives Vermont a
bad image. Who the hell's going to throw it all over down in
the rat race and buy peace of mind up here when word gets
out there's somebody in Vermont can program the goddam
weather and a man's sex machine, too?"

"You ought to get your aunt to put a hex on all those
screaming creditors of yours, Aldrich," the Abbé proposed
wickedly.

"You should be run out of that business, too," the realtor
blustered on. "That business of cheating and fucking over all
those condominium buyers with false advertising and the rest
of it. Why didn't you hire a realtor to represent you? He could
at least have lent his professional integrity to the project. Because of your blood line you may have dishonest parts of you
that you're not even aware of, parts that you have no control
over. A realtor would have understood this. Would've put
forth an affirmative image to the public . . ."

"I didn't hire a realtor to sell condominiums for North
Hollow because I couldn't find an honest realtor to represent
the place," Aldrich told the man archly. He appraised the
other faces in the blue-tinted mirror, saw that he was gaining
an ally in the ex-mental hospital orderly, who seemed to share
the universal old Vermonter's smoldering suspicion that he
had almost certainly been screwed out of a larger profit on his
inherited land because of a fast-talking realtor. But the alli-
ance failed to materialize as the drunken realtor screamed:
"You goddam bug fucker, Aldrich!" and threw his beer glass
at Aldrich's reflection in the mirror when he meant to throw it
at Aldrich instead. The mirror shattered and shards of glass
fell down all over the stacked liquor bottles. Everyone stared
dumbly at the peeling plastered wall behind the mirror.

25

"Wherever you go, Aldrich, calumny, rage, evil intent and the severing of the bond of men's hearts go with you. How is it possible?" the Abbé Gaston demanded, shaking his head in evident bewilderment.

At his side the realtor burst into wracking sobs: "All the suppressed rage, frustration and antagonism I feel from jostling among an overpopulation of brother realtors in this place of exploitation called Vermont during the current recession has busted out again because of this person! I've never met a man, black or white, who infuriated me so much!" he cried, head down, into one arm now, pounding the bar gently with another fist. Beside him, the ex-orderly patted his back consolingly: "That don't come from the wind, realtor. That be in the blood. His Great-aunt Zebidiah once turned a psychiatric doctor up at the hospital into a raving lunatic hisself . . ."

"No more for you, Aldrich," the bartender said stonily.

"I can't be shut out of the communion of men this way," Aldrich whined. "My wife has left me. I'm about to die of loneliness, as is. So much is beyond my control and they keep heaping blazing coals on my head. Men I've never met before have accused me of being the root cause of all the problems of their life when I'm only a kindred soul at best . . ." His bleary mind searched for the words: "All I did was drop anchor in this state, only to have the anchor chain drag my ship down behind it . . ."

There was a silence while they considered his bizarre analogy with consternated and knitted brows. Then Gaston spoke somberly: "Before you return to the community of man, you must undertake a penitential season, Aldrich. You must exclude yourself from other men and look inward on the perniciousness of your nature, trying to understand from whence it comes, and what you must do to correct it. You have sinned seriously against God, Man and Nature . . ."

"Can I spend it at the Abbaye des Neiges?" Aldrich asked hopefully, thinking ecclesiastical property might perhaps be a safe place to wait out his creditors.

"No, you cannot. Spend it at North Hollow, in the private hell you've created."

"How will I know if I've done penance?" Aldrich asked. "Will I feel differently?"

"We'll feel differently toward you. That's how you'll know. Meet us here in a year's time, on the very anniversary of Tricky Dick's resignation, 'n we'll tell you if you've changed or not," the ex-orderly told him. "Let's make a pact 'n swear that we'll all be here at this hour of the evening next year. Join hands 'n we'll swear on it."

"Done!" Aldrich agreed as they put their hands together on the bar before the seated Abbé.

"Someone's hands are cold as ice on this bright hot summer night," the realtor intoned distantly.

"Mine," Aldrich acknowledged meekly, wriggling his clammy uriniferous-smelling hand out of the pile to gaze at it speculatively, wondering if that condition were somehow a certain indication of his interior moral crumblings.

"Go forth now into the night," the bartender ordered solemnly.

"Yes, go forth . . ."

Aldrich went out into the evening to start up the pickup again, amazed at the hour of beginning darkness at the number of bats that flew everywhere among the trees.

CHAPTER 4

That Penitential Season

However: He went grudgingly into his penitential season. The habit of fighting back was too well ingrained. Out of summer and through the nipping days of fall he waged a holding action, tried negotiating with the banks, the utility company and the endless lists of other creditors for more time. Meanwhile, he worked at diddling yet another urban black Fresh Air Foundation who were determinedly interested in buying North Hollow for a children's camp. But that last hopeful prospect soured by degrees with all the new disclosures the Foundation's lawyers kept unearthing in the County Records Office and courthouse docket, then finally died on a bitter day in mid-October when two black attorneys—the one a squint-eyed bantamweight, and outright menacing; the other, dignified and tall in pinstripes with a mouth that visibly trembled as he tried to control his fury—knocked on Aldrich's door and demanded he sign a rejection of any claim to funds already in escrow because of his gross misrepresentations about the clear title availability of the property.

From habit, Aldrich balked. Bantamweight allowed as how both Joe Frazier and Muhammad Ali were heavy contributors to the fund. Tall, dignified Pinstripe turned a labored half circle and pointed to the middle distance across the North Hollow lake where a huge, square-headed, close-cropped black man in a black overcoat with turned-up collar leaned heavily against the flanks of a black Cadillac limousine.

"Which one is it?" Aldrich whispered.

"It's Joe," came the dual answer, "the family man with all the kids. He's mad, Aldrich!"

Aldrich signed the rejection forms quickly, tucking his own unread copy into his jeans. He was heedless of the brittle leaf-crackling departure of the lawyers, instead smiled and waved effusively at Joe Frazier because he was rich and famous. He thought of running after the lawyers, apologizing to and shaking hands with the heavyweight, then decided against it after an alternative thought that Frazier's anger might not be the instantly cooling variety, and a snowbound winter alone at North Hollow with a wired jaw was quite a bit more penance than anyone expected of him. So he contented himself instead with smiling and waving and calling out: "Hi, Joe! Hi, champ!" Yet Joe Frazier kept a stony silence all the while. Nor did Frazier move at the approach of the lawyers until they shoved him rudely away from the side of the car, face down and sprawling into the leaves at the side of the lake. The Cadillac lurched away out of North Hollow, and it was then Aldrich knew he had just been diddled.

He ran screaming his rage at other people's cruel duplicity around the end of the lake and attacked the papier-mâché Joe Frazier furiously, kicking it to shreds beneath the ratty old overcoat, then setting fire to the destruction for good riddance. Then, exhausted from his rantings, he sat down to watch the vanquished burn, scarce consolation, however, to that day's certain knowledge that the North Hollow enterprise was henceforth truly finished. It was only a matter of time.

The last leaves turned and disappeared and the long rains that came before the snows turned the papery white birches gray and forlorn in the fogs that refused to lift out of North Hollow for days on end. Hunting season came and went with a minimum visitation and abuse by the hunters and

Aldrich was somehow pleased that he could find only two spent shells to dig out of the wooden walls of North Hollow in this, its second full hunting season of existence. The utility company spoke its final no on the day that the first tentative snow came and quickly melted, and that night, midway through Walter Cronkite, the power died. Aldrich sighed briefly in the aftermath of darkness at the notion that the fading withdrawal of the grandfatherly face from the screen signaled the real beginning of his period of isolation from the community of man. So be it.

Later that night, after he had moved out of his apartment and into the tennis pro shop that he converted to kerosene and candlelight, Aldrich walked about the place in the glow of the clear full moon, enthralled despite himself at the white-capped beauty of the mountains to the south where the snows had not melted. He pondered his future survival: Aldrich loved winter, prided himself on his private and continually self-delighting defenses against the seasonal depression that short, stark days and endless snows in the North Country brought to so many others, hiking suicide rates, hastening the days of terminal illness, confirming the sadness of alcoholism.

Instead Aldrich got high snorting in the dreadful rushes of Arctic air that others sought to hide from, found a pleasing mystery in the glare of green ice in the wintry streams, came bang! awake on nights of the fiercest cold at the crack of rifle fire, only to nod sheepishly back to sleep at the realization that a wad of sap had just exploded in the limb of a nearby tree. He loved all of these things in winter and knew he would survive, hands down.

He knew how the animals worked the winter, too, but they were not always to be imitated. Even now, before Thanksgiving, the preparations were under way. The geese from Canada had already flown south in great V-shaped wedges. Soon the scavenging raccoons and skunks would go into hibernation. (The skunks, curiously, horny for mating, quit hibernation in the deep awful cold of February, and frequently got nailed on their way home to the burrow by the great horned owls, who considered a spent, happy skunk quite a delicacy, it seemed.)

In subsequent days, walking about the damned acres of his failure, Aldrich saw that the deer were coming down from the hills for winter after the hunters had gone away. After this second snow, during the fragile half day it lasted, he found the tracks of a forage yard being marked out, as if the deer could not wait enough for winter to begin. Aldrich would wait with him, more patiently though, and when the first real storm of hip-high snows flashed over the Northeast Kingdom, that deer would be his meat for the winter.

He found where a black bear was hibernating. He filled his bird feeder almost daily now, glad for the chattering company of blue jays and chickadees, sparrows, woodpeckers and grosbeaks, marveling in late November at their compromise and cooperation when, in times of ample food, they were strictly separated by species:

Nature delighted him then, even if men did not.

That was the sticking point: the perfidy of men. In his penitential season, it was quite impossible for Aldrich to feel penitential because he felt so completely wronged instead. He thought of this often during his late-afternoon meditation period when he sat in the pro shop with his carefully apportioned share of Bourbon, looking northward past the tattered flapping nets of the tennis courts across the three miles of tundra that led to Quebec Province. The tallying of the number of slings and arrows sent against him was countless, he considered. America, Vermont, other men's economy, other men's government, their taxes, their lack of understanding, their horrid intolerance had all conspired mercilessly against this well-groomed young entrepreneur from Kansas. Penitence indeed: What bullshit! The Abbé Gaston was crazy if he thought Aldrich was the only one that needed to drag the cross around through the snows for a winter. What about environmentalists who had put moratoriums on all his construction starts? Or bankers who had priced mortgage money right out of reach? Or those liberal jackass legislators who had voted the American worker into the realm of tin godship, notwithstanding the fact that they were taxing his employer, Aldrich, out of existence?

Wrathful, impotent to avenge, he read and reread his favorite consoling book, *Six Crises,* and wondered how his hero, Mr. Nixon, was doing during his penitential season. He caught the 6 P.M. news daily on the truck radio (ever since the power had been cut) and worried over Nixon's phlebitis, the possibility that he might lose the San Clemente estate that Aldrich liked to think of fraternally as the Nixon North Hollow. Aldrich wrote Nixon several letters, explaining who he was, how they were kindred spirits, vilifying the conspiracy that had brought them low and urging the exiled leader to recall that he had known grim days before. What of the aftermath of the 1960 election? (Aldrich assured Nixon he believed the Democrats had stolen that one with Illinois and Texas ballot stuffing.) What of the time of the Nixon hegira from California to New York when Nixon himself believed his political career was over and done with? Cheer up, Mr. Ex-President, Aldrich told him, they can't keep a good man down.

After his fourth letter to Nixon, Aldrich received a polite, formal card of thanks from San Clemente that buoyed his spirits immeasurably, restored some vestige of his ancient indomitable courage so that he felt adequate again to operate his special wintertime food-gathering shakedown game.

He sent the boiled head of a lake trout (eyes intact) along with a label to the home offices of his favorite Cap'n Snows Chowders and protested indignantly to its evidently distressed management that he had found it just so in a can of fish chowder. That begot him a letter of regret that hinted sadly at the possibility of employee sabotage and a free case of fish chowder. Dinty Moore Beef Stews obliged him with two full cases delivered to North Hollow by an area sales representative who apologized profusely for the discomfort caused to Aldrich, his wife, and two children when they had discovered the bleached bones of a raccoon's head at the bottom of their traditional Thursday-night Dinty Moore Beef Stew dinner. Aldrich allowed to the representative that his wife and children were away shopping in Burlington and the grave, unsmiling representative allowed how it was just as well since he had to tell Aldrich man to man that the main plant lab had determined the bones were the hand of a young monkey.

"Monkey meat?" Aldrich had begged incredulously, then stepped outside and effortlessly vomited his bilge, his own graphic imagination victim of some nitwit lab technician's gratuitous one-upmanship. Aghast, the representative inquired after Aldrich's favorite alcohol and rushed off toward the village of Inglenook, to return with a case of Jack Daniel's Bourbon whiskey, an unexpected and particularly prized bonus since Aldrich had tried and failed in two previous attempts to dun a case of same out of those arch and scornful gentlemen down in Tennessee.

He found skunk cabbage in a jar of Rosoff's Kosher Pickles and a glass eye (from a Barbie doll left in one of the condominiums) in a can of Budweiser beer. Rosoff capitulated in dumbfounded ethnic exasperation, but Aldriches, evidently, were not unknown to Anheuser-Busch. A third claim-pressing letter from Aldrich, whose righteousness by now was so self-convincing that he actually believed he had found the eye of a Barbie doll in a can of Bud, drew sharp exception from Anheuser-Busch's legal counsel. Their reply spoke gravely of courts and court costs and slander and libel, and Aldrich, who by now had set his sights on a whole truckload of beer, decided he had had enough of courts, lawyers and adverse judgments in the one year past to make do for the lifetime of any highly unreasonable person, and thus withdrew his claim.

By Thanksgiving, though, he had amassed a considerable larder that he thought would see him through to spring. It wanted but fresh meat and he waited greedily for the hip-high snow that would send the buck he had spotted to the forage yard, where Aldrich would kill him when the odds were clearly on his side. He would store the butchered meat safely in the sub-basement of one of the unheated condominium buildings. Aldrich's mouth positively slavered with anticipation when he leafed through his collection of twenty or so marvelous recipes for preparing venison.

There was but one last thing to do, he considered, in his preparation for getting through the real winter, and that was to put his irksome penitential season to work for him to keep the restless horde of creditors at bay until spring so he might at least have a little peace and quiet to go along with his lonely estrangement from the community of man. So he wrote letters to all his creditors telling them about his penitential season. That plan backfired, however, a genuine miscalculation, the merchant mind viewing Aldrich's penance with a keen and squinting suspicion. To a man they thought he was going on the lam, and an army of process servers descended on North Hollow all through November, so that in no way could Aldrich yet consider himself to be lonely.

CHAPTER 5

Thanksgiving at Great-Aunt Zebidiah's

He went to the tumbledown farm of the witch, his Great-aunt Zebidiah, for Thanksgiving.

She did not invite him, rather he invited himself, his seasonal terror of loneliness that began with Thanksgiving and ended the day after New Year's growing apace in him days before the feast, so that he drove to the old farm in the Notch beyond Inglenook and with a feigned elaborate casualness inquired after her plans for Thanksgiving dinner.

"If you come, Dwight David, bring your own food. I'm on welfare, you know."

"I know." Aldrich winced, stung as ever by the fierce prideful tone of her voice that betrayed how implicit was her delight in ripping off the state. Zebidiah Aldrich was the only citizen of Inglenook on welfare. Aldrich learned that fact to his ear-burning dismay in a public place when he first stormed into Inglenook in the late summer of '69 to collect his inheritance, the five hundred acres on which North Hollow was erected.

Until that summer he had never seen his kinswoman either, and when he went the first time to introduce himself, he was frankly appalled. Zebidiah was a wizened and spiteful old woman, who lived for her wars against the citizenry of Inglenook. The farm that Aldrich's Kansas mother with pretensions had never seen, but always spoke of as "quaint and very New England-like," was a run-down near ruin with an

35

old Cape Cod-style house that had not been painted for half a century or more. The roof of the barn had long since collapsed inward from snow loads. The outbuildings were in various stages of tilt, and lichens and mosses clung to everything, including trees and shrubs, because the Notch was a kind of canyon that the original Aldrich ancestor had deemed the perfect natural bastion against Indians, Canadian Frenchmen, lawmen and creditors. He had not considered that the sun never penetrated it long enough to dry it out. In its center, like the lagoon of Black Orpheus, was a deep, deep pond that mad Zebidiah fancied was the entrance to hell, and which was long polluted and useless since the time that some prankster Inglenook kids had stolen an oil tank truck and driven it into the water. Now, like a disintegrating ocean liner, it clung to the bottom, occasionally disgorging a raft of oil that bubbled slowly to the surface.

On Thanksgiving Day, just before noon, he drove into the Notch with two plucked pheasants that he had shot out of season the day before, a bottle of bonus Jack Daniel's, a bottle of Rosoff's pickles, a loaf of French bread and one can of cranberry sauce. Smoke rose turgidly from the main chimney of the house as Aldrich pulled up before it, then sounded the horn for Zebidiah to come out and shoo away her three cows who stood resolute and menacing before the door and refused to move. Zebidiah's cows were scrawny starved beasts, each with the mean, evil look of a crazed longhorn steer. Aldrich always suspected that they were not herbivorous as Nature had intended them. They lived in the house with their mistress since the barn had fallen in, and now lunged past her into the interior when Zebidiah opened the door to discover what was the matter.

"What's wrong, chickenshit?" she cackled. "Afraid of my poor old cows?"

For Thanksgiving, she wore a faded old two-piece Victorian suit. Pine cones and mistletoe dangled from a red ribbon that wound through the dirty snarls of her hair. Aldrich climbed from the pickup and carried his packages inside, overcome as usual by the pervasive musty odor of nearly forty years of the Burlington *Free Press* that lined the walls from floor to ceiling in tightly packed stacks except for the window openings; they were Zebidiah's artless but effective concession to the principle of modern insulation.

Inside, the cows retired to the dining room, one slumping down heavily into the straw that Zebidiah kept there for them, the other two standing side by side and staring myopically outward through the small panes of the big eight-over-eight window. Aldrich observed that it was time for the dining room to be mucked out and hoped that Zebidiah would not prevail upon him to do it after Thanksgiving dinner.

In the kitchen a fire burned in the old fireplace with its twin Dutch ovens. Beyond the kitchen, in what was formerly the living room, was the disheveled mess of Zebidiah's bedroom. The three upstairs rooms were closed off. Water came from an outside well. Plumbing was an outhouse. It was dismaying enough to Aldrich to think that some relative, near or distant, lived in this kind of squalor, but more dismaying still was the fact that for all Zebidiah's boasting about being the only citizen of Inglenook, Vermont, on welfare, she had an enormous and elegant-looking color console TV that Aldrich, rich or poor, would have considered a great extravagance.

"What have you brought to eat, Dwight David?" she demanded greedily. "Something good I can chew on with my poor old lady gums?"

"Two pheasants I shot just yesterday. Some bread and pickles and cranberry sauce . . ."

"What's in the bottle?"

"Whiskey. Jack Daniel's. A gift from a friend."

"Shit. You don't have no friends. You fucked somebody over for it, didn't you?"

"Aunt Zebidiah, I have spoken to you about your language before."

"And I have told you I like to keep it colorful. Except for

testing out imaginative new epitaphs on the populace of Inglenook and watching my TV set, I wouldn't have a reason to do anything but lie down and die."

"Would you like a sip of my whiskey, Zebidiah?"

"No, I drink my own wine, the stuff I make myself."

"What do you make it from?"

"Things I find in the forest. Secret things that make a good bubbly ferment. It distills out to about a hundred and forty proof."

Aldrich, not unaccountably, thought of Macbeth, the witches, their toads, the hearts of furry forest creatures. He poured a glass of his whiskey and sipped it cautiously, watching Zebidiah glug down her wine with great gasps of satisfaction. He grew annoyed with her that she watched the TV screen fixedly with one eye.

"Do you think we could turn the TV off for a while and talk, Zebidiah? I have something to say to you, something that's been bothering me for a couple of months."

"I can't turn it off. I got to watch the preliminaries to the football games. We got to eat them pheasants before two o'clock, too, Dwight David, 'cause I'm always too excited to eat after the kickoff. What is it you wanted to talk about?"

"It's about sex, Aunt Zebidiah . . ."

"I never get any," she told him mournfully.

"You try, though. Some man I met in a bar in Manchester told me you tried to seduce a Baptist minister in Plainfield one winter night . . ."

She took a long gulp of her wine. On the instant her eyes grew fibrous and distended, her mouth spread wide in a great grin of pleasure: "I did? Tell me about it, Dwight David. I disremember completely."

"You stood in the snow in his front yard bare naked on a twenty-below night with a candle in your hands that didn't flicker once in a thirty-mile wind . . ."

"I did that? This little old Vermont lady you see before you did that?" The notion positively delighted her; she clapped her hands and clacked her toothless gums together in anticipation: "What happened, Dwight David? Did I get him? Did I lay with him?"

"He called the police and they took you to the state hospital in Caledonia County."

"Too bad. I wonder how I got down to Plainfield to try seducing him in the first place?"

"Maybe you flew, Zebidiah," Aldrich told her wrathfully.

"If I hear one more person say that about me, I'll start believing it's true, that I do fly when the blackout comes upon me."

"What's the blackout, Zebidiah?"

"That's when I do the things I disremember. The sex things. It amazes me to hear some of the shit I get myself into when the blackout comes on me. Did you hear anything else I did?"

"You made one of the orderlies at the institution impotent. He lost the equivalent weight of his penis every day and died about two years later."

"He deserved to die. He's the son of a bitch who jilted me when I was a young woman and turned me into this toothless old cliché of a New England spinster that Norman Rockwell should have immortalized on a *Saturday Evening Post* cover . . ." Her attention was completely diverted for some moments as she watched the televised highlights of a Buffalo Bills–Miami Dolphins game. O. J. Simpson ran outside ten, twenty, thirty-three yards while Zebidiah pounded her fists on her knees in excitement and screamed "Zap that nigger!" at the screen. A Miami tackle dutifully brought Simpson down on the Dolphins' twenty-one-yard line, and Zebidiah clapped her delight.

"How'd you do it, Zebidiah?" Aldrich asked.

"Move that tackle into position so fast, do you mean?"

"No, make the ex-lover impotent."

"Power of suggestion, that's all. Plus his silly ass superstitious certainty that I was a witch, and therefore his thing wasn't going to get hard ever again no matter what he went and fantasized.

"But he died."

"That wasn't my fault. That was the work of some of my friends at the happy farm. He went from lead poisoning they introduced from time to time into his food. Cumulative effect. Ex-orderly Stanton was a genuinely cruel prick toward his charges. It gave them no end of delight to see that tight-fisted fucker who wouldn't spend money on a doctor turning yellow and scrawny while his hair and teeth fell out at the same time."

"But, Zebidiah . . . that's murder."

"Not if you're a certified nut, it isn't."

"How did you hear this?"

"I see some of my old friends from time to time."

"You shouldn't know people like that, Zebidiah."

"A person has to have friends."

"All these visitations to that institution, all this talk about your sexual escapades . . . well, it's embarrassing to hear it, and it just isn't good for the family image, Zebidiah."

She sniggered at the notion, her mouth spread wide in a preposterous and mocking grin, the gums a fascinating mélange of purple and liver-spot coloring as if they had been tattooed: "Family image, Dwight David? Forget the horse-shit. We got none. There might be some general sympathy for an old lady on welfare who goes eccentrically daft on the average of once a year, but not for the likes of you who put the name Aldrich on so many bad checks and court dockets all over Vermont, and built that wooden circus you call North Hollow over there on your inheritance land. You even embarrass me, Dwight David, and I didn't think I'd ever be in a position to say that to anybody."

"I had a lot of bad luck, Zebidiah," Aldrich whined, hoping to deflect her slings.

"The only bad luck you had was in being born an Aldrich, Dwight David. That made you the inheritor of a long-established tradition of rascalry, thievery, sexual perversion, treason, sedition, blasphemy and apparently, in my case, gratuitous witchcraft. There's nothing redeeming at all about us."

"In Kansas, we were proud of our name. We always believed we came from an old Vermont family of English extraction that established in this country before the Revolution," he said defiantly.

"You did. On the face of it, that's exactly what you come from. Except that in England we were gypsy tinkers who set sail for a new life in America on the King's prison ship and never lost the habit of being brigand gypsy tinkers and weren't made to live in peace with any neighbors. We've been on the wrong side of every war since, and including, the Revolution. You should have been here in Inglenook during World War II. Your Great-uncle Wesley came out for the Nazis at town meeting not long after Vermont declared war on Germany, and before the rest of the country got around to it. This here Notch was a goddam fortress against the world during those years, let me tell you . . ."

She poured herself more of her wine, then stood up and unaccountably swirled about in her long tattered skirt, admiring herself in a tall gilded mirror that was propped up against the insulating stacks of the Burlington *Free Press*. Bizarre narcissism, Aldrich judged. What a family we are. Moral reserves absolutely zero, and worse, he understood all that about himself. From the dining-room barnyard the cows came out to watch Zebidiah's giddy dance and something in Aldrich clicked awake with the terrible fear that his great-aunt was flirting with him, had sexual designs on him.

"I'd better get these pheasants on to cook, Zebidiah, if you want to finish eating in time for that game."

"Oh, fuck the game, Dwight David. When you come right down to the wire, the Super Bowl's the only thing that counts anyhow. Let's you and me party and dance a while.

Our family always was so somber and grave. What was Thanksgiving like out there in Kansas? Tell me about it."

"Somber and grave like it should be. All things considered, Kansas isn't the most exciting place to live in this country."

"Neither is Vermont. And for an Aldrich it could be downright dangerous. Dance with your old aunt, Dwight David. We might die tomorrow. Somebody might shoot us."

"I don't want to dance and I might be leaving Vermont soon, Zebidiah. I'm working now on selling North Hollow to a camp foundation from New York City," Aldrich lied.

"You'd better hurry, Dwight David, because there won't be a North Hollow come next spring."

He was raking the coals of the fireplace, preparing the grate for the two pheasants that he had stuffed and basted and wrapped in foil that morning. Zebidiah swirled and dipped preposterously before the mirror, smiling toothlessly at herself all the while.

"How do you know there won't be a North Hollow next spring?" Aldrich demanded angrily. In truth he was frightened she was right. She had already called a number of things in the past with amazing accuracy, told of his divorce from Liddy right down to the week of the month.

"Because I had a dream, and my dreams are never wrong. It won't be there come spring, I promise you that."

"What the hell's it going to do? Self-destruct?"

"No, nothing supernatural. Some of it's going to burn, some blow up, and some more just fall down. . . . It won't happen all at once."

"Zebidiah, you're crazy! Don't say things like that to be mean just because I don't want to dance. You've had too goddam much to drink."

"And I'm going to have more, too, to assuage my hurt over the fact that my own nephew won't dance with his old aunt on Thanksgiving Day."

"My insurance has been canceled. There's no way I can

get an insurance company to write a policy on that place again. If you're right, I'm a complete loss except for whatever those five hundred acres will bring if everybody gives up and retires their liens against it. Who's going to do it to me?"

"I don't know. I didn't see any faces. But the first thing they're goin' to take out is the dam on the lake."

"Why the dam?"

"Obvious reason, stupid. You can't fight fires without water, and if the lake goes there's no water except for throwin' shovelfuls of snow on the blaze. They're goin' to leave one building standin', though."

Aldrich gulped more of the Jack Daniel's, heedless of the smoke that rose from the pheasants he had put too close to the coals. He filled Zebidiah's glass and she sipped at it greedily, turning to watch herself in the mirror, daintily extending one crooked finger of her gnarled, arthritic-looking hand.

"What building, Zebidiah?"

"A little tiny buildin' with a tennis racket on the wall. That's all that'll be left of North Hollow come spring."

"That's where I live," Aldrich said mutely. "It's thoughtful of them to spare me."

"You won't die, Dwight David, but Liddy will. I saw that in another dream."

"She will?" The notion positively delighted him. Balm to his fractured ego, vengeance for her treachery in divorcing him. But in an instant he grew apprehensive again: "But, Zebidiah, what about my alimony?"

"I didn't see anything in the dream about that. How much is she payin' you?"

"Five hundred a month as long as I stay away."

"Huh. You got it made, kid. That's more than I get from the welfare people."

"How will she die? Violently?"

"A virgin. In the dream she died a virgin."

"She's no goddam virgin," Aldrich said scornfully.

"Well, in the dream she's all dressed in white like on her

weddin' day and lyin' on the front steps of a church. All dressed in white like I would've been if that pecker ex-orderly Stanton hadn't compromised my virtue, then jilted me afore the war . . ."

Zebidiah cast her arms about herself and bowed her head in a parody of grief, and Aldrich, knowing the sign, grew tense and ready and neatly dodged her when she ran at him so that she slammed hard into a wall of Burlington *Free Presses* and was knocked to the floor. He stood above her, staring down wrathfully at the dazed figure: "I thought you told me you weren't going to do that again, Zebidiah."

"That damn alcohol made me do it, Dwight David. I had nothing to do with it."

He reached down and pulled her to her feet: "Have you any more prophecy, Aunt Zebidiah, before we eat our Thanksgiving dinner?"

"Only one, Dwight David. The Super Bowl. Steelers versus Minnesota. Hands down the Steelers are goin' to win."

CHAPTER 6

Armageddon

Zebidiah, alas, gave faultless prophecy.

In the first week of December when the land was cold enough to receive and keep the snows, Aldrich's unknown enemies began the destruction of North Hollow. At one o'clock of a Tuesday morning Aldrich woke to the dull thud of an underwater explosion that cracked the dam of the lake he had created and let loose a tidal wave of water that raged off downstream toward Inglenook and took with it one of the town's secondary wooden log bridges on its westward rush toward the Winooski and Lake Champlain. Then, certain of North Hollow's isolated aridity, they burned down the first condominium cluster, the Aspen House, four nights later.

In the midst of the blaze, when the temperature was a wind-driven fifteen below out of the Arctic of Canada, Aldrich staggered out of the pro shop and stood near the fire, mesmerized by the flames, yet comforted somehow by the warmth and his observation that the fire walls he himself had designed would have done an admirable job of containing the destruction had they been considerate enough to torch but one unit of the Aspen House, instead of six simultaneously.

No fire trucks came from the village of Inglenook since everyone knew that the lake was gone, that the road to North Hollow was still unplowed since the last storm, and that Dwight David Aldrich had not paid his property taxes in two years and had no bright prospects for bringing them up to date in the near future. So Aldrich, making his own token gesture at saving the structure by throwing ineffectual shovelfuls of snow on the conflagration until the Aspen House simply collapsed between the fire walls into six neat piles of burning embers, listened in vain for the air to be rent with the screech of sirens, and cursed the citizenry of Inglenook for not making their token gesture, even if it were as little as a satanic communal round dance about the blaze to proclaim their joy that the North Hollow Development Company was evidently on its way down the road to extinction.

Paranoid about his enemies, sleeping out the night in fitful snatches, Aldrich was certain that someone in Inglenook had done the dam and the Aspen House.

He told the sheriff his suspicions in the morning when that officer bucked his jeep through the snow to inquire dutifully, though somewhat disinterestedly, after the blaze. The sheriff assured him property burning was not in the local tradition and suggested accidental causes. Aldrich insisted emphatically that the fire had been set since the utility had been turned off in mid-October and there was no possibility of an electrical short.

The sheriff, a wry desiccated man who did not like Aldrich since the days when heady, full of piss and vinegar Aldrich stormed town meetings and tried to get the electorate of Inglenook to renounce nearly everything but their names, declared that Aldrich had set the fire himself to collect the insurance. Blunt Vermonter logic that was. Stung, seething with righteousness, Aldrich ran sacked his filing cabinet to show the lawman his lapsed insurance policies.

Defeated, the sheriff set to his police work and found the snowshoe tracks of two persons leading off toward the border, then a jerry can—five gallons Imperial rather than U.S. gallons —and swiftly closed the case: "Quebecois. Out of my jurisdiction."

He bade Aldrich goodbye, promised he would send in a report to Montpelier, and drove bucking and crashing through the drifts back to Inglenook. Dumbfounded, Aldrich spent the rest of the day trying to remember who hated him so much in Quebec Province.

About two weeks later, on Christmas Eve, they dynamited the Chamonix Cottage with a curious and artful precision so that it collapsed inward into a neat package, looking for all the world like a prefab building waiting for assembly. At the time, Aldrich, terrified of his loneliness in the midst of a festive season, had fled to Montreal for any company he could find. The day before he left, walking for exercise through the snowfields, he discovered he was talking to himself incessantly with emphatic Latinesque hand gestures about the continuing demise of Mr. Nixon, the announcement of the traitorous forthcoming remarriage of his ex-wife Liddy that he had read in the Sunday New York *Times* the week before (to Stephen Hodges, of all people, the very affianced that Aldrich had stolen her away from!), the collapse of the Vermont land binge and consequently his fortunes, and other diverse and equally rancorous considerations until it came to him with a sudden trembling that he might be going mad. In Montreal he spent three nights with a gimp-legged hooker who solicited him in a blizzard on St. Catherine Street, and she was evidently as happy for his company as he was for hers. On Christmas morning they exchanged presents, and she roasted a small Christmas turkey for *son gosse américaine* and threw in two bottles of a good Bordeaux, for none of which was Aldrich charged over and above her regular fee. All, Aldrich considered, in the seasonal spirit of generous giving.

From Montreal, Aldrich remembered to send a Christmas card to the Nixons.

When he returned to North Hollow on Saturday night, he saw resignedly the additional destruction and waited until late morning to go into the village to buy the *Times* and inform the sheriff, who knew already what had happened and showed Aldrich the blasting caps he had found at the site.

Not surprisingly they read: "Fabrique au Canada." Again, jurisdictional.

In two weeks again, in early January, they took out the Park City Lodge by aerial bombardment and at least forced Aldrich to concede that his destroyers were for real, for by then he was beginning to think they were ethereal and otherworldly. The deftness of their strike astounded him, so much so that even though he stood guarding North Hollow with his rifle in hand, not a thousand feet from where Park City was flattened beneath a mushroom cloud of smoke and fire, he did not think to raise the weapon and blast away at the stolen Cessna that banked off a mere couple hundred feet above him and headed northward toward Quebec. Instead he had waved after them for a long moment because the two men inside— evidently pilot and bombardier—had waved and wagged their wing tips at him, and when he finally thought to fire at them, they were already a distant speck in Canadian airspace. After that, Aldrich was questioned by federal marshals, for the plane had been stolen in Sherbrooke and flown illegally into Vermont.

In the third week of January they pulled down the Steamboat Springs House. At the time Aldrich was away in the capitol at Montpelier, making a halfhearted defense against a foreclosure. When he returned, in full darkness, he saw the additional damage and went inside to read *Six Crises,* daring until morning to think optimistically that a snow load had collapsed the roof.

Just after dawn he spied the Caterpillar tracks, saw that they had hooked a chain around two of the outrigger support struts Aldrich had designed to enhance the suggestion that the building resembled a steamboat superstructure, and simply pulled the struts off their foundations, collapsing the roof. The tracks disappeared again toward the border, dragging the tow chain behind it. Aldrich went for the sheriff.

"Quebecois again, I reckon," the sheriff judged laconically as he had done already four times in the recent past. Before he could mouth the words "Out of my jurisdiction" the last resistance to anything welled up in Aldrich: "Bullshit! You can't get across the border driving a goddam Caterpillar tractor!"

They followed the tracks on snowshoes across the windy tundra and the tracks made an abrupt ninety-degree left turn toward the Interstate Highway.

"God Almighty, I don't believe it, but I think I know where we're goin' to find that Cat . . ." the sheriff spoke.

It was neatly parked in the nearby Vermont State Highway maintenance garage with a thank-you note taped to the control lever. The sheriff and Aldrich stomped about in the cold, the gravel of the garage floor crackling beneath them.

"I can't move in with you and watch that place every minute," the sheriff said quietly, a faraway speculative look in his eyes. "We can't rightly expect the State Police to do it either. Could you afford to hire a private guard for the place?"

"No. I really let myself get fucked over in the divorce settlement. I only get five hundred bucks a month . . ."

The sheriff snorted his contempt: "It's a goddam shame anybody would have to pay alimony to a grown man who could work just to get rid of him. . . . But think hard, Aldrich. By now you must have some idea who's behind it. Who wants to wipe you out like this? Any former employees?"

"I think my ex-wife Liddy has something to do with it," Aldrich said vengefully. "She's about to remarry and I'll bet she's trying to clear the decks of her past, to get even with me for having to divorce her because of her prurient extramarital escapades. Can't you get up a warrant for her arrest and have her brought in for questioning down in Boston?"

"Horseshit, Mr. D. D. Aldrich!" the sheriff raged. "Horseshit, I tell you! Lydia Welsh is one of the finest, most beautiful girls in New England! She couldn't have anything at all to do with this. She doesn't have any of that terrible, tin god, bug-fuckin' cruelty in her like you have!"

"I think your position is rather prejudicial, Sheriff. Open-minded objectivity is the first requisite for an effective law-man."

Apoplectic-looking, the sheriff advanced on Aldrich, who was backed into the treads of the Caterpillar. Then he calmed himself, took deep breaths until the muscles of his jaw stopped quivering, then spoke quietly: "You aren't goin' to stop her marriage that way, Aldrich. I won't let you. Especially now when she's got the chance to tie the knot with a decent fella like Stephen Hodges instead of a low-down, cheatin', grubbin' bug fucker like you! Stay away from my daughters, too! Here?"

The rage overwhelmed the lawman again and he smashed his fists together hard and Aldrich winced with the suggestion that his head was intended to be between the great ham hands. Aldrich was frightened now: The sheriff had two marriageable daughters. They were ugly. He loved them. At the point of a gun he had already warned lonely, horny Aldrich away from them.

"I'm sorry, Sheriff, for getting you so angry. I didn't know you and Liddy were such close friends," Aldrich tried to calm the storm.

"I love that little girl, Aldrich. I never will forget how good she was to us when my wife died three years past. How she showed the girls how to cook and keep the house clean. How she took care of the young one when her period come while her sister was away, and I was runnin' around like a jackrabbit not knowin' what to do. . . . It's goin' to be good to see Liddy again down at that weddin' in Boston next week. It promises to be a damn fine blast."

"You're going to Liddy's wedding?" Aldrich asked, the pain of his awesome rejection passing through him like the shafts of spears. Tears flashed suddenly to his eyes: His exile was cage-like in its completeness then, all-inscribing, isolating him even from the widespread knowledge of his ex-wife's remarriage that must have been the most talked-about event in Inglenook for a month. Aldrich, who had once owned the beautiful Liddy, must happen now upon that news in the pages of the *Times* . . .

"There's twenty-five or thirty from Inglenook goin' down for it. You should see the present we're goin' to give them, one present from all of us together."

"What is it?"

"The widow Fletcher's house on the Common, the one she left to the village in her will."

"But why?" Aldrich shook his head dumbfoundedly. "The Welshes have more money than God. The Hodges have even more than the Welshes. Why would anyone need to give them a house for a wedding present? Nobody gave me a house when I married Liddy. Nobody gave us much of anything."

"Tough one, Dwight David. Sounds like her folks seen you comin' a long way off. Besides, I hear tell that the circumstances of your marriage were rather bizarre, if that's the right word to use. I mean, I'd think twice about handin' over a fat present to some bridegroom that showed up bare-ass naked to his own weddin'."

"You don't understand, Sheriff . . ."

"I don't care to, Aldrich. I don't want to know anything else about you. My goddam head is about ready to explode right now from all the problems you've brought into my once peaceful little jurisdiction. But to answer your question about the wedding present, we're givin' them the house because we want Liddy and Stephen Hodges to come back and settle in Inglenook."

"Back to Inglenook?" Aldrich smiled in wonderment at the naïve hopefulness of some people. Hodges was a Wharton MBA. Liddy, now at Harvard Law, clerked summers in her father's firm. They were doubtless getting set to storm Boston as the complete professional couple. The widow Fletcher's gift house would never be anything more than an occasional retreat for them.

"Damn right! Inglenook needs good young people like them if it's ever going to grow in the future. With his business training we can offer Stephen the town manager's job right off the bat."

"They'll never come back to Inglenook, Sheriff," Aldrich said stonily.

"Well, maybe not while you're here, Dwight David, but from the look of it back there at North Hollow you might not have too much more reason to hang around these parts come spring. If your enemies keep at it with their current gusto, there shouldn't be anything standin' by mud season."

"Move on?" Aldrich asked dumbly, hearing the words bounce around the Highway Department's corrugated garage with a tinny echo. "Move on to where?"

"To where you come from, I reckon. It was out in Kansas, wasn't it?"

And face the ignominious judgment of Abilene that Dwight David Aldrich had tried to knock the world on its ass and quite evidently failed: Never!

"Yes, that's where I came from," Aldrich agreed.

The sheriff handed Aldrich the snowshoes: "We'd better haul ass back to the jeep, Aldrich. I'll have to call the boys at State and tell 'em somebody took their Cat for a ride and left the garage door unlocked."

Outside the garage they struggled into the snowshoes and started the trek back across the plain toward the remnant of North Hollow. Two does bounced across the whiteness before them, not fifty yards away, and the sheriff dropped reflexively into a shooting crouch, aimed and fired, though he had no rifle. Aldrich grew bemused at the motion, thought to ask the question that was forming in his mind: "Do you think some of the boys from town might be cleaning out my assets at North Hollow, Sheriff, to make sure I'll leave so that Liddy and Hodges can feel free to come back?"

"Nope." The sheriff spat emphatically into the snow.

"Not Bixbee the general-store keeper, or some of those boys I couldn't pay who did the wiring and finish carpentry and the stonework on the fireplaces?"

"Couldn't pay? Wouldn't pay is more like the truth. But no, you're long past your hour of terror with them. There was a time about two years back when I had to stop in the Towne Tavern every night around closing to make sure those boys weren't all liquored up and gettin' set to come out here and burn you out, but Liddy paid them all off and the trouble blew over."

"She did? You're kidding?"

"I'm not kidding. She got her father, Mr. Welsh, to put up the money and he paid back every last cent was owed those boys. I bet you didn't even know that, did you, Aldrich?"

"She never said a thing. Not a word."

"That's probably because they wanted to make sure that money didn't get waylaid en route to the rightfully intended."

Aldrich shrugged: "Well, at least I realized some sort of profit out of my marriage, even if I found out about it belatedly."

"In this case I'd say you profited by keeping your life, Aldrich. Those unpaid boys were in a mean, mean mood."

"I should have fought harder for more alimony from those Welshes!" Aldrich suddenly raged. "I spent four hard years of my marriage trying to build a good home and a fortune for that bitch, and her family turns me out when they don't have any more use for me on five hundred lousy dollars a month!"

"What a terrible injustice!" the sheriff howled his derision. "One of the worst crimes against humanity I ever did hear of, let me tell you, sir! Shit, Aldrich! The way I got the story you didn't have too many moral aces in that sloppy deck of yours, otherwise you were goin' to face two separate charges of kidnapping."

"It wasn't kidnapping. It was amorous detainment. No one was held for ransom, after all."

"You crossed three state lines both times. That's kidnapping, Aldrich. At least it is for the rest of the citizenry."

Aldrich said nothing. They were at North Hollow now

and the sheriff grew distracted looking into the ruin of the Steamboat Springs House. He pointed to a collapsed section of interior wall that Aldrich had finished off in cheap green lumber. Drying, the wood had contracted, and ugly tufts of equally shoddy, bargain-rate, flood-damaged insulation had begun marching outward through half-inch gaps between the planking. The lawman yanked off a section of the insulation with a gloved hand and held it up before Aldrich: "You sure did use some cheesy goods in slappin' these shit boxes together, Dwight David."

"Some refer to the method as low-cost housing. It is not illegal as far as I know."

"No, it's just immoral instead. Especially after you tack on the sales price and that run-away finance plan you come up with that the Attorney General's office down in Montpelier got so curious about a couple of years back."

"Is there anything else?" Aldrich asked him stonily.

"No, I'll go now. My high blood pressure has had about all the outrage it can stand today."

Aldrich unstrapped his snowshoes, preparing to hand them over to the other, when he suddenly dropped them in the snow and threw his arms about the sheriff, holding him tightly in a bear hug. Surprisingly the man did not clutch in panic, only pushed Aldrich off gently after a long moment.

"You're lonely, huh, Dwight David?"

"I just wanted to touch another human being."

"I don't doubt it. For a man that's not been sentenced, you're livin' pretty close to a prison existence. I don't know how you can stand it, Dwight David. I think you'll have to leave here pretty soon. Your destroyers are goin' to make sure of that anyhow."

"You think it's the only thing I can do, don't you?"

"Yes. And like I said, Liddy and Stephen won't come back while you're here."

The sheriff turned and carried away the snowshoes to the jeep, climbed in and drove off without waving. That was when Aldrich resolved Lydia Welsh was never going to remarry. Especially that jackass apostle of liberal benevolence named Stephen Hodges.

The wedding day.

By early afternoon of the Saturday of Liddy Welsh's marriage to Stephen Hodges, Aldrich had already shown himself twice in the village to corroborate his alibi that he had never left Vermont with the few souls of Inglenook who had not gone down to Massachusetts for the festivities. He caught the 1 P.M. news from Burlington on the truck radio, but there was no mention of Liddy or her death.

He walked agitatedly about North Hollow for about forty-five minutes and was on his way back to the truck for the 2 P.M. news when he heard the shrill cries behind him and turned to see Aunt Zebidiah striding with a giant's progress across the snow on her cross-country skis. She wore the long-skirted two-piece Victorian suit of Thanksgiving Day and a great fur hat on her head. Beneath the hat, Zebidiah's face was near rapturous in its joy.

"Dwight David! Dwight David! I was right! Exactly what I dreamed came true! I seen it on the telly-vision not twenty minutes ago! Lydia dead down in Boston Town! In a white dress like a virgin all covered with blood! It happened at eleven o'clock afore noon!"

"Oh sweet Jesus, thank you!" Aldrich moaned. A bolt of pain passed through him, delicious like the thrill of orgasm, and he grabbed at his crotch because he thought he was about to come in his shorts from the delirium.

"Where did she get it, Zebidiah? Where did the bullet hit?"

"Right in the left teat. It was plain as day on the telly-vision. All blood red on her white dress . . ."

"Right through the heart? What a shot that guy is! The groom, Zebidiah? Did you see the groom?"

"Shocked! That's what the man on the telly-vision said. He was shocked! It showed how they took him away in the ambulance to the hospital. They gave him oxy-gen from a tank 'cause he couldn't breathe so good."

Aldrich grabbed Zebidiah and hugged her tightly, and together they did a hopping little dance of joy, though for different reasons, the slats of her skis clacking and popping in the cold like snapping fingers.

"I was right, Dwight David! Wasn't I right? Us Aldriches got to stick together!"

"Yes, Zebidiah, you were right! Absolutely right!" Aldrich agreed. Zebidiah bent to release the skis and they danced and hopped some more in the snow.

After a while he kissed his great-aunt fondly goodbye and went back to the pro shop to wait for the State Police who would surely come to North Hollow with a warrant for Aldrich's arrest and extradition to Boston.

CHAPTER 7

A Saturday Night
in Vermont

A little forward now in time.

Except for losing a portion of the lobe of his right ear at Liddy Welsh Aldrich Hodges' funeral, nothing much happened for more than three weeks after the burial until the early darkness of a Saturday evening in mid-February when a snowmobiler decapitated himself on the fluttering net of the tennis court.

Aldrich, nodding gravely over his underlinings in *Six Crises,* heard the snowmobile's distant approach, then grew wary as it drew very close to the pro shop and remembered one of the sheriff's warning that they might next begin shooting at him. When he heard the sharp crack! sound that was like a rifle fired in bitter cold, he dived to the floor, expecting the shattering of windows.

Instead the snowmobile crunched with a medium bump into the side of the hut, the motor dying with a sputter. Aldrich decided on the instant that it might be wired with dynamite and dived head first through a window, picking himself up and racing off about one hundred yards from the shack, heedless of his cuts and bleeding. He held his ears against the explosion, then, when it failed to occur, chanced his way back in a wide arc around the hut. By moonlight he saw the headless apparition in a blood-spattered blue snowmobiler's suit and guessed sadly what had happened. The head lay about twenty feet away, cleanly severed. The goggles had popped off into the snow nearby.

The victim was Minyard Turner, the woodchuck hit man that Aldrich had hired to assassinate his ex-wife Liddy in Boston on the day of her remarriage to Stephen Hodges.

Minyard's head had a surprised look on its face and Aldrich spoke to it for a while of his problems, and his loneliness, but declined for the moment to speculate on future prospects. He suspected, though, that the head had been drinking, and when he lifted it up and smelled its breath, he grew righteous and told it it had just been rewarded for its indulgence.

Aldrich unzipped the snowmobile suit and out fell a pocket flask of Four Roses, from which he took a long belt. Then he looked for identification in the body pockets, and finding none, decided instead to take the head into Inglenook for identifying.

He first returned to the hut, bandaged his cuts, boarded up the window he had dived through with some scrap lumber and canvas, then carried outside a blanket to cover the body so he might impress the sheriff with some suggestion of reverential gesture. He placed the head in a plastic trash bag, went to the pickup, deposited it beside him on the front seat and drove away to the village.

A sense of expectancy at the prospect of a social encounter welled up in Aldrich: He positively trembled at the notion of whipping the blood-dripping head from its sack, certain of the revulsion and horror it would inspire among the Saturday-night checkers players and hangers-on in the general store who had actually run him out of town a scant three weeks before on the night of Liddy's death; his sense of drama, keen and inspired, could barely await the moment of unveiling. But there was a stir of apprehension in the midst of this unaccustomed euphoria despite his profound relief at this sudden gift of eternal silence, the way there must needs be in everything these days: If their anger with Aldrich had not yet cooled, the unfriendly villagers might cite some medieval Vermont law about taking down your tennis nets by Thanksgiving and use that pretext to outright lynch him.

In minutes more he drove up beside the gas pumps outside Bixbee's General Store. A light snow fell inside the arching glow of two lamps over the pumps and there was the usual collection of old, listing cars about that told Saturday-night checkers was under way. Aldrich carried the head inside. He felt immediately the waves of animosity emanating from the five old men seated before the potbellied stove. Two played checkers while three others looked on. Predictably, all five wore black armbands, badges of the public sorrowing of Inglenook over the death of Liddy. To a man they scrutinized his bandaged right ear closely. Bixbee, the storekeeper, pronounced stonily: "I can't extend you no more credit, Aldrich."

"That's not why I'm here, Mr. Bixbee."

"Well?"

"Somebody on a snowmobile decapitated themselves up at my place."

They grew interested. There was a slight perceptible shift of bodies toward him.

"Who was it?" one of the checkers players named Bullfring asked.

"I don't know. I've never seen him before. The body was too heavy for me to load on the truck, so I brought in the head instead."

"That was somewhat kind of you, Aldrich," Bixbee said conciliatorily.

Aldrich opened the trash bag, and fixing the old men with his idea of a fierce theatrical gaze, whipped out the head, grasping it by the hair. The five regarded it with level curiosity.

"That's Minyard Turner," one of them, Orenfiester, spoke, pointing his pipe at the head. "He looks kind of surprised, I think."

59

"Poor Minyard," Aldrich grieved.

"Did you know him, Aldrich?" Bullfring asked. "I thought you said you didn't know him."

"No, I didn't know him. I guess he's not from the village, huh? He was drinking, it seems. I don't think he felt much."

"Minyard always did have a problem with the firewater," one named Redmond spoke. "When his wife was still alive, I'd sometimes go up to his place when he was drunk and passed out and muck out that cow barn of his and milk the cows. Them animals'd be standin' almost to their knees in the shit and howlin' to have the milk taken."

"He was a lazy bastard. His father was a lazy bastard before him," Bullfring judged.

"Still he didn't go on welfare that time when his barn fell over and killed all the stock. You've got to give a man credit for that."

Aldrich absorbed that barb, the inference to Great-aunt Zebidiah, thought instead of plunking down the dripping head on the checkerboard from anger.

"Yes, and furthermore," Redmond said, "if you ever went out to Minyard's place you were always served good wine and beer."

"That's true," was the general agreement. Then: "Where's the rest of him, Aldrich?"

"Out at my place. I covered him over with a blanket from respect."

"It's good what you've done, Aldrich, bringin' in Minyard for identification like that," Bixbee congratulated. "Maybe I can extend you a little more credit after all. What'd he hit? A fence?"

Aldrich hesitated, thought of lying, but decided it might be worse when the truth came out in the coroner's investigation: "He crashed into the top wire of a net of one of the tennis courts. . . ."

"You could've taken it down."

"There's no law." Aldrich stood his ground. "Besides, he was on private property."

"Not too much credit, though," the storekeeper advised. "Well, we'd better call the sheriff, then go out and get the rest of poor Minyard."

They rose to dress with the ponderousness of old men and started outside as Bullfring rang up the sheriff and Bixbee ran a wet mop over the drippings of Minyard Turner's blood. Aldrich returned the head to its plastic sack and Orenfiester— who rode up front in the pickup with Aldrich—held the sack on his lap while he worked at lighting and relighting his pipe.

"Fine cold night, isn't it, Aldrich?" the man opined.

"Yes, it's quite beautiful," Aldrich answered, scanning the heavens across a vast arc of newly arrived dark clouds that ended in a fiery red glow east of Inglenook in the vicinity of North Hollow.

"My place is on fire again." Aldrich sighed resignedly, hoping it was not the pro shop where Minyard Turner's headless body lay near enough to cook.

"Maybe we'll catch whoever it is this time," Orenfiester said. "I don't much care for North Hollow but before I die I'd at least like to know who really hates it so much."

"Yes," Aldrich agreed. "So would I." He knew they would never catch his destroyers, though: In his mind they had taken on a spirit quality again despite the telltale markings of snowshoes, Caterpillar cleats, cross-country skis and their ebullient friendly wavings from a stolen airplane. They had to be somewhat, to take advantage of a brief trip to the general store with a head that needed identifying to put the torch to yet another building. But Aldrich was game: The pickup roared along the road, bouncing the last few hundred rutted yards until it slid to a halt before the pro shop, where there were no arsonists in evidence, needless to say.

The Alta Lodge was afire, the flames rushing skyward with a sound like the low rumble of a jet engine. The pro shop still stood and Minyard Turner's headless body lay unscathed beside it. When everyone had collected they strode toward the body and found a note pinned to the blanket covering. The snow all about was beaten down by the hooves of horses that led away inevitably toward Canada and safety.

Aldrich opened the note and read aloud to Bixbee, Bullfring, Orenfiester, Redmond and Rausch.

Dear Aldrich:

Are you now become a murderer in addition to your crimes against Nature, the laws of economics, professed goals of social reform and beautiful, beautiful Liddy, your ex-wife, who is now doubtless in heaven? Where's this man's head, you savage? Did you use a chain saw to undo it? Vermont, in addition to all its other problems—high unemployment, recession that is really depression, capricious snowfall, absentee foreign investment, high taxes and a near standstill lag in second-home construction—does not, I repeat, *does not* need a chain-saw murderer. Such an additive problem to the already existing stresses in this little state of mind might cause the complete panicked collapse of social order. I shall phone the sheriff forthwith and acquaint him with the problem for your own good.

But, to more important business.

As you see, there are only two buildings of any particular substance left in North Hollow to deal with. Tahoe House and the Sangre de Cristo Mountains Recreation Center. I'll do so at my own leisure, but promise to spare the pro shop so you'll at least have a roof over your head until warmer weather returns.

Since this is our first communication, I'll tell you that it was I who assassinated Liddy for reasons that will be made known to you when the time comes. This missive from your evidently activist enemy, a genuine North American Scarlet Pimpernel, defender of revolution and eradicator of social injustice everywhere, those very things you so cruelly disavowed one unforgettable day in 1970 when you destroyed the commune of North Hollow.

Vive la libération Québecois! Vive PLO! Vive IRA! Eritrean independence! Black Nationalism! Etc.!

"What revolution, Aldrich?" Bixbee asked, keenly perplexed.

"The one that was going to happen in America in the late sixties, early seventies that never got off the ground."

"I heard about that one," Orenfiester said. "That was about the same time all those young fellas was goin' to Canada to beat the draft."

"Yes," Aldrich responded lamely. He turned with the others to watch the roof of the Alta Lodge collapse in an uprushing blizzard of sparks. From the corner of his eye he caught sight of the village volunteer fire truck lurching up the road after the sheriff's jeep. His mind, dazed now with the blunt proof of his most certain speculation, turned a kaleidoscope of faces through it. Faces from the pre-North Hollow Development Company days of the commune that Aldrich and Liddy his wife and her long-time affianced Stephen Hodges, who lost out to Aldrich on the very day of his wedding, had founded together. Faces of the twelve other permanent commune members who had sat about planning mostly ineffectual anarchy against Washington and the military and the political Right to even up the score over Vietnam before Aldrich had seen his chance to clear the decks and gain sole control of North Hollow once the major buildings had been framed up and closed in and were ready for the interior finish work.

From greed Aldrich turned patriot-informer and blew the whistle to the local field office of the FBI the day before a number of the communards were preparing to descend to New York and terrorize the super-chauvinist hard-hats working high steel on the World Trade Center in Lower Manhattan with sniper fire. In his deal with the feds, Liddy and Hodges were also to be exempt from prosecution (though neither knew there was a deal) and on the morning of the surprise raid Aldrich contrived for them to be away with him in Montreal. Returning, North Hollow commune, soon to be North Hollow Development Company, was deserted and silent as the aftermath of a massacre, though in fact there had been no shoot-out. . . .

Now Aldrich stared north past the glow of fire and wondered which of the betrayed had evidently escaped to Canada, found out the name of his accuser, and periodically crossed the border to wreak havoc on Aldrich's shoddy commercial dream. Who among them was so deranged and full of hatred that he took the life of innocent Liddy into the bargain?

Then the sheriff ran toward them from his jeep, his gun drawn and shouting at the top of his voice: "Hands up you bug fucker, Aldrich! Some anonymous citizen just called and said you went bonkers and cut off some guy's head with a chain saw!"

"But I didn't . . . !" Aldrich protested feebly, throwing his hands up as the sheriff slammed him hard into the wall of the pro hut.

"He didn't, Sheriff," Bixbee affirmed, hauling down the lawman's gun. "It's Minyard Turner who's dead and he cut off his own head drunk-drivin' on a snowmobile. Aldrich here brought him in for identifying. Also, Aldrich got a letter from the guy who killed Liddy down in Boston. It's the same anonymous citizen who called you and is burnin' down all the buildings here at North Hollow."

"Did that bug fucker sign his name?" the sheriff demanded.

"Of course not, stupid," Aldrich answered. The notion bemused him, then sent gales of laughter tearing out of his eyes. He supposed they thought he was mad. The sheriff took the letter from him, scanned it briefly beneath the flashlight, then read aloud the portion about Vermont's problems and the added stress of having a chain-saw murderer running about.

"He's not so dumb for being a radical and a murderer," the sheriff opined, and there was a general agreement about that. "Still, it's good to know he's the murderer and not you,

Aldrich. Bullfring and some of these boys here was your alibi that you never left Inglenook that day but I always did feel you was involved in it. That if you didn't do it yourself, you hired somebody to do it. Your Great-aunt Zebidiah thinks so, too. She's been in three or four times since then to tell me that . . ."

"Zebidiah!" Aldrich hissed. "God! Even family can't be loyal!"

"Well anyhow, I'll send a copy of this letter to the police down in Bean Town. It should clear up any lingerin' doubts they have about you."

But Aldrich was unhearing. He stared in blank-eyed fascination at the turning dome light of the old fire truck that stood nearby, heard the ragged idle of its engine: "Why is the fire truck here? There's no water."

"A token gesture, Aldrich," the fire chief said. "It's just to show you that if there was water we might be able to do something for you. It was neighborly of you to bring old Minyard in, after all."

"You're very kind," Aldrich told them each in turn as he shook hands with them when they prepared to depart, taking Minyard Turner's head and body with them. He stood for a time and watched as the sheriff's jeep and Bullfring's station wagon followed after the fire truck back to the village, then turned about to watch the Alta Lodge burning fiercely to the ground, comforted despite everything by the fact of human contact when it seemed so long since he had even shaken hands with anyone. He slept well that night, came awake in the morning with a vague feeling like optimism.

By noon though, after he had threaded the endless ribbon of his problems through his mind once more, the burgeoning optimism had dissolved. Withdrawal, now become an easy habit, returned to claim Aldrich, so much so that when he saw in the distance five or six of the village women trudging single-file through the snow to North Hollow carrying covered dishes of food, he bolted and ran to a grove of fir trees rather than face them. Bundled, with the uniform obesity of older country women, they resembled Russians crossing a blizzarded steppe.

He peered through the trees as they knocked on the pro-hut door, then watched as they put the covered dishes down in the snow and scribbled a note that they shoved into a crack in the door. They left in the same orderly file as they had arrived, marching off perhaps to a car that he presumed they had left at the plowed end of the road.

For no reason at all, it seemed, Aldrich began crying amid the trees: Ah, how it was possible to both love and hate the inscrutable Vermonters.

CHAPTER 8

The Five-Acre
Hit Man

Liddy Welsh Aldrich Hodges' death—assassination by a high-powered rifle on the steps of an Episcopal church in a Boston suburb—had electrified New England with its stunning anomaly. The vendetta technique of olive-skinned peoples came with violent intrusion into the bastion of the Brahmin.

Disappointingly, no stab of pain had passed through Aldrich at the moment of his ex-wife's dying. He imagined it would be so, a searing bolt of acknowledgment that, if nothing else could be called simple in his life these days, he had at least achieved a clean vengeance against Liddy for daring to divorce him, for daring to trifle with the pillars of the massive Aldrich ego by presuming that another marriage meant another chance of equaling the romantic ardor she had known with Dwight David Aldrich of Abilene, Kansas.

The day of her death, after Zebidiah had given him the news, he had gone home to the pro hut to pour himself a congratulatory drink and wait beside the phone he had had reinstalled a scant three days before for the call of confirmation from the hit man Minyard Turner he had sent down to Massachusetts to murder Liddy Welsh.

Only Minyard had not killed her.

After an hour or so of fidgety waiting for the call, when Aldrich supposed a State Police car would make its way into North Hollow at any moment, Minyard Turner phoned from Manchester, New Hampshire.

"Nice job, Minyard," Aldrich congratulated him. "Where are you now?"

"Where I been nearly all day. In the parkin' lot of a Howard Johnson in Manchester with a broken drive shaft on my fuckin' truck. I'm waitin' here for a guy from a junkyard to bring me another one."

"But, Minyard . . . she's dead . . ." The realization that she was dead and the revenge was not Aldrich's at all convulsed him with fear, sent him scanning the horizon in every direction for a brother hit man.

"How'd she die, Aldrich?" Turner asked. "A heart attack?" There was no apprehension, just a level curiosity to know.

"Somebody shot her with a rifle the way you were supposed to."

"Well, it wasn't me, Aldrich. And I got a goddam Howard Johnson manager who's been tryin' to kick me out of this parkin' lot since early mornin' to prove it."

"Then who?"

"I don't know. Maybe she had another ex-husband who wanted her dead. You ain't gonna try to take back that five acres you deeded me for the job, are you?"

"Did you do the job?"

"No, but I was goin' to. That is, I intended to."

"You didn't do it though, Turner."

"I know a lot, Aldrich. The cops might like to know as much as I do. My cousin Hiram knows a lot, too. It'd be a nice gesture if you'd give Hiram about five acres also. Otherwise, Lord knows what Hiram might say if he went 'n got hisself drunk."

"You're just a fucking Vermont dirt farmer, is what you are!" Aldrich shrieked at him.

"And you're just a goddam frustrated lady killer, you are!"

Minyard Turner laughed a long raucous laugh at the notion of his own humor, then slammed down the phone on

Aldrich's ear. Aldrich leaped to his feet in a tight fighter's crouch and began punching at illusory mocking likenesses of Minyard Turner that rebounded up from the floor after every spring with robot-like precision. But in another minute, as he grew tired, Aldrich became terrified anew that he had no part in his ex-wife's dying. Who then? What other motive? What bastard had dealt such a low blow to Aldrich's sweet joy of revenge? He yanked on a jacket, seized the loaded Winchester from the wall, scanned the early darkness for phantom gunmen infused with someone else's purpose, dashed outside along a weaving dodging path to the pickup and raced into town for the safe company of anyone who had not that day gone down to Massachusetts for the wedding.

At the general store the Saturday-night gang numbered only Bullfring, Redmond and Orenfiester. They did not play checkers, instead sat before the potbellied stove in a grave, pipe-stem-punctuated conversation. On the store counter a portable TV played soundlessly, evidently in waiting for the 6 P.M. newscast from Burlington. At Aldrich's entrance they rose from their chairs, a community of suddenly stricken men, their ancient animosity toward him miles away gone and diffused. Orenfiester even dropped his pipe to the floor. Bullfring, apparent proprietor for the day in Bixbee's straw hat and apron, coughed nervously as he stared downward at his feet, on which he rocked to and fro: "You happen to hear any news on your truck radio this afternoon by chance, Dwight?"

It was the first time in long memory that Aldrich had heard his Christian name spoken in the village of Inglenook. He wondered how the man knew it until he remembered all the bounced checks he had left about. He looked to the wall beside the cash register and saw one of his own taped now beneath a No Acceptance sign. Bullfring followed his eyes. Symbolically, the proxy storekeeper removed the bad check, tore it into tiny pieces that he threw into the potbellied stove.

"I know about it, Mr. Bullfring. My Aunt Zebidiah told me."

"Who the hell would do it?" Redmond begged. "And on her goddam wedding day. You'd be the only likely suspect seein' how she threw you over like she did, but everybody knows you didn't leave North Hollow all week."

"She didn't throw me over, Redmond. I had to divorce her to get rid of her," Aldrich lied.

"That ain't the reason, Aldrich," Orenfiester told him bluntly, the well of his sympathy for Aldrich evidently a shallow place at best. "Nobody here in Inglenook is quite sure what the reason is, but I'll bet it was 'cause of that young fella Hodges she was gonna marry today that you divorced her. That's what I always thought happened."

Aldrich snorted his contempt. "Hodges! Don't be absurd! Hodges was nothing to Liddy, only a laborer here when North Hollow was a commune. I took Liddy away from him on his original wedding day . . ."

"Aldrich is a blind motherfucker," Bullfring intoned mirthfully, slapping his knee.

"What do you mean, Bullfring?" Aldrich demanded. "You'd better make it good."

There was no direct answer. They were gossipy old men: The conversation took off, heedless of Aldrich's presence on the day of his ex-wife's dying.

"He used to come here with her every Sunday noon to pick up the New York *Times*," Bullfring avowed. "They bought wine and Wisconsin cheese and fruit and went off to have a party at the Maple Leaf Motel in Byerville. There's many from town here seen his jeep parked there every Sunday afternoon. Lots drove over after Sunday dinner just to check them out . . ."

"That can't be true," Aldrich protested. "While the commune was together nobody was permitted to buy an establishment newspaper like the *Times*."

"Well, he done it, Aldrich. I remember him especially 'cause he was a good-lookin' boy whose checks never bounced, 'n he had the *Times* on order every Sunday. Bixbee can tell you that also."

"That traitor bastard!" Aldrich hurled, slamming an ineffectual footfall into the floor. "Thank God Liddy never lived to consummate a marriage to a man of so little principle! I tell you, I'm happy she's died and gone to heaven today!"

The three looked at Aldrich as if he were quite mad: The result of the perverse, self-serving Aldrich logic was an actual rush of joyous tears to his eyes. In the next moment the sheriff came through the door. He seemed startled at the sight of Aldrich, then slowly removed his hat. From the rheumy glaze of his eyes, Aldrich knew that the lawman had somewhere been crying this day. A genuinely well-deserved sorrow, Aldrich thought: you sweet old uncle lover you.

"Have you heard the terrible news, Dwight David?" the sheriff asked, his voice choked with phlegm. He sank heavily into a chair near the door and Aldrich noted involuntarily that he wore an old-style tuxedo with a Scotch-plaid cummerbund. There were bloodstains—doubtless Liddy's—on the white waistcoat and the frayed-looking satin lapels of his jacket. An unexpectedly elegant-looking belted cashmere overcoat was thrown loosely about his shoulders. A Russian-style fur hat returned to sit atop his head. It occurred distantly to Aldrich that he had never before seen the sheriff dressed in anything more formal than a hunting jacket. His daughters came in behind him, their faces tear-swollen, mascara running amok from their eyes across fat Breughel maiden cheeks that framed identical tiny mouth slits, fiercely red with dime-store lipstick, ugly as the business end of a blowfish. They wore long shapeless evening gowns fashionable in the fifties, or even forties, that may have been castoffs of the women of the rich who summered in the big places down on Lake Champlain. The gowns made the sheriff's daughters look even fatter than they were. Aldrich recalled that the only suggestion of Liddy's that the sheriff could not abide was that his daughters be given subscriptions to *Vogue* and *Cosmopolitan*. Too bad.

Now the daughters each lay a consoling hand on their father's shoulder, the youngest whimpering as she may have done all the way back from Boston. Behind them, ten or twelve more of the Inglenook wedding guests edged through the door. Outside, the doors of more cars of the caravan slammed firmly in the night. More footsteps shook the plank steps of the general store, then the abrasive signal bell above the door jangled once more and fell silent. They were all inside: More than thirty of the citizenry of Inglenook, husbands and wives, old and young, fanned out in a semicircle behind the sheriff and his daughters. They had cried that day, even Starbuck the mason, a huge, fathomless man whose silences had always unnerved Aldrich (frightened him even) since the time that Starbuck had contemptuously pushed aside Aldrich and his principles of leverage and simply lifted a 250-pound chunk of fieldstone to a fireplace facing, holding it in place with one hand while he chinked it expertly with the other. Aldrich always took considerable pains to make certain Starbuck was paid for his work. Now the giant seemed spent and stoop-shouldered under the burden of his private anguish, as though he had just finished carrying the chunk of fieldstone all the way from Boston.

They were in communal shock. Aldrich had absolutely no idea how they were going to respond to him. He stood all alone before the potbellied stove, feeling its heat on his backside, scanning the tortured faces for a clue, overcome by degrees with the eerie feeling that they were looking not at him, but through him, seeing at once on some tableau the scenario replay of the decided end of that much proclaimed divinely ordained marriage down in Massachusetts. Then he realized with a jolt that the scenario was actual, being played out in soundless detail on the screen of the TV set behind him on the store counter. Aldrich turned to see his Liddy quite dead, sprawled midway up a long rise of church steps just as Zebidiah had foretold it, the wedding dress billowing about

72

her in the wind spattered with the blood of her exploded heart.

All about the victim there was pandemonium. Stephen Hodges, Liddy's husband for the seconds it took to descend the church aisle to the place of her death, wept hysterical tears hunching over her as two identically tuxedoed members of the wedding party tried repeatedly to pull him to his feet. Danton Welsh, Liddy's father, held up Big Janie, Liddy's mother, who had evidently fainted dead away. Even he looked as though he was in rigid shock, about to fall over. Good, Aldrich cheered to himself, recalling that Danton Welsh had never made any secret of the fact that he loathed Aldrich. Aldrich was in a kind of nervous delirium. Would he begin dancing beside the stove? Involuntarily he put a hand to his face to test if he were smiling. He turned furtively to watch again the faces of the returned wedding guests.

"Me . . . it's me . . . l" Starbuck stumbled over the words, gesticulating wildly toward the set.

On the screen Dickie Welsh, Aldrich's pear-shaped ex-brother-in-law lately of Harvard Divinity School, pointed wildly off camera to Starbuck and the sheriff, who had already drawn his gun. The two raced off, scrambling over the unattended form of one of Liddy's bridesmaids whose face in close-up Aldrich did not recognize, and who lay fainted, though not dead presumedly, since she still clutched a floral bouquet with two hands to her breast.

The camera eye followed after the sheriff. Across the street from the Episcopal church was a statue-drenched Catholic church from one of whose twin belfries the killer's shot had evidently come. The sheriff and Starbuck dodged cars in the crossing, along with an actual local cop who appeared from nowhere and five or six liveried chauffeurs who had sprung from the line of limousines on both sides of the street. Behind Aldrich in the general store, the returned Vermonters became a howling mob, cheering on their lawman and neighbor Starbuck, screeching for vengeance in the name of God and Liddy. Frightened now, Aldrich turned about in time to see Bixbee knock over an entire display case of canned vegetables and bagged dog food because he evidently could not remember how to get around it, then stumble dementedly over the carnage past Aldrich to turn up the sound of the TV set, something Bullfring, Redmond and Orenfiester, who stood hopping and madly gesticulating beside it, might have done on request.

The action on screen was being narrated by a stuttering voice which might have been that of the cameraman who took the incredible footage that very morning. Arriving at the Catholic church, the sheriff and Starbuck flung themselves savagely at the doors. The doors were locked. No matter: In a bobbing sequence of film clips as the camera was presumably being run toward the neighbor church, the giant Starbuck ripped the church door from its hinges and threw it down the steps. The would-be avengers surged inside, the camera following after them, its lens become suddenly frozen and cautious in the semi-darkness of the interior, slowly panning the gaudy painted walls as if it thought to find the murderer masquerading among the ragged clusters of rapturous saints marching altarward along the walls.

The sheriff and the local cop ascended the steps to the choir together with breathless footfalls, then each took one of the belfries. In the general store the silence was so absolute that Aldrich believed he could even hear the footsteps climbing the belfry staircases. His bowels twitched with fearing and a dollop of sweat cut loose from the middle of his back and plunged down his spine. Every face had an absorbed fearful look on it, and the sheriff leaned far forward in his chair, eager as anyone to know the outcome of the drama as if he had not been a participant to it all. The next shot cut to the outside and the lens became telescopic, zooming up the twin belfries to show the sheriff and the cop shrugging their shoulders in bewilderment at each other across the distance that was punctuated by a large Latin cross. Nevertheless they both looked relieved. Aldrich decided the assassin had gotten out the back way.

In the store the relief was general, except for the sheriff, who stomped the floor angrily and cursed out loud: "Goddammit, that was stupid! Any fool should've figured he'd be long gone out the back way past the altar by the time we got there! Them two lawmen were idiots!"

Except for Aldrich, everyone agreed with that judgment. As if they were watching Kojak or Cannon or McCloud. Aldrich was appalled at the effortless transfer, the universal detachment. For them, evidently, the reality of the event was so numbing that they had simply shunted it into the realm of a television serial's safe predictable violence. On screen the camera eye returned across the street to the Episcopal church steps. There, Stephen Hodges sat sobbing boundlessly into his knees, his weeping parents trying vainly to comfort him. Danton Welsh still stood rigidly holding up his wife, Big Janie. Aldrich's friend the Mohawk high-steel worker named Charlie Wishing Ten Fingers (he had only seven) held a visibly shuddering Little Janie, Liddy's sister, against the embroidered, buckskin of his full tribal regalia. His cousin Sybaritic Hawk stood beside him. Perhaps it was the anomaly of Indians among Episcopalians that drew the camera lens into a close focus on Charlie's face: It roamed the broad strong nose and the high cheekbones. A single incredible tear gathered in the pouch below the left eye, then tumbled over the ridge of the cheekbone, falling to the corner of Charlie's wide mouth as he stared down at Liddy's motionless form with so undescribable a noble savage grief on his face that even Aldrich was moved. Sybaritic Hawk, who was almost always stoned, was a great wreath of a sardonic smile, some hint, Aldrich guessed, of his judgment on the hopeless irony the day contained. The camera showed that Charlie held Little Janie to him with one arm; the other was extended down to Dickie Welsh, who sat like the bridegroom on the steps and cried with equal intensity into the back of Charlie's hand while

Sybaritic Hawk softly patted at his head. Then the final footage shifted to Liddy: An elderly man, evidently a doctor, shook his head in confirmation of the obvious, then stood aside as Stephen Hodges was helped by his parents to the side of Liddy's body. The final shot showed him lowering his wife's wedding veil over her face. Amen. The announcer voice told harshly that a warrant had been issued for the arrest of Lydia Hodges' ex-husband, Dwight David Aldrich, a Vermonter. A commercial break ensued.

"But I didn't kill her!" Aldrich blurted out. "I don't know anything about it!"

"He never left North Hollow this day, Sheriff," Bullfring said defiantly. "There's three of us here can swear to that fact."

"Routine questioning is all." The sheriff spoke tiredly. "There's two Boston detectives flyin' into Burlington to take you back with them. Your ex-father-in-law got them to swear out the warrant on you. He thinks you did it. He hates you, I hear tell."

"Fuck him!" Aldrich raged. "That candy-assed patrician! That tin god martinent motherfucker!"

Before the dazed mourners Aldrich did a little dance, punching with lead-weighted fists at the bloodied, broken-nosed apparition of Danton Welsh, who had once been a famous Harvard boxer. A month or so after his marriage to Liddy, Aldrich had gone half a round with him and been knocked decisively on his ass to punctuate whatever private and decisive point Danton Welsh was interested in making.

"Stop that foul-mouthed denunciation, Aldrich, you bug fucker!" the sheriff ordered. "There's women and children here present!"

A barely perceptible ripple of lynch-mob malice traveled across the wedding guests' faces and Aldrich made haste to apologize before the shock of their grief suddenly turned to a quest for vengeance and instant justice and they strung him up outside on a lamppost. It seemed to work: They returned to staring dull-eyed at the TV screen where two average-housewife models laundered competitively in the advertising business' new Assault Thy Brother Product style, and ended up giving all the apples to new Cold Water Cheer. Then a Mercury Monarch took on a Mercedes for a quiet-ride test and won that one hands down. When the news coverage returned it was about Henry Kissinger and SALT talks diplomacy, and Bixbee, bored perhaps with the end of violence, switched off the set.

Then there was a silence so deep that the only sound was that of the coals crackling in the stove and the fizzle noises of the TV set cooling down. Aldrich had absolutely no idea what the near-catatonic Vermonters might do until the sheriff unexpectedly began crying a little and broke the stillness with a blubbering judgment: "It was the saddest damn thing I ever did see . . ."

Then they were all crying, another paroxysm of communal grief that Aldrich thought might have done better service in the event of the complete destruction of their village, rather than for the death of a single person. Still, Aldrich found it in him to cry also, but not for the same reason: Self-pitying tears coursed down his cheeks at the certainty that no one would ever love Dwight David Aldrich the way they had loved his Liddy. A great sadness. Especially when Dwight David Aldrich had so profound a need to be loved.

The sheriff, bawling violently now, stood and lurched at Aldrich with his arms thrown wide open and his hands cupped and menacing like the claws of a bear. Aldrich grew terrified at his approach, anticipating the man would squeeze the life out of him with a single spine-cracking hug, then was mightily relieved when it turned out the lawman had only come to commiserate, not kill. He wrapped his arms about Aldrich, holding him tightly to the bloodstains of his lapels, pummeling Aldrich's back softly as if he were burping a baby!

"Poor, poor Liddy," the sheriff moaned. "Oh that poor beautiful girl . . ."

"Poor Liddy," came the garbled chorus from the weeping wedding guests of Inglenook.

"That poor family of hers," the sheriff surged on. "Poor Mr. and Mrs. Welsh, and poor Little Janie and poor Reverend Dickie . . ."

"Oh the poor Welshes . . ." came the chorus part.

"Poor, poor Stephen Hodges," the sheriff continued. "Twice on the threshold of perfect joy, but it just wasn't in the cards . . ."

"Poor Stephen Hodges . . . it wasn't in the cards," the chorus returned.

Sheriff: "The poor parents of Stephen Hodges . . . Poor Dr. Hodges and Mrs. Hodges . . ."

Chorus: "Oh the poor senior Hodgeses . . ."

Sheriff: "Poor Charlie Wishing Ten Fingers, who was their good friend and loved them so much . . ."

Chorus: "Oh poor, poor Charlie . . ."

Sheriff: "Oh Inglenook . . . for what we have lost . . ."

Chorus: "Oh poor lost Inglenook . . ."

Sheriff: "Poor Dwight David Aldrich . . . for everything . . ."

Chorus: "Oh poor old Dwight . . ."

That last keening lament convulsed Dwight David Aldrich with shuddering sobs, the wellsprings of the bottomless self-pity he felt. He lay his head on the sheriff's broad shoulder, staining its cloth with tears, and thought comfortingly to himself: My exile is ended. Now I am returned to the community of men.

Bixbee the storekeeper brought a chair, and the sheriff lowered Aldrich into it.

Aldrich, for his own reasons, cried nonstop for perhaps two minutes, the orbs of his fists held tightly to the sockets of his eyes while he rocked back and forth in his chair, the sheriff clapping him tightly by the shoulder, in anticipation perhaps of the unmanly prospect that Aldrich would rather be prostrate with his grief on the floor. The assembled of Inglenook wept and blubbered along in perfect union with the one-time village outcast.

Ours is the deepest bond of sharing, Aldrich consoled himself as his wracking sobs wound down to a ragged engine idle of snifflings: They'll never refuse me loans and credit after this. He opened his eyes to confront the blustery faces and begged in his best-remembered little-boy-with-a-skinned-knee voice: "Cou' I pwease have a hanky-chief?"

Obliging handkerchiefs flashed forth everywhere before him and Aldrich chose the large blue workingman's bandanna of Starbuck the mason. It was crumpled, used and smelling of sweat, and Starbuck, evidently loath to relinquish it, simply held it tightly to Aldrich's nose and encouraged him to "get rid of that headful . . ."

"It's goin' to be all right, Dwight," Starbuck crooned consolingly, patting at Aldrich's head. "The pain can't last forever. It may seem like your heart just wants to bust now, worse even than when she went 'n divorced you that time, but the pain always passes after a while. Nothin' can hurt forever . . ."

That was when Aldrich blew it and became the village outcast one more time: He stood abruptly, yanking his nose from the pinch of Starbuck's fingers: "Why the hell can't anybody get that story straight?" he fumed. "She didn't divorce me! I had to divorce her! Everybody in town knows she was cheating on me with that bastard Hodges!"

"They were having a love affair, Aldrich," Starbuck said stonily. "They were two fine young people in love. That's what it was."

"The state calls it adultery, Starbuck."

"Government ain't always right, Aldrich . . ." Starbuck warned, knotting the big bandanna in a couple of fierce ties so that one end began to look convincingly like the head of a homemade truncheon.

"They were adulterers," Aldrich snarled back, "and that's why I divorced her."

"Not on the day of her death, Aldrich," Starbuck menaced softly.

"Come on, Aldrich, you've got to go." The sheriff spoke urgently, grabbing his arm and moving him toward the door. "You're to be on an eight-thirty flight out of Burlington. The troopers should be here to pick you up right about now."

They approached the door, but Aldrich, charged full of stung righteousness and generally heedless of the quickening sea change in the place, surged on to a pleasant prospect: "I haven't been to Boston in over a year, I'll bet. I can't remember how long it's been since I've been on a plane and I love to fly. I love having Bourbon and water, especially when it's a night flight. You can forget all your problems and leave them behind you, and it's a gas to try to make time with the stewardesses. It's something to look forward to even if I have to go there in irons. At least I get a free plane ride out of all this crap."

They got through the resistant line of mutterers to the outside and Aldrich felt a sharp dig in his ribs as the sheriff whispered hoarsely: "Run, you damn fool!"

The sheriff knew his people to a fault: The mob was already pouring through the door not fifteen paces behind them when Aldrich finally understood. He ran for his life, sprinting around the sheriff's car to the passenger door, and was inside pleading for police protection before the lawman even got his door open. All variety of missiles—cans of fruits and vegetables, cartons of milk, a length of sausage, numerous eggs, a whole chicken, fresh apples and oranges and an unaccountable bag of charcoal briquets that landed on the hood right before Aldrich—rained down on the old car. The dome light was smashed, then the rear window, and looking back, Aldrich saw with perfect minuscule clarity that a quart can of Contadina Spaghetti Sauce had landed on the rear seat with the shards of broken glass.

The starter motor ground for what seemed an interminable time while the sheriff pumped the accelerator fiercely and muttered about a vapor lock. Aldrich thought he might be killed. He thought that especially when he turned to look through the passenger window and saw the giant Starbuck's face not a foot away, staring at him with a vacuous, almost moronic gaze, heedless of the cans thrown blindly from the other side of the car that bounced off his back and head continuously. His mouth moved as if he were trying to say something, and Aldrich, in dumb fascination, actually lowered the window a little to hear the words and the clamor on the outside.

"Tell him to hold it to the floor. It's flooded."

"Hold it to the floor, Starbuck says," Aldrich told the sheriff. "It's flooded."

The sheriff held the accelerator to the floor and the engine sputtered and roared into life as a can of something crashed into the front windshield, turning it to a rather artful frieze of shattered glass about an uncracked oval that still could be seen through. As the car lurched into motion, Starbuck's great ham fist that Aldrich had just decided was defused came crashing through the passenger window, nailing Aldrich solidly on his cheekbone, throwing him into the sheriff's lap with a hard brush against the steering wheel. Stunned, he jerked himself up again in time to hear Starbuck raging after them: "I loved her, Aldrich! Do you hear me, you fool! I loved her more than you . . . !"

The sheriff flew down the rutted track and simply plowed through the snow diagonally across the Common rather than drive around it. Aldrich found that his nose was bleeding. He peered desperately through the broken rear window to see if any other cars were being started in pursuit, then grabbed the sheriff's arm in panic: "Sheriff, they'll kill me! Don't let them kill me!"

The car slowed abruptly to a safe speed in the icy ruts and the lawman sighed miserably: "Just look at my goddamn car, Aldrich. How am I goin' to tell that bug-fucker claims agent it was attacked by a howlin' mob of my own constituents? He'll never believe me. By Jesus, you do have the devil's own ability to unleash the howling beast in men's souls . . ."

"Will they come after us?"

"No. They'll all go over 'n open up the Towne Tavern 'n get good 'n drunk so they'll be sick 'n hate 'emselves before church tomorrow mornin'. Starbuck'll probably punch a couple of holes in the bar before he's done for the night, 'n I'll have to arrest him tomorrow when he comes out of services for malicious damage, but that's all part of the game . . ."

"Animals!" Aldrich judged furiously. "They behaved like animals! I'm going to press charges against every last one of them!"

"No you're not, Aldrich," the sheriff said bluntly. "I won't let you. These are tacit people. You just tapped once of the deepest-flowing rivers of rage there can be. When they understood it wasn't for Liddy you were weepin' and cryin', but for yourself . . . Thank the Jesus Lord you're still alive!"

The sheriff drove perhaps a mile further out of Inglenook, then pulled into a turnabout to wait for the troopers who would take Aldrich to Burlington. In the silence Aldrich got to wondering again who could have done it to Liddy if Minyard Turner and Hiram his cousin never made it closer to Boston than Manchester, New Hampshire, that very morning. Beside him the sheriff began his snifflings again, twice blowing his nose loudly between his fingers and flailing the snot through his broken window to the snow outside. . . .

"A lot of men seem to have been in love with Lydia Welsh at the same time," Aldrich judged softly, not a trace of irony in his voice now.

"Yes, it does seem that, Aldrich," the sheriff answered.

It came then to Aldrich that the assassin might be one of the lovers rather than an enemy. Someone who sought to deify the beloved object before the new husband Hodges took her irretrievably away into Life. If so, did that necessarily make the assassin an enemy of Aldrich? Maybe not: So far it looked as if the guy had gone and done Aldrich a good turn into the bargain. . . .

CHAPTER 9

Predator Americanus

Only one trooper came for Aldrich.

He sat handcuffed in the rear seat behind a heavy mesh screen for the 100-mph ride to Burlington Airport with a police dog who did not like him. Every time Aldrich shifted position or tried ingratiating himself with the trooper by complimenting his driving skills, the dog crouched lower and growled more menacingly and Aldrich sweated from fear in his heavy parka and remembered that dogs were supposed to be prescient about whoever was most vulnerable to attack from the odor of that very sweat.

About ten miles from Burlington the trooper told him to shut up or the dog would rip him to pieces.

At Burlington International Airport, Aldrich was handed over by the trooper to two Boston city detectives in the airport manager's office, unshackled from the easygoing state of Vermont hardware that permitted relatively free movement of his arms before him and reshackled into a convincingly deterrent-looking Boston city police harness with a short lead of chain that allowed his arms but a few inches of motion in any direction. Affronted by that professionalism, its mean implication of criminality, Aldrich protested to the detectives. In response one detective stonily read him a statement of his rights, something the trooper had already done when he took custody of Aldrich from the sheriff.

At the flight gate, a curious crowd gathered to watch

Aldrich being escorted aboard the Delta jet. Stung righteous with his accidental innocence, he sought to assure the onlookers: "It's all right. I'm completely innocent. I'm just going down to Boston for routine questioning. This little proceeding is a complete waste of the taxpayer's money. See how your hard-earned dollars are being spent." He gestured with an exasperated but conspiratorial jerk of his head at the two detectives on either side of him, who were soundless, looking straight ahead.

"Have they finally caught up with you for all your goddam fraud, Aldrich? Or do they consider you're responsible for the assassination death of your former wife down in Boston today?"

Aldrich blanched, grew defeated on hearing the voice from the North Hollow past that would never quite go away. It was Skiffington, a Canadian of British extraction, the only one of the condominium purchasers who had ever actually taken up residence at the place. He had sued Aldrich for fraudulent misrepresentation when the roads stayed unplowed, the power was cut off and every pipe in his apartment subsequently burst during a particularly bad freeze. Now he stood glass in hand at the entrance to a small bar across the corridor from the flight gate. He looked drunk and spoiling for a fight, though Aldrich had always judged Skiffington could not punch his way out of a paper bag. Simultaneously the two detectives rushed a hand under their suit jackets to their shoulder holsters.

"I say, Aldrich, have you gone and murdered your former wife down there in Boston on her wedding day?"

"Does it look like I'm down there in Boston, Skiffington, you shithead?"

"Shut up, Aldrich!" the detective on his right snarled. "We don't want this turning into a full-scale riot."

But it already had, after a fashion: Everyone within hearing seemed to know of Liddy Welsh Aldrich Hodges' assassination. A kind of collective dread look came over the thirty or so departing passengers, onlookers and flight personnel that ranged about the gate. Inevitably, fascinating to Aldrich, children were held up by fathers or grandparents to see the handcuffed murderer over the heads of adults who crowded the seating-area railing: as if you could not begin soon enough to impress an American child with a clear-cut moral lesson if you could find one anywhere these days. Strung in harness between two detectives, Aldrich would doubtless do for this season's preachment.

"Tell your children that innocent men are also led away in chains!" Aldrich hurled, rattling the chain of his harness before him. "Teach them to speculate compassionately beyond the symbols of incarceration! Teach them of the spirit of justice and the deep, abiding fairness of our American ways that will yet be proven . . . !"

"Shut up, Mr. Martin Luther King, or I'm gonna cold-cock you right here in front of your captive audience," the same detective warned in a low voice, squeezing Aldrich's arm painfully. "I hear all that Kunstler horseshit down in Boston every time I go to testify against some bum who ends up beating the rap because of lawyer oratory. I can't be responsible for how I might react to it at this here Vermont altitude . . ."

"I'm not a liberal," Aldrich assured the cop earnestly. "I was a YAF in college. I supported Nixon both times. I've even corresponded with the gentleman . . ."

"That won't buy you spit, Aldrich. I'm a loyal Democrat all the way. I wouldn't piss on the roses out there in San Clemente. It won't buy you safety either, if you see my meaning, pal."

Aldrich followed the upward thrust of the detective's head. Skiffington had thrown the heavy-bottomed rocks glass from which he had been drinking. It traveled a high parabolic curve over the heads of the onlookers, turning end over end and flashing like a crystal comet as it drew near the glare of ceiling lights. Aldrich watched in dumbfounded fascination, amazed at a drunk's prowess, as it reached the apex of its trajectory and began a faultless descent straight at Aldrich and his two wardens. The cop to the left actually drew his revolver as if he meant to blast it out of the air. The talking cop to the right simply stuck out his arm and snatched it away from its predestined crash into Aldrich's head. Aldrich and the thirty-plus onlookers sighed in communal relief. The Democratic detective studied the glass carefully, uncharacteristically sniffing its odor with the pouty-lipped elegance of his Gallic counterpart, Inspector Clouseau, turning it about with dainty fingers.

"Scotch, I would judge," he spoke authoritatively. "A good upper-medium brand, say Dewar's White Label or Cutty Sark . . ." He passed the glass to his fellow, who concurred just as Skiffington started screaming again from the entry to the bar.

"I say, anyone, has it landed yet? Is Aldrich bleeding or unconscious?"

"You missed by a goddam mile, Skiffington, you idiot! You couldn't hit the side of a barn with a cow flop ten feet out!"

In real alarm Aldrich's detectives began herding him outside onto the tarmac toward the jet in advance of actual boarding. He resisted, doing a hopping little dance in retreat, trying for the sight of Skiffington in defeat over the heads of the onlookers. In an instant they parted as Skiffington evidently turned human battering ram. The last sight of him that Aldrich caught as the Boston cops whipped him around a corner into the jet-roar night was the fleeced Canadian being brought down by the same trooper who had ferried Aldrich in from Inglenook.

"You rotter! You corrupt fraudulent rotter, you!" Skiffington got off in a voice wet with frustrated tears.

"Only the stupid allow themselves to be defrauded, Skiffington!" Aldrich hurled back through the night, laughing deliriously as he joined the detectives now in their rush to follow the flight attendant who clutched the hem of her skirt close against her knees as she ran. She bounded up the steps to the entry door, and while she stood banging on the outside for someone to open it, the Democratic detective on Aldrich's right pleaded Heaven and his cohort on the left: "*Madre de Dios!* Pray to God this guy doesn't know anybody on this plane or we'll all be tangled wreckage somewhere between here and Boston . . ."

On board the jet Aldrich was marched down the aisle to the gaping stares of seated passengers. Blessedly, a profound relief to Aldrich himself, he knew no one among them. He sought once again to assure them he was no criminal, however, and chanted all the way down the aisle: "It's just routine questioning, folks. Don't trouble your heads. I'm not the guilty one. We're going down to Boston to find out who the guilty one is, you see."

"Shut up, Aldrich, or I'll gag you," the Democratic detective growled at him.

"He's a criminal," an old lady explained to a child, presumedly her grandson.

"I'm not at all," Aldrich told the child, smiling benignly, wishing his hands were free to pat the little towhead. The Democratic detective twisted his arm painfully and dumped Aldrich unceremoniously into the middle seat of the rear bank of three on the plane's starboard side. Aldrich was belted tightly into place.

Up front, the flight attendant who had led them aboard evidently spilled the beans about Liddy Welsh Aldrich Hodges' assassination. From his vantage Aldrich could see perhaps halfway up the aisle. In moments the grim look like dread began slithering from passenger to passenger toward the rear of the plane. Full-grown adults knelt on seat cushions like children to stare back at Aldrich and his wardens unabashedly. Feigning industry, a concern for passenger comfort, the pilot, copilot and three flight attendants all came aft for a look at the New England Monster. Across the aisle from Aldrich the word arrived to the final uninformed soul. A portly, sixtyish man who sat alone, he leaned forward to assume the grim look like dread from a woman of identical age who pointed at Aldrich and spoke out loud clear as a bell: "He's the guy who murdered that girl down in Boston on her wedding day. He's her ex-husband. Can you believe he's right here?"

The news rendered the portly loner speechless. He grew flushed and excited, lewd and glowing as if he had just seen Aldrich the lady killer in a masturbatory fantasy. Perhaps he hated women. Wished for the death of a wife.

"Oooo mah gawd . . . !" came the first ejaculation, doubtless a violent mixture of pleasure-pain. The man grabbed up a newspaper from the seat beside him, snapped it open and held up the front page to Aldrich. Dead Liddy lay center stage in full-color reproduction. Above her an alliterative headline screamed out: BRAHMIN BEAUTY BLITZED IN BOSTON!

"Jesus . . ." Aldrich judged softly. "Jesus H. Christ . . ." he whispered again, appalled at how big the thing had become. The two detectives were evidently equally stunned. They were not nearly ready for it when the fat erotic lunged out of his seat at the threesome, seeking to shake Aldrich's hand: "Sir, I am proud! I tell you, sir, I am proud to meet you!"

"Sit . . . sit down . . ." Aldrich said feebly, trying to raise his shackled hands for protection before him. To either side of him the cops came violently to life, flinging off the wellwisher. The Democrat drew his revolver, shoved the fat man fiercely into his seat again and held the gun pointed at the head of the cringing form: "You try that again, sickie, and I'm gonna blow your ass off!"

"My God . . ." Aldrich judged witlessly again. He stared across the aisle at the sickie, who no longer cringed in fear of the Democrat and now ogled Aldrich with open admiration. The rest of the plane passengers and crew were numb-faced automatons, unmoving and myopic-eyed, appalled evidently at the reality of the Democrat's drawn, menacing revolver. On either side of Aldrich the detectives breathed heavily from their exertion. The Democrat took quick, small gasps of air to bring himself under control, then spoke in a mute, wondering tone: "You are getting to be quite a famous man despite yourself, Mr. Dwight David Aldrich."

"Will there be photographers at the airport?" Aldrich dreaded, thinking of the reaction of his mother in Abilene, Kansas, to the sight of the prisoner Aldrich in chains between two cops.

"There may, but they won't get to see you," the one on the left spoke. "We've got it all arranged to get you out a back door. Photographers are the least of our problems, though, friend Aldrich. We're more worried about some gun-toting members of the wedding showin' up to settle the score for the day."

"I need protection," Aldrich whined to his wardens. "Those people are going to try to kill me."

"I need a drink," the Democrat said flatly. He pushed the call button for the hostess, who began a cautious progress toward the rear, her toothy Delta Air Lines smile barely masking the trepidation she felt.

"Yes?" she asked, staring fixedly at Aldrich, the look of fearing gradually become speculative now, as if she were trying to decide whether Aldrich had done in his Liddy or not.

"My partner and myself would like a drink," the Democrat spoke. "I want a scotch and soda and he takes rye and ginger."

"I want a Bourbon on the rocks," Aldrich told her. "Make it a double."

"You're a prisoner, Mr. Aldrich. I can't serve you a drink. I can't serve anybody anything anyhow until we're airborne."

"When we're airborne give the prisoner a double Bourbon on the rocks, miss," the Democrat told her sweetly. "He didn't do it."

"I didn't think so, if you really want to know. He doesn't look like the criminal type. He's much too clean-cut-looking."

"He's a nice boy," the Democrat agreed. "This whole trip is a waste of the taxpayer's money."

"Tsk! Tsk!" she judged. "The reasons they invent to rip you off. You should see the size of my paycheck after all the taxes are deducted. Hey, would you mind putting the gun away for takeoff since he didn't do it? We could be in some real trouble if you accidentally blew a hole in the floor of this bird. . . ."

She turned and marched forward again to dispense the official version to the crew and Aldrich suddenly hoped the captain would make an announcement of his innocence over the loudspeaker. But no matter, really: Across the aisle the sickie looked clearly crestfallen after hearing the news. The woman in the seat before him tapped the head of the man before her and told him in her clear bell tone: "He didn't do it. The cop said so himself. It's a waste of the taxpayer's money. A real rip-off." Dutifully the word traveled forward as the plane lurched gently and taxied away from the terminal. By lift-off Aldrich felt generally smiled upon and commiserated with. Below in the night the winking lights of Burlington and the moon-reflecting ice floes on Lake Champlain dropped quickly from sight as the jet banked sharply and headed southeast toward Boston.

Their drinks came moments after the cockpit turned off the No Smoking sign. The detective on the left took the cuffs off Aldrich, who massaged his wrists with emphatic relief, though they did not hurt at all, then autographed a cocktail napkin for the hostess, whose mother's most treasured possession was the autograph of the onetime super-gangster John Dillinger.

"Thank you for buying this drink for me, sir," Aldrich told the Democrat. "One really doesn't expect the milk of human kindness from the police, after all."

"Think nothing of it, Dwight David. There's lots more milk where that came from. It needs but the way. I'd do anything I could to get you sprung on a technicality, pal, but I have to make sure it doesn't beget me anything more than a slap on the wrist."

"Why? Because you know I'm innocent? Cops can sense that about prisoners, I've heard tell . . ."

"Horseshit. Nothing at all psychic about this old cop, Aldrich. I've been conned by beatific-looking matrons who've done in their husbands with an ax. No, it's because of Danton Welsh that I'd like to help you find a loophole."

"He's a very cultured gentleman who's a partner in one of Boston's best law firms," Aldrich said automatically.

"He's a prick," the detective said emphatically. "Believe me, Aldrich, I've know him a lot longer than you were married to his daughter . . ."

Aldrich turned to see the classic tremble of the Democrat's jaw as he ground his teeth together in a private rage. Then he took a hard bite on his drink: "That's an off-the-record opinion, by the way, friend Aldrich."

"Yes," Aldrich answered. "You're right. He is a prick. Some of the things I could tell you about him . . ."

But the cop silenced him with a wave of his hand. They flew over the Green Mountains, the moon glistening below on the glare ice of the open snowfields of an occasional mountain farm. They crossed the Connecticut River into New Hampshire and began the descent for the mid-flight stop at Manchester. Aldrich thought of Minyard Turner, the foiled hit man and his cousin Hiram, wondered if they were still in Howard Johnson's parking lot fixing their broken drive shaft. Close to landing, he looked out the window for the lights of a Ho Jo's, but could not see one anywhere. Aldrich sighed. He conceded sadly he would have to deed Hiram five acres also to keep him quiet.

After Manchester, the jet sprinted the last lap to Boston in twenty minutes. Aldrich waited with his detectives until the plane emptied of his well-wishers, who waved him goodbye, and the disgruntled erotic, who made no bones of his disappointment over Aldrich's innocence, then was shackled back into his handcuff harness, marched outside to the boarding area that had been cleared of civilians but was infested with State Police, then shunted out a rear service entrance to an unmarked police car that waited on the runway side of the terminal. Aldrich and his wardens sat in the rear seat; a third detective drove swiftly along a service road inside the airport fence and exited into the Sumner Tunnel traffic through a gate held open by a security guard. When the car emerged from the tunnel, beneath the steel-girdered maze of the Fitzgerald Expressway, the Democrat's closed-mouth partner on Aldrich's left said for no reason at all: "This is Boston."

"Yes," Aldrich agreed. And I am returning in irons to the place of my triumphant marriage not five years before.

The car pulled up to a rear entrance of the main police station on Berkeley Street, where again—sublime comfort to Aldrich—there were no photographers. He was led inside, mugged and fingerprinted, then taken to a room for interrogation. The Democrat and his sidekick shook hands with their prisoner at the door, wishing a continuing plague on the house of Danton Welsh. They were replaced by an interrogator named Mugiani. Mugiani was fat, short, fiftyish, balding and hollow-eyed, his head wafted about by a cloud of smoke from a stogie cigar that he pulled with a continuous lip-smacking staccato. There was an unspeakable air of wearied indifference about him, Aldrich thought, as if they had not yet come up with the crime that could shock him.

"*Predator americanus*," Mugiani said abruptly through the cigar, standing with his hands to his hips before a seated Aldrich, watching his prisoner with narrowed eyes.

"What, sir?"

"*Predator americanus*. Your ex-wife's dying words. Your genus and species apparently, at least in terms of her private classification. But everybody knew who she meant. At least ten people on the list mentioned that *Predator americanus* was her personal designation for one Dwight David Aldrich of Inglenook, Vermont."

93

"What list?"

"The list of those who called in since the killing to assure us that you're the most logical suspect and ought to be summarily executed without benefit of trial. That list headed, by the way, by her father, that elegantly persuasive civil libertarian son of a bitch Danton Welsh, a gentleman who views the matter of some people's civil liberties on a very selective basis. That is to say, I'd imagine he could be appeased by the spectacle of your beheading before a massed audience on a grim, drizzly day on the State House steps . . ."

"Can I see who else is on the list?"

"Sure. There's nineteen so far, and they aren't all your ex-wife's relatives by a long shot."

"No, some were my friends," Aldrich agreed sadly, checking down the three-page list of names and addresses. Even his banker from Burlington was there: he who would save his vice-presidency by pointing to the defaulting felon Aldrich conveniently jailed for life. Stephen Hodges was there and his ex-brother-in-law, Dickie Welsh, and also nearly every member of the betrayed North Hollow commune, whose desperation to see Aldrich hang was evidently keen enough to risk giving out Quebec and Ontario Province addresses though they were technically still fugitives in America. Dear Lord, what a passel of enemies I have managed to accrue, Aldrich thought with headshaking dismay. The only glad note was that neither his friend Charlie Wishing Ten Fingers nor Charlie's cousin Sybaritic Hawk was on the list. He handed the pages back to Mugiani, who threw them disinterestedly onto a desk top.

"This is a depressing crime," Mugiani extemporized, waving the reeking cigar in the air. "Especially depressing in New England, if you consider our long-standing traditions of tolerance and civility, personal self-reliance and dispassionate tacitness. It's so out of character for sweet New England if you see my meaning . . . bizarre and foreign, a method worthy of a bunch of crazy wops in Palermo. One thinks of restless heat, the wedding procession moving slowly through winding, sun-baked lanes, then zap!—capo A evens up the score with capo B by taking out his beautiful daughter on her wedding day, right before the Monsignor on the church steps with all of Sicily nodding sagaciously over the meaning . . ."

"I have an alibi," Aldrich told him determinedly, bringing the detective back to the reality of the American present. "A whole Vermont village will swear I never left my place today until I heard the news about Liddy's death."

"We checked that one out too, Aldrich," Mugiani said almost nonchalantly, trimming the chewed end of the stogie with a penknife, "and you're right, you never left your place in Vermont until we hauled you down here on an airplane."

"I didn't hire anybody to do it either. I don't have any money to pay an assassin."

"You're right again, friend Aldrich, you didn't hire anybody for money. You might've thought a bit about deeding off some of that nearly ruined five hundred acres you've got up there to some shit-kicker Vermont hunter to put a few slugs in the traitorous Lydia Welsh provided he could find his way down to Boston . . . didn't you, Aldrich? . . . but this was no shit-kicker rifleman. The guy who did this number was a pro. First-rate."

Aldrich barely recovered from his shock over Mugiani's dead-center perception, sputtered out chauvinistically: "There's guys up in Vermont could knock a pimple off a mouse at two hundred yards, Mugiani . . ."

"Regional pride is most commendable, Aldrich, but as I seek to imply, your man didn't make it, and just as well. Because if he had gotten in numero uno's way, we'd have a dead shit kicker on our hands to boot."

"How . . . ? How did you know about Minyard . . . ? Did he call you, Mugiani?"

"Minyard who?"

"Minyard Turner, my shit kicker," Aldrich blurted out uncontrollably. "He's stuck in Manchester, New Hampshire, with a broken drive shaft on his truck."

"Lucky Minyard," Mugiani judged. "Charmed lives have curious ways of manifesting themselves. And if you want to do Minyard another favor, Aldrich, you'll give him a call in Manchester after I release you a little later tonight and tell him not to think about crossing into Massachusetts with that rifle in his truck or I'll have his ass in prison for one whole no-parole year. Guaranteed."

Aldrich smiled inwardly at the notion of Minyard Turner safe and distant in a Massachusetts prison for a whole year and unable to collect his promised five acres: He had absolutely no intention of warning the shit-kicker hit man to stay out of the Bay State and Mugiani's clutches.

"That kind of thinking is going to backfire on you, Aldrich," Mugiani growled his annoyance through the cigar. "You can't ever see the forest for the trees, can you? If Minyard goes to the pokey he's going to blow the whistle on you, pal, and then I have to go the whole route and arraign you and you'll go to jail too because you'll never be able to raise the monster bail that'll be set by some chickenshit liberal judge who's afraid of crossing Massachusetts' outstanding moral bully, your ex-father-in-law, Danton Welsh. See what I mean?"

"Are you a psychic or something, Mugiani?"

"Pasquale Mugiani, whom you see before you with a bum liver, misfiring kidneys and a chronic ulcer condition, is but a weary servant of the law, brother Aldrich. I won't call myself a psychic, but I've long since learned to read the evil in men's hearts. Yours is an open book with glaring print, Dwight David. Real ethical pornography. But it ought to be called *Twice-Told Tales.* You've got a forerunner. The designation *Predator americanus* wasn't a Lydia Welsh original. Her mother, a fine and long-suffering lady by the way, has been calling her husband the super-lawyer exactly that for the twenty or so years he's refused to give her a divorce since her love turned to the grinding hate that the lady has managed to conceal admirably well in public places. . . . Bet you didn't know any of that, did you, Aldrich?" Mugiani asked the question in the quiet voice of restored control as if he realized abruptly that his hatred of Danton Welsh had set him to screeching.

"No, I guess I didn't know the *Predator americanus* part. You really hate the gentleman, don't you, Mugiani?"

"Words alone cannot describe the way I feel about Mr. Danton Welsh, brother Aldrich. That son of a bitch civil libber has conned more juries in this state, gotten more guys that I had an airtight dead-to-rights case against acquitted on some horseshit technicality than I can remember. Guys that were so fucking guilty they went into bars across the street from the courthouse and bragged about it. Talk about justice being blind!" the detective raged, smashing a fist into the desk top beside him. "Danton Welsh has even managed to bind and gag the lady. On two separate occasions when he got the bastard acquitted, he has caused this hard-nosed, blunt-speaking, long-time professional cop who's turning apoplectic before you right now to break down sobbing hopeless tears right in the courtroom. Another time I went home, called in sick and stayed drunk for four days. My dreams are especially frightening to me since they all have to do with vigilantism when I keep wishing for erotica. . . . Aldrich, you wouldn't believe some of the things I could tell you about that ex-father-in-law of yours."

"You really don't care if I'm guilty or not, do you Mugiani? You'd really get your jollies out of helping me beat the rap because it would turn Danton Welsh apoplectic for once, wouldn't you?"

"Tsk! Tsk! Don't make the mistake of totally unfounded presumption, dear Aldrich. My hatred is real, but it's not the blind variety. I, Pasquale Mugiani, am a good cop, not a paragon of rectitude like Danton Welsh pretends to be, but honest enough to walk with sprightly step. If I thought you had any more to do with your ex-wife's death than that fumbling attempt to send Daniel Boone down from Vermont with a slightly used flintlock musket, you would have been arraigned already and your ski parka taken away for safekeeping. And when it came time to stand trial, I'd nail your ass to the cross and, for once, have the help of Danton Welsh to do it. So, as I imply, the Boston Police Department has not given you carte blanche to flout the law."

"Yes, sir, I understand." Aldrich feigned humility. "Am I free to go, then? You don't have any further use for me?"

"Yes, you're free to go, Aldrich, but be careful out there in the world, because I do have a use for you."

"Which is?"

"Bait, brother Aldrich. Once you beat your way past all those about to be disappointed photographers and newsmen hanging around this place, it'll only be a matter of minutes before Danton Welsh knows you're loose. Then I'm hoping like crazy that super-lawyer comes after you. Because if he does I'll be ready to pounce right on his ass for violating your civil liberties. You might say I'm hanging you out as a target."

"You're wasting your time, Mugiani," Aldrich told him, pitying Mugiani's naïveté a little now. "Strong-arm stuff isn't Danton Welsh's style. I may hate his guts for my own reasons, but I've always respected that high-minded Brahmin ethic of his. He's a gentleman who wouldn't traffic with Mafia methods. What that towering rectitude and dry Episcopal scorn of his can't do to an enemy is venturing into the uncharted wastes of punishment and abuse . . ."

"Horseshit, Aldrich." Mugiani waved his cigar annoyedly through the text of Aldrich's dissertation. "I've changed my mind about springing you this instant. I'm off duty now. Come on, let's you and me hop down to the Combat Zone for a couple of drinks together and I'll tell you a few goodies about Danton Welsh that might surprise you. I think your head could stand some rerouting about the perfect illusion of who and what Mr. Danton Welsh is supposed to be. All that glitters is definitely not gold, sir . . ."

CHAPTER 10

The Plastic Woman and Other Devices

Aldrich left the police station a free man with his new friend, Detective Sergeant Pasquale Mugiani, by the same rear door that he had entered in irons. They exited down a narrow lane toward the lights of Stuart Street, crossed the thoroughfare to the opposite sidewalk and started walking toward the Combat Zone, Mugiani pointing mirthfully across the street to the Police Headquarters main entrance, where about twenty members of the press stood stomping about in the cold waiting for the sight of Dwight David Aldrich of Inglenook, Vermont.

"I love going to the Combat Zone," Aldrich told the other, excitement rising in his voice, the delicious tingling of erection uncurling in his shorts. "I love the skin flicks and the sexual devices and all the fetish equipment in the porn stores."

"Have you seen that new full-size inflatable woman doll, Aldrich? It's amazing," Mugiani enthused, the tiredness dissolving from his eyes in a blur that astounded Aldrich. "It's just like the real thing. The cunt's made out of some special synthetic stuff that even simulates contractions. It comes with a jar of lubricant that smells just like a cunt, too. A buddy of mine who hates his wife has one and he gets off on it every night. He says the doll moves fifty times better than his old lady ever did. He even has a record he plays along with it of some dame moaning and screeching like she's getting fucked with a two-by-four . . ."

"Je-sus Ch-rist," Aldrich judged in a soft whistle, fully erect before the Greyhound Bus Terminal and covertly arranging his parka over the evidence as two overweight black women carrying a single metal trunk waddled toward them from a loading platform. "God Almighty, a plastic woman! I wonder how much they cost, Mugiani. If I can afford it, I'm going to take one back with me. I haven't been laid since Christmas."

"It should set you back about two hundred bucks. It sounds like just what the doctor ordered for your exile up there in North Hollow, Aldrich, my friend. What's the matter? No hookers up there in Vermont?"

"In Vermont? Are you serious, Mugiani?" Aldrich snorted at the cop. "We don't have any of that kind of stuff up there. Lovemaking is free if you happen upon the occasion. The only problem is that the ratio of men to women is lopsidedly in favor of women. That is to say that every time I chased a girl in a bar in Vermont, there were about three other guys breathing heavily right behind me. It makes for harrowing competition."

"Ow. The ugly head of Aldrich's regional pride rearing up again. Keep Vermont green as long as you've got the erogenous sewers of Massachusetts to wade through a mere hundred fifty miles away, huh? Well, what can I say, Aldrich? Your kind of hypocrisy at least has some suggestion of a constructive principle to it. You'd keep the rot from the lily only because you happen to live in the lily and that fundamentalist prudery you're all shot through with would be sorely troubled by the enticing nearness of a Combat Zone and all its paraphernalia that evidently turns you on, and worse, you'd be absolutely terrified at the thought that some neighbor might see you there. . . . So, we add your hypocritic and self-serving support to a coterie of real moralists, and *voilà!*—the lovely lily lives to uncoil in splendor yet another season, and the children of Vermont, if they even care, have been deprived of still another reason for vilifying their elders . . ."

"You'd make a real middling-fine piss-pot poet, Mugiani," Aldrich kidded him. "You're so alliterative and musical it would take two days for the good citizenry of Vermont to realize they were being scorned for their moral rectitude instead of being praised."

"Fuck that kind of moral rectitude"—Mugiani spat out the ragged end of his stogie—"that's the province of home and family, where it should be. But that's all. Out here in the wild-animal park with its profusion of unregistered hand guns and villainous natures, the righteous theory that clamors to turn off an escape valve like the Combat Zone is getting set to wreck the ecological balance of things. That is to propose to you, Aldrich, a very fundamental maxim which every citizen should know, but only wise cops seem to: Society needs a way to get its rocks off. And what with declining outlets available to us given that local wars or even border skirmishes are unpopular since the debacle of Vietnam, and that pro football has an unfortunately limited season, and that not everyone has the stamina to run ten miles around the esplanade along the river Charles, I submit to you, Dwight David, with no undue facetiousness, that there remains but kite flying, baking marijuana brownies and this bittersweet little place as a way out . . ."

They halted before the profusion of advertising posters in the airline ticket offices on the ground floor of the Statler Building and the detective pointed across the intervening square to the traffic jam of expensive suburban cars cruising the hookers before the strip joints on the alternate sidewalk.

"There stroll the ladies, dear Aldrich, who are the salvation of the illusion of not a few happy marriages in Waltham, Wellesley, Neponset, Lynnfield, etc. . . . Hey, Lola! Hey, you bippie sweetie, you!" Mugiani called across to a tall black girl in platform shoes who had just backed away from somebody's elegant Lincoln in evident disgust over the bride price. Aldrich was delighted with Mugiani: The dour detective grinned like a satyr now and waved the lit end of the stogie in the air like a beckoning flare.

"Hey, Pasquale! How you doin', Pasquale honey? What you doin' out tonight?"

"Showing life to a friend, Lola. Hey, anybody over there under eighteen?"

"Pasquale, you know we don't let no teen-agers in this here line. You call this under eighteen?" she screamed in the midst of her laughter, yanking off the shiny black shoulder-length wig of the girl beside her, who was white and also quite, quite bald. Mugiani convulsed with laughter, slapping his stomach fiercely as the bald one chased screeching and cursing after her hair that the one named Lola passed off with a deft fake to another black girl who tossed it onto the roof of one of the cruising expensive cars. Everyone watched hypnotically as the car swung around a corner, then suddenly accelerated and burst toward the changing green light at the end of the block. The bald white girl ran helplessly after it and was gone and Mugiani grew serious and dour again, calling out to the laughing Lola: "Hey, Lola, any Italian girls working that line over there?"

"There ain't no dago girls here, Pasquale. Just dago men. I always warns them about you, honey, like I promised you."

"That's good, Lola," Mugiani approved sternly. "Men only. Like it should be. Have a good night now there, sweeties."

"Bye, Pasquale. Bye, honey," came the non-Italian hooker chorus from the opposite sidewalk, a little wistful even, Aldrich thought as he moved on with the detective, watching the fluttering of handkerchiefs after them over his shoulder in the darkness. Crossing the street through twin lines of moving cars that Mugiani halted authoritatively with a wave of his hand, Aldrich gave a low whistle of disbelief: "I'll bet none dare call that last little exchange I overheard hypocrisy, do they, Mugiani?"

"Let 'em call it whatever the fuck they want, friend

Aldrich. I find an Italian girl working the streets in my area and I promptly invade the province of her home and family. That is to say, I have a little talk with her father, brothers, uncles, the closest male relative I can find who's big enough to conclusively blacken her eye in time for Mass next Sunday. To date the Mugiani method has proved faultless. Not a single repeater. But of course you don't find too many Italian girls working the streets to begin with . . ."

"I expect not. I must say your special defense of your tribal ethic is laudatory, Mugiani, given the welter of other peoples getting their rocks off in the Combat Zone who must overwork and constantly beleaguer you, and merely don't happen to be Italians . . ."

"Tsk. Tsk. Don't be a smart-ass, Aldrich. There's not a taint of flattery in that coil of snakes you just mouthed. Every man has a special weakness. I've got a wife, two daughters, sisters, nieces, old aunts. I've got responsibilities toward all of them. When I see some little bambina who reminds me of my two daughters out there strutting her brand-new tits, I get livid to protect her from herself, to take the nigger pimp she's probably got and rearrange his face into a genuine papier-mâché African mask . . ."

Aldrich glanced sideways at the cop, startled at the fury in the voice, amazed at the distended, fibrous glare of the normally tired eyes. Mugiani grabbed the fence that ringed the Trailways Bus Terminal for support, chomped hard on the stogie for a long moment. Then he whipped out his wallet that fell open automatically to a blurred snapshot of two young girls standing before a car: "Here, Aldrich, look at my daughters. They're pretty, aren't they? The oldest is fifteen, her sister is thirteen. There are girls on the street even younger than the little one selling their bodies now."

"Yes, they're quite pretty," Aldrich lied, holding the wallet up to the arc of streetlight above. In truth, like the daughters of the sheriff of Inglenook, they were ugly, though evidently just as beloved. A professional weakness in lawmen, Aldrich decided, pitying Mugiani the objects of his passion.

"I won't . . ." Aldrich said reflectively.

"You won't what, Aldrich?"

"I won't go anywhere near them."

"You'd better not," Mugiani growled, pocketing the wallet again. "It's good that we understand each other, Aldrich. We might be friends before this is over yet, but of course my family will have to remain off limits. Come on, I'll buy you a drink."

Mugiani led the way along Stuart Street through the blasts of diesel fumes from the Trailways buses. At the corner of Tremont Street the detective chased off a gaggle of four queens with identical gold earrings who did an impromptu high-kick routine to a rhythm of contemptuous offerings aimed at the crowd of well-dressed and generally middle-aged couples descending the steps of the Shubert Theatre after the last performance who were now loading into taxis and private cars.

"That's the way, fairylanders. Keep up the strident and belligerent militancy," the cop told them evenly, spitting out more tufts of the stogie. "Then it will come home to you with terrible swiftness that the middle class will not do without its theater, but will quite happily do without the kindredness of the third, fourth or fifth sex, or whatever you call yourselves these days, and bingo!—every gay bar in this iniquitous belt will be closed up tighter than a flea's ass. Gentleman, believe me, I know that of which I speak. Now, move it on."

"I hate queers," Aldrich ground out savagely as the four slashed their way, muttering and cursing, along Tremont Street, then turned the corner of a building and disappeared into a parking lot. "They make me sick to my stomach."

Mugiani shrugged, waving his cigar: "I don't doubt it, Aldrich. Not for a moment. Given the smallness of your moral reserves and the consequent need for reinforcing righteousness, those poor gentlemen make a perfect and obvious target for someone like you to pounce on."

"I've never had sex with a queer, Mugiani."

"You have, Aldrich."

"All right. But it was only once. It was in the YMCA in Abilene on a hot summer night and I was very curious. But I didn't enjoy it. I want you to understand that."

"What the fuck do I care, Aldrich? If you didn't enjoy it you were stupid. If you decide you're going to do it, you should at least decide you're going to enjoy it . . ."

"They don't bother you one way or another, do they Mugiani?" Aldrich asked, staring perplexedly at the cop.

"As far as I'm concerned, Dwight David, the gay boys are all part of the sweet balance of the universe. If one hundred percent of the male population were straight, that would mean I would have to be one hundred percent apprehensive about some guy trying to get into my daughter's panties. But say twenty percent is gay and eighty straight, then I've already got a twenty percent chance of relief. See my point about balance? Besides, the gays are very helpful to inquisitive cops like me. They always have their ear to the ground where the whispers zig and zag, so they know things. Also they break easily under questioning."

"What bizarre reasoning, Mugiani," Aldrich judged, shaking his head. But the detective only shrugged, already in motion, aiming for a news vendor on the opposite corner who announced the news of Liddy Hodges' death to the Combat Zone. Mugiani took a final-edition Boston *Globe* from the kerchiefed woman, who would not allow him to pay for it, and shoved beneath Aldrich's nose a three-column headline proclaiming that the assassination victim's former husband, a Vermonter named Dwight David Aldrich, had already been extradited to Boston for questioning. Beside Aldrich's three columns was the same church-steps death picture he had already seen reproduced in glaring color on the front page of the Montreal paper during the flight down from Burlington.

But now it was done in a blurred, almost indiscernible black and white, and the banner headline (comforting to Aldrich) spoke mournfully, rather than trumpeting, the news: WEDDING-DAY TRAGEDY IN BOSTON.

"They still haven't got your picture, Dwight David. I'm surprised Danton Welsh hasn't provided the news services with a bushel of reprints by this time."

"If he hasn't, it can only be because he hasn't kept a single photo of me around to remind him of the person he must hate more than anyone else in the world. That probably represents the first miscalculation ever in his life."

"Oh, I assure you, friend Aldrich, that Counselor Welsh has made a few in his time. In fact, I like you so much I'm even going to tell you about one tonight. How does your new celebrity status read, by the way, Dwight David? The way you'd like the folks out in Abilene to hear it?"

"No. Shit, no," Aldrich said miserably. "They somehow came by the news that I was under investigation for a time by the Vermont Attorney General's office. Oh God, I hope Mother doesn't get a squint at this. . . . Maybe it won't play in Abilene. What do you think, Mugiani?"

"It'll play, my friend." The detective patted Aldrich's shoulder consolingly. "Guaranteed it will play. Danton Welsh may even have dispatched someone from his law firm out to Abilene by now to make certain. Your sainted mother may open her front door tomorrow morning to find a copy of the Boston *Globe* left by some kind newspaper boy on her front porch during the night. Then, sadly, the good woman will be bitterly disappointed over her first cup of coffee to learn that you, a poor boy from a desperately poor welfare family who rose to such apparently dizzying heights of prosperity in one relentless surge, who married a New England beauty from a family of impeccable background that you contrived to keep your mother from meeting because you were embarrassed by her, who became the heart-swelling fulfillment of a mother's dream to be rammed down all the neighbors' throats since they knew your father was a no-good drunk who kicked off from cirrhosis . . . Well, Aldrich, she's just going to find out, poor lady, that her overachiever son was arrested on suspicion of murder in Vermont where all was not as she was made to believe, and to her further dismay she will find out that you were divorced by the beautiful Lydia Welsh over one year ago. Then I suspect the lady will get weepingly down on her knees and pray the neighbors don't find out what it has been the cruelest blow of her life to learn . . ."

Stunned, near reeling from the shock, Aldrich pressed his hand flat against the pane of a porn-shop display window for support. Tears flashed to his eyes and his voice beseeched the squat detective hoarsely: "Mugiani . . . how do you know everything?" It came to him in a crippling instant that he had been naught all along but a consummate self-deluder who had even come to believe the roots he had invented for himself. Only now he heard gales of scornful New England laughter that assured him no one else had bought the story as unquestioningly as the storyteller had, that naïve young man from Kansas.

"Mugiani, have I been so obvious? Have I always been the butt of a joke I didn't even know existed?"

"How should I know, Dwight David? I've never been invited to any of Danton Welsh's cocktail parties. I don't expect I ever will be either."

"Then how?"

"Not psychic, as I assured you. One could intuit a bit about your past by listening to you a bit, but never really get close to the bedrock facts that Danton Welsh elicited simply by having his new and, as it turned out, decidedly undesirable son-in-law's background completely investigated."

"That treacherous double-dealing motherfucker!" Aldrich howled his fury, slamming his hand hard against the porn-store windowpane that, miraculously, did not shatter. Before him, inside the window, was the king of all dildos, an enormous silo-shaped appliance fully two feet long. Aldrich pointed at it energetically to the cop: "You see that, Mugiani? If I had Danton Welsh here right now I'd shove that thing up his ass and turn it on for eternity!"

"Shhh . . . Quiet, Aldrich. A crowd will gather. Think of your station in life," the other jibed. "Uncharacteristically, you have the blunt rages of an ethic. Remember, you come from a good Kansas family with the big house in Abilene and that enormous ranch out near the Colorado line. It's too bad about the horse shying at the rattler and throwing your daddy off that time he was out riding fences to make sure the hands—all forty of them—had done their mending properly. But, as you yourself have often sadly intimated, it was a blessing he finally died since the best that could be hoped for in the aftermath of the concussion that came from striking the fence rail with that fine tousled head of his was the afterlife of a vegetable. Something you couldn't bear to think of when he'd been such a strong, proud man all his life. Of course, all this tragedy had left your poor mother so distraught that there was no consideration of her traveling East to meet her new in-laws. And furthermore it had incapacitated her so much that there was no possibility of her meeting with your mother-in-law Mrs. Welsh when she volunteered to travel West to meet the lady . . ."

"I don't like you at all, Mugiani."

"Perhaps not now, D. D. Aldrich. But you will. Because as I intimated you are about to become privy to a Danton Welsh secret, a well-intended gift from your friend Pasquale Mugiani, a veritable royal flush of a bit of knowledge that will enable you at the very least to pick up a substantial number of your ex-father-in-law's playing chips when the moment seems propitious . . ."

"What is it, Mugiani? Tell me right now," Aldrich begged, grabbing at the detective's coat sleeve.

"A little later, Aldrich. But I'll tell you now I'm doing this because I like the idea you have tender feelings about your mama. I loved my mama, too," Mugiani sniffled, instantly milk-eyed, whipping out his wallet for proof of devotion. "Look, I carry her Mass card with me everywhere. Some days I look at it as often as ten times a day. I think it was a blessed thing you did, screwing an extra five hundred a month out of Danton Welsh on your divorce settlement for your mama out in Kansas."

"It made me a proud son to do that little thing for my mother, let me tell you, sir!" Aldrich enthused as he and the detective stood pummeling each other's shoulders in mother-loving camaraderie before the dildos and plastic vaginas in the porn-store window, heedless of a group of Taiwanese merchant seamen who stared at the two Americans with unabashed curiosity.

"I even got that tight-fisted prick to set it up so the checks were issued monthly from a Vermont bank so Mother would never be the wiser about me not being the source of the gift. . . . Hey, Mugiani, how do you know about that, too? That was supposed to be super-secret . . ."

"Brace yourself, friend Aldrich, but anything about you in any connection whatever to Danton Welsh is general knowledge among the Brahmin fellow travelers of the Welsh family. That is to say that the very day Lydia Welsh issued you your final set of walking papers, the gristmill of society was set in motion by Danton Welsh and Stephen Hodges' mother, both of whom earnestly resumed the task of uniting their two houses, which effort, alas, ended in today's tragedy, in which I, as a good policeman, really ought to be more interested. . . . Anyhow, all of this I learned from an ex-law partner of Mr. Welsh who has no special love for the gentleman, believing him to be as crooked a barrister as I do. The upshot of these rumors set forth on the wind, however, will hardly please you, Dwight David. The reason for your divorce was not given as the actual 'Cruel and Unusual Punishment' stipulation of the Divorce Code, but rather the sad whisperings have it that you were a sexual impotent . . ."

"Are you out of your fucking mind?" Aldrich shouted,

lunging at a gloating apparition of Danton Welsh with a roundhouse right whose fearful proximity sent the Taiwanese scattering along the sidewalk in flight. "Me, Mugiani? Me impotent? Find a whore! Find one for me right now! I'll make her scream so loud the whole Combat Zone will stop to listen to her! I'll do it right here on the sidewalk!"

"I don't doubt it, Aldrich. I don't doubt it for one moment. But look, you're creating a scene. People are stopping their cars. Some are leering openly. I can't have this. Obscurity is a requisite for the pursuit of my art as a policeman. That is to say, nobody, but nobody, must ever convey home to Danton Welsh the startling news that Pasquale Mugiani and Dwight David Aldrich were window shopping for dildos and other apparati in the Combat Zone when that august civil libertarian and defender of the rights of the downtrodden rich is doubtless at home praying we're extracting a confession from you with rubber hoses down in the basement of Central Police Headquarters . . ."

"I understand, Mugiani," Aldrich said quietly, taking deep breaths to calm himself, waiting a long moment until his breath smoke exploded in even puffs into the cold night air. He began walking again beside the detective: "Tell me more, sir. Tell me all you know."

"Well, the rumors allow as how the Welshes found out early on in your marriage that you'd completely misrepresented your background from an old Harvard crony of the grand seigneur who hailed from Abilene. But they were saddened rather than infuriated and chose not to confront you with your deceit because old Danton figured, however pathetic your insecurities about who you were and what you came from, there was still a good deal of commendable drive and ambition in you and that boded well for the genes of the male grandchildren he was so eagerly expecting. And of course there was sensitive Lydia, who would be crushed if she ever found out about all those lies . . ."

"Go on," Aldrich told him stonily.

"Well, there was the trifling business about all the money you borrowed from old Danton and some friends in the name of North Hollow that they have long since written off with the IRS while telling the Social Register crowd that they did it because of Lydia, notwithstanding the fact that they originally did it because they thought they were going to make a surefire killing on the rape of Vermont. Then there was the business of paying off some workmen who'd done carpentry and masonry work up there at North Hollow. This however was no act of generous consideration by Danton Welsh for those men and their families, but rather a calculated attempt to embarrass you, needless to say. Then the divorce settlement payoff to your mother came off as pure, unmitigated salvation at the hands of an excellent Christian who was nothing less than appalled when the poor woman phoned from Kansas to beg him to save her miserable house from being sold for taxes. Need I continue, Dwight David, or do you get the idea?"

"I think I understand, Mugiani."

"Good. Now that you've been properly primed by a look up the anus of the world Danton Welsh created for you unbeknowst to yourself, why don't we step into this here little bar and have a look up the puckering anus of Danton Welsh?"

CHAPTER 11

Danton Welsh:
Ersatz Brahmin

Inside the bar a melon-breasted mid-thirtyish interpretive dancer slinked along an elevated catwalk trying to drum up a little expectancy for what was evidently to be the final definitive lowering of her sequined panties to bare the prize to a roomful of generally balding and spreading middle-aged men who were more attentive to conversations with each other than to the stripper on high. Vaguely Aldrich noted that she was badly out of synch with the bump-and-grind music and that nearly all the men somehow resembled Pasquale Mugiani. He noted also that the ill-lit place had matte black walls and reeked of stale beer, stale cigars and urine, and considered comfortingly that it might be some perfect metaphoric departure point to a netherworld beneath the Combat Zone where he might escape the humiliation the vengeful Danton Welsh had heaped upon the head of Aldrich. Down there, for certain, he would never meet a friend of Danton Welsh's either.

"Have a seat, Dwight David," Mugiani invited. "Have a glass of consolation on me. Sorry to pull the rug out from under you like that, but I thought it better you should know your vestigial family pride is nonexistent. In case you got into a conversation about it again."

A bartender automatically brought a drink and placed it before the detective. Aldrich ordered a double Bourbon on the rocks. Overhead a drum roll raced to a deafening conclusion as the stripper wrestled artlessly out of her panties, hooking them on the spike heel of one shoe, so that she hopped a little on the other to regain balance until the cloth came free. Mugiani clapped a limp moment at the sight of her triumphantly displayed crotch that she turned about twice in full circle before leaving the catwalk, then said mournfully: "She's already five years over the hill, poor thing." Aldrich, remembering that he was supposed to be an impotent, clapped dutifully also for a moment, then said in an even more mournful tone: "I'm going to leave the country, Mugiani. I'm going to renounce my citizenship and never return. I'll become a British subject."

"And give up your fling at the American dream? Tsk! Tsk! I had hoped for more from you than that, Aldrich. Especially now since I'm about to even up the score between you and Danton Welsh, my friend . . ."

They were interrupted by an overweight and nervous nail biter in his mid-twenties perhaps who whispered briefly in Mugiani's ear, then was introduced to Aldrich; "Dwight David, meet Little Georgie. Georgie, this is Dwight David Aldrich of Inglenook, Vermont, who was extradited tonight to Boston for questioning about his ex-wife's murder. Georgie is a veritable film cliché known as a paid informant. Georgie bats right-handed about fifty-five percent of the time. Georgie knows who killed Lydia Welsh."

"He's innocent." Little Georgie pointed meaningfully at Aldrich.

"I know that, Georgie. What certitude are you peddling that's worth just twenty dollars to me?"

"Let's pee together, Mugiani. Like we always do."

"Order me another drink, friend Aldrich, while Georgie and I go and make a froth upon the waters. Believe me, the legendary communion between a criminal and his priest doesn't even bite the heels of the intensity that this cop and this public-spirited citizen have known together. I'll be right back, sir."

Mugiani returned from the men's room in less than a minute with a look of annoyance on his face.

"I tell you, Aldrich, the underworld at heart is naught but a bunch of romantic idealists."

"Who did it?"

"Danton Welsh. Had his own daughter killed, that bright object of his furious and unlawful passion, to make certain her heart would not be venalized by yet another interloper."

"I believe him, Mugiani!" Aldrich smacked a fist into his palm. "That bastard is absolutely capable of it!"

"No, you don't, Aldrich. You just want revenge on that worthy. Danton Welsh may have coveted the very air his daughter breathed, but she had a practical place in his game plan, too. Her marriage to Stephen Hodges, finally consummated, would have been a stunning personal coup for the fiercely upwardly mobile Counselor Welsh. I know that of which I speak, Aldrich, for Danton Welsh came East to Harvard from a town in Kansas so small it would have thought your rustic Abilene to be the Paris of the Plains . . ."

Aldrich grabbed Mugiani's arm so unexpectedly the other almost fell from his bar stool. He stared incredulously at the cop, seeking out the lie, but the sardonic crunch of Mugiani's jaw about the stogie told him there was no lie. Aldrich withdrew his grip from the arm, just shook his head numbly: "You're not kidding at all, are you? He really did come from Kansas. . . . God Almighty! What an irony! The way that bullying fucker used to rasp me about my prairie origins! He'd find ways so subtle to humiliate me at dinner parties that I wouldn't even know until days later that I'd been humiliated . . ."

"Do control yourself, friend Aldrich, or no more informants will come forward because you're creating notoriety. Take solace in the knowledge that you, showing up at Danton Welsh's estate, having come all the way from Abilene on a ten-speed bicycle for the purpose of claiming the lovely Lydia but four days before her marriage to the divinely ordained

Stephen Hodges, turned Danton Welsh's terrified heart to the coldest of cold iron in his breast. That is to say, he saw the old beast of himself in you, a grasping, ambitious, unprincipled sort of animal that he had long since veneered over with urbanity and the studied nuances of endless inbreeding. You reminded him of hardscrabble days when he'd almost convinced himself he'd been a Stephen Hodges all along. Even his children have no notion about his real past. So as I imply, Dwight David, you've already shafted the good counselor even though you didn't have the satisfaction of knowing it. He took great pains to make certain that you'd never find out that his reaction to the sight of his beloved daughter, the bride all in white, being married by benefit of clergy to you, the groom, stark naked except for the wearing of a Mohawk chieftain's headdress against the background of beautiful Lake Champlain, with no small complement of Boston society smiling catatonically on at the felicities, was a heart attack. He spent nearly all of your honeymoon in the University Hospital in Burlington."

"Wonderful! Absolutely wonderful!" Aldrich said, hammering the bar in unrestrained glee, so that Mugiani hauled down his arm, righted Aldrich's overturned glass and warned him sternly this time about creating a scene. But Aldrich was off and flying, charged by the possibility of the havoc he might wreak with his new knowledge on Danton Welsh's future days. His would be a vengeance of Kansas proportions, Aldrich thought deliriously. No small day of Puritan ignominy spent in the stocks of a New England village common; but rather a full seven days of the Kiowa with Danton Welsh staked out to an anthill and kept ingeniously alive through unremitting pain as the Indians of Kansas had known how to do.

"You shall taste the sweetness of your forsaken roots!" Aldrich spoke out loud to no one in particular, not really certain when he said it what he meant by saying it.

"Nice tits, huh, Aldrich?" Mugiani jabbed at his arm,

bringing him back from exquisite death on a Kansas anthill. The bump-and-grind refrain had come on again and a light-skinned black girl with oiled orbs of breast that were high and pointed of themselves began her slink along the catwalk in her sequined panties which were black when her predecessor's had been silver.

"She's prettier than the last one," Aldrich said, noting that the bar's patrons seemed generally more interested in the art-less dance of seduction this time around. But that was all: Aldrich ordered a refill of his overturned glass and sat staring myopically at his great wreath of a smile in a circle of mir-rored glass on a pillar behind the bar, positively prescient with the pleasure of his forthcoming vengeance.

"Tsk! Tsk! Careful, Dwight David. Your youth is showing all over your puss." Mugiani shook a finger at him. "Don't go flying off in the face of all things at once concerning Danton Welsh or your attack will have the effect of buckshot at long range. The knowledge that he came from Kansas isn't the real chink in his armor anyhow."

"It'll do for now. I'll send a form letter denouncing his fraudulent misrepresentation of his past to everyone in the Boston Social Register. I'll force him to commit suicide. He'll be left with no alternative. He couldn't stand to see himself as an outcast and pariah . . ."

"Your innocence is a belligerent one, Aldrich," Mugiani sighed. "What are you telling the bluenoses at best? That someone of their apparent membership was so ashamed of his roots and poverty-ridden past that he invented a new past complete with forebears for himself so he could come on as an equal trading partner? I could give you even more ammo for your letter, Dwight David. About his phony birth certificate here in the county records that alleges he was born in Aix-en-Provence, France. About the phony death certificate that al-leges his parents died in an automobile accident on the outskirts of that city when Danton Welsh was but two, and are buried there in the American cemetery, which grave, by the way, French authorities are unable to locate. About how Danton Welsh was given over in custody to a maiden aunt who scrubbed down cathedrals or something like that and lived in an outback town called Rouen, where she would have been completely overlooked by Bostonians galavanting around Paris, Deauville, Cannes, etc. . . . About how he somehow falsified his records at Harvard to read in complete accord with everything else he falsified. About how he got some dotty old dame up in Manchester to spread the word about hów she'd been a bosom buddy of that same aunt who'd never existed and who, unfortunately, also kicked off when young Danton was but twelve, leaving him provided for in an excellent French lycée, for which transcripts also exist, needless to say. . . . You know, Aldrich, it suddenly occurs to me for the first time that the unimpeachable Danton Welsh must be a very sad little boy way down deep inside. I mean, it's the sacred shit of Jay Gatsby if you follow me, a genuine strangler of an American cliché, an attempt completely to obliterate an unwanted past. Our man even meets once a week with a French lady who teaches at BU for a conversational hour to keep the level of that alleged mother tongue of his up to adequate. It's a goddam wonder somebody else hasn't found out about him by this time. With so many snakes wriggling around in the basket of his old life, you'd think one of them would've reared up and bit him by now."

"I am the snake from Danton Welsh's past," Aldrich pronounced dramatically, appraising a slit-eyed, agreeably determined image in the mirror before him.

"No, Aldrich, you're the snake in Danton Welsh's present. As am I and a few other brother reptiles. His impeccableness is beyond being hurt by the old life at this stage of the game."

"I'm still going to send my letter, Mugiani."

"Then prepare for it to backfire on you, Dwight David. You're just a little boy peering uncomprehendingly through the window at the Brahmin Christmas Quadrille. Do you think on hearing your news that Boston society is going to drum Danton Welsh out of town the way the Army gives dishonorable discharges? No way. They'd choose not to believe it rather than admit the good attorney fooled them. Also he has a fine track record among those folk, has given generously of his time to foundations and fund raisings, etc. And, if I may be indelicate, your own history is now widely known, friend Aldrich, which history would seem to undermine your credibility as chief accuser. It won't wash."

Crestfallen, Aldrich stared unseeing at the black stripper, feeling the storm tide of his avenger's euphoria ebb swiftly away to a real tiredness that presaged the beginning of a drunk. Danton Welsh was invulnerable then, safe behind a Gordian knot of circumstance that even Mugiani had been unable to unravel even though he seemed to have known about the Kansas other life for years.

"How did you find out about Danton Welsh's past, Mugiani?" Aldrich asked. "Did you have him investigated?"

"Nope. The thought never occurred to me to have him investigated. I never suspected that he was anything but what he seemed to be. Besides, technically, it could be called harassment, and there was no way I was going to get directly in front of a salvo from super-lawyer on that charge. That was courting sure demotion. No, I first knew all was not holy in the Holy Family when somebody anonymously sent me photo copies of two conflicting birth certificates, one from France and the other from Kansas . . ."

"Just like that, Mugiani? I mean, out of a clear blue sky?"

"Not quite. The covering letter said they were a gesture of sympathy from a well-intended citizen who had seen me break into an unmanly flood of tears outside the courthouse when Counselor Welsh got sprung one very guilty bastard whom I had handed to the County Prosecutor in an airtight bubble. . . . Other gestures of sympathy arrived from time to time until I knew everything I'm telling you now. I still don't know who it was."

"I'll bet it was Big Janie," Aldrich declared flatly.

"Who's that?"

"The woman you spoke of back at the station, ex-mother-in-law, Mrs. Danton Welsh. Her real name is Olivia, but her children started calling her Big Janie when they were all just little kids and it took."

"I met her years ago. She's a fine lady. Sending surreptitious little love notes to tearfully frustrated Italian cops doesn't seem like her style."

"She's got a good act," Aldrich judged softly, not unloyal when it came to his ex-mother-in-law, whom he pitied, who had tried in her own timorous way to forewarn him of impending eruptions of the volcano of her husband's malice toward Aldrich. "In fact, I'd say she's got a very good act considering how few people know she's an alky who has to be shipped out to some dude ranch in the Southwest to dry out periodically. Or that she sees a shrink here in Boston three times a week as a result of being hopelessly cowed into every kind of submission by you know who, that same worthy who established such a pattern of righteous abuse that his three children had absolutely no uncertainty as to where their duty lay, and contrived to heap dung on their mother's head every time their father had a notion to berate the poor woman . . ."

"Caution, Dwight David, your voice is rising again," Mugiani warned, gripping Aldrich's shoulder another time. "Calm yourself and look at that nice twat up there." The detective gestured to the catwalk, where the black stripper had peeled off her panties and was humping a defiant pelvis at the world to a drummer's final upbeat.

"You know, Aldrich, something else that's redeeming about you besides your mother love is your mother-in-law love. That strikes me as bizarre since I hated my mother-in-law in the traditional manner. However, it implies that occasionally on the chill terra infirma of your devious heart a campfire for two persons was allowed to be lit. It impresses me that you could feel love for Big Janie Welsh the way I feel for my mother, my wife and my daughters."

"Love, shit. It was the bottom line of civilization. Anybody that couldn't feel sorry for Olivia Welsh when Big Daddy the Commonwealth's chief moralist, ex-wife Lydia the insufferably beautiful altruist, brother Dickie the twenty-two-year-old pipe-sucking octogenarian of Harvard Divinity and sister Little Janie the trampy cellist prodigy turned to after-dinner games at the lady's expense would have to be a gorilla. I used to dread the possibility that she'd excuse herself with a sick headache and go up to her room, because then the archery target became me . . ."

"Hmm. What progress we're making, Aldrich. What layers we're stripping away. Have another drink on me, sir."

"Emily Dickinson . . ."

"Say what, Aldrich?"

"Emily Dickinson, the lady poet, the recluse of Amherst and all that horseshit."

"What about her? She's dead."

"Lucky Emily. When he was in his cups one of Danton Welsh's most reliable methods of berating Big Janie was to assure her he'd been born a century too late. Otherwise he might have presented himself as a suitor to that lady genius who was the only one he could conceive of as worthy of his intellect and sensibilities. When the fantasy really reached ape-shit proportions was when old Danton saw himself single-handedly changing the course of nineteenth-century American literature by bringing his adoring wife Emily to Boston to help preside over the salon he established in his great house on Beacon Hill where guys like Mark Twain and William Dean Howells wandered to and fro mouthing fiction. Yuk! What an ass! Those were the times even a well-calculated opportunist like myself couldn't conceal irreverence. The astounding thing was that his three children were in grave and complete agreement with their father that their poor alcoholic mother who sat in the same room peering into the cloudy depths of a quart of scotch couldn't hold a candle to the likes of Emily Dickinson. Those little sessions in comparative literature used to end with an hour-long reading of his lover's poems by Daddy Danton, with tears streaming down his face all the while. . . . Jesus, think of it! The man who might have wasted Emily Dickinson! Lucky American literature! Lucky, lucky Emily!"

"He settled for a lot less than Emily Dickinson in the end," Mugiani said thoughtfully, blowing a tracer of stogie smoke in the direction of the stripper who clattered backstage off the catwalk after her act wearing only her platform heels and a look of abject boredom on her face.

"Big Janie wasn't such a bad lady given half a chance, Mugiani," Aldrich defended her.

"That's not who I'm talking about, friend Aldrich."

"Who then?"

"This lady," Mugiani snarled fiercely, whipping a black-and-white photo from a deep pocket of his billfold and slapping it down hard on the bar before Aldrich.

"She's beautiful," Aldrich said involuntarily, struck by the radiant face framed between twin curtains of long dark hair. The eyes were almond dark and wide and somehow just a trifle mournful-looking, Aldrich thought. On the instant he decided he knew everything about her and why Pasquale Mugiani carried the photo.

"She's only fifteen years old," the detective rasped, taking a hard bite on his drink and draining it right to the bottom.

"And Italian Catholic, a prostitute, and client of Danton Welsh. . . . Am I right, Mugiani?"

"She was a prostitute. When she was twelve and one half years old. A very energetic little cocksucker whom Danton Welsh, given the convoluted nature of his ethic, plucked from the very streets of this Combat Zone and contrived to turn into a lady whose services were reserved for the pleasure of

Danton Welsh alone. In those days of being twelve and one half she had frizzy hair, bad teeth and skin, and knew very little English since she and her mother were illegal aliens hiding out with some cousins up in the North End. Now, as you can see, young Angelina Frippi of Messina, Sicily, has lovely straight hair, lovely skin and teeth, speaks English in a fluent and charmingly accented manner and will be a naturalized U.S. citizen in three short years since Danton Welsh bypassed certain legal technicalities by making her his ward. Also she goes demurely off to convent school each day like a nice Catholic girl from a good family should, wearing subdued and tasteful tweeds and knits of Counselor Welsh's choosing, and is allowed visitations in the living room of her mother's also subdued and tasteful apartment by young men who match the prototype young man of the good barrister's specifications. Also, mother and daughter receive allowances which, by the way, are quite generous. In short, Danton Welsh has fulfilled God knows what dirty-old-man fantasy by transforming a child hooker into a beloved spirit quality on the threshold of the nunnery. Doubtless he thinks he saved her, and thereby appeased the annoying twitch of whatever dregs of conscience remain to that astute sixty-year-old Christian gentleman when he visits the lovely, virginal fifteen-year-old Angelina Frippi twice a week to perform upon her body whatever perversions my mind will not permit me to imagine . . ."

Beside Aldrich, Mugiani spat furiously on the floor, then held out his glass with shaking hand to the bartender, who filled it wordlessly to the brim, neglecting to add any ice. The detective drank greedily, then put down the half-emptied glass on the bar with a great outrush of air through pursed lips.

"I'm sorry, Aldrich. Normally I don't drink so much. That girl is the same age as my oldest daughter."

"How'd you find out about it, Mugiani?"

"Divine intervention. Nothing less. One night, just like to-

night, while walking these same mean streets here in the
Combat Zone, I picked up that little bippie to take her home
to her family for a talk. That's when she started haranguing
me about all the trouble this big-shot lawyer friend of hers
was going to make for me. *Mama mia,* Aldrich, I grew absolutely giddy at the news that little girl told me! Talk about the
guiding light at the end of the tunnel. A God-sent beginning
of the end to all those years of impotent hatred when Danton
Welsh seemed the most invulnerable person I'd ever encountered . . ."

"Is it fair to ask why you haven't made a move on him
yet, Mugiani?"

"Because I can't obviously unless I get the bambina or
her mother to testify against him. Which they won't. And
crashing through the bedroom door into the midst of one of
their trysts with a cadre of camera-wielding off-duty cops is a
violation of Danton Welsh's civil rights that would put Pasquale Mugiani out of the retribution business for good and
all. . . . No, you're working for me now, friend Aldrich. Keep
the bambina picture; I've got plenty more. She's your ace for
the time you need it. And you're going to need it. He won't be
satisfied until Dwight David Aldrich of Abilene, Kansas, is re-
duced to metaphorical dog-food scraps. I know that of which
I speak. I'll leave you now because my good wife has dinner
warming for hours for me. One thing to remember, Dwight
David, before we part."

"What's that Detective Sergeant Mugiani?"

"He loves her. Believe it or not that awful gentleman
loves Angelina Frippi."

"That's nice," Aldrich judged. "By the way, since I'm
working for you, do you think you could advance me a little
cash?"

"Why?"

"The plastic lady I'm supposed to take back to Vermont
with me."

Mugiani shrugged: "Fair enough, brother Aldrich."

The cop counted off two hundred dollars from a wad Aldrich did not think a cop should be carrying and plunked it on the bar before Aldrich. He nodded a terse good-night and exited the bar, heedless of some other informant perhaps who tried to get Mugiani's ear and was pushed rudely aside.

CHAPTER 12

Aldrich's Only Friend

The plastic lady cost only $139.50.

The porn-shop proprietress threw in the vaginal lubricant and a catalogue of fetish devices free. She was an obese dying woman with a lewd mouth ringed with a bizarre black-cherry shade of lipstick who speculated out loud even as she took Aldrich's money on the problems of a young man who needed a plastic woman to take home to his bed. For his part, Aldrich whispered a definitive "Fuck you, lady!" when he exited the store, crimson-faced at the unconcealed guffawings of four suburban husbands who pawed the offerings in the magazine section.

With his $60.50 profit, Aldrich thought of inflating the lady and spending the night with her at the Ritz-Carlton before returning to Burlington the next afternoon on the prepaid flight ticket Mugiani had assured him was awaiting him at Delta Air Lines. Then he thought better of squandering the money when he remembered it was more than a year since he had seen his one true friend, Charlie Wishing Ten Fingers, who lived in a tin-sided hut in an abandoned quarry in nearby Saugus while he worked high steel on a new building going up near the Boston waterfront.

Aldrich hailed a cab and directed the driver to Saugus. At the end of a development of mean little houses where the paved road gave out and became a dirt track that headed bumpily up a hill to the quarries, the driver refused to go any further.

"Wouldn't that be a pickle? Robbed and shot to death up in them quarries? That is, if this bucket even made it up the hill to begin with."

"You've got to trust somebody. Just once in life you've got to put yourself out for somebody," Aldrich pleaded, remembering the distance was more than a mile on this cold February night.

"That's what a real refined-looking black gentleman told me the night he set me up for a mugging in Roxbury. See the nice false teeth I got for my trouble." The cabbie brandished an upper plate before Aldrich. "No way, pal. I bought that shit once, but no more. The public is a pack of dogs. After twenty-two years in a hack I know what I'm talkin' about. My idea of the perfect retirement would be to move in with a colony of baboons. They're supposed to be more civilized. Pay up and walk, buddy."

Aldrich paid, but did not tip the driver, who swung the cab rapidly about and clattered off down through the files of development houses, blaring his horn in the night as if to celebrate his good fortune in still being alive. Resigned to a hike, Aldrich tucked his plastic woman beneath his arm and started up the road to the quarries, wondering for the first time if Charlie or his cousin Sybaritic Hawk would even be there. At the lip of the first huge crater he picked his way across heaps of slag that shifted beneath his feet, sending occasional head-sized rocks plunging over the edge to land with a loud crackling echo on the frozen surface of trapped rainwater below. Overhead, there was an intermittent moon and Aldrich peered closely about the crater for the reflection of the hut's corrugated tin sides every time the light broke from behind quick-scudding clouds. Ten minutes and two craters later he saw the glow of a campfire, though not the hut, behind a jumble of boulders that stood at the edge of a blind corner of the pit. Aldrich cupped his hands and called down to the place: "Charlie! Charlie! It's me, Charlie! Dwight Aldrich!"

He felt the poke of a gun barrel in his back and threw up his arms in reflex, dropping the woman in her cardboard box, who plunged over the edge of the crater more than a hundred feet to the ice below.

"Lydia's wedding gift, per chance, Dwight David?" Charlie's voice asked tonelessly. Only the length of a rifle barrel away, the Mohawk smelled pungently of the bear grease he used to slick down his hair.

"Don't be ironic, Charlie. Needless to say I wasn't invited to the felicities like you were."

"And for that you killed her? A bit of overreaction on your part, wouldn't you say?"

"I loved her," Aldrich whined. "Why does everybody think I killed her? I never even thought about it, Charlie."

"You did. Every ex-husband does."

"All right, I did. But it was only a fleeting thought. A momentary madness more than a year ago. I loved her too much. My heart was broken when our marriage ended. I can't tell you how I felt today when Aunt Zebidiah came to North Hollow to bring me the news. I was devastated."

Behind him Charlie sniggered as he lowered the gun: "I expect you were delirious with joy, Dwight David. I expect you just plain jumped up and down with happiness. I have to confess that among all the white eyes I've ever met, I trust you the most. That's because the truth in you is always the absolute polar opposite of what you say. Unerringly so. You're the only man in America with a forked tongue who's completely trustworthy."

"Thank you, Charlie," Aldrich said, turning about to face the tall Mohawk, who cradled a Winchester in the notch of three missing fingers on his left hand. He still wore the ceremonial embroidered buckskins that Aldrich remembered seeing on the six o'clock newscast film of the wedding tragedy though now it was mostly covered by a tattered old loden coat against the cold. The three feathers in his hair glistened silver in the moonlight and the long hair shone jet black and oily from the bear grease. Charlie's eyes looked hopelessly saddened by the day's events, Aldrich thought, yet somehow there was a glint of determined anger in them too that made Aldrich wary and he sought to diffuse the anger with his own ready tears that started effortlessly from his eyes: "You must be the only friend I have, Charlie. I've just been released from the police station. There's a list with nineteen names on it fingering me as the chief suspect in Liddy's murder."

Charlie shrugged, hiking the rifle over his right shoulder. "I'm surprised it isn't longer, Dwight David. You fucked a lot of people over since I've known you these brief five years. Wittingly and unwittingly. But mostly wittingly. Think of it."

"The world of business is a tough place, Charlie. Things go on there that you wouldn't understand. It's a rough-and-tumble game that spawns losers because everybody can't win. Only the strong survive."

"Yes, I remember Mr. Nixon your hero affirming the sacredness of that selfsame law, the coda of the white eyes. Only look what it got him for all his resoluteness. Do you still consider that you and that gentleman of San Clemente are living parallel lives, Dwight David?"

"Yes, after a fashion," Aldrich said morosely, wiping away the tears that had evidently not brought down their man. "We've both reached some kind of nadir. I don't expect you've heard, Charlie, but except for a couple of buildings which may be gone by the time I return tomorrow, North Hollow is pretty much razed to the ground. What's worse is nobody has a clue who's doing it except that they seem to be based over the border in Quebec Province. All my hard work and struggle going right down the chute before my eyes and I can't even guess who they are or why they're doing it to me . . ."

"Can't you, Dwight David?" Charlie snorted loudly, the snort echoing and re-echoing around the rim of granite crater. His eyes twinkled with bemusement now, beyond irony, and clouds of chilled breath smoke rose about his head, making his face somehow luminous and ghostly in the moonlight. Impulsively, Aldrich moved further away from the edge of the pit behind him: "Who are they, Charlie?"

"For certain, my friend, it's got to be those twelve lost revolutionary communards of yours who split the scene from North Hollow when you set the federals loose upon them some summers back and ended up in sole control of the plant that had been built up with no small amount of their sweat and tears."

"What I did was patriotic, Charlie. You said so yourself. They were going to harass and kill some of the high-steel workers on the World Trade Center to underscore their dirty leftist opposition to Nixon's Vietnam policies because the construction workers supported their President's plea to give him time to bring the war to a just and honorable close. . . . They were going to murder patriots, Charlie . . ."

"The word 'patriotism' on your lips, Dwight David, merely proves that that much-maligned ideal has been put to all sorts of defenses by all sorts of scoundrels for all sorts of reasons. The North Hollow gun club that was on its way to the World Trade Center for a little sniping action thought they were the patriots and the steel workers a pack of fascists. There you have it. Who's right? No, I never told you I thought you were acting like a patriot, Dwight David Aldrich. No one will ever tell you that. I simply agreed that something had to be done because I would not permit anyone taking gratuitous potshots at my brother workers, most of whom, despite their politics, were good family men who didn't deserve being wasted by the children of the rich experimenting in violence. Those were the terms of my support, Dwight David. I spelled it out very succinctly for you."

"They used to practice up on that range of theirs above North Hollow. Some of them were real Deadeye Dicks with a rifle. Do you think one of them could've killed Liddy today?"

"Probably one of them did." Charlie spoke thoughtfully,

peering far down into the bottom of the crater. "But only to get at you, not because they decided Lydia and Stephen Hodges had anything to do with the original tip-off to the feds. However, that was a genuine miscalculation on somebody's part because they almost certainly have no idea how badly your and Lydia's relationship had deteriorated. What sardonic comedy. That beautiful girl wasted for a misconception that her death would savage you. Tsk! Tsk!"

"Charlie . . . !" Aldrich started, gripping the Indian's left arm in a sudden panic. "Charlie, what if they try to kill me?"

"What if? They might try to kill you, Dwight David. It won't bring back any of that money you diddled them for, but at least it will assure somebody that you won't be able to make another fortune. You consider that you're at the nadir of your life now, but if you live you'll rise again. Men like you always do. Yes, it might be a great comfort to someone to know you weren't going to make it a second time after shedding the debacle of the first attempt with no more punishment than a hand slap in bankruptcy court. After all, Dwight David, you really haven't paid your dues . . ."

"I thought you were my friend, Charlie. It sounds like you think being dead is a very good idea."

"Only if it saves you from yourself. What greater love? Lord knows what harm you might do yourself on the next go-round. What went over the edge, by the way?"

"My plastic woman. I hope to hell she's still O.K."

"What plastic woman, Dwight David?"

"The one I'm taking home to Vermont with me to help make it through the winter. She's fantastic, Charlie!" Aldrich enthused, instantly forgetting his enemies from the commune days who might seek to kill him. "She's just like the real thing only easier to get along with. Life size, inflatable and portable, with a cunt that simulates contractions. The guy who lent me the dough to buy her has a friend who has one and he gets off on it every night. The friends says it's fifty times better than his wife ever was. You ought to get one for yourself, Charlie . . ."

Before Aldrich the Mohawk's eyes beseeched heaven. A long low whistle escaped his lips. He lay down the Winchester and reached up to pluck one of the three feathers from his head, then decisively snapped it in two, letting the pieces flutter toward the edge of the crater, where they sped off into the depths on a sudden slipstream of wind.

"Great Manitou," Charlie intoned, his arms extended upward, "protect this poor red man from the power of the white eyes, for now it is clear nothing is beyond them. They have even conquered the ultimate want and are a fiercely brave people who fear to tempt absolutely no perversion known to man . . ."

"Oh, cut it out, Charlie, will you? It's only a convenience until the real thing shows up again."

"Doll fucker. If you showed up on the day of Lydia's death with anything more significant in your mind than your anticipation of getting it off with a plastic doll, I'd be keenly disappointed. That's another reason I suppose I like you so well, Dwight David. It's because you're so completely dependable. Come on, let's go get your playmate. If we hurry we can still make the eleven o'clock news. Are you hungry? Cousin Hawk made a good venison stew."

They descended into the quarry down a long narrow seam of exposed white quartz that flawed the granite and had evidently years before sent the cutters off to work another face, leaving behind a natural rampway. At the bottom, where the ice crackled loudly beneath their weight, they found the plastic woman unharmed, one grotesquely bent uninflated arm lying outside on the ice where a corner of the cardboard box had popped open on impact. Aldrich followed his friend across the ice. They came ashore on a pebble beach that made the same reverberating noise in the quarry as a pebble beach washed by the sea.

"I saw you on television, Charlie. On the six o'clock news before the cops came for me."

"How did I look, Dwight David?" Charlie seemed uncharacteristically eager to know. He stopped to concentrate on the response and Aldrich grew amused at the notion of a viable narcissism somewhere down deep behind the mien of stoic noble savage Charlie always projected to a somewhat awed world at large.

"You looked fine. Very handsome and stoic. Very much the noble savage. You looked especially dignified because that asshole Reverend Dickie and hot-pants Little Janie were crying their eyes out all over you. You shed only a single, very profound tear. Everyone noticed it. It was the dramatic highlight of the entire film footage . . ."

"More so even, do you think, than the moment when Stephen Hodges lowered the wedding veil over poor Lydia's dead face?"

"Easily, Charlie."

"Ahhh. I did well then, Dwight David. At the time I questioned whether it was tolerable to display any emotion at all, then decided to allow the single tear. I hope that its effect did not seem too well calculated, but an Indian cannot be too cautious of emotional display in the white eye's world. I must wait until later. In late spring, when I return home to Lake Champlain and am safe among my own people, I can divest myself properly of my grief over Lydia's death."

"You loved her Charlie, didn't you?" Aldrich whispered softly, delighting in pouring quarts of salt into the wound while it obviously stood so painfully open.

"Yes, if I must confess it to you. I knew Lydia since she was only twelve years old. . . . Yes, I loved her. I have never known such a beautiful woman."

"Everybody loved her. It got to be so goddam boring the way everybody loved her."

"Boring to you only, no doubt. If Lydia was bored by the way everyone loved her, then being married to a crass and self-serving curmudgeon like you must have provided the perfect counterpoint to her problem. That would make you an absolute bargain of a husband instead of the considerable liability that everyone has always thought you were."

"That talk is boring too, Charlie. Especially on the day of her death. It's not like I haven't heard any of it before. She won't be made any happier hearing this noise while she's fleeting on her way out there through the universe to the place of Afterlife . . ."

Aldrich made a dramatic sweep of his right arm across the night sky, plotting the course of dead Liddy's passage through the fleece of swift-moving cloud tumbling over the face of the moon. Charlie took full heed of the solemnity of the moment, stood at ramrod attention, the clenched fist of his good right hand clutched tightly to his heart while his dark sad eyes scanned the indicated arc of the passage, searching perhaps for the billowing white wedding gown of his lover. For one wildly irreverent moment before he bit hard on his lip to bring himself under control, Aldrich thought of Mary Martin as Peter Pan.

"Go softly, Lydia, into that dark night," Charlie intoned in a distorted borrowing from the poem. "Other lovers follow after you. You shall not be lonely long."

"It's too bad whoever killed Liddy didn't think to kill Stephen Hodges along with her," Aldrich ground savagely into Charlie's poetic metaphor of the Otherworld, "because then that poor fleeting sprite wouldn't be lonely at all tonight. She'd have her little Stevie with her up there in eternity . . ."

The end of Charlie's rifle barrel rose so swiftly to bruise the tip of his nose that Aldrich thought he himself had just been shot up a nostril.

"Shut up, Aldrich! Something must be sacred for you somewhere! You cannot violate everything everywhere you touch! I won't let you! I loved her!"

"Charlie, put the gun down! Please! It might go off!" The cold metal rested right between his eyes on the bridge of his nose and he could feel the powerful tremble of the Mohawk's anger transmitting right up the barrel. Across from him, Charlie's face was suddenly the most hate-filled mask Aldrich could imagine. The lips were curled back in a snarl. The cheek muscles popped and contracted in a spasm of fury.

"Charlie, if you kill one of the white eyes, they will make it bad for you. Even one like Aldrich whom nobody would particularly miss. You could not return home to Champlain when the spring comes."

The voice of Sybaritic Hawk: Aldrich turned a wary eye to see the fat and dumpy, perpetually stoned cousin of Charlie Wishing Ten Fingers staring at them somehow speculatively, rather than in any real alarm, his head moving moronically to and fro on the fulcrum of his neck as he pulled in either direction with his hands on the long black braids of his hair. Like Charlie, he still wore the embroidered wedding-day ceremonial buckskin; a large dark stain coursed down the front of his shirt as if he had missed his mouth with a full ladle of his venison stew.

"I think I knew you were here, Aldrich," Hawk said. "The air felt charged and electric in the hut so that I had to leave. Rage and bitterness bounced and ricocheted everywhere off those tin walls. The din of ping and pang was nearly deafening. I . . ."

"You're stoned, Hawk," Charlie told him flatly. "Save the shaman spiritualism for Tribal Council Week when all those brother hopheads of yours come round to visit. Hear?"

"All right, Charlie. But he's still not worth it. If he's meant to be dead, the white eyes will do it for you. After the killing, I made it back to the family place in Milton about ten minutes before you did. There was a war party of about twenty Episcopalians trying to break into Danton's gun cases so they could ride out after Aldrich. It was Danton himself who locked the library and posted a guard at the door. Someone of their tribe is almost certain to take a potshot at Aldrich here, so that no one of our tribe will have to bother . . ."

Charlie took deep gulps of air to calm himself. The gun came away from Aldrich's head and Aldrich exhaled the hard knob of his fear like the issuing of air from a bellows. He touched a hand to his forehead: It was hot and wet with dollops of sweat in the chill of a twenty-degree February night.

"Aldrich is my friend," Charlie said simply after a moment, placing his right hand firmly on Aldrich's shoulders. "Aldrich is not meant to be dead."

"Tsk. Tsk. Well, let me tell you, Charlie, he's not my friend," Sybaritic Hawk surged on. "The honor is all yours. He's nothing but a bug-fucking treaty breaker as far as I'm concerned. You can tell just by looking at him. General Custer's own vanity, a mighty river of white eye's sincerity a whole mile wide and a half inch deep. For a smart up-and-coming subchieftain, Charlie, you're pretty dumb when it comes to the business of Dwight David Aldrich . . ."

"Shut up, Hawk," Charlie growled at him. "Dwight David knows you're zonked and running off at the mouth, so you're just wasting your abuse on him. Why don't you go back to the hut and try turning in for the night?"

"No, I'm going to slide on the ice and war-hoop for a while. If I go back to the hut, I'll never be able to sleep with all that goddamn pinging and panging against the walls. I can watch for the Episcopal vigilantes, too. Listen for the mating cry of the horned owl. If I see them, I'll sound it three times in warning."

"You're a good old Indian, Hawk," Charlie said wearily. "Did you manage to spill all the stew when you put that stain down the front of you or is there still a little left for Dwight David and me?"

"Eat yourself sick, doormat of the white eyes. I only spilled a thimbleful. Hurry home so you can both watch your dead Lydia on the eleven o'clock news while you eat supper . . ."

While they watched, Sybaritic Hawk raised a full-throated war whoop and charged off the pebble beach onto the ice, slithering twenty feet or so across the crackling surface while he fought for balance before he fell flat on his ass with a convincing whoop like pain. Aldrich hoped fiercely that his coccyx had been broken or at least bruised. But Charlie only shrugged and began grinding off through the pebbled expanse toward the hut while Aldrich took giant steps to keep up with him.

"I'm truly sorry for what happened back there, Dwight David," Charlie said as they began picking their way through the jumble of hip-high boulders that guarded the approach to the hut. "It's been an awful day of conscience. Beautiful Lydia dead and poor Stephen Hodges so heartbroken he couldn't even speak when they brought him back to the house from the doctor's office this afternoon, and I feel like I'm responsible for everything that's happened."

"Why? What the hell did you have to do with her death?"

"The war canoe. I set the whole chain of events in motion way back when. If it weren't for the war canoe, Lydia would have married Stephen five years ago and she'd still be alive and the mother of beautiful children today. I would have been a godfather to one of her sons instead of a pallbearer at her funeral . . ."

"Don't knock the war canoe, friend Charlie. It was a foxy ploy that served me well. When history records the more ingenious devices that ever turned victory into rout, Aldrich's war canoe is going to be right up there with the Trojan Horse . . ."

"Aldrich's war canoe . . . Curse it!" Charlie stormed, spitting furiously into the coals of the campfire before the tin-sided hut, narrowly missing the flame-blackened pot of savory stew that hung above the coals. He leaned the Winchester against the hut with a loud clang. Aldrich set the plastic lady down beside it.

"Here, Dwight David, take a bowl and fill it. We'll go inside and watch the news."

Aldrich filled his bowl with stew after Charlie had filled his, then followed the Mohawk into the hut, where he was nearly overwhelmed by the trapped-air stench of bear grease, drying wool work clothes and the acrid burnt-chemical odor of a glowing-red heater element suspended too close to the slabs of styrofoam insulation tacked up around the walls.

"It stinks in here, Charlie," Aldrich told him bluntly. "You ought to air the place out every once in a while."

"I don't notice it anymore," Charlie said disinterestedly, reaching down to turn on the sound of the portable TV set that played silently since Sybaritic Hawk did not require sound when he was stoned. On screen the commercial break was ending and the busy, urgent music of the 11 P.M. newscast surged into the hut. The announcer's face appeared head on, and he began speaking immediately of the "sensational Boston wedding-day tragedy."

"I don't understand, Charlie, how an educated Indian like yourself could put up with living in this kind of squalor."

"Don't concern yourself, Dwight David. It's none of your affair. I have my reasons. Good reasons for an Indian."

"You make good money working high steel, Charlie. Union wages. You and Hawk could afford to rent a nice apartment someplace in town. You could afford to live like human beings."

"You can't build campfires on the floors of nice apartments in town and most of the money has to be sent home anyway to the family on Champlain. Life in this quarry suffices well. Leave it alone."

On screen was the by now widely recognized shot of dead Lydia in blood-spattered wedding gown sprawled across the church steps.

"I don't think I can eat this stew, Charlie," Aldrich judged abruptly, putting his bowl brusquely aside on the plank floor and wiping his hands emphatically on the nylon of his parka as if to rid them of germs that might have swarmed to them out of the stew and over the lip of the bowl. "I mean, I don't want to insult you, Charlie, but God knows what's in the stuff. I mean, Sybaritic Hawk probably chopped the ingredients right here on the floor with a rusty knife and threw them in, splinters and all . . ."

Aldrich was carefully searching his hands for sign of infection when Charlie threw his bowl of stew at him full in the face, then reached over with his good right hand to grab a clumps of Aldrich's hair and begin shaking him furiously while Aldrich howled with surprise and pain. Pieces of meat and vegetable flaked away from his eyes from the fierce agitation at the roots of his hair until he could see that the hate-filled mask of Charlie Wishing Ten Fingers was operative again and that the blunt jabs of his nubby left hand were in the direction of the TV set, where Lydia's announcement photo that had appeared in the Sunday *Times* stared back a long moment from the screen. Charlie's words tripped and fell all over his rage. His voice was choked and near incomprehensible as he sought to gain ascendancy over the newscaster's solemn tones.

"Do . . . do you remem . . . do you remember her . . . ? Lydia! She was your wife once! You white-eyes pig! Do you remember when she shared your bed and she loved you even when you were too indifferent or preoccupied to love her back? Oh, Aldrich, you're a husk of a man! Something in you is dead! Twisted and sick! There's beautiful dead Liddy on the TV screen and all you can think about is my hygiene and some shit in your stew . . . !"

"Poor Lydia . . . poor, poor dead Lydia," Aldrich chanted in fear of his life as Charlie began an upbeat Mohawk kind of keening in rhythm to his whipping about of Aldrich's head. Aldrich prayed his hair would not come out by the roots; he used his two hands to scrape the dregs of spattered stew from his face and hairline and the front of his parka rather than in any attempt to fend off Charlie's iron grip, because he was afraid any resistance might send the Mohawk into a real paroxysm of rage. He patted tentatively at the skin of his face and decided he had not been burned badly enough to cause any blistering.

On the TV screen that weaved and bobbed in his vision, the engagement photo of Lydia dissolved and the camera eye honed in on a view of Danton Welsh's Milton preserve that was totally lit in the early darkness. Two State Police cars guarded the tall-gated entry, keeping away the curious. The newscaster spoke with hushed wonderment about what went on inside that palatial manse, moralized about sudden tragedy making kindred souls of lord and peasant. Despite the controlled painful motion of his head, Aldrich sniffed delightedly at the notion of the remaining four Welshes sorrowing for real like their peasant kindred, tried envisioning them as genuine hair-tearing, breast-beating lately arrived hyphenated Americans rolling on the floor for good measure, but in another moment gave up his fantasy with the dejected realization that they would not.

The newsman told that ex-husband Dwight David Aldrich of Inglenook, Vermont, had already been questioned and released by Boston police. Aldrich's head came abruptly free of Charlie's grip as the Mohawk, suddenly witless with pleasure, pointed at his own apparition exiting Danton Welsh's driveway on his Harley-Davidson. Two State Troopers snapped to attention on either side of the gate as the cycle gained the roadway. The final footage showed Charlie Wishing Ten Fingers roaring off down the road, his shoulder blanket flapping behind him in the wind. He had not worn a crash helmet as the law required and Aldrich wondered vexedly why the troopers had not seen fit to do their job and arrested him for the violation.

"Did you see that, Dwight David?" Charlie jabbed his arm excitedly. "Did you see that final fade-out? The awesome poignancy of the lone, noble, quietly sorrowing Mohawk riding off toward the horizon in the fast-declining light . . ."

"Yes, on a motorcycle. Yes, it was very poignant. You almost pulled my goddam hair out by the roots, Charlie."

Charlie looked at him annoyedly, distracted from his singular vision of Mohawk majesty: "You have to learn to observe the conventional norms, Dwight David. Or in your particular case of unqualified self-absorption, learn to pretend to observe the conventional norms. When the tragic death of a woman who lay in your arms for four years is reported on TV, you must remember to look saddened at the very least. Tears would be helpful, too, even if their origin is self-pity. Otherwise, someone more appalled than myself might reward your sociopathic behavior with a lot more intensity than a bowl of chow in the face or a few tugs on your golden locks."

"You're right, Charlie. Someone might. I've got to be careful. Listen, tell me something. What was it like back at the house after Lydia got wasted. I'll bet everybody sat around and cried like crazy, huh?"

"Sorry to disappoint you, Dwight David, but it was a dignified and marvelously upbeat kind of mourning. We went right on with the wedding reception as if the bride and groom were there with us. Drinks, food and dancing to two bands. I left early as you saw on film because I don't know any of the white eyes' dances. But that was the reason the house was all lit up. They were having a party for over one hundred guests. I'm sure it's still going on."

"But that's grotesque!" Aldrich stormed. "They're uncivilized! They're behaving like savages! Who ever heard of dancing at a mortuary?"

"They were honoring Lydia, Dwight David. They were honoring her beauty and the way she loved life with such a passion. They were remembering all the fine generous things she did for people. It was the way Danton wanted it. No tears for her father's bright prize, he kept saying. It was the only way a consummate aristocrat like Danton Welsh could have acted. What an incredibly admirable person! Stephen Hodges couldn't talk when they brought him back, but he sure did dance. Danton dragged him on the floor the minute he came into the house and spun him around and around to bring him out of the daze and the two of them just jitterbugged and did the Charleston together nonstop for about twenty minutes. It was wonderful, Dwight David! Everyone stood around laughing and clapping with tears streaming down their faces. You never saw anybody's hired musicians put out like that band did today. Simply wonderful! What courage!"

Aldrich supposed he was scowling darkly, furious at the certainty that Danton Welsh triumphed everywhere and always. Charlie's face was uncustomarily rapturous at the recall of the death revelers. In another moment Sybaritic Hawk came ponderously through the door and sank to his knees before the TV screen, turning off the sound, though not the picture, throwing a derisive middle finger repeatedly at the unsmiling newscaster.

"You've known Danton Welsh a long time, haven't you, Charlie?" Aldrich asked, remembering that he had early on in his marriage been inanely jealous of the closeness of Charlie and his father-in-law, who could barely suffer the sight of Aldrich.

"I've known Danton since I was twelve, Dwight David. He taught me to play chess and hunt and ride a horse. He sent me through college and grad school. He was a father to me when I never knew who my own father was."

"He's a good friend to the Indians," Sybaritic Hawk blurted out. "He has often defended the Mohawks in court. We have made him an honorary chieftain."

"You've wasted a lot of time admiring Danton Welsh, Charlie," Aldrich snarled at the other. "There are things I've found out about him that you wouldn't believe."

"What kind of things, Aldrich?"

"Prurient things. Sexual improprieties. Background discrepancies. I've got the goods on Danton Welsh. Enough to cause him real trouble. All that glitters in that man's life is definitely not gold, sir."

"Leave it alone, Aldrich. I warn you. I won't let you do anything to Danton. Any cheap-shot blackmail on your part would backfire on you anyhow. It would make it quite obvious to a lot of people who know you that you've managed to sink even lower than they thought possible. Danton has been plagued by trouble enough from you already. The loss of Lydia today is the crowning stroke."

"That was somebody else's revenge. Not mine. I'm going to get mine and a face-to-face admission from old Danton that it's had its effect on him."

"I'm telling you I want you to forget what you know." Charlie leaned menacingly forward. "You've done enough damage to people and things in New England. Leave Danton Welsh be and get on your ten-speed and pedal back to Kansas the same way you pedaled out here . . ."

"Don't tell me what to do, Charlie. I'll only pedal back to ignominious defeat in Kansas if Danton Welsh agrees to do the exact same thing, because that's where that bastard friend and patron of yours hails from. A little old sodbuster town in Kansas, not some gilt villa in Aix-en-Provence, France. Bet you never knew that one, did you?"

"I've known that for years, O dispossessed youth of Abilene whose father died of cirrhosis of the liver, whose disadvantaged mother is living on the dole from Danton Welsh. I knew that since the night before I left for college when I made him my blood brother. He told me many things then. He told me about Kansas also."

"Many good Mohawks know of this now," Sybaritic Hawk said. "No one speaks of it, though. If Danton doesn't want the white eyes to know, he must have a good reason. They'll never know from us."

"Try this one, Charlie." Aldrich spat out the words: "Your friend, patron and blood brother is romantically involved in a clandestine relationship with a fifteen-year-old ex-hooker. Fifteen! It's illegal, immoral and disgusting! Do you think many good Mohawks could keep that one to themselves?"

"She is an Italian girl named Angelina Frippi," Charlie told him levelly. "She was sucking cocks in dark hallways at age twelve and a half when Danton found her and rescued her. She's his ward now. She's on her way to becoming a beautiful, well-educated and finished lady. When her time comes, she will marry well and no one will think to concern themselves about her past. Danton is keen on helping those who are disadvantaged through no fault of their own . . ."

"Jesus Christ!" Aldrich raged, pumping an irate fist on the planking of the floor. "Is there anything you goddam Mohawks don't have a tolerance for?"

"One thing, Aldrich . . ."

"Yes?" When he looked up the roundhouse right was already on its way. It slammed into his left cheek with the power of a freight train and bowled him over so that he smashed his head against the plank floor. Charlie was on him in an instant, clipping his neck in the vise-like grip of the two-fingered left hand, the nubs of the three missing fingers pressing harshly on his windpipe. With his good right hand Charlie punched repeatedly at Aldrich's face while Aldrich tried vainly to push off the Mohawk, who had locked his knees tightly about Aldrich's middle. Charlie Wishing Ten Fingers' face was absolutely ecstatic with a great broad grin of pleasure that he was deriving from his task. Aldrich tasted the first rush of blood from his battered nose just as Sybaritic Hawk pulled Charlie off his victim and onto the floor, simply sprawling his great weight across the attacker to hold him down. Charlie fought and kicked for a while, trying to throw off the heavyweight peacemaker, then gave up in apparent exhaustion, staring blankly for a long moment at a bleeding Aldrich, who sat up now, searching gingerly over his face with his hands for other occasions of cuts and bleeding than the torrent that coursed from his nose. Aldrich watched warily as the look of blank incomprehension turned to pain and sorrow and the single telling tear burst gigantically from Charlie's left eye and ran a plumb-line drop down the cheek, signaling the new wind of the sea change: Aldrich had seen it all before.

"Aldrich is my friend," Charlie moaned, rapping his forehead on the plank floor. "Why am I doing these awful things to my friend?"

"Love has strange manifestations," Sybaritic Hawk extemporized wryly, climbing off his captive. "No two people go at it the same way. Yours is a violent head-on confrontation, Charlie Wishing Ten Fingers. Dwight David's is an exercise in diplomatic maneuver, a treaty with a confusing welter of subclauses because it always has fiscal considerations. Come on, Charlie, let's you and me go outside and dance that demon out of you with a good old Mohawk two-step around the campfire. There's fresh water in that milk can over there, Dwight David, to clean yourself up. Here's a clean face towel . . ."

Sybaritic Hawk pushed Charlie unprotestingly through the door and Hawk's measured chanting began immediately and Aldrich could hear the steady thump of their work shoes circling the fire before the hut. He poured some of the milk-can water into a washbasin and began washing at his cuts and bruises before a small shaving mirror, relieved at least that his nose was clotting and evidently not broken and that none of the three cuts on his forehead would require stitching.

In time he became aware of the odor of burning rubber that was not from the closeness of the glowing heater element to the styrofoam wall and rushed outside to where Charlie and Sybaritic Hawk, both oblivious of Aldrich and lost in a howling trance to the swift measured footfalls of their dancing, circled the $139.50 plastic lady. She burned with a furious roar atop the pyre of the campfire, sending four- and five-foot tongues of flame licking into the dark sky, eerily reflecting the bobbing silhouettes of the dancers all over the quarry walls.

Aldrich looked up over the rim of the crater to the glow of lights of the Boston skyline to the south where there was community and reason and law and order and marveled with headshaking bewilderment at his own special ability to turn a simple visit to a friend to something akin to a descent into hell.

He thought better than to protest the judgment of the Mohawks on the plastic lady from the Combat Zone.

CHAPTER 13

Some Conversations about Funeral Arrangements

On Sunday morning Aldrich woke to the ground-shaking reverberations of a series of muffled explosions in the quarry. He pulled back the rain cover of the sleeping bag the Mohawks had given him and opened his eyes tentatively, afraid of the pain, touching softly in exploration at the puffiness of his right cheek grown large enough to nearly occlude the sight of his eye. Across from him, the width of two floor planks away, Sybaritic Hawk lay bundled up in his sleeping bag, awake and staring at Aldrich with a look of moronic detachment. A dried trickle of brown emission that may have been the night-time burpings of his own venison stew coursed from one corner of his mouth. The morning smell in the closed confines of the hut was appalling. Aldrich gritted his teeth against nausea.

"What was that noise, Sybaritic Hawk?" Aldrich asked him after a minute. "It sounded like an explosion."

"Charlie's throwing a few sticks of dynamite onto the ice out there to break it up so the local kids won't have any reason to come down and skate on it tomorrow while we're away at Lydia's funeral. Tomorrow's a school holiday. If they find the hut when we're not here they're liable to torch it and steal the radio and TV set. Or if they start talking around town about our little setup here, the cops might get inquisitive and find out we've tapped a nearby source of electricity that Boston Edison doesn't know about and isn't billing us for.

Kids are dedicated merciless little bastards when they put their minds to it, Dwight David. Remember *Lord of the Flies?* A disturbing book. I can readily empathize with Piggy, let me tell you. We've shared the common bond of victimization. Not a week after I finished that book a gang of about twenty little white-eyed monsters dressed like Indians burned us out of a quarry in Danvers when we were working steel on the Hancock Building. I was home alone the afternoon they came. Charlie was away in Boston. They tied me up and poked at me with their cute little playthings weaponry for about a half hour before they grew tired. Their understanding of where best to induce pain on a grown man's body was sheer breathtaking instinctual genius. Never felt anything like it. Until the minute they left I didn't know whether or not they were going to throw me into the fire . . ."

"Cruelty is everywhere, Sybaritic Hawk," Aldrich delighted in telling him, wincing from the pain of speaking. "It takes all sorts of forms. Why, for instance, did you have to put the torch to my plastic lady?"

"She wasn't right for you, Dwight David. Not your type at all. Not nearly well-bred enough. Remember your roots and family background. Surely some debt is owed there. Charlie reasoned we were doing you a considerable favor anyhow. Such perversion as the plastic lady might prove to be your real sexual palliative from habit and easy accessibility. It would be womankind's absolute loss for a warm, generous person like yourself who has so much to give to go that route. The thought of you not fathering children in this life is nearly unbearable."

"How much abuse do you think one person is supposed to take, Sybaritic Hawk?" Aldrich asked miserably, not feigning anything, unzipping himself from the sleeping bag and picking up the shaving mirror to appraise the welter of cuts and bruises on his swollen face. "I'm further estranged from the community of man right now than the Ancient Mariner ever knew. Get off my fucking back a bit."

"You haven't seen anything, Dwight David, if you still consider that Charlie Wishing Ten Fingers is your one last true friend on earth. Even though I don't like you, I'm being compassionate now for a change. Use that off-color information you've happened onto against Danton Welsh and you've lost Charlie too. And maybe your life into the bargain, what with that incredible temper of his. Be warned. Danton is the father Charlie always wanted. You break the peace treaty with Charlie over Danton and there'll never be another chance at male bonding with that noble Mohawk . . ."

Then Charlie Wishing Ten Fingers pushed through the door and entered the hut, a rush of Arctic air and swirl of snow flurries blowing in with him. He crossed the plank floor in two quick steps and pressed his face and hands near the glowing heater element on the wall.

"Whew! It's about ten degrees out there right now. That little disturbance I created upon the waters ought to refreeze nice and lumpy and generally unusable in about three hours or so. How do you feel, Dwight David? Is there much pain?"

Aldrich, sullen and staring fixedly downward at a knot on the floor, did not answer, and Charlie put his good hand firmly on Aldrich's head and forced it backward so he could look into the battered face. Normally inscrutable, the Mohawk winced at the morning-after testament to his handiwork. A small whistle escaped his lips. Aldrich thought he looked generally contrite.

"Forgive me, Dwight David, if you can. That time-bomb temper of mine goes off very rarely, but when it does the result is usually astounding to behold. The morning after is like waking up with a colossal hangover and a clean slate of memory. I can hardly ever remember what I did . . ."

"You did this to me, Charlie." Aldrich grabbed at the puffy right cheek, tweaking it reproachfully between thumb and index finger in an unrealized parody of the Sicilian curse. "You also did some primitive Mohawk Druid's dance around the flames of my burning plastic lady, for which you owe me a hundred thirty-nine dollars and fifty cents. I want it, too."

"No way, doll fucker. Burning that graven image was an act of charity. Faultless testimony of my deep-seated and abiding love for you. I couldn't be the friend of a man who embraces unnatural acts so effortlessly as you seem to, broad-jumping the hurdle of every moral stricture that hoves into view. . . . And come to think of it, Dwight David, I'm the only friend you've got, if I recollect properly, but for your Bible-toting mother in Abilene, who I imagine is not so vehement a foe of the flesh that she would endorse plastic instead. . . . She too might find the plastic lady somewhat repulsive."

"I don't like the idea of Mother's name being brought into this sort of discussion, Charlie," Aldrich warned, standing abruptly, stung by a cramp of pain in his left thigh that had him tottering on his feet. "There are certain irreproachables in life, after all. There have to be. Certain sacred spiritual places that every man needs for survival out in this god-awful world. I'm not ashamed to say that. I measure my ethical conduct from day to day by my dear mother's expectations of her only son. How would you like it if I opened up with a big salvo on your mother, mister?"

"I wouldn't care. You couldn't mount a big enough salvo to ever touch a sacred place in my mother with even a casual half-ounce piece of shrapnel. There isn't any sacred place. She was a terrible drunk and prostitute on self-destruct who finally kicked off from uremia. I haven't a clue who my father was. In the face of that background, I'm afraid my ethical resources are entirely my own. As for sacred places, unlike yourself, inasmuch as there's no mother, there's no other middling American convenience like flag or apple pie either. Only my belief in the indissolubility of the Mohawk nation and my profound respect for Danton Welsh, about whom you'd better not make any mistakes . . ."

Wary of yet another pummeling, Aldrich chose discretion, extended his hand to Charlie and spoke with forked tongue: "Let's bury the hatchet, Charlie. Let's cut the recrimination. What I got last night, I had coming to me. This morning the idea of blackmailing Danton Welsh seems repulsive to me. The plastic lady is an unmanly perversion. I don't know how I've sunk so low. It must have something to do with my isolation in North Hollow. It's affected my mind. I actually gloated over Lydia's death because I saw it as a personal vengeance. I want to go with you to that funeral service tomorrow to mourn her properly and demonstrate my true feelings for her. I want to get down on my knees to Danton and ask him to forgive me for the past if possible. I want . . ."

"You want but the truth, Dwight David, and finding it will be the fruitless quest of your life," Charlie told him, exhaling a weary sigh and irritably knocking aside the extended hand. "You can't go to that burial tomorrow. No one will want you there. Someone is liable to go berserk and try to kill you."

"But why? I've repented, Charlie. Everyone will be able to see that. They can't deny me the right to mourn the woman I loved. Anyhow, it's time for me to rejoin the community of man. I've been away all winter. I'll cry so bottomlessly tomorrow that people won't fail to be moved. I'll bet that Danton Welsh and Stephen Hodges will be so touched they'll both come up to me after the service is over and embrace me. I'll bet they invite me back to the house to Danton's study for a drink with them . . ."

"To Danton's study where the guns are kept? Yes, they might invite you there, Dwight David. But not for a commiserating drink. You can't go, don't you understand? You'd blow it. Even if you started off equaling St. Peter's own legendary crying jag, some supercilious grimace would find its way onto your face to prove you were only there to see Lydia victoriously into the ground. To see Stephen Hodges' tears of loss and hear the choking in Danton's voice. Revenged in one fell swoop for your small-minded grudges all around."

"I have excellent control of my facial expressions, Charlie. They'd never know."

"They'd know. Your heart is an open book, Dwight David."

"You're the second person to tell me that since yesterday. The first was a police detective."

"Then it must be true. The police never lie. You mustn't think of going."

"Hey, Charlie," Sybaritic Hawk interrupted irritably, "are you going for the *Times* or what? It's your turn if you can spare time enough from the repartee to walk down to town to get it."

"All right. Sorry, Sybaritic Hawk. I'll go now. I have to phone the Welshes to find out what time the funeral service is being held while I'm down there anyhow."

"Get French bread for breakfast, Charlie. And some strawberry jam. Check the *Times* to make sure you've got all the sections and take Dwight David with you because you know I can't stand to be alone with him. If they have any of those little boysenberry tarts I like so much at the bakery, get me a dozen, O.K.? If they don't have boysenberry, apple, lemon or blueberry is all right. And I'm all out of rolling papers. Please don't forget those because a case of the munchies is essential for those tarts be they boysenberry, apple, lemon or blueberry. Or whatever. Get anything they have, because there's a long afternoon of TV ahead of me and I don't want to miss a bite."

"Lydia died yesterday, Sybaritic Hawk," Aldrich reproached him in a low mournful voice, trying for a moral one-upper. "Do you think you could forgo the pleasures of the senses for just one day in her memory?"

"No. I'm honoring her in my own way. Sitting shiva, as the Jewish brothers say. In life, Lydia loved me for my erudite gourmandise, my slovenly fat. She loved to watch me eat. A true religious experience, she always called it. The sacred cult of the Sumo wrestler. If she's up there today looking down on us, I won't be the one to disappoint her. She'll see the Sybaritic Hawk she always loved best."

"That makes no sense," Aldrich said, shaking his head in dismay. "That makes absolutely no sense at all . . ."

But he was already through the door and into the fierce cold outside at Charlie's urging. The ashes of the dead campfire shifted about in the intermittent downdraft that blew into the half-circle hollow sheltering the hut; blackened, unburned pieces of the plastic lady's hands and feet lay in perfect, spread-eagle symmetry beyond the periphery of ash, and Aldrich stopped for a moment to kick dully at one of the feet, thinking that the vague, powdery outline of legs, arms and torso that connected the remnants must be like that of an immolated victim near center zero at Hiroshima. Above was a sky of very dark, snow-pregnant clouds. A depressing day into the bargain of batterings and bruises.

Aldrich followed Charlie along the periphery of dynamited ice and up the quartz rampway that ascended to the lip of the crater. In five minutes, they were down the hill to the edge of town in the same mean little development where the taxi had discharged Aldrich in fear the night before. Each and every house had an identical living-room picture window, and in nearly every picture window was framed a more or less identical lamp atop a table, and almost universally, it suddenly occurred to Aldrich, the occupants of the house, some already dressed and others still in bed clothes, were clustered about the lamp, staring out the window with unabashed curiosity at the progress of Dwight David Aldrich and Charlie Wishing Ten Fingers through their little suburb. Charlie did not seem even remotely aware of their presence. He thought instead of his task on the phone.

"The first thing to do, Dwight David, is take the bull by the horns. I'll call Danton directly, and we'll end the business of your invitation to tomorrow's feast of weepings out in Milton straight off. So you'll have no doubts about your welcome."

"Let me speak with him at least, Charlie. I think I can convince him to let me come."

"Suit yourself. It'll spare making me the translator of Danton's hatred toward you. But you won't convince him, I'll bet."

"I've convinced him of a lot of things before, friend Charlie. He's parted with money I needed when he swore up and down he had absolutely no intention of doing so."

"That was when Lydia was alive and still your wife, friend Aldrich. You lost your collateral yesterday. Some enemy of yours wasted her. Remember?"

They were silent until they came to a glass-walled telephone booth on the edge of a service station closed for Sunday. Charlie stepped inside and dialed the Welshes' unlisted number in Milton. He kept the door open, and in the cold his breath smoke exploded in puffs against the panes. Even in the wrappings of his ragged old loden coat, Charlie Wishing Ten Fingers was an imposing, powerful figure, Aldrich thought involuntarily, half consoling himself for his limp defense against last night's beating by the Mohawk. Six feet two inches tall, a hard, lean workingman's body without the hint of a tall man's slouch, as physically noble an Indian as ever lived, except for the fact that he was a half-breed: Of that Aldrich was certain, though Charlie raged against that possibility whenever it was suggested to him that his unknown father had been a white man.

Aldrich had seen that anger operative almost the first time he had encountered Charlie at Danton Welsh's farm on the Vermont shores of Lake Champlain near Shelburne. When Lydia had grown giddy over pre-dinner cocktails and told Charlie teasingly that she had spied on him dyeing his dark brown hair the brilliantine black of Indian hair, knew that he applied something to the exposed skin of his body to match the genuine flesh tone of his cousin, Sybaritic Hawk. Then Big Janie, Lydia's mother, had tried entering the jest, already drunk before dinner, and the thing had become a monster that got away from them so that Charlie had stood, shaking with speechless fury, and then stormed out of the house and back to his village. To Aldrich, that incredible paroxysm of Charlie's was unforgettable and it made him wary ever after in his dealings with the Mohawk. He would also never forget the dawn of recognition of what it was that so disconcerted him on first meeting Charlie, caused him to pinch himself to force him to look the other straight in the eye: In the midst of the handsome face of perfectly convincing Indian features, Charlie's eyes that had been murderous that day with hatred were incongruously pale gray.

Someone answered the phone in Milton—a secretary or receptionist evidently who questioned Charlie at some length, then switched the call to Danton Welsh. In the Sunday-morning cold of Saugus, Charlie spoke commiserating words to his friend Danton, applied the balm of Mohawk spirit imagery to the passage of the dead with the same deft assurance as he had once applied the perfect tinctured healing mudpack to an armload of Aldrich's painful bee stings. He activated the single profound mourning tear from his left eye, and as it plunged down his cheek, he told Danton Welsh it was falling. Inside the phone booth he began a sad, measured dirge of Mohawk chanting in time to the stomp of his heavy-booted feet, his head snapping back and forth to the rhythm of the plaint like a doll's head bobbing on a fulcrum of rubber neck. Astoundingly, in an interim of silence when the movement of Charlie's body continued nonetheless, it came to Aldrich that the dirge was being sung in response from the other end of the line. One-liners in Saugus begat one-liners in Milton. Simple guttural grunts their like in kind. Then there was two-part harmony. Shuffling close to the booth, stomping his feet against the cold, Aldrich actually heard Danton Welsh's voice mouthing the strains of Indian keening, felt the terrible reality of Lydia's loss rising and falling through octaves of pain, wondered how far away the Episcopal minister was from the sounds of this consoling primitivism.

Only none of this ought really to surprise him, Aldrich reasoned: He had long since digested his incredulity over the strange communion between his ex-father-in-law and Charlie. At first it had unnerved him, made him competitive and jealous, until he half-convincingly reminded himself that Charlie was, after all, only an Indian, someone with whom Danton might feel less challenged and more at ease than with the man who shared his daughter's bed. Still the memory rankled Aldrich, the recall of how archly his attempts at normalizing relations with Danton Welsh had been dismissed that midsummer of 1969 when he had first dared venture back to the Shelburne farm after marrying Lydia.

Then he was made conclusively to feel like an outsider, an inlander who did not understand the customs of New England, an incognoscente in the mead hall of old school ties where Danton Welsh of Harvard and Charlie Wishing Ten Fingers of Dartmouth drank and sang affably together. Aldrich, graduate of the State University of Nebraska, was a student of architecture. Danton Welsh, whose fief in suburban Milton centered on a great Georgian-style brick edifice, whose farmhouse in Vermont was a comfortable and sprawling old restored Cape, gave it bluntly to be known that he had no further need of architecture, all good taste having declined with the dawn of the nineteenth century.

In time, a few short weeks after the timorous return of Aldrich and Lydia to her father's house, Aldrich had been deftly maneuvered to the farthest periphery of a glowing summer society of poets, painters, Morgan-horse breeders, forensic scholars, glider pilots, civil libertarians, Canadian yachtsmen, hunting buddies, fishing buddies, wind-instrument ensemblists, summer-stock thespians, Harvard theologians, Middlebury College academicians, bored inherited wealth, lots of important Mohawks who were always coming by for free legal advice for their never-ending wars against the government, and—most dumbfounding of all to Aldrich—Stephen Hodges, who had apparently awakened one morning from the shock of finding he was not actually married to Lydia and simply returned at Danton Welsh's behest to take his rightful intended place in that society.

Aldrich, from the terrace, looked in. With him, soul mate by default, was Big Janie, his mother-in-law, the sad fact of her alcoholism formally confirmed that eventful summer. Danton Welsh contrived skillfully at institutionalizing their kinship of pariah, making of them an anomalous, ghostly duet of an unwanted opportunist of a young man helping a drunken older woman stumble about seeking safety beyond the perimeter of Danton Welsh's fierce intolerance for either of them. Recalling this punishment, the ravages wrought in his own breast by the unreconcilable warring odds of pity for and detestation of Big Janie's awful condition to which he had gotten shackled, Aldrich ground his teeth in the Sunday-morning cold of Saugus, Massachusetts, and determined he would witness how Danton Welsh buried his splendid, traitorous daughter Lydia on the morrow.

In the phone booth Charlie's chanting came to an end and he spoke English now with his friend Danton: "I supposed you might bury her there, Danton, though I wish she could be buried in Vermont, on Champlain near her Mohawk friends. She loved it there so in the fall, on the crisp clear days when the lake was so blue and she could look across to the foliage colors on the New York side. . . . Well yes, her mother's family is a very old family and I can understand how this would be important to Big Janie. . . . Yes, three hundred fifty years is a long time. . . . It is a noble lineage, Danton. Don't ever doubt it. Lydia's being buried in hallowed ground. I mean, the Breckenridges were all the best things a family could be in American life, Revolutionary War heroes, unstinting patriots, first-rate merchants and philanthropists. Yes, I know . . . all that, and . . ."

Except unto this generation, Aldrich thought ruefully, stomping outside in the cold: when the last Breckenridge alive anywhere, Olivia Breckenridge Welsh, was a pathetic

and beaten alcoholic. Now see the last possible use Danton
Welsh had for the poor lady after he had already usurped her
social standing as a launching pad for his career, fleeced her
of her assets, changed the name on the gates of her family's
estate to Welsh, caused her to bear his children, who despised
their mother for her trouble—in short, built up the dynasty of
Welsh atop the hastened ruins of Breckenridge: He chose to
extol the memory of her ancestry on a day like today when it
suited him, even when he had nothing but scorn for the lady
herself. He prepared to lay the first dead Welsh among the
moldering bones of a noble race who had not ever lived in sod
huts on a prairie. Oh, you ravening Kansas rustler!, the words
raged inside of Aldrich. You were worse a thousand times
than I could ever have thought of being!

"Don't cry, Danton," Charlie said to the Kansas rustler,
the turnabout of emotion in the Indian's voice so unexpected
that it dragged Aldrich away from his private fury, set him instead to listening keenly to the exchange: "Why think about
that at a time like this? I never begrudged you a moment for
what happened. It was so completely and unintentionally an
accident. . . . No, Danton, I don't think it was divinely ordained because I don't believe in the divine, and I don't think
you need go exploring through the plague stations of Christian morbidity looking for an answer either, especially now
when you'll need to call on so much of your strength for tomorrow's burial. . . . Of course I forgive you, Danton, if it
makes you feel better to hear me say it. But after seventeen
years, what's left to forgive? Losing three fingers to your chain
saw obviously hasn't meant the end of my life. It's just meant
adapting to other methods. . . . No, no, Danton, please don't
revert to that Bible Belt fundamentalism of yours again, or I'll
confess to my annoyance with you in no small whispers. . . .
Because it's insulting, that's why. If you won't let Kansas or
the Baptist terrors of your youth all hang out with any of the
white eyes, then don't lay it on me every time you get a few

too many in you. It's no compliment as far as I'm concerned . . ."

Aldrich stared blankly at the figure in the phone booth, mesmerized by the motion of Charlie's two-fingered left hand tapping out a loud staccato beat of his rising annoyance with Danton Welsh on the frosted glass pane before him. Incredible to find this out now after five years of knowing Charlie but never once daring to ask how the fingers had gone: from embarrassment or guilt or fear perhaps of whatever curious, unnamed power it was that Charlie wielded over people through the use of that nubbed, claw-like appendage that hypnotized his listeners when he sinuously punctuated the air with it as he spoke. Lydia had called it his king's scepter. His cousin Sybaritic Hawk alleged that it was the inflated head of Charlie's inner cobra. Aldrich could hardly ever remove his eyes from it when the serpentine motion began. . . . But a chain-saw massacre by Danton Welsh of all people: What marvelous irony! Aldrich thought. No, better still, what perfect incest! What deservedly perfect incest: In the soft summer Champlain nights when Danton and Charlie had eyes and minds only for each other to the exclusion of everyone else, when the jurisprudential arguments of two fierce intellects (Aldrich frankly admitted to being farm team when it came to playing in that league) raged on into the early-morning hours, how many times had Danton Welsh finally given up his king to his opponent, Charlie Wishing Ten Fingers, from a burgeoning guilt compelled by that blunt reminder of one of his life's very few acknowledged missteps weaving before him in the half-light of his study?

"I haven't failed you, Danton. It hurts me to hear you say that. If you say it one more time I'm not coming to the service tomorrow. I don't have to put up with this kind of abuse from you. You're drunk, Danton, and you'd better lay off the stuff right now or they'll be carrying you up that hill to your own daughter's burial to society's obvious judgment. . . . Yes, Danton, I thank you for all that. I thank you for Hotchkiss and Dartmouth and Harvard Law, but I warned you when I was an undergraduate that I was going to live my life as an Indian and you were wasting your dough on Harvard and that you weren't going to get a pinstriped Boston Mohawk lawyer for your trouble. . . . I don't care if it embarrasses you to have to introduce me as a riveter with a law degree. If it doesn't bother me, it needn't bother you. We're not family after all. . . . Oh, Danton, please don't start that crap about me being the son you always wanted again. It's really exasperating. You hurt people when you drink too much, Danton. It's the only thing about you I can't abide. I was absolutely mortified those times you started in vilifying Reverend Dickie for being unmanly and calling him the pimp of God and demanding to know why he had to be five feet six inches tall and pear-shaped when he was no more responsible for his genetic short-changing than for his inability to fly . . ."

They argued like lovers, Aldrich thought, his eyes agleam, staring at Charlie, who cleaved the air outside the phone booth with the claw hand in some totally uncharacteristic parody of a Levantine's passion for semantics. Lovers! Yes. Good thunder! What high-grade ore was being mined from the deepest veins of the mighty mountain that was Danton Welsh on this day that his daughter lay out cold and dead on the mortician's slab! The mother lode discovered at last, a wealth of information that no enemy of Danton Welsh as dedicated as Dwight David Aldrich should ever be without.

"Stop talking about it, will you, Danton?" Charlie went on, a real annoyance in his voice now. "We were both half oiled that day. It was stupid to try to clean up that brush in the condition we were in. Anyhow, I didn't feel a thing. It was the cleanest offing of any man's three fingers that ever occurred. . . . Yes, I am bored with your sloppy crying, but here's something that ought to restore your equilibrium, Danton. Dwight David Aldrich is standing right beside me. He requests permission to come to the service tomorrow. Well?"

Aldrich stiffened, trying to decipher the response in

Charlie's face that regarded him rather vacantly for a long moment until he suddenly held the phone away from his ear and grimaced with pain as if a thunderclap had just exploded over the wire.

"He says no, Dwight David. Definitively."

"Let me speak with him, Charlie," Aldrich begged, grabbing the phone away from the Mohawk.

"Danton?"

"Yes, Aldrich? I really have nothing to say to you. Especially today of all days."

The voice slurred over the words: The wide vowels of a Kansas twang unleashed by the drink came unmistakably to Aldrich's ear.

"Danton, you can't make me stay away. She was my wife. I loved her."

"I won't have you at that service, Aldrich! Big Janie won't either! We don't want you anywhere around!" The voice was apoplectic now, wildly out of control, its edges fraught with furious tears like a child choking to find the right invective in a child's argument: "You've left your ugly mark on Lydia's life, Aldrich. . . . Dirtied and sullied everything you've ever touched. At least allow her to go cleanly into her grave. . . . I don't care what that wop detective Mugiani says. . . . I don't care how many alibis you've got. . . . You're as responsible for her death as if you'd pulled the trigger yourself. You were the one who turned traitor and ratted on the commune members who must certainly have killed Lydia yesterday in revenge. . . . Stay away, do you hear? Stay away or someone might take violent exception to your presence!"

Over the wire Aldrich heard clearly the plop sound of alcohol being poured into a glass, heard the dull thud of the bottle as it was set down hard on the leather-top desk in Danton Welsh's study.

"Danton, you're overwrought," Aldrich tried at soothing him. "I can understand the shock you must be feeling. But

Charlie's right. That booze isn't going to do you one bit of good . . ."

"Don't you dare try pitying me, you fucking indigent Kansas dirt farmer, you! You loathsome Baptist cretin! You unprincipled opportunist rattlesnake with a dead drunk father and a mother living on the dole from me!"

"It takes one to know one evidently, Danton. Was yours a more privileged upbringing out there in little old Holcomb, Kansas? No reprobates in the Welsh family closet that you can recall and have obviously tried to forget?"

"What . . . ? What did you say . . . ?"

The phone slammed down abruptly on Aldrich's ear, but not swiftly enough to disguise the certain tone of fearing in the other's voice. Aldrich looked delightedly into the receiver's skein of holes as if he expected to see the blanched, shaken face of Danton Welsh peering back at him, trying to decipher how far he had pried the lid off the coffin of the old Kansas life, what were the possible limits of the terror Aldrich might unleash upon him. Aldrich hung up the phone in triumph, thought warmly of his new friend Pasquale Mugiani, speculated on the real havoc he might wreak on the day he confronted his archenemy Danton Welsh with the photograph of beautiful little Angelina Frippi . . .

"That ought to sober the bastard up," Aldrich told Charlie emphatically as he exited the phone booth.

"You're a cruel guy, Dwight David, to make that man recall forgotten truths on the nadir day of his life."

"He's a cruel prick to bar me from attending my own ex-wife's funeral."

"No, he's not. He understands full well why you want to be there. You mustn't go."

"I'm going. Now more than ever. I'll call Hodges. He'll take me there with him. Nobody can ask me to leave if he brings me to the service with him."

"Are you crazy? I imagine Hodges would like to kill you

right now more determinedly than any other enemy you've got, considering all the trouble you've caused for him."

"Why? I had nothing to do with it. I'm going to call him right now."

"Dwight David . . . don't! Imagine what kind of shape he's in today."

"I could comfort him, Charlie. I was always good to Hodges. I never implicated him as corespondent in the divorce, after all."

"You seem to forget that was part of the deal for Lydia's agreement not to press kidnapping charges against you. On two occasions. Stephen Hodges was murderously irate about that concession, I seem to remember."

"He forgave me. He got Lydia, didn't he?"

"For all of the time it took to march backwards down the church aisle." Charlie spat disgustedly. "Go ahead and call him, Dwight David. He lives in Back Bay. Maybe he'll convince you you aren't welcome, and I won't have to weary myself for the rest of the day with fruitless argument."

Aldrich dialed Information for Hodges' number, wrote it in the film of his breath fog on the glass pane before him that quickly froze the digits into perfect frosted clarity. He phoned the Back Bay apartment. His hands sweated despite the chill and his stomach danced nervously. A man's voice answered the call.

"Yes, may I help you?": It was not Stephen Hodges.

"I'd like to speak with Steve Hodges."

"Who's calling, please?"

"This is a friend of his, Dwight David Aldrich." He was conscious of divulging his name with a musical lilt: Trying to obfuscate it, perhaps, or trying to infuse it with a good-natured resonance that implied innocence of intent.

"Jesus H. Christ . . ." the voice judged softly. "I don't fucking believe it. Of all people . . ."

"May I speak with him, please!" Aldrich grew frantic at

the notion the phone might be slammed on his ear again as Danton Welsh had done.

"I'll find out if he wants to talk with you. What shall I say you're selling today? Burial plots?"

Aldrich absorbed that barb in silence and listened, trying to hear any imprecations or threats of violence, but there was only a garble of hushed voices, then complete quiet. The receiver was lifted and a sorrowing voice, phlegm-coated, came at Aldrich over the wire. Oh, mine enemy from the boudoir has succumbed to boundless grief, Aldrich thought delightedly. He pictured Hodges still clothed in his wedding-day tuxedo, meticulous but for the stains of Liddy's blood across the front of it. His face would be gaunt and hollow-eyed and very, very pale. He would grip hard on the telephone table to keep from swaying and collapsing to the floor.

"Hello . . . Aldrich?"

"Hello, Stephen. I'm very sorry."

"I loved her so much, Aldrich. There was always something in the way of our happiness. First you, now an assassin's bullet. It just doesn't seem fair . . ."

Hodges broke into little shuddering sobs punctuated with quick jabs of apology—"Forgive me . . . I'm behaving so badly . . ."—while Aldrich, aflame with curiosity, tried speculating on who might be with Hodges in the apartment: "Don't apologize, Stephen. She was your wife, after all. Hey, who's there with you, by the way?"

"My best man and four ushers. All guys from the pre-political college fraternity days. All reasonable, intelligent, clean-cut men totally unlike that gun-toting revolutionary riff-raff you conned into putting up North Hollow for you. Those same persons who it now seems certain killed dear Lydia since the police say you had nothing to do with it. Killed her to avenge your treachery! Oh, my heart is so broken, Aldrich. . . . We were both so innocent, she and I, to let you intrude on our lives the way you did. . . . To have to suffer so much simply for having casually encountered you at an antiwar protest out there in Nebraska when you weren't even against the war to boot. What karma! What criminal injustice!"

"Stephen . . . about the funeral . . . I want to be allowed to attend tomorrow."

There was a long pause while Hodges' strained breathing came over the wire and Aldrich had time to trade a shrug with Charlie Wishing Ten Fingers indicating the bereaved widower's indecision. Then the voice returned, cold and completely under control now: "If it were up to me, Aldrich, I'd encourage you not to be absurd. I'd assure you that nobody wants you there after the job you've done of dragging the Welsh name into places they didn't even know existed. . . . But the bizarre fact of the matter is that I finished speaking with Danton Welsh not a moment before you phoned and he told me that in the event you contacted me I was to tell you he's given his permission for you to attend the service. I can't for the life of me understand why. . . . He sounded very drunk . . ."

"I doubt very much that Danton Welsh was drunk, Hodges." Aldrich rushed archly to the defense of the man he had just terrified into acquiescence with his disclosure of the Kansas past. "You yourself should know better than that. Danton simply realized that I have a right to be there. She was my wife, after all. She loved me."

"Loved you, Aldrich?" Hodges actually spat. "She pitied you. She couldn't believe that anyone could be so obsessed with success and moneymaking. She said you'd so little time for her or any other human being that you'd ended up battening on your own entrails by the time she'd left you . . ."

"She said that? My Lydia said that about me?" Aldrich begged miserably.

"That was the tame stuff, Aldrich," the voice continued, lurching—despite the phlegm-coated sorrowing—into grinding gears of merciless pleasure taking. "She told me about all those times you were impotent with her. She told everyone.

Wow, that must have been an incredibly romantic couple of winters that I agonized over for no good reason at all. Dwight David Aldrich, King of Vermont and anything else he could get his grubby hands on, lying there beside my Lydia with a wet noodle between his legs. Sure, castrato, you're welcome to come to the service tomorrow. I'll phone Danton and Big Janie right back to make the way doubly safe for you. It would be just wonderful to see you again, old buddy, by the way."

"You don't seem to be quite keeping the spirit of mourning, Hodges. You seem on the verge of turning this into a literal triumph. All men suffer from impotence, you know. I had colossal worries, Hodges. All you did was build foundation footings and frame up buildings. I had to worry about raising capital, placating my partners and the banks and the goddam environmentalists, everything . . . Hey, are all those guys still there listening to this, Hodges?"

"Sure they are. They're rolling in the aisles, asshole. My best man Sutherland is here doing a Dwight David Aldrich fertility dance. That is to say, he's hopping all around the place in festive fashion with a very limp, but wildly swinging dick hanging outside his pants . . ."

"Stephen . . . ?"

"Yes, Aldrich?"

"What are you wearing right now?"

"I'm wearing my wedding tuxedo. It's stained with Lydia's blood."

"And yet you find reason to profane, though it's not even twenty-four hours since she died . . ."

A sob—swollen with an agony of guilt—rushed at Aldrich from the Back Bay apartment. How easy, Aldrich thought. Hodges' voice came behind, growling now with unmistakable menacing: "How perfectly able you always are to find the mark, dear Aldrich. Uncanny ability. I hate you for that ability. But I digress. Yes, come to the service tomorrow. We'll expect you. We look forward to it, in fact . . ."

"I want you to tell that to Charlie Wishing Ten Fingers, Hodges. He's here with me now."

"What's an honest man like Charlie doing with a crooked son of a bitch like you?"

"He's my friend. He has been for years."

"If he's your friend, he's the only one you've got left."

"Maybe," Aldrich responded, thinking of his mother. "Here, you talk with him."

Aldrich handed the phone to Charlie, who only shrugged, and looking properly mournful, told Stephen Hodges the expected: "If there was only something I could say, Stephen. . . . Yes, I understand Stephen. . . . All right, if you say so. I think it will cause a lot of unpleasantness, but he seems determined to be there. . . . Goodbye, Stephen, I'm sorry again . . ."

Charlie handed the phone back to Aldrich, who returned it to its cradle and stepped outside the phone booth.

"Danton Welsh changed his mind, Charlie. Right after I dropped that little morsel about our shared Kansas past. He phoned Hodges to say it was O.K. for me to show."

"This smells like an invitation to a beheading, friend Aldrich. That wedding party may end up beating your brains out for you."

"Don't be insane, Charlie. At Lydia's funeral? They'd never. . . . They're all a bunch of limp-dick preppies, anyhow."

The notion was so preposterous Aldrich discounted it immediately. With Charlie, he walked to a nearby drugstore for the Sunday *Times*, then to a French-Canadian bakery where they loaded up with provisions for Sybaritic Hawk's mourning orgy and carried them back to the tin-sided hut in the quarry.

CHAPTER 14

A Halting Progress
Toward the Bier

Monday morning, February 11, 1975: Lydia Welsh Aldrich Hodges' very last day in the freer air above the earth.

At 8 A.M. Aldrich left the quarry with Charlie Wishing Ten Fingers and Sybaritic Hawk and marched in solemn trio down the hill to the storage garage in Saugus where they kept their identical Harley-Davidsons. For the funeral both Mohawks wore the same embroidered buckskins they had worn at the wedding only two days before. Black heavy woolen blankets were draped about their shoulders. Aldrich, cleaned and cosmetized since the pummeling he had received at Charlie's hands, wore a black watch, fleece-lined raincoat on loan from Sybaritic Hawk and dark sunglasses to hide the distinctive rings of bruise that surrounded both eyes.

On their way through the mean little development to the town, a teen-age boy, one of the ones evidently liberated by that day's school holiday, sprinted from the front door of a house with a Polaroid camera in hand and asked if he might take their picture. Charlie Wishing Ten Fingers immediately acquiesced on the condition that he be given a copy of the photos, and sent the young photographer running back to the house for a jar of Vaseline to smear the lens and create the blurred image of 1890s daguerreotype.

"We can pretend we're recently subdued plains Indians on our way to the Territorial Governor's funeral," Sybaritic

Hawk spoke earnestly, willing prisoner of the mythical red Indian narcissism both Mohawks shared to an unnecessary fault.

"We go to his funeral because we're forced to by the white eyes," Charlie declared, snatching up the baton and rushing off on his quarter mile. "But we go proudly defiant and subtly display our defiance so that no other red man who sees the photo will doubt our intention." Charlie shook the clenched fist that seemed to be everyone's current liberation symbol, clutched it tightly to the front of his shoulder blanket at breast level. Sybaritic Hawk grunted his approval and followed suit, thumping his own breast in a mindless parody of the mea culpas. In another moment Aldrich realized both Indians were looking at him rather speculatively as if from a great distance away.

"I don't think you need to be in this photo, Dwight David," Charlie told him levelly.

"Why not, Charlie? I want to remember this day, too. It's important to me also."

"You don't look right. You're too twentieth-century-looking. You'd immediately seem anomalous and thwart the desired effect of the photo by turning it comical when it means to be solemn and noble. This is a sad day of Indian mourning, after all, and the photo's meant to imply memorabilia. Besides, you're not an Indian."

"Yeah, Dwight David, you look like a greaser in that raincoat and shades," Sybaritic Hawk judged. "You look like a 1950s minor gangster on his way to a Mafia funeral in an about to be repossessed third-hand Cadillac. Get the kid to take your photo alone and you can remember what period in time you represented despite yourself on the day of Lydia's funeral . . ."

But the kid, evidently no small romantic on his own, had already foreseen the problem and emerged again from the house at a run carrying a western hat and an enormous motheaten raccoon greatcoat for Aldrich. Arrayed in the coat and hat, his sunglasses removed, Aldrich turned to the Mohawks for their judgment. Charlie sighed deeply, then shrugged his shoulders in defeat: "Welcome the new Territorial Governor to this day's memorabilia, Sybaritic Hawk."

They stood against the backdrop of a winter-bare lilac bush for four separate takes, Aldrich reminded each time by Charlie that on the day of his ex-wife's burial he was not supposed to smile. The smeared-lens polaroid gave forth blurred, ghostly last-century images of two Indians and a white man standing on the edge of infinite prairie perhaps looking for all the world as if they actually were on their way to a Territorial Governor's funeral. Despite himself, the vengeful pleasure he meant to derive from the day's events, Aldrich was strangely touched by the photos, made uneasy, as if he were seeing a past incarnation of himself, a harbinger of his own mortality that at the age of thirty-four he still considered himself too young to be bothered about.

"It's as if we're already dead," Sybaritic Hawk said quietly as they began walking down the hill again with two photos of their own after the teen-ager had taken his pick. "It's as if we're the spirit remnant of an already lived life remembering how it was. We look very strange dressed as we are."

"We're not dead!" Charlie ground out savagely, his intensity startling in the early-morning quiet so that Aldrich instinctively shied from his side. "Wearing Indian garb in 1975 doesn't mean we're vestigial fools when we try to spark new life into the customs of an old nation! It proves we're more determinedly alive than anyone! We have a purpose! And what about Dwight David Aldrich? Do you think he's given up the ghost, Sybaritic Hawk? He's got the strongest life force I've ever encountered. Do you consider for a moment that he's done wreaking havoc everywhere he touches down upon the earth?"

"No, you're right, cousin Charlie. That's all the proof I need. Now I know I'm not dead. But the thing that really bugs me about every one of those photos is the look of our eyes," Sybaritic Hawk said, studying the photos closely again as he waddled down the hill. "It's real pristine innocence, I think, unnatural in grown men, very disturbing. It's like looking at three people and suddenly realizing that these guys are inveterate victims rather than victimizers, that no matter what they proposed doing in life it was all beyond their control anyhow . . ."

Charlie Wishing Ten Fingers seized the photos from his cousin's hands and tore them fiercely to pieces: "That little exercise in narcissism was a foolish digression. And that kind of ridiculous fatalism put a lot of quitter Indians under the ground with exploded livers because they just gave up and drank themselves to death. Shut up, Sybaritic Hawk! Don't ever speak of this to me again! We're in this life to hoe our own row and that's all there is to it!"

They were silent except for the snorted exhalings of Charlie's anger winding down until they reached the storage garage and brought out the motorcycles. Aldrich rode behind Charlie, who rushed off down U.S. 1 toward Boston in the face of a chill wind that was nearly unbearable when they crossed the Mystic Bridge over the harbor and the wind came due east and uninterrupted from the Atlantic. Above, obscuring the tops of the tallest buildings that rose up out of the city beyond the nub of Beacon Hill, a dark bank of cloud hung pregnant with promised snow. Dismal day, Aldrich thought, clapping first one ear and then the other fiercely against the cold as they moved off the bridge and southward on the Fitzgerald Expressway toward suburban Milton. Dismal day, full of dismal portents. Perfect day for a genuine old-fashioned New England Puritan funeral. J. P. Lovecraft spirits ranging about the dark and murky air, Emily Dickinson being read over the coffin at ground level, not a ray of random sunlight anywhere to illumine that big fat scarlet A that somebody should have sewn onto dear traitoress Lydia's breast. Oh, sweet revenge! Aldrich joyed. Bless the sublime prowess of whoever's Saturday hit man! Am I going to enjoy this little leave-taking . . . !

In Milton the first light snow began as they sped through the rolling-hills horse country beyond the town, shattering the stillness of great fir-tree-rimmed estates with the roar of barely muffled engines. At the gates of Danton Welsh's fief, two State Troopers manned a checkpoint with a list of the invited mourners. Aldrich saw that his name was added in pen to the bottom of the typed list and a notation beside it specified that he was to be admitted only in the company of C. Wishing Ten Fingers.

"You're responsible for this person, Mr. Wishing Ten Fingers," the older trooper spoke. "No crazies from him today, understand? There's a lot of important people in there, starting with the governor. He acts up and we book him for disturbing the peace."

"Isn't he the guy they extradited from Vermont Saturday after the killing?" the younger trooper asked.

"Yep."

"Hmmm. Who let him go?"

"Patsy Mugiani."

"Hmm. Bait."

"Yep."

"Hmmm. Maybe today?"

"Nope. A fruit fly couldn't get in there without a gate pass today."

"Hmmm. Where's your crash helmets, boys?"

"A lady we all loved is dead in there today and all that concerns you is whether or not we're wearing crash helmets," Aldrich tried accusing. "What barbarous inhumanity!"

"It won't work, Aldrich," the older cop told him drily. "Your reputation has preceded you. Besides, when it comes to moral bullyship you're just a plain bush-league rookie standing at the gates of the all-time champ, Mr. Danton Welsh."

"I really ought to march right in there and tell him that. I

171

really ought to tell Danton everything you've said. I doubt he'd take to it very kindly."

"Tell him any fucking thing you want, Mr. Aldrich. Only remind him that the same uniformed turds of crypto-fascists he's always laying into in the courts and widely read newspaper interviews are outside his gates guarding his ass against some part of his much-beloved criminal element whose misunderstood humanity he's always defending. Tell him if we had a choice, we'd leave."

"Yeah, Aldrich, you tell him that for us!" the younger cop snarled, advancing aggressively toward Aldrich so that the older trooper had actually to restrain him. Charlie revved the cycle engine, preparing their escape: "We'd better go in now," he told the older trooper. "We didn't come here to fight about Danton Welsh."

"There isn't a neutral place in Massachusetts where that name can be dispassionately spoken," the older trooper rasped as they moved away. "And I don't care if his goddam daughter is being buried today in there! Bay State lawmen pee collectively on her grave!"

They moved slowly up the hill toward the Georgian mansion and Charlie Wishing Ten Fingers whistled long and beseechingly: "How do you do it, Aldrich? How are you always able to let loose the most obscure rage in men's hearts?"

"I don't know," Aldrich told him, thinking it was as profound a source of wonderment to himself as anyone.

They rode past the house's main entry that was guarded by another trooper and onto the large cobbled courtyard before the stables where perhaps twenty or so expensive, funereal-looking cars were being parked by a number of valets. Charlie and Sybaritic Hawk switched off their engines and the three dismounted after being told the other mourners were all gathered in the house, Aldrich doing a gawky little shuffle on the cobblestones to relieve the chill stiffness of his legs until he almost fell over dead at the sight of Minyard Turner and his cousin Hiram unloading cordwood from their evidently repaired truck into the woodshed beyond the paddock. Hiram saw Aldrich first. He nudged his cousin and Minyard turned to wave effusive greetings to Aldrich, who was ashen-faced and actually trembling now at the certainty that his two would-be hit men had carried the concealed weapons of Lydia's intended dispatch into the veritable police state that was Danton Welsh's fief today.

"Someone over there unloading firewood does not seem to be an enemy of yours, Dwight David," Charlie spoke. "In fact he seems downright joyous to see you."

"That's because I owe them money. They're from Inglenook. They're coarse unfeeling characters who wouldn't think anything of walking right up to me in the middle of a burial service to ask for it, either. Let me talk to them before things get worse than they are now. They've got to respect the dead for my sake," Aldrich whined self-pityingly, wondering to himself how it was continually possible for Dwight David Aldrich to be so heaped upon.

He walked quickly away, leaving Charlie and Sybaritic Hawk waiting near the cycles, and drew up face to face with Minyard Turner, who spat a wad of tobacco juice onto the fast-collecting wisps of snow at his feet.

"What the fuck are you doing here, Turner?" Aldrich demanded in a fierce whisper.

"Sellin' my firewood to Danton Welsh, that's what. Like any good Yankee, he ain't too bereft of his daughter's dyin' to fail 'n spot a good bargain. Wood's eighty dollars a cord here 'n we struck for sixty. He's ahead, I'd say."

"You're mad, Minyard! Why the fuck didn't you turn around and go back to Vermont after you fixed your truck?"

"'Cause Vermont's uphill and Boston's downhill, 'n how the hell do you expect me to make it back uphill under this here load when the drive shaft broke comin' down to begin with?"

The terrible woodchuck logic that always inevitably defeated him began, and Aldrich, despite himself, fell into the hypnotic rhythm: "You could've sold it in New Hampshire. You could've driven it up to Concord and sold it there."

"Are you crazy? Them granite-chip fuckers wouldn't give you more 'n forty dollars a cord for it, 'n I wasn't goin' to leave it there for free in Howard Johnson's parkin' lot."

"But why here? Why on this day did you come here of all places in Massachusetts? It defies all logic . . ."

"No, it don't, Aldrich. I didn't know the name of anybody in Massachusetts 'cept Danton Welsh, so I called him 'n told him I knew Liddy when she lived at North Hollow 'n how she was a good girl 'n it's too bad she's gone, but did he want to buy some nice dry cordwood? We squatted and haggled for a while, then he said yes to sixty, so here I come."

Aldrich stared blankly for a long moment at the sagging old ten-wheel logger behind the two, its frame all hung over with mud chains and tow cables and faded Wallace stickers from campaigns past; it was Minyard Turner's predictable notion of what constituted a perfect unobtrusive vehicle for a contract job on the streets of downtown Boston.

There is a curious justice, Aldrich decided suddenly, thinking for the first time in a long time that the universe wherein he lived was not the automatic fail-safe province of whatever little bitch godling had had it in for him these past five or six years running. Some benevolent principle had caused Minyard Turner's drive shift to snap, keeping Dwight David Aldrich from a surefire, no-bail, one-way trip to the pokey. What desperate, mindless lengths his passion for vengeance had driven him to! It astounded him now, smiling reflexively at Minyard's 60 IQ simpleton-grinning, rotten-teeth cousin Hiram, that he had ever actually sat down to negotiate with the two, had ever grown tingly with excitement at Minyard's proposal to construct a box with gunsights big enough to hold the assassin and cover it over with ten cords of firewood atop the bed of the truck! Faultless camouflage: The end pieces of six-inch logs were even fashioned into a trapdoor that could be raised to permit the bullet's egress. Viewed up close, even touched and probed, it was nothing more than what it appeared to be, a couple of tons of firewood on a truck. On its shakedown cruise, lumbering past a target range of head-sized half-gallon wine jugs like a mobile log fort crossing the snows, it had performed faultlessly, making Aldrich, Minyard and cousin Hiram heady and drunk with the notion of their death-dealing prowess. Now Aldrich stood shaking his head at the recall: What a curious capacity for unreality develops in wintry Vermont in those who choose not to commit suicide: The Boston police would have apprehended them in moments. . . .

"There are two troopers down at the gate and one in front of the house, Minyard. What if they ask about that box you're uncovering there on the truck?"

"There's more than that. There's about twenty altogether roundabout. Welsh must be a really powerful fella. But if they ask I'll just tell 'em it's the box we use for haulin' around them raccoons we sell to the pet-store guy. Next question?"

"The guns?"

"In the fake wall behind the driver's seat just like always. Unless they got X-ray vision there's nothing to worry about. But they won't bother themselves. Me 'n Hiram are just good old Vermont boys sellin' a little dry firewood is all. They can see right off we're not your criminal type."

"I couldn't stand for anything else to go wrong now, Minyard. Things are quite bad enough."

"I don't doubt it. I don't doubt it for one single minute, Aldrich. But we'll just unload our wood and stay out of harm's way. You want a ride back to Inglenook after the burial's done?"

"All right," Aldrich agreed, thinking he would turn in his return flight ticket for cash. "I've got to go now. My two Mohawk friends are waiting for me."

"Je-sus! Ain't they a sight?" cousin Hiram judged, shifting his chew of tobacco from one cheek to the other while he waved to Charlie and Sybaritic Hawk across the stable yard.

"This is the strangest funeral I ever did hear tell of. There's maybe ten more Injuns all dolled up like them two down at the house, Aldrich. There's colonials, too. Colonial men and colonial women, 'n . . ."

"What colonials?" Aldrich asked.

"The Inglenook Fife and Drum Corps, and its Ladies' Auxiliary," Minyard pronounced with measured contempt, punctuating with spurts of tobacco juice on the snows. "About thirty altogether. Them same fellow citizens of ours who make such fools of themselves dressin' up like they was two hundred years old 'n already dead 'n rushin' off anywhere to march for any fool reason where there was a parade. . . . Also, Saturday's weddin' party is still dressed in their weddin' clothes. Bloodstains and all! There's hardly anybody to speak of in a decent Sunday suit like there should be at a funeral."

"We talked a bit to Stephen Hodges, didn't we, Minyard?" Hiram spoke.

"Yep. He's a good old fella himself. He said he didn't ever bear us any malice for helpin' you kidnap Lydia that time we took her to the monastery on that mountain. He said he always figured you tricked us into goin' along 'n didn't know what for. I allowed as how everybody knew we weren't the two brightest fellas in Vermont and, yes, that's exactly what did happen."

"I wonder how benevolently and forgivingly he'd respond if he knew what you were on your way to do in Boston just two days ago," Aldrich growled at them.

"I'd plead no intelligence again," Minyard surged on. "It'd work, too. But you know, Aldrich, I can't help speculatin' what might've happened if there was two assassinators there Saturday instead of just the one who did it. It might've turned into a real shoot-out to see who was goin' to get first crack at her!"

Aldrich stared blankly at the killer animation that rose in the other's face, appalled at the notion of his own mindless collusion with the man, afraid of the monster he had set loose

who had not yet taken its kill. Minyard Turner was truly a
home-grown Vermont psychopath. Bonkers. If Lydia was a
five-acre hit, God only knew what you could get for ten. The
President of the United States and a year of national mourning for fifteen in second-growth scrub. Aldrich sought to
defuse the killer lust, contract the widely dilated pupils of
Minyard Turner's eyes: "We should be thankful for what happened, Minyard. It was a terrible thing we were going to do.
Be thankful you're alive, too. The cops told me whoever did it
was a Deadeye Dick. A real pro. He might really have done a
number on you, Minyard."

"Like fuck, Aldrich! If I was there, I'd a got that other as-
sassinator before he ever got out of that church across the way
where he took the shot from. I'd a been there at the back door
to blow his ass off for takin' out my doe when I had my scope
on her first!"

"I can't talk to you anymore, Minyard. I've got to go to
Lydia's service," Aldrich pleaded. Involuntarily he put a hand
to his head. His hair was nearly completely wet from the thin
flakes of melting snow, his forehead damp in the low-twenties
cold from the sweat of fear at his encounter with mad
Minyard. "You'll wait here for me, Minyard?"

"I reckon so. I won't get my check from Danton Welsh
until it's over anyhow. You don't forget them ten acres either,
hear Aldrich? Five for me 'n five for cousin Hiram."

But Aldrich was already gone, hastening back toward
reason and an impatiently waiting Charlie and Sybaritic
Hawk.

"Have you stalled them off, Dwight David?" Charlie
asked. "Or are they going to embarrass you by trying to
collect in the middle of the burial service with all those
worthies standing about?"

"They'll wait till later," Aldrich told him stonily.

"That's a relief. One less rent to display in your mourning
clothes today. Cast an eye over yonder at brother Hodges, his
best man and ushers. I knew this was an invitation to some-

177

thing violent and punitive for you. From here I'd say it looks like a paddling . . ."

Aldrich turned to see Stephen Hodges, instant widower, and the four male members of his wedding party standing in the grove of tall pines that lay between the stables and the estate's guest house. They wore only their wedding-day tuxedos and no overcoats against the cold, and standing in the quiet dimness of the pines with wind-whipped snow squalling around them, they had the ghostly look of apparitions rather than human avengers. Aldrich, trying to master a new terror, blinked his eyes and wished them to dissolve. But they did not, and certified their realness with the loud clap of wooden paddles smacking on an open hand. True to Hodges' description on the telephone the day before, these were all good old conservative pre-political protest days fraternity boys. What irony, thought Aldrich, I used to be one of those mothers myself . . .

"Come on over, Aldrich," Hodges called out to him, his voice still cracking from the pain of loss. "We'd like a word with you."

"Those assholes are going to try to pulverize me with those fraternity paddles, Charlie," Aldrich said. "On the one hand I'm supremely contemptuous of their method. On the other hand they could kill me . . ."

"What's this all about, Stephen?" Charlie Wishing Ten Fingers demanded sternly. "You told me on the phone yesterday that Danton had given permission and it was all right for Aldrich to be here for the burial."

With the two Mohawks Aldrich had advanced to the edge of the grove where the three stared a long moment at the would-be avengers five, all of whom seemed somewhat uniformly bleary-eyed, red-faced and splotchy as if they had been drinking nonstop since Lydia's dispatch. Stephen Hodges was convincingly the worst by far, though, since he had obviously been long crying into the bargain. Aldrich stared raptly at the front of the bridegroom's tuxedo, appalled despite his satisfaction over Lydia's dying by the reality of her blood smeared on the cloth, some distant and unaccountable place in himself even touched by the meaning of Hodges' evident refusal to take it off.

"You should change out of that tuxedo, Stephen," Charlie told him quietly. "Lydia had no particular taste for the macabre. She wouldn't have approved of being remembered this way."

"I'll never change out of it!" Hodges wailed, more tears charging from his eyes as he grabbed his lapels, proffering them toward Charlie as if he thought the Mohawk had somehow missed seeing the stains. "I'm going to die in this tuxedo Charlie! I haven't got anything left to live for!"

Penetration at last, Aldrich considered: Stephen Birch Hodges hanging on for dear life to the whipping tail of a real raging monster of human emotion. God love! Nothing impossible. Even Lydia, who had twice perfunctorily mounted the altar beside him and once actually said "I do," would finally have found something compelling about her father's choice for her mate today were she around to see Hodges' tall blond sleepy blue-eyed healthy handsomeness disintegrating into the sharply etched planes and dark discolorations of his abject anguish. Gone for good that naïve guileless candor so boringly devoid of subtlety or sting that incessantly mouthed the cant of lovingkindness, pacifism, racial brotherhood and especially romantic love when Lydia would have settled for good old eros instead. Stephen Hodges: heretofore a passionless man. Seeing him today, even Lydia might have approved of the use her death was being put to. Human sacrifice not in vain. . . .

In a moment Aldrich grew aware that Charlie Wishing Ten Fingers, who stood beside him, was glaring at him openly.

"Stop smiling, Dwight David," the Mohawk told him fiercely, "or I'll break your goddam neck!"

Inside the pine grove, one of the ushers, a squat, balding ex-Harvard classmate of Stephen Hodges from St. Paul named

Porker Pode drained the last of a pint of whiskey and threw the bottle vaguely in Aldrich's direction, though it fell far short, shattering on a rock. Then he stumbled away from the others, walking over the shards of broken glass, coming right up to Charlie and extending his hand to be shaken: "You are, I take it, sir, an Indian?"

"Obviously, sir."

"Then you'd know what rules apply to the running of the gauntlet since I seem to recall that particular test was an invention of your people. Will it be cricket to hit Aldrich in the head with our paddles as he runs through, for instance?"

"No, it won't be cricket to hit Aldrich in the head. And he's not running anybody's gauntlet as long as I'm responsible for him in this place. You're drunk, whoever you are . . ."

"I'm Anthony Pode. My friends call me Porker. In the beginning the name hurt me terribly, but I've gotten used to it, even turned it into a social asset because it suggests a convivial good fellow, see? My grandfather was a famous Indian fighter in Minnesota during frontier days. My blood line just won't permit taking any guff from a red man, see? Now, Aldrich has caused a great deal of suffering and harm and this is the way we've decided to deal with it . . ."

"Yes, get your ass over here, Aldrich!" Stephen Hodges ordered. "Line up like we practiced, boys. Forget the head. From the looks of those shiners on his eyes, somebody's already been there. Concentrate on the buttocks and genitals! Knock the balls right off him!"

"I said Aldrich is not running anybody's goddam gauntlet," Charlie snarled at them. "He was permitted to come here as a mourner. For God's sake remember your ages. You're behaving like a pack of terrible little preppies. It's laughable."

"I won't permit any of your intolerable Indian interference, sir! Remember my blood line, sir!" Porker Pode threatened, menacing the air with his paddle too close to the tall Mohawk's head. Charlie Wishing Ten Fingers snatched the paddle from Pode, raised his leg and broke it in two over his knee and threw the pieces at the feet of the drunk descendant of the famous Minnesota Indian fighter, who was plainly startled with fright: "You little prig, you! Your dumb smugness reminds me of somebody born fifty years old! There will be no running of any gauntlet!"

"Exactly right. Aldrich is an invited mourner."

Surprised as the others at the sudden intrusion of the familiar low rumbling authoritative voice, Aldrich turned to see Danton Welsh, hatless and wearing a dark overcoat thrown loosely about his shoulders like a cape, emerging from the pine grove to the right. If he had gotten drunk the day before, there was no measurable evidence of it this day. On the morning of his oldest daughter's burial, Danton Welsh was still an extraordinarily handsome man in his early fifties, his hard athlete's body perfectly tailored and perfectly groomed. No appreciable vengeance taken there, Aldrich thought miserably, deciding that, battered and bruised as he was, he himself must look like a falling-down wino in comparison to his one-time father-in-law. There was a little sadness for Lydia's loss about her father's eyes, but only a little, and it disappeared quickly beyond the hard stare of his evident displeasure over the blubbering condition Stephen Hodges had gotten himself into: "There won't be any running the gauntlet, Stephen. Put away those foolish paddles."

"But, Danton, he's got to!" Hodges whined in response. "He's got to be punished, Danton! My wife is dead and he's the cause of it! We practiced this for hours yesterday after he telephoned. Just let us run him through once. We know how to put a couple of good dents in Dwight David Aldrich!"

"Oh, Hodges, don't be such an ineffectual Wasp! I thought I was getting better goods in a son-in-law. What the hell is a paddling going to do to the warped mind in Aldrich? Look at him over there. He's positively gloating at your puny alternative to any real ability to punish him. You're only begetting a fiercer contempt. Give me those paddles now."

"No!" Hodges raged, "I'm going to get one shot at him

today if it's the last thing I do!" Hodges started forward toward Aldrich at a run, but Danton Welsh intercepted and tripped him neatly to the ground, snatching away the paddle on the way down and flipping it behind him into the grove, where it clattered against the limbs of a tree and fell to the ground. Snow came down more heavily now, perfecting the awful day, sissing through the grove of pines, obscuring somewhat the hoarse breathing of Stephen Hodges, who stared up in stunned disbelief at the immobile face of Danton Welsh. Then tears swelled from Hodges' eyes as he stumbled to his knees, a certainty that he was bested and spent, and Danton Welsh put a consoling hand to the widower's shoulder. Still a member of the family then, Aldrich thought: Danton would push him far and reward him well; it merely demanded an occasional show of fealty.

"I have a better way, Stephen. Trust me to handle this. Lydia was my daughter and I loved her as much as you. Come, Pode, and the rest of you, take Stephen down to the house. Go in through the kitchen and get yourselves cleaned up so no one sees you looking like this. Let's have the rest of those paddles now, and any more liquor you've got on you."

Like sheep they handed the three remaining paddles and two pints of whiskey to Danton Welsh, who put the lot off to the side, breaking the whiskey bottles by throwing one atop the other. Then they headed off toward the house, a vague concentric ring about Stephen Hodges, disappearing eerily into the swirling snow, ethereal wedding party.

"How are you, Danton?" Aldrich taunted his enemy.

"Vengeful, Aldrich. Simmering with possibilities to achieve your destruction. Since you've somehow come by the horrifying news that I'm naught but a fraud from the plains of Kansas, then for me you've just become the universe's one other most unscrupulous soul."

"That's very Christian of you to put it that way. Are you the one perchance who's been bombing and burning North

Hollow Development Company of Inglenook, Vermont, to ruin?"

"Don't be ridiculous. That's totally incompatible with the Danton Welsh style. It's certainly got to be those commune people you betrayed. I'm talking about spiritual destruction. I'm going to hit you right in the abstraction that will cripple you for the rest of your days. When I find it, that is."

"I don't think you will. I don't think there is such a place anymore. I should be standing here today absolutely broken-hearted that the woman I once loved so much, the woman I tried so desperately to become a financial success for because I had to grovel impecuniously in the face of her father's money, is being lowered away for eternity. But I'm not. If anything I feel quite a bit like gloating . . ."

"This is neither the time nor place for that kind of talk, Dwight David. Stop it!"

Predictably, it was Charlie Wishing Ten Fingers eternally keeping the peace. Curiously, Danton Welsh seemed to notice the two Mohawks standing on either side of Aldrich for the first time: "Oh, hello, Charlie. Hello, Sybaritic Hawk. Thank you for coming today."

"Don't mind Dwight David, Danton," Charlie told him. "He isn't thinking or talking straight today."

But Danton Welsh had suddenly grown reflective, staring with perhaps unseeing eyes at the layer of snow that was fast covering the carpet of dead pine needles at his feet. Then he spoke, still not lifting his eyes.

"You know, Aldrich, I never thought I'd hear myself say it, but I do have a modicum of pity for you in one regard. Lydia treated you pretty badly. But of course, if you'd cleared out when you were supposed to before her intended marriage to Hodges, it would never have happened. Hodges was perfect because Hodges is quite rich, and a beautiful, vacuous girl like Lydia hopping through life from lark to lark, from antiwar protest to this women's lib silliness or whatever was current needs the advantage of a rich husband to retreat to. In a sense, I suppose, it neutralizes her capacity to do too much harm. Look what she did to you, after all. Turned you into a hod carrier when you were meant to design majestic edifices instead. But then what positive good are we privileged to receive from a daughter who left her betrothed standing at the altar and took off with you because the alternative looked more interesting? Not much, I guess. Oh well, the bishop should have arrived by now. Let's go down and bury that sweet flapper daughter of mine . . ."

Aldrich traded an incredulous look with Charlie and Sybaritic Hawk, stunned near rigid by the absolutely unexpected truth of what Danton Welsh had said. Then Lydia's father turned and marched off down the road toward the house, and the three followed quickly behind him. In moments more when all four stepped off the road to allow the passage of the bishop's car to the parking area, Danton Welsh turned to face Aldrich again.

"Aldrich, there's one thing I've forgotten. You are not privileged to stand with the main body of mourners today. You are to stand conspicuously alone and apart from us. The family wants it that way and the Hodgeses do also."

"I won't do it," Aldrich said flatly, any softening toward Danton Welsh he might have felt instantly hardened again by the sublime and condescending method of their petty vengeance. "I'm standing with the others. Right next to the goddam governor if I want. I warn you, Danton, that I have a trump card of information that could make lots of trouble for you. A real ace."

"I don't doubt it, Aldrich. But never play your card until the right moment. This, as any smart boy from Kansas who knows there's still a future to be lived out there would realize, isn't the right moment . . ."

Aldrich weighed his words a long minute, then shrugged: "Where's the conspicuously alone place, Danton?"

"That little knoll up to the right of the family graveyard. Go to it now. You're not to enter the house either."

Aldrich split off from the other three and climbed up toward the graveyard, hearing Danton Welsh ask of the two Mohawks: "Did either of you say anything to Aldrich about Kansas?"

"Of course not, Danton," Charlie told him. "He told us. He knew already."

"Hmm. Damn. Who?"

CHAPTER 15

The Saddest Day
in New England

Aldrich, standing conspicuous and alone on his outcast's knoll in a deepening snowstorm, watched the procession of mourners ascend the long gentle rise of meadow from the house to the private burial ground where the faded etching on the tombstone of the first interred Breckenridge read: 20 June 1785.

Dead Lydia came first in a simple pine box atop an ancient farm wagon that was drawn by two of Danton Welsh's prize Vermont Morgans guided by the estate's old Irish gatekeeper, another of Lydia's lovers, who wept uncontrollably into the neck of the horse he walked beside. The Inglenook Fife and Drum Corps came behind, led by the sheriff, who also wept and whose wig was on crookedly. The members marched four abreast in slow military precision, the ten pipers silent, the ten drummers tapping a mournful dirge into whose rhythm every mourner seemed to have fallen with unconscious step. Starbuck the mason brought up the rear alone, huge and awkward-looking in colonial garb, banging a single, measured beat on a big bass drum slung before him. He cried unceasingly also and Aldrich found himself suddenly wondering with absolute perplexity how she had done it, how she had gotten to all these guys who walked behind her coffin with broken hearts. She, Lydia, with the world's lowest threshold of boredom, its least capacity for tolerance. Lydia, who feigned interest with near manic zeal because, *au fond*,

there was naught but the enlarging ice cap of her nearly totally self-absorbed disinterest. Not one of them, evidently, had
ever come close to seeing through her. Who could say what it
had been? Whatever it was, to Aldrich's eternal ignorance, she
had taken her secret with her to the grave.

The Welsh family came next.

There were only four of them: Danton, Big Janie, Reverend Dickie and Little Janie. But for a brother who had committed suicide in Mexico before her marriage to Danton
Welsh, Olivia Breckenridge was the last of a moldering line.
By now some old aunts had died off, and ties to distant
Breckenridge relatives had more or less lapsed (in keeping
with Danton Welsh's purposes, Aldrich suspected), so that
today there were none of the usual vaguely look-alike cousins,
nephews or nieces bringing up the rear. For certain there were
no Welshes. If any existed, they were long since metaphori-
cally dead, plowed in under the distant Kansas sod.

Aldrich might have wept himself at the sight of Big Janie.
Today, slung in a harness of alcoholic defeat between her husband and her son, both of whom pretended solicitousness for
the woman they so despised, she looked pliant and destroyed
as if the steel rod of the life force that kept straight the human
back and propped the shoulders high had simply snapped in
two. She wore a simple black overcoat and her hair, covered
on top by the small triangle of a black scarf, hung long and
gray and lifeless to the collar. The face that from the old
photos had once been beautiful was puffy now from the drink
and dark, atrabilious circles clung beneath the eyes. She
looked, Aldrich considered, as if her fondest wish might be to
be allowed to drop in her tracks and disintegrate into the
earth, all trace of her covered by the driven snow. If there
were a hell, there had to be a special place in it for Danton
Welsh, for what he had done to this woman. . . .

Little Janie, whose name really was Jane, walked beside her brother Dickie. For the day of her sister's burial, she
was an Indian from the Southwest, Pueblo or Hopi perhaps,

clad in a severely tailored black blouse and black calf-length skirt over high soft-leather boots, lavish Indian silver jewelry at her throat and waist and festooning both arms, covered only by the sleeves of the blouse that stuck out of an embroidered sheepskin vest. Her hair, blond in reality, swept long and straight and dyed fiercely black to the level of her buttocks. A beauty like Lydia her sister, she had inherited the regal Breckenridge nose and the thin-faced high cheekbones and the combination made her more stunningly an Indian woman than Aldrich considered any real Indian woman could be.

At seventeen, just beginning her dalliance at Wellesley, she had already a vaunted reputation for her sexual preference for blacks, and today Aldrich scanned further down the line of march, looking for an institutionally angry black male face beneath a snow-covered Afro, fairly typical of the studs little Janie had been leading around by the nose ring since she was about thirteen. But there were no blacks to be seen, or none that he could discern yet, and Aldrich wondered if Danton Welsh had finally laid down the law for Janie about who his daughters were intended for, and nailed shut the door. But in the last analysis, he doubted it. If there was an acknowledged Catch-22 in Danton Welsh's life, it had to do with blacks: The Commonwealth's chief civil libertarian and liberal policies exponent simply could not give vent to all those primal hatreds that Aldrich knew damn well were deep down there in Danton Welsh. . . .

As to Little Janie, Aldrich found he did not dislike her particularly: Absorbed about herself as Lydia had been, she had been massively indifferent to the nearness of Aldrich to her life, and Aldrich had returned neutrality for neutrality, grateful enough for not having to post eternally wary guard on that front at least when there had been so many others to cover.

Reverend Dickie, though, the family's recessive gene, Aldrich positively despised. Lately of Harvard Divinity and a nervous breakdown from too much concentration on the moral irresoluteness of the world, he marched today between clinging mother and Hopi sister, wearing his lift shoes with the two-inch heels that always made the fact of his shortness more apparent, if anything, clothed in a dark overcoat whose tailored cut, as ever, reminded Aldrich of a round-top circus tent with billowing sides as it traced the outline of Dickie's (né Dickie) perfect pear shape. Now snowflakes scampered across his absolutely bald pate, and his eyes—deeply socketed on either side of the Breckenridge nose that did not work for Dickie—were wide open and myopic, which meant that he was thinking, a process that had the effect of making Dickie look unaccountably moronic: doubtless applying the theologian's thumb rules to the strange reality of his sister's death.

In the beginning Aldrich had tried for Dickie's friendship, somehow amused by and drawn to Danton Welsh's unwanted son who had an impossible sense of timing, who was always starting serious abstracted conversation about morality, virtue, the Virgin Birth, ecumenical responsibility or some such topic right at the beginning of cocktails or at half time in the Super Bowl or when his father's determinedly disinterested hunting and fishing buddies came around to reminisce and pound the tabletop in good-fellowed camaraderie. Poor Dickie: Ever out of synch, never seeming to recall the last outburst of his father's furious impatience with him, his virile animal's distaste for Dickie's flaccid jokes that all dealt with slightly impious clergymen, he would invariably be banished from the circle of the intelligent, the witty, the macho or whatever was playing that day by curt dismissal: "Shut up with that stuff, will you, Dickie? Save it for the ninnies at Divinity in Cambridge."

Early on in Aldrich's marriage to Lydia, Reverend Dickie learned that the only means he had of pleasing his father was to vent his spleen on Aldrich. He had taken to it with uncommon avidity, despite all the Christian clergyman's abstractions. Like a hapless mongoose in mid-life who suddenly discovers his chief purpose lies in trouncing cobras, he had come snarling after Aldrich's Kansas roots, his Baptist rearing and state university education, tearing open cruel wounds in the fabric of a past for which Aldrich was largely unaccountable, all to his father's applause and appreciative laughter. When attacking Dwight David Aldrich, there was no possibility of bad timing: Danton Welsh would suspend anything to listen. Aldrich would never forgive Dickie Welsh that studied viciousness that brought his father's approval.

The Hodges family came after the Welshes.

Stephen Hodges, still wearing only the bloodstained tuxedo, was yoked between his parents in much the same helpless way as was Big Janie between her husband and son. Stephen Hodges' father was a shaggy-browed, quizzical man who puffed eternally on a pipe and had offered Aldrich sincere congratulations on his marriage to Lydia as if his son, who had also intended marrying her, were no kin to be partisan about at all. Stephen Hodges' mother, who was the great good friend and co-conspirator of Danton Welsh, had fainted outright on the shores of Lake Champlain when stark-naked Aldrich had spirited her son's betrothed away. She was the power to be reckoned with in that family, and from his vantage Aldrich saw that her face had neither sorrow nor irony in it, only a grim, forward-looking resolve that made him wince with the memory of how hard she had smashed his face the first time he had encountered her after the wedding day. By all means he must stay out of her way today.

The members of the wedding party came next, the best man and three ushers of Stephen Hodges, each paired with a college friend of Lydia's, the same eight people, but for Porker Pode, who comprised the wedding party on the first try in the summer of '69. Unlike Stephen Hodges, the men wore overcoats now over their tuxedos, and the bridesmaids wore coats over their gowns, the three gowns of the evidently still unmarried ones identically the same, while the fourth wore her wedding dress. To Aldrich the women seemed as uni-

formly bleary as the men, as if they too had been off somewhere drinking in the face of the repetitive unreality that
dogged the efforts of Stephen Hodges and Lydia Welsh to live
together as man and wife.

Seven Mohawks came behind the wedding party, all
dressed in full tribal regalia, though Charlie and Sybaritic
Hawk were the only ones who wore blankets over their shoulders. The other five, all men, and all chieftains from the wearing of their feathered bonnets, marched abreast while Charlie
and Sybaritic Hawk followed behind. Aldrich recognized the
five from the days on Champlain in his first summer as Danton Welsh's son-in-law. They were all from New York State
and all members of the tribal council and frequently crossed
Champlain from Plattsburgh seeking free advice from Indian-
rights champion Danton Welsh in an expensive cabin cruiser
belonging to one of them, Tom White Stag, who was reput-
edly a millionaire. Today the feathers of the war bonnets
whipped wildly to and fro in the wind, framing faces that
were dark and inscrutable, telling nothing, though Aldrich
was certain they mourned on the inside like the white old-un-
cle lovers: Lydia had spent a long time fawning over them,
too.

Of all the Indians, only Charlie Wishing Ten Fingers' sorrow was manifest on the outside.

After them came Welsh family friends, a gaggle of thirty
or so of them marching in no particular order except that
Danton Welsh's law partners and their wives seemed to be
leading the pack. Many were conversing with each other and
there appeared to be a general sad shaking of heads. A very
old woman whom Aldrich did not know was being helped
along by two young men who had once been members of the
SDS with Lydia. The Irish gatekeeper's wife and fortyish unmarried son who had never left home, nor bothered to fall in
love with Lydia because he did not like women, brought up
the rear. The son wrestled a covered fiddle up the hill,
and the mother carried a violin case beneath each arm, and

Aldrich was ruefully certain that the remaining three members of the Welsh family string quartet—Danton, son Dickie and Little Janie—meant to pay their own special notion of homage to their lost cellist member Lydia by playing appropriate concerti over her remains today in a snowstorm. Ghoulish preoccupation, Aldrich judged: There would not be a dry-eyed serious music lover anywhere about. Still, the one compliment Aldrich would not begrudge his dead Lydia was that she was a very fine cellist indeed.

Last, before two rifle-toting State Troopers who squinted through the snow in every direction, was the permissible union of Church and State, the Episcopal bishop and the governor of the Commonwealth, both close friends of Danton Welsh, who walked side by side gravely talking and nodding together.

Now the two Morgans drawing the rattling hearse of a farm wagon passed before Aldrich, the Irish gatekeeper suspending his crying for a long moment while he stared at Aldrich standing bareheaded in a blizzard on his outcast's knoll with the mute-horror look of a man who thinks he is seeing a ghost.

"Is that ye, Aldrich? Are ye real?"

"Of course I'm real, asshole. What do you think?"

"Ah, I wasn't sure, ye know."

But that was all: He pressed his blubbering face to the horse's neck again, moving the team toward the entry in the stone wall that surrounded the graveyard, dead Lydia bouncing a bit in her cheap pine box as the wagon wheels covered the rutted approach to the top of the hill.

In another moment, crossing a foot thickness of exposed root, the wagon lurched heavily, jarring the coffin hard against the vehicle's side, and Aldrich saw with a spine-thumping threshold to delirium that it had begun an almost imperceptible backward slide toward the end that was open for want of a tailgate. The wagon lurched again as the horses dug in for the final pull to the level ground of the burial place and the backward slide quickened and Aldrich decided this day of required humiliation was yet to be his, that his vengeance on Danton Welsh was about to be perfected, that a giant paint-brush dripping with the bright colors of the comic macabre was about to be splashed across the funereal tints of Lydia Welsh Aldrich Hodges' death-day landscape if her coffin should take off out of that wagon and flip end over end like a giant pogo stick gone on to cartwheels all the way down the hill through the funeral cortege to pile up unceremoniously against the house at the bottom, maybe spewing out limp Lydia somewhere along its course for good measure. A funeral a lot of people in New England would never forget for sure in the same way that no one could forget her two wedding days. Aldrich cheered the gathering slide, clapping his hands together lustily, hissing in his urgency to have the coffin clear the end of the wagon bed, then overhang space. It did: by one inch, then three, then a whole foot until it slammed into the massive chest of the sheriff of Inglenook, who led the Fife and Drum Corps behind the wagon. Grunting, running to keep up with the horses, the sheriff pushed his beloved one's coffin back into the wagon and held it there, panting at Aldrich: "I seen that, Dwight David. I seen how you wanted her to go. I ain't gonna forget that either. Hear?"

"I don't expect you will," Aldrich agreed miserably, the outcast of the Blue Hills of Milton, Massachusetts, instantly again. But no matter, really. The day would yet turn to the macabre: It waited but the means. For now Aldrich had to stand the reproachful stares of the line of pipers and drummers marching slowly past, the giant Starbuck who brought up the rear looking for all the world like his fondest wish might be to stuff the coiled body of Aldrich into the orb of his bass drum and roll him down the hill straight at the house instead. Impossible nakedness is mine here on this little hillock, Aldrich judged. Danton Welsh, in prescribing it, knowing as ever exactly what he was about: Punishment by Patricianness. No blunt rages here. No one but Charlie Wishing Ten Fingers would acknowledge the presence of Dwight David Aldrich this day with anything even approaching moderate civility, he guessed.

But there was one defection, if only for a moment's recognition before it was stilled as traitorous: Big Janie, in the passing line of Welshes, smiled and waved meekly to Aldrich, her friend by default during that first summer of his marriage spent on Champlain. Aldrich responded in kind, reading for one instant a look of conspiracy in the otherwise bleary eyes and he knew then for certain who had given Pasquale Mugiani his information about the buried past of Danton Welsh. Danton Welsh cast a long moment's speculative look at his wife, and Aldrich knew that he too knew also.

Then they were all marched past, only Charlie Wishing Ten Fingers further acknowledging him as expected, and the service began, the majority of the mourners ringed about the outside of the stone wall that contained the small graveyard. Inside among the ancient markers were but the Welsh family and Stephen Hodges and the bishop staring down at Lydia's coffin that had been placed atop a lowering device over the open grave. The snow fell very wet and heavy now, clinging everywhere, covering the petals of Lydia's already wilted bridal bouquet that Hodges the five-second husband had weepingly placed atop the pine box.

Danton Welsh read from the lover Emily Dickinson:

> Because I could not stop for Death,
> He kindly stopped for me;
> The carriage held but just ourselves
> And Immortality.

Sobs broke out of the mourners, the bridesmaids of the wedding party instantly convulsed with shudderings, one of the onetime SDSers actually slumping down on the snow-covered stones of the wall and weeping bottomlessly into clenched fists held to the sockets of his eyes.

Oh, traitorous, hypocritical Lydia! the words raged within

Aldrich: How you would have loved your own leave-taking! Your old man playing to the gallery, dry-eyed and absolutely certain of the effect he is creating, sharing the sacredness of his well-known affair with the spirit lover, spooning the sugared pablum that recluse lady cooked up out in Amherst into the mouth of babes and other dupes come to watch your lowering away in a snowstorm. . . . Lest ye forget the sweetness of that once living Lydia Welsh. Or the majesty of her father's sorrow. Come to think of it, you've also been had, Lydia. This is his day, not yours. They'll be speaking of that nobleness in Boston drawing rooms for ages to come. . . .

Danton Welsh, shining now with the radiance of one who has accosted Death and found it wanting, put away the volume of his lover's words. The bishop took over for a short eulogy of convenient lies and then the string instruments were brought in for the finale, portable chairs set up for the three musicians among the graves of the Breckenridges, and after a weighty pause, Danton Welsh announced they meant to play Lydia's favorite piece, Albinoni's Adagio in D Major.

The music crept sinuously into the silence that was absolute except for the siss of falling snow, the whistle of wind through the branches of pine overhead. It was the saddest music Aldrich had ever heard, music that affected him despite himself each time he heard it, and he had heard it often because it truly was Lydia's favorite music, an incomprehensible tonal anesthetic that brought her a rare calm in her normal whirl of manic frivolity. When they lived together at North Hollow she had sometimes played it for hours, resetting the needle at each conclusion until she would finally drift off into peaceful sleep, her face of the disparate parts become a composite beauty at rest that Aldrich would study for wondering hours.

Remembering this, Aldrich softened: a grievous mistake. Seeing the bent, still heads of the mourners, convinced their animosity toward him must have diffused and scattered in the sad strains of the Adagio, he decided to rejoin the community of man and committed the error of leaving his exile's hillock and going toward the graveside to join the others. Those closest to his approach stared at him somewhat uncertainly, and even Danton Welsh seemed for a moment not to know what to do until Dickie Welsh threw down his violin and raced animal crazy through the Breckenridge tombstones and over the low stone wall at Aldrich's throat, raging somewhat incoherently about not defiling his sister in death as he had done quite enough defiling in life.

Then Dickie was upon Aldrich, powered by his evident madness and totally unskilled as a fighter, tumbling Aldrich over and over down the hill away from the grave in barrel-rolling pursuit of the two Morgans who fled toward the stables in terror dragging their clattering wagon behind them. Dickie Welsh pulled at Aldrich's hair and actually bit at his eyebrows as Aldrich, remembering the low contempt he had always had for Dickie's physical prowess (Danton Welsh, a leader of the Massachusetts Antiwar Coalition, had actually invited Dickie to try enlisting for Nam in hopes the experience might somehow change him), broke out into gales of laughter. But he stopped when he felt the incredible flash of pain, like a white-hot iron touched to the lobe of his ear, then felt the hot sticky wetness of his own blood on his neck. When he looked up, a very surprised Dickie Welsh was sitting in the ground cover of snow, removing the bitten-off piece of ear from his mouth.

He held it up to show his father, who had swiftly descended the slope toward the warring twosome, and that was when Danton Welsh did the absolutely least expected thing in the universe and completely lost his cool, pounding Dickie furiously on the head in keeping with his evident delirium: "Good Dickie! Good brave Dickie! That's the son Daddy always wanted . . . !"

CHAPTER 16

Recherche
des Temps Perdus

Aldrich, notch-eared, a certifiably complete specimen of the puzzle that was *Homo sapiens* but for one eternally missing piece, rode home to Inglenook, Vermont, with Minyard Turner and his cousin Hiram in the old ten-wheel logger after a patch-up job at the Milton Community Hospital. Minyard drove, giggling at Aldrich's demise, slugging occasionally on his own corn whiskey. Hiram took the passenger window that could not be raised, spitting the effluent of his tobacco chew into the white maw of the howling blizzard. Aldrich sat between them, touching the smarting, bandaged, newly defined rim of the ear, sometimes crying because of his absolute incomprehension of how the hatred of himself sown by Danton Welsh had taken such eager root in persons two or three or a seeming infinity of times removed from the epicenter of their monstrous confrontation: The assembled mourners had actually cheered Dickie Welsh's witless feat at his sister's graveside. The only outrage had come from Charlie Wishing Ten Fingers and the two rifle-toting State Police. It was Charlie who had angrily conscripted Danton Welsh's Mercedes-Benz against Danton Welsh's protest and rushed a bleeding Aldrich off to the hospital. Aldrich, despite the shocked numbness he felt, thought enough to take retribution wherever he could, and allowed himself to bleed copiously all over the Mercedes' hand-crafted upholstery. . . .

In the truck, grinding home along the Interstate past the

barely discernible lights of Manchester, New Hampshire, Aldrich twisted the rearview mirror toward him for another close look at the damage, then grew bottomlessly despondent all over again: It was a genuinely characterless wound, he considered, an undisputable loss. Not a whit of compensation in it anywhere, unlike Moshe Dayan's universally recognized glamorous eyepatch or the Hathaway shirt model's reward for his particular bludgeoning.

Even a long purposeful facial scar done with a stiletto would be better. Witness Wendon K. Wylie, Aldrich's junior high school classmate in Abilene. A fat, potato-faced nonathlete with receding hair and tiny, deep-set, frightened eyes that sought everywhere to ferret out the next potential attack of schoolboy cruelty before it became his agonizing reality, he had been set upon one Saturday night in Denver by a knife-wielding Mexican simply gone amok. The slashings of his face had healed to a sinister handsomeness, making him look hard and cruel and inscrutable all at once. Sensing his new potential, he had shed pounds, developed a taut lean body and shaved the last straggling wisps of hair from his head. Trading on his mutilations, on the curious unnamed power they imparted, he had been the first male of his class to lose his virginity. Hallowed event: That sent an insanely jealous Aldrich off and running in hopes of closing the gap within a year, though, in fact, it had taken more than three. Wendon K. Wylie went on to cut a fabled swath through the senior high girls. At graduation he was voted Most Likely to Succeed and Most Popular. Staring at his reflection in a mirror, he had not at all disliked what he saw, it was generally agreed. . . .

"It's a clown's remembrance," Aldrich judged miserably of the severance as he righted the angle of the rearview mirror. "No one would ever believe how it happened."

"Winters won't be so bad, Aldrich," Minyard chuckled. "You kin wear a hat over it or an ear jock like them skiers. But the summers'll be rough, specially if you're lookin' for tail. Women always notice that sort of stuff. It distracts 'em so they can't never take their eyes off the goddam thing. Can't see the whole man for the missin' piece. They'll always be tryin' to figure out if a horse reached down 'n bit it off or what happened. It'll absorb 'em too much to respond to your fawnings 'n advances."

"I'll let my hair grow long. I'll have it curled and wear it over my ear," Aldrich said distantly. Not inexplicably he thought of Prufrock, saw himself as an old, white, curlyhaired man taking the waters at various seasons in New England and the Caribbean, lonely and possessed of a sad secret, jerking his head away in terror from the innocent fondlings of rich tipsy widows scouting with bejeweled fingers beneath the opulent, lovely hair, having to leave sixty-day worldwide cruises in mid-progress because everybody on ship had got to wondering what ailed him. . . .

"Wonder what they did with the piece of your ear the young reverend bit off?" Hiram spoke through his wad of tobacco. He chuckled too, and brown spittle rolled down his chin.

"I expect they'll put it in a bottle of alcohol, label it 'morsel of villain' or something like that and display it in one of Danton Welsh's trophy cases."

"They sure do things with style, them Welshes," Minyard avowed, gulping down more of his corn liquor and passing the bottle to Aldrich, who refused.

"Yes, I guess that's what fatally attracted me to the bastards in the first place, if the truth be told." But that was all. Aldrich was glad when Minyard switched on a Country and Western station and he did not have to talk to the two woodchucks any longer. Live nasal voices sang mournfully of love and all the good it did you and Aldrich concurred with the unerring wisdom of just plain country people. Outside the blizzard raged and, crossing the spine of the White Mountains heading for the Vermont line, they began circling around cars evidently stuck for the night in drifts, Minyard assuring them each time it was not his goddam Christian responsibility to

199

stop and inquire if anyone needed aid. Inside, the old truck heater gave off like a blast furnace and it was not uncomfortable, though intermittent squalls of snow blew through Hiram's open window.

The unstoppable behemoth rumbled into snow-buried Vermont about 8 P.M. and made the rest of the distance to Inglenook by midnight. Minyard and Hiram refused to drive the extra two miles on to North Hollow and left Aldrich off in the village center. He walked home, leaping and plunging through the drifts, and was exhaustedly abed in the proshop by two in the morning after building a fire in the potbellied stove, vaguely comforted by his realization that whoever was about the destruction of North Hollow had evidently declared a moratoriun for his weekend away in Boston. Decent of them, he supposed.

The Welshes did not consign the missing piece of Aldrich's ear to a trophy case; they returned it to Aldrich instead. It arrived by special-delivery mail a week to the day it was bitten off, a somewhat shrunken and yellowed waxy-looking half-moon-shaped flap of skin with the measured indents of teeth marks along the severed edge, resting on the bottom of a six-ounce jar of formaldehyde that was neatly packaged against breaking in a small wooden box. The bottle was labeled simply: "Separated Ear Portion of D. D. Aldrich." There was no accompanying note.

Aldrich placed the bottle on a shelf midway up a wall. At night, illumined by moonlight, the severed lobe glowed with an intense ghostly phosphorescence, and during the first couple of nights after its installation, Aldrich woke abruptly many times to stare at it with a flesh-crawling trepidation, convinced of its particulate mortality, its restless wandering through the universe of souls, its ceaseless crying out for the rest of Aldrich to hurry and catch up with it. A piece of me already out there and impatiently waiting, Aldrich thought unhappily, cursing his peasant-minded morbidity when spring was not far off, when his penitential season would be over, when Aldrich *comme* Phoenix meant to rise in shining radiance from the metaphorical ashes of the emotional debacle of his marriage to Lydia (and the real ashes of the commercial debacle of North Hollow) and begin again a new life of riches and power and remarriage to a girl whom he determined fiercely would be even more beautiful than Lydia and whose money would be easier to get at. . . .

On the morning after the third night of intermittent sleeplessness, Aldrich put the bottle containing the severed lobe into his pocket and drove down to Lake Champlain, where he sneaked onto Danton Welsh's farm, drove across a frozen pasture that was concealed by a windbreak of fir trees from the caretaker and his wife who stayed winters in the main house, and continued on over the thick frozen ice of the lake until he came to the approximate mid-point between the Vermont and New York shores. There he chopped a hole in the ice and consigned the restless glowing scrap of himself to the murky deep. Then he went home and ceased thinking about his mortality and slept a deep and refreshing sleep that night. And every night thereafter for about two weeks until the Saturday evening that the would-be hit man Minyard Turner decapitated himself drunk-driving on a snowmobile and the North American Scarlet Pimpernel burned down the Alta Lodge and left behind a note assuring Aldrich that his penance for past transgressions committed in Vermont was not ended with the assassination death of Lydia which he had perpetrated and that the irrevocable destruction of North Hollow was forthcoming.

After that Aldrich barely slept at all. As February turned into March, he sat up long hours of the night guarding the dark snow-covered landscape of North Hollow with his rifle against the next terrorist attack. He thought constantly while he watched, plying the memory trails to the recent past, closely scrutinizing the seeming army of hurt, angry or betrayed faces for the one with the motive more stupendous than anyone else's, yet also the one so unapprised of Aldrich's current affairs that he saw the killing of Lydia as a means of punishing Aldrich.

By degrees Aldrich got all the way back to his first meeting with Lydia Alexandra Welsh, in early spring 1969, an instance of familiar duplicity from the word go since Dwight David Aldrich pretended to be a fevered Vietnam War-protesting, SDS-loving, anti-anything-on-the-political-right radical when he was actually an ultrareactionary Young American for Freedom whose fondest hope was that the U. S. Air Force would mount recorded history's ultimate, all-time high-density bomber armada and pound the livin' bejesus out of Ho Chi Minh's North Vietnam before June graduation when Aldrich's draft deferment was slated to end.

PART TWO

Aldrich and Lydia
–1969

CHAPTER 17

The Rooster Priestess

Lydia Welsh, granddaughter of a famous suffragette named Leila Breckenridge who had once chained herself to the White House fence, took up the cudgels in her generation against the Vietnam sojourn and traveled the Midwest in a Chevrolet van from one besieged academic island to the next organizing timid objectors to strident militancy, setting up radical presses to turn out proselytizing literature for the edification of a citizenry that still thought the Government in Washington was a pretty good Joe by about a seven-to-three margin, and demonstrating multitudinous techniques for violent disruption of that same Government's functioning to underscore the point that some folk lurked upon the land who did not consider the Government in Washington to be much of a good Joe at all. From far northern Minnesota south to Tennessee, from Colorado east to the Pennsylvania line, Lydia Welsh in her bright-red-for-revolution Chevy van full right up with radical manifestos, stolen rifles and blasting caps was known to the dedicated fringe as the Pacifist Queen. In retrospect, Aldrich considered, the Vietnam War turned out to be a real boon for Lydia: For the life of him he could not imagine her explosive torrents of energy finding a proper outlet in the Junior League.

With her traveled Stephen Hodges, a poet and her fiancé, and a Mohawk Indian named Charlie Wishing Ten Fingers, a recent Harvard Law graduate who was their friend from Vermont. Hearing of her entry into Nebraska, the very Pasionaria of the Midwest's grudging participation in the new American Revolution on her way to the university, Aldrich, who lunged with easy hatred at obvious totems of diametric persuasion, swore to his brother YAFs that he meant to crown his six years of generally uninspired cum laude scholarship at Nebraska with the undeniably symbolic act of squashing a bunch of non-union grapes in Lydia Welsh's face, hopefully before a wire-service photographer: so that no one would mistake what Dwight David Aldrich thought of Lydia Welsh, Cesar Chavez and his unionizing, radicals, liberals, war protesters, draft resisters, hippies, long-hairs, pinkos, queers, women's libbers, the memory of Martin Luther King, Chicanos, blacks, Walter Cronkite, the Ivy League establishment, the American Indian Movement and any number of other things that were unseemly, subversive, unmanly, unwholesome and un-American. . . . This, until he got a close-up look at the goddess face he meant to spatter.

Aldrich, whose need for women was perfunctory and scheduled, whose prowess as a lover begat no excited whisperings in coed dorms (done humping, he always reapplied his jockey shorts after carefully washing his privates and retired to bed to sleep alone), fell instantly in love with the Pacifist Queen. So much so that, arch-reactionary gone mindless, he followed hypnotically after her when she led a band of fifty or so partisans through the front doors of the university Records Office to liberate the place in protest over the administration's ready acquiescence to channel classified information to the Selective Service. On her right marched Stephen Hodges carrying an American flag; on her left was Charlie Wishing Ten Fingers, who bore the red flag of revolution mounted on a bamboo pole; between them, beautiful, fanatical Lydia Welsh, La Pasionaria incarnate, dressed in flowing-robed imitation of the Marianne of Revolutionary France, cradled a very agitated-looking rooster in her arms. A name tag hung down from one of the rooster's legs, and the name tag said he was called Nixon.

Inside, with the building's doors chained behind them, Stephen Hodges set about his kindly, sensitive young man's special task of quieting the heavyset Records Office ladies who whined and whimpered pathetically about mutilation and death at the hands of radicals and Communists. Charlie Wishing Ten Fingers cut the phones and supervised the dumping of about twenty filing cabinets of grade transcripts into a big mound in the center of the largest room. Aldrich, remembering suddenly what he was supposed to be, grew saucer-eyed with incredulity at the notion that he was expected to join some satanic pacifist's dance around a bonfire of blazing transcripts that would probably end up taking the Records Office building with it for good measure.

Aldrich opened his mouth to protest, but no words came forth, cut short by the beginning of Lydia Welsh's awesome incantation against the American War Machine, a lynx-throated priestess' tirade of imprecation that rose from some deep, almost libidinous place in her, alternately infused with hatings and tauntings and gloatings and graphic promises of what the women of America might do for all those boys in Vietnam if only they were allowed to come home. Good God Almighty! How Aldrich grew excited in the midst of her denunciation of war! The first flutterings of erection were triggered within him and he gazed rapturously at the long-robed priestess whose uplifted face and wide-flung arms beseeched Eros rather than Heaven, hoping that the bulging of his eyes and his crotch and his vaguely realized hoarse pantings were passing for peace-loving fervor. But no matter. For whatever reason, she had them all aroused, chanting and clapping and stomping their feet oblivious of Aldrich's private passion. So much so that when she turned to Charlie Wishing Ten Fingers, took the hapless rooster Nixon from him by the legs and decapitated the bird over the pile of transcripts with one dramatic slash of a machete, she near brought down the house with a ceiling-rattling crescendo of pacifist war cries.

Much ritual solemnity here, Aldrich decided ecstatically, having just come in his shorts. The priestess Lydia held out the headless Nixon at arm's length, and Nixon obligingly anointed the transcripts of the potential dead with geysers of rooster blood pumped out by the frenetic twitchings of his brutally surprised autonomic nervous system. In minutes more, when Nixon no longer twitched or shuddered, nor had any more blood to spare, Lydia Welsh contemptuously flung him out the window at a confused-looking gaggle of ten or so campus police who stood in the quadrangle below, talking to each other over two-way radios evidently, though they were within touching distance. After Nixon went the bloodied transcripts, tons of paper blowing against the quadrangle buildings in a stiff spring breeze. Aldrich, seeking his introduction, wanting the instant approval of the woman he had decided to marry, planted himself firmly beside Lydia Welsh at the task, gleefully hurling armloads of records out the open window with a mimicked antiwar slogan applied to each cast into the wind, distantly and amazedly aware that his joy in destruction was appeasing some deep anarchistic place in himself that he would not ever have admitted existed. He grew too joyous, in fact: so that he stopped in mid-stride on perhaps his tenth trip from the diminishing mound to the window at his realization the the Rooster Priestess was no longer in motion, but stood appraising him with a very slit-eyed, skeptical gaze.

"You're kind of new at this protest business, aren't you there, guy?"

"I was in Chicago last summer, Lydia, for the Democratic Convention," he lied desperately. "I was beaten by the police . . . The pigs . . . It was awful . . . They hit me more than fifty times in my kidneys with their nightsticks . . ."

Her gaze traveled purposefully up and down him as more record chuckers stopped to listen: On the instant he understood what was wrong: He wore clean chino slacks and Bass

Weejuns, a blue button-down Gant broadloom shirt and camel-colored Jack Nicklaus golf sweater; he was clean-shaven and took his very blond, blue-eyed head to a barbershop punctually every two weeks. He did not look like any other male in the room. Also he recognized not a few people from among the mob of protesters who, if they thought hard enough about it, would remember Dwight David Aldrich as the spitfire pianist in the YAF's patriotic and nostalgic Roaring Twenties band who ground out all those rag solos the well-to-do, conservative twenties alumni so loved, to raise contribution money in front of the football stadium on Saturday afternoons. Blessedly, today, because of the stiff wind, he had not worn his straw boater that would make him instantly recognizable.

"Mister, the police, even the Chicago police, do not beat up clean-cut young men dressed for summer in Lacoste tennis shirts and Bermuda shorts. And if they pummeled your kidneys more than fifty times but nine months ago, you'd still be peeing blood. Can you go into that men's room over there and pee me a cup of blood, mister?"

"No, Lydia, I can't," he said mournfully, "I . . ."

"Charlie . . ." she called out to the Mohawk, who was not yet aware of what was happening.

"Yes, Lydia?"

"A fink, I think. He doth overcompensate mightily in all ways. Better attend to him."

Charlie Wishing Ten Fingers came quickly across the room from where he had been assigning stations for the sit-in marshals.

"He says he was in Chicago for the garden party last summer. He says the cops whaled the daylights out of his kidneys. He won't pee me a cup of blood. I think he's feds, Charlie."

The Mohawk scrutinized Aldrich up and down in turn, but the prepared hostile stare quickly vanished, was replaced by a bemused smile instead. In the midst of the arrestingly handsome Indian face framed between twin curtains of jet-black hair, the incredible gray eyes twinkled with mirth: "If he was in Chicago last summer, Lydia, he was shopping at Brooks Brothers. That's all. He's not a fed. Given even the convoluted reasoning of our G-men brothers, the feds do not send archetypal Midwesterners to spy on tattered, bearded, surplus-store-clothed riffraff such as we. They send look-alikes schooled in minimal cleanliness who buy from the stacks at Benny's Army and Navy, not anomalies. No, this gentleman, in my opinion, is a radical voyeur, an instinctual political conservative drawn like moth to flame toward the power of our movement that repels and fascinates him at the same time. A part of him is disgruntled with himself, dissatisfied that the intellectual basis of his political credo is no more than a moron's automatic reflex to an initiated action from the political Left, like an eternal rally in tennis that's made prisoners of the players. If this person seems to you to overcompensate, Lydia, it's hardly to disguise a government informer. That would make it altogether too obvious. It's because he's desperate for your approval so you'll let him stay around and learn from you. Aren't I right, friend?"

"Yes," Aldrich gushed at him, "you're exactly right. It's perfect! Thank you for putting it so perfectly for me. I hadn't thought it through that far . . ."

"Charlie Wishing Ten Fingers, are you funnin' me?" Lydia demanded vexedly. "Are you playing games with the Pacifist Queen herself? I'm not running a crisis center for ultrareactionaries with self-doubts about being the All-American Boy. This is war. He goes when the fat gray ladies over there waddle their way to freedom with our list of demands for the administration. Otherwise, if his dear conservative conscience reactivates somewhere further along the line when the going gets tough in this little sit-in of ours, all we'll get for our trouble is a state's witness who can identify people."

"That gentleman won't leave your side, Lydia. He'll never

turn state's witness either just to save his ass as long as you're involved," the Mohawk taunted her, delighting in her anger. "That gentleman is in love with you, Lydia Welsh. He can't take his eyes off you. Look, the crotch of his pants is already wet."

The ten or so demonstrators who stood about them, overhearing the confrontation, guffawed with laughter as Aldrich, asinine now with embarrassment, folded nearly double, covering the front of himself with his hands. Stephen Hodges, who stood beside Charlie, and who had looked very concerned at the Mohawk's judgment that Aldrich was hopelessly in love with the woman he was to marry come June, seemed to think the matter of Aldrich's spotted crotch was very funny indeed. He extended his hand to Aldrich in a warm greeting: "How do you do? I'm Stephen Hodges, a peace-loving poet from Massachusetts. Lydia's my fiancée. We're to be married in June. Our families have known each other forever."

"Charmed, I'm sure," Aldrich told him, instantly appraising the weakness and liking Hodges for it. "I'm Dwight David Aldrich of Abilene, Kansas. I'm a grad student in architecture. My family's big in ranching and meat packing back home."

"I'm Charlie Wishing Ten Fingers, if you haven't already guessed," the Mohawk introduced himself, holding up the nub of his two-fingered left hand. "I'm a Mohawk Indian from St. Albans, Vermont, and a graduate of Harvard Law School. I have no idea who my father was, and a very unhappy memory of my mother, who is quite dead now."

"I'm sorry for you, Charlie," Aldrich said. "It must have been very hard growing up."

"It taught resourcefulness, I will admit, Dwight David. However, for future reference, one is not permitted to pity Charlie Wishing Ten Fingers on any account."

"I understand, Charlie. I'm sorry," Aldrich whined, frightened of the warning in the suddenly smoldering eyes. "Will you be in Vermont this summer? I could visit you on your reservation. I'm going there after graduation to claim my inheritance. Five hundred acres of prime land outside a village called Inglenook. It's been in our family since before the Revolution."

"Inglenook . . . ?" Their three faces were screwed up in identical consternation.

"It's not on the map. It must be pretty small. A real hamlet. It's near the Canadian border. It's a quaint New England village with white houses and red barns whose chief industries are sugaring and candle and harness making and carving wooden salad bowls in the old Vermont tradition. The people are self-reliant farmers and artisans who come from good English stock and are disdainful of the encroachments of Big Government on their lives. They are unstinting when a neighbor requires help and love to join together in house and barn raisings, singing lustily all the while. Marriages are often celebrated on the village common, where fiddlers play music for dances so old their origins are unremembered, and . . ."

"He absolutely gives me the creeps," Lydia Welsh said flatly. "He's talking about the New England poor and thinks there's romance in them there dirt farms. I'll bet he's never been east of the Mississippi except by travelogue."

"The Vermont town meeting is working democracy in one of its purest forms, Dwight," Stephen Hodges chimed in, hapless politicized poet evidently borne away on the strains of Aldrich's long-dreamt pastoral symphony. "If you intend remaining in the state after you collect your inheritance and becoming part of the Vermont Experience, then you'll find the town meeting an excellent forum for educating the subsistence-level unlearned in the methods of radical activism. Just this year we were able to elicit a condemnation of the Vietnam War, though only by a one-vote majority, from a town full of people who could scarce believe they'd kicked the sacred cow of the American military right smack in the udder. I tell you, Dwight . . ."

"These unschooled people, properly politicized, will be

ones who'll man the trenches in Vermont's forthcoming class war when the rich carpetbaggers who own more than half the state get kicked the fuck out!" the Pacifist Queen avowed. "They'll claim the state for the masses again! No tepid reformist bullshit here! The tiny wedge of Vermont will be a red-hot radical spike sticking right into the heart of an ugly capitalist America! We'll become the officially recognized underground railway station for persecuted dissidents on their way to the freer air of Quebec! America will know when it wakes up from its Nixonian nightmare of self-delusion that one of its numbers dared pee unfearingly into the wind! *Nous sommes Vermontois!*"

There was a lusty round of clapping at that. Aldrich, who did not like what she said, but loved the way in which she said it, stared at Lydia Welsh in rapt adoration: He was all the more determined to marry her now. What a catch for the political Right! La Pasionaria, who howled for revolution and dismemberment of the Establishment everywhere across the overlays of Bible, Wheat and Corn Belts, whimperingly abed with her husband D. D. Aldrich, who would school her in the enlightened dictums of Goldwater cum Wallace conservatism in the placid hurricane's eye of lovemaking's after-climax. Lesson done, he would call forth the terrible storm of his manliness again, unleashing it at her protective resistance with brute, yet pleasing sensuality until she began to rage on the Right, a well-coiffed Medea who fell automatically to the task of vilifying at the mutest mention of names like Kennedy, Chavez or King . . .

"We'll be in Vermont this summer, too, Dwight," Stephen Hodges said. "Come and visit with us. Lydia's and my family have farms right next to each other on Lake Champlain, near Shelburne. We're to be married at the Welshes' and we move right next door to the Hodgeses for the rest of our days. My family's given us the place, all seven hundred acres, for a wedding present. We'll be true Vermonters working the land."

"It sounds like it's going to be a nice life," Aldrich conceded painfully, awed at the notion of wealth that gave away seven-hundred-acre farms for a wedding present.

"It's going to be an active life," Lydia said. "Politically active. We intend taking over the state and turning it into a showcase of radical affirmation. I'll be governor of Vermont within ten years. We may secede from the Union."

"Lydia dear, why don't you invite Dwight David to your wedding in June since he'll be in the state?" Charlie Wishing Ten Fingers prompted. In response Lydia regarded the Mohawk defiantly for a long moment, hands planted firmly on her hips. "Charlie my friend, what the fuck are you up to? What's the ulterior motive in you that's trying to shove Mr. Straightsville from Abilene here in on top of us? Of what use could he possibly be to you? Look at him. Look how he looks. He doesn't look like anyone else here . . ."

"The next time you come to help us protest, Dwight, you'll have to wear the proper battle fatigues," the Mohawk said with mock seriousness. "It's important that one look like a protester when one protests."

"I could roll on the floor," Aldrich volunteered. "I could dirty my clothes."

"Oh my God," Lydia groaned. "Listen to him. Doesn't he understand that the look is intrinsic? It comes from the inside. It is not achieved by soiling Brooks Brothers."

"Lydia, don't be so prejudiced," Hodges told her. "The possibility that we of the Left might allow our righteousness to grow as monstrous as the righteousness of the Right is intolerable. What does it matter how he looks? Yes, Dwight, do come to our wedding if you're going to be in Vermont. I invite you."

"Don't you dare ever speak to me that way again, Hodges, or there won't be a wedding or a happily ever after!" Lydia snarled at her fiancé, the deep-throated growl of the she-lynx returned to her voice again. "And invitations to my wedding are not unilaterally given."

"I'm sorry, Lydia. I spoke too quickly," Hodges groveled, sickening Aldrich, who did not consider women worth groveling to at all, who resisted the temptation to slap the queenly arrogance right off the superbly beautiful face. "I just thought it would be nice for Dwight to come to our wedding if he were going to be in Vermont, that's all."

"Yeah, marvelous. It wouldn't be much of a wedding at all without old Dwight. O.K., Aldrich, you're invited. I wouldn't miss seeing what Charlie Wishing Ten Fingers has up his sleeve for you for the world. If you're gay, Charlie, and trying to get it on with Dwight here, you sure are going about it the hard way. Why don't you just ask him?"

"Lydia, do you ever quit?" Charlie's eyes beseeched Heaven, more weary than annoyed. "The day is going to come when you'll have to stop riding roughshod all over people, when you're going to have to stop mouthing the first irresponsible thing that comes to your mind. Your beauty isn't going to cover for you forever."

"What day are we getting married, Stephen?" Lydia interrupted. "I can never remember the date."

"June twenty-sixth, Lydia."

"Yeah, that's it. See you at Morgan Kingdom Farm, Shelburne, Vermont, on June twenty-sixth, for the festivities, Dwight. Dress as conservatively as you like. Stephen's parents will definitely approve. Mine won't give a shit. All right, everybody, let's get this show on the road," she urged. "Everybody to their places and I'll take care of radicalizing the stout ladies before we turn 'em loose with the demands . . ."

She marched off, Hodges the desperate, stung lover trailing in the wake of her momentum. Aldrich stared after her, his mind aflame with the certainty that Stephen Hodges, poet for peace, might somehow be unhorsed along the way to Morgan Kingdom Farm by June 26, a scant two months away. He shifted his gaze to see Charlie Wishing Ten Fingers studying him closely.

"It can be done, Dwight David Aldrich," the Mohawk told him. "As you can see, it's not the love match of the century."

"Are you gay, Charlie? I mean, like she suggested?"

The right hand shot out, grabbing a bunch of Aldrich's shirt, pulling Aldrich's face very close to Charlie's angry mask: "Do you want to die? That is, do you want me to strangle the life right out of you here?"

"No, of course not," Aldrich stammered. "It's just that you sure are going out of your way to be nice to me."

"It's Lydia's happiness I'm thinking of, friend Aldrich. She deserves better in life than a Stephen Hodges."

CHAPTER 18

The Siege of Love

Aldrich the suitor's formal courtship of Lydia Welsh lasted through twelve days of siege by the State Police and Nebraska National Guard, during which (strong testimony to the deep, fierce roots of Aldrich's ultra-right politics) the greening of Aldrich the radical voyeur was not even a remote possibility: He simply understood that the first step toward expelling Stephen Hodges from Lydia's bed was to stick out the sit-in longer than Hodges, and as long as the Pacifist Queen herself, who would doubtless stick it out the longest.

On the morning of the second day when the university physical plant engineers turned off the water, heat and electricity to the Records Office building, the ranks of the liberators thinned dramatically from fifty-four to six in response to the administration's promise of a fair case-by-case hearing before an instantly created Disciplinary Committee. In the silent aftermath of their parting when the echo of Lydia Welsh's unbelievable tirade of imprecations against the deserters still resounded about the rooms (Aldrich decidedly shocked at the graphic precision of invective from the woman he so loved), there remained but Lydia, Aldrich, Stephen Hodges, Charlie Wishing Ten Fingers, a squat, acned girl from Staten Island, New York, named Inez Yona, who said repeatedly that she had nothing to lose by staying, and most surprisingly, one of the stout, gray Records Office ladies named Dora Pffiefenberger, sixtyish and recently widowed, who now lived all alone on a two-hundred-acre farm some twenty miles from the university and made no bones about the fact that she was only staying for the company.

Outside the Records Office, by day, beyond the defense perimeter of State Police and National Guard (who had two very real-looking howitzers pointed at the building), an unindictable horde of cheering students urged the very indictable five protesters and Dora Pffiefenberger to an interminable occupancy for the sake of ending the Vietnam War; inside the Records Office, three fervid radicals, one horny pretender, evidently suicidal Inez Yona and lonely, lonely Dora Pffiefenberger—victims all together of revolutionary spontaneity and very poor planning—ransacked vending machines for food, and rationed out the carbonated water of Coke dispensers for drink after they had drained the dregs of every last faucet in the building.

Outside the Records Office, by night, beyond the somewhat relaxed cordon of State Police and National Guard (the two very real-looking howitzers spotlighted for emphasis), a potentially indictable group of twenty or so hard-core supporters held a candlelight prayer vigil, the cheering horde of students gone home to rest, evidently the better to cheer on the morrow; inside the Records Office, in the low-forties unheated chill, the six huddled all together for warmth on two blankets on the floor of the main office with Inez Yona and Dora Pffiefenberger claiming the middle between the other bodies, Inez whimpering self-comfortingly at the prospect of a starvation death that her parents might still call noble sacrifice, and stout, gray Dora sighingly assuring them that this was the happiest she had ever been.

Aldrich lay beside Charlie Wishing Ten Fingers to the right of stout Dora, feverishly exhaling tiny, concealed breaths to drive away the sweet-smelling smoke of the joint Charlie always toked on before dozing off, lest the evil weed (Aldrich spoke gravely of allergy to four bemused young people and sympathetic Dora) somehow impair his ability to keep watch over the high mound of Dora and the low mound of Inez Yona on the physical proximity of the woman he loved and Stephen Hodges: He, Aldrich, would find a way to put a stop to even their most surreptitious lovemaking the moment it began.

But no matter, really. On the first night nothing happened. On the second, mystified though overjoyed at the sound of Hodges' painful wheezings and gasping for air, Aldrich learned that his rival was an asthmatic. On the morning of the third day, it was a kindly, solicitous Aldrich who helped Charlie Wishing Ten Fingers escort Hodges to the front door of the building and yield him up for emergency medical treatment to the bristling point-blank rifle barrels of perhaps forty Nebraska state cops. It was the same Aldrich who, certain that Opportunity had just given him the nod, defiantly assured those cops of Charlie's warning that the building was set to be torched if the two did not return inside within two minutes and that, if necessary, Dora Pffiefenberger's volunteer status could be upgraded to hostage.

And it was that Aldrich again who heard his name being called with lynch-mob intensity from behind the green perimeter of National Guard and looked over to see a gaggle of thirty or more brother YAFs shaking a collective menacing fist at him. In response he merely shrugged his shoulders, hoped the look on his face was properly apologetic: How could he tell them now that his was a complex innocence? That the decision to return inside the building was made in his heart? That he was at work on their behalf, on the conversion of the Pacifist Queen? He waved them a doleful goodbye, then extended his hand to shake to the captain of State Police in command, who took it reflexively, imitating the grave, knowing look of Aldrich's face as Aldrich told him reassuringly: "Don't worry. This will all work out in the end. You'll see."

"Take care of Lydia for me, Charlie and Dwight." Stephen Hodges gasped out the words. "Take care of my dear, lovely fiancée . . ."

"I will," Aldrich told him.

"He will," Charlie confirmed.

Get well, Aldrich was about to tell him, then thought better of it, hoping Hodges would die instead, the obstacle conveniently removed. With Charlie he turned to walk back into the building, eager to begin the unfettered pursuit of Lydia Welsh. Unlike Charlie, he did not respond with clenched fist to the roar of zealous approval that came from the unindictable horde, and wished that his brother right-wingers everywhere across the American landscape might understand his meaning if the film footage then being shot by a TV cameraman made it to the national networks. Once inside the Records Office building again he thought so intently about his beloved Lydia that he forgot to think about his beloved mother, who watched lots and lots of television every day at home in Abilene, Kansas.

On the fifth day, when the university president affirmed flatly for the third time that he would not negotiate with the protesters, and rations were down to two chocolate Oreos and a cup of flat soda water apiece, Inez Yona experienced a sea change. The chill wind of doom that blew out of the Arctic of a dead romance reversed to blow hot and sweet out of a lush tropical place when she stuck her head out a window to see her old boy friend standing inside the cordon of National Guard, holding up a huge sign with the assistance of two troopers that proclaimed mightily: "I love you, Inez! Please Come Out!"

She went. In less than a minute, heedless of the entreaties of Lydia and Charlie, who begged her to remember the principles of the Revolution.

"Oh, fuck the Revolution!" Inez Yona screeched, trying to drag Charlie with her to undo the chains on the door so she could get out. "I just stayed because I wanted to die. Now I don't want to die. I want to get married and have babies and a nice house. What do I want a revolution for? Huh?"

Charlie undid the door chain and set her free and they watched out the window as her short, fat legs churned across the intervening stretch of lawn and she fell into the arms of her lover amid the booing and general howling disapproval of the unindictable horde and the clapping and cheering approval of the State Police, National Guard, Aldrich's brother YAFs and a fair-sized contingent of the local VFW post who had been screaming most of the day for the twin howitzers to open fire on the building.

"Isn't that beautiful?" Dora Pffiefenberger blubbered, patting at moist eyes with her handkerchief. "He's a nice-looking boy, too. I wonder when the wedding will be?"

"That bitch!" Lydia Welsh actually spat. "Talk about the triumph of the American way! She'll tell her wanting-to-die story to those cops and they'll never even book her, I'll bet! They'll just send her home to get herself good and patriotically fucked!"

"She'll also tell them we've got no weapons and we're on a two-cookies-a-day food ration," Charlie said. "When they know that they're liable to rush us and there isn't much we can do about it if that happens."

"We could break up a couple of chairs and use the legs to crack a lot of pig heads before they get us!" stout Dora Pffiefenberger enthused, swinging her arm at illusory rows of riot cops that she was bowling over like candlepins. Aldrich marveled at her: Slumbering somewhere deep inside her was an evidently anti-authoritarian dwarf that began awakening the morning of the third day when Hodges had quit. By now, the fifth day, it had changed into a monster that raged about the pointlessness of fifty-five years of a life that had never incurred as much as a traffic ticket, that had paid taxes incessantly, that had never dared contest the majority viewpoint about anything, that had plodded dumbly. Doubtless lightheaded from the lack of food, she had spent most of the day swiftly pacing the hallway outside their room, like someone hallucinating, muttering invectives against Nixon, Vietnam and her dead bastard husband (who was a bastard evidently for going and dying on her), stopping occasionally to slam one of her thick ham fists into the wall, or other times to kick it, so that once when Aldrich went out to check on her, he saw with irony that the only real physical damage the Records Office building had suffered had been caused by stout Dora Pffiefenberger who worked there.

Because they actually had no weapons it seemed safe enough for Aldrich to join in the revolutionary rhetoric: "Jesus! If only we had a couple of rifles! They'd get us in the end for sure, but there'd be a couple dozen pigs dead for the cause of peace, you can bet your sweet ass!"

He pantomimed for good measure, grabbing up an imaginary rifle, thrusting the butt to his shoulder and firing out the window, pumping furiously on the crank of a Winchester: "Pow! Pow! Got that mother! Pow! Pow! Pow! . . ."

Aldrich left off firing and hauled down his rifle to see Lydia appraising him thoughtfully: "There was something about you, Dwight . . . something too American, I guess, that made me doubt your pacifist revolutionary credentials. But now . . ."

"It's all right, Lydia. I forgive you. We all make mistakes. What Stephen said was true, you know. We can't let the right-eousness of our cause transfer over to impair our judgments about people who don't look quite right, of all things. We might lose a good soldier for it . . ."

She slept with Aldrich that night for the first time. They lay together on one of the blankets in the darkest corner of the room. Charlie smoked a joint lying on his blanket in another corner, staring unblinkingly at the ceiling. Dora Pffiefenberger careened along the hallway, punching and slamming, inventing new blasphemies to score the memory of her husband and his traitorous dying. Outside was the muted glare of spotlights in a rainy night, clouds of steam rising past the windows as the rain touched down on the hot lighting equipment and instantly evaporated. Beyond the incessant low cackle of police two-way radios was a continual soft-voiced chorus of "We Shall Overcome" sung by the die-hard supporters who had still not gotten themselves arrested and burned their vigil candles under the cover of umbrellas. A sweet, somehow comfortable night, considering their circumstance.

Inside, making love, Aldrich was not entirely happy. The reality of having Lydia, so ardently fantasized for five days, was not nearly so good as the fantasy had been. She hardly moved at all, punctuated the romantic darkness with an unvarying staccato of uh-uh-uh grunt sounds that made Aldrich think that for her it was a lot like work and she was simply rewarding him for being a good old radical boy, after all.

"Hurry it up, will you, Dwight?"

"I want you to have an orgasm, Lydia."

"I don't need one. They don't do anything for me. You get yours off. That'll be enough for me."

"Lydia . . . Lydia, could you talk real low and sexy and say 'fuck' a lot the way you did when you butchered the rooster? Could you do it like that again, only don't say anything about Nixon this time? That really turned me on."

"Why can't I say anything about Nixon?"

"He's repugnant," Aldrich lied. "I'd absolutely lose my erection."

"I have to use somebody's name. That pre-sacrificial incantation of mine is a prepared text that it took me months to put together. How about Agnew?"

"He's no good either," said Aldrich, who, if anything, liked Agnew even better than Nixon.

"Who, Aldrich? Make up your mind quickly, will you?" she urged annoyedly, checking her watch, thrusting her hips hard upward at him to hasten the end of the thing.

"Gene McCarthy."

"I can't, Aldrich. He's a good guy. How can you expect me to call him a rat shit fuck like Nixon?"

"Just pretend, Lydia, can't you? Don't think of what you're saying. Just say it. It won't work for me unless you use a liberal's name. My fantasy will be interrupted by flashes of rage if you insert some goddam right-winger's name in the blank space."

"Oh, all right," she sighed, slowing the thrust of her hips. "Forgive me, Clean Gene, for what I'm about to do."

She began excoriating the name of Gene McCarthy in the snarling she-lynx voice that came from the deep libidinous place within her, gyrating her body sensuously beneath Aldrich for the first time in rhythm to the measured torrent of abuse she normally kept in store for Richard Nixon. Aldrich grew thrilled at the sound of her hatred harnessed now against the Left, rose and fell upon her mightily, feeling a nameless, new power in himself, storm trooper of the Right about the simple business of dominating the Left by the most natural of all means, turning this beautiful vessel of absurd political notions into a whimpering sexual slave. He fantasized the two of them abed, saw the taut young bodies moving in perfect harmony, panned in for a close-up shot of her face that was delirious with ecstasy begging him to thrust at her harder until he opened his eyes a moment to look at her and saw that it was in fact true, that her eyes were wide and ecstatic, that between her bursts of castigating Eugene McCarthy she actually was begging him to fuck her senseless, calling out the name of Aldrich with the same worshipful enthusiasm that Aldrich would have reserved for the name of Nixon. Great conservative victory, this!

Then she was gone: Perched on the edge of an orgasm she did not require, she rushed to it screaming, Aldrich rushing after her, the big, brave storm trooper in him not a little frightened at her intensity, wondering despite himself what his back was going to look like after she got finished clawing at it.

"Oh, Aldrich! Fuck me, Aldrich. Fuck me hard with that big Middle American cock of yours! Oh! Oh! Oh! Fuck you,

Mr. Gene McCarthy, you right-wing hatemonger, you! You hawkish, cold warrior tyrant! You childish mind with a nuclear arsenal for a playhouse!"

Then Aldrich roared to climax, yelling and yelping, feeling as if he had just begun a dizzying fall into a mile-deep vortex as she spread wide her legs, pounding her heels furiously on the floor, cursing and screeching at the memory of his enemy, McCarthy, who had once avidly hunted Alger Hiss and other pinkos for the House Un-American Activities Committee. Now Aldrich saw the bottom of the vortex rush up to meet him, and he slammed into it hard, his body convulsing with fierce spasms he could not control, his intensity in turn frightening the lover Lydia not a little. He opened his mouth, preparing to sing his triumphant love song, bellowing in deep-chested baritone straight at the snarling she-lynx of the Left: "Nixon! Agnew! Nixon! Agnew! Nixon! Agnew!"

"Oh, Gene McCarthy, God bless the memory of your defeat by Jack Kennedy in 1960!"

"Nixon! Agnew! Nixon! Agnew! Nixon! Agnew!"

Aldrich collapsed in exhaustion, whimpering a little in awe at the notion of vastly expanded new sexual horizons yet to come with the Pacifist Queen. Inside him was a great contentment, a certainty of conservative vindication, Aldrich's humble offering to his hero Nixon. See what I have done for you, my captain! Just fucked the pants off your dedicated enemy on the Left! He thought of pulling out of her now and curling up for a well-deserved sleep, but remembered the admonition of his brother YAFs that the most certain means to complete domination of a woman was to pretend tenderness after coitus when women were easily the most vulnerable of all the earth's creatures. So he began to pretend: Moving slowly within her, stroking her breasts with his hands, curling his stomach against hers where the layer of their sweat made rippling pok! sounds as the vacuum broke and sealed. He opened his eyes to smile at her and saw from her completely unexpected menacing gaze that the she-lynx still had her fangs. She thrust him rudely outside her and he yelped with the pain.

"What was all that shit about Nixon and Agnew, pal Aldrich?"

"Just venting my rage, Lydia darling. That's all."

"Well, if there's a next time, don't try venting it in me."

"Very bizarre sex," came the judgment from halfway across the room. Aldrich looked up to see Charlie Wishing Ten Fingers and Dora Pffiefenberger standing together, staring unabashedly through the dimness at them.

"My husband used to yell like that," Dora said. "But it was mostly about animals, bulls and buffaloes and things, not about politicians."

"Doesn't it embarrass you in the least to be standing there looking at us lying here without a stitch of clothes?" Aldrich demanded testily.

"We're all in this together," Dora said, and for an instant of panic Aldrich thought she meant to take off her clothes, too.

"We'll leave, Dwight David," Charlie apologized. "We were just concerned about all the noise. Dora and I will go to another room and leave you to yourselves."

"We couldn't see any of the particulars anyhow," Dora told them. "Just the general outline."

"Well, lest you remain forever ignorant of the fact, Dwight David Aldrich is particularly well-hung." Lydia laughed coarsely, grabbing the stem of Aldrich's half-limp penis and hauling it up to demonstrate. Aldrich, torn about equally between his prudery and his pride, merely smiled inanely in the darkness, then grew alarmed again as by now half-witless Dora Pffiefenberger cackled lewdly in response to Lydia's assertion, then rushed over for a closer look at the proof. Charlie sprinted after her, intercepting her about ten feet from where the two lay.

"That was vulgar and disgusting, Lydia," Charlie told her harshly. "That was completely uncalled for."

"I love seeing you angry, Charlie," Lydia pressed on. "I love seeing that stoic Mohawk cool of yours completely blown. And I know exactly how to do it, don't I? Action, reaction. More predictable than one of Pavlov's little doggies. Just flap the scarlet cape of Lydia's sexual escapading in front of this superbly intelligent Harvard Law grad and he slams head first into the brick wall behind the cape every time. Watch this, Dwight, if you really want to see those gorgeous gray eyes of Charlie's light up the darkness . . ."

She dropped her head and kissed the tip of Aldrich's penis as Aldrich, fearing Charlie's anger, tried pushing her away. Above them, the Mohawk responded with a quick, painful-sounding intake of breath, the gray eyes becoming suddenly fibrous and distended in the half-light as if they were on the verge of popping from the pressure of a fury dammed up behind them.

"Damn you, Lydia!" Charlie snorted his anger. "You go too far! You won't always be able to get away with the things you do! You'll have to pay your dues like the rest of us someday!"

Aldrich fully expected to be set upon, but Charlie made a harsh grab at Dora Pffiefenberger instead and whirled her about, rushing her toward the door, Lydia laughing wickedly after them, pleased no doubt with the pinpoint accuracy of the damage she had done. Aldrich, for his part, sighed a vast relief, was not at all surprised to find on touching a hand to his chest that his heart was pounding like a pile driver.

"That could have been very bad, Lydia. He's a big boy," Aldrich acknowledged, ashamed of his fear.

"I love seeing Charlie angry. I love getting behind that regal hauteur of his to the place where his wolverine lives and then setting loose that nasty little beast. Sometimes I have fantasies of Charlie just going bonkers and mauling the living shit out of me and then making this incredible soft love to me when I'm all whimpery and cracked and bleeding . . ."

"Is that what you fantasize?" Aldrich demanded angrily.

"Is that what you were thinking when I just made fantastic love to you, Lydia?"

"No, when you just made fantastic love to me, Dwight, I was enjoying my other favorite Charlie Wishing Ten Fingers fantasy, the one where Charlie rides bareback and stark naked and streaked with war paint across a prairie on an Appaloosa horse. When I want to I can always climax just at the point that Charlie sweeps me up behind him on the horse and saves me from the mean white-eyed motherfuckers. Poor Hodges. If he only knew who I was getting off on . . ."

"It's Charlie you love," Aldrich said miserably. "Why aren't you sleeping with him instead of making mischief in other people's lives like mine and Hodges'? It's obvious he's got it bad for you."

"Can't."

"Why? Because he's an Indian?" Aldrich hoped, preparing to be properly derisive.

"God, no, not that. Nobody cares about that. I lost my virginity ages ago with Sybaritic Hawk, Charlie's cousin. No, it's because of my gorgeous, super-indulgent civil libertarian father whose foot falls upon the earth I absolutely worship. The only thing he ever asked of me, way back at the onset of puberty, and literally made me swear to on a stack of Bibles, was that I would never become romantically involved with Charlie, even though it seemed like the most natural possibility in the universe. And because Daddy wanted that promise so intently, I said yes and thereby precipitated America's most tension-ridden platonic relationship. Oh God! What a bitch it's been! Six-plus years of reminding myself never to get stuck in the same room alone with Charlie because the old libido might get unhinged and I'd end up trying to rip his clothes off. To say nothing of the intimate possibilities of skinny-dipping parties, camping trips and ski trips, and never visiting Charlie when he was at law school in Cambridge without taking my cretinous brother Dickie along as a chaperone. Oh dear." She lay back heavily on the blanket, exhaling a great sigh. "Why does so much of our energy in life have to be sexual?"

Aldrich lay back beside her, cupping his hands beneath his head. Not nearly so overwhelmed by life's burden of sexuality as Lydia Welsh, he was also emphatically relieved to learn that, for Lydia's purpose, the very handsome Charlie Wishing Ten Fingers was consigned for life to the reservation. He paused a weighty moment, then began laying the earnest groundwork for the future.

"You know, Lydia, you and I together could make a real mark for the cause of peace. It's too bad about Hodges, though."

"What about him, Aldrich?" She grew cautious, guilty perhaps.

"He's frail."

"I'm not. I know how to take care of him."

"He's not your type, Lydia."

"Yes he is, Dwight David. He's just what I'm looking for. A gentle, low-premium insurance policy for the future when these heady days of pot and protest are over. Even a nation of automatons like America that so willingly snaps to when its leaders run the flag up the pole can't abide a Vietnam forever. It's got to bottom out sometime soon. And when that happens, I don't want to be stuck with some restless and much-decorated veteran of the street wars who won't be able to find his next calling until about 1980 or so. I've got to think of my future. I'll never get to be governor of Vermont without a peaceful-looking consort. Besides, my father's really pushing for him, and he's from our gang. It makes things so much easier."

"What's our gang?"

"Boston . . . you know . . . like in the bad novels. The horsey set. Not western saddle, however."

"And me? From Kansas, alas, but with no asthma and a brilliant future as an architect ahead of me?"

"A good-looking boy. A little rough around the edges. A prairielands' Tom Jones."

"But that means I get the girl," Aldrich delighted, raising upon one elbow and tweaking her nipples for emphasis. She pushed his hand roughly away.

"Not this time, Dwight boy. Don't push it. I don't want it."

"You're a snob, Lydia."

"No I'm not. Just preferential. I've watched Stephen Hodges' privates grow a little bit bigger every summer on the shores of Lake Champlain since we were little kids. I know exactly what I'm getting when I say 'I do.'"

"He has no passion!" Aldrich wailed at her. "He's just not a passionate man at all!"

"I'm tired of passion. I've already had a mad affair for nine months in Italy with a German. Once is enough. I've got all my stories about him down pat and ready to be embellished for my daughters. Now, have we covered all the bases?"

"I'm still coming to Vermont to collect my inheritance after graduation, Lydia. I'll come to visit with you and your family. We can talk. You might find yourself changing your mind about Hodges once you've had a little distance from me to think about it."

In the dim light he saw that her eyes were assessing him quite coolly and analytically as if from a very distant place. Then she smiled wanly and touched a kiss to his lips. He tried to gobble the fingers, but she snatched them too quickly away.

"My family, Dwight, aren't easy people to visit with. The kind of jokes we enjoy are mostly about other people whom you wouldn't know, so you'd feel very left out of things. It would be quite a lonely visit and visits aren't meant to be lonely. Besides, your own plans might be suffering some disruptions. I'm quite sure, for instance, that you aren't going to graduate."

"Not graduate?" His eyes were bug wide with surprise and he sprang to a sitting position. "Not graduate? But why?"

"Because as soon as this last stand at the Alamo in defiance of the Selective Service is over, the best you can hope for is to be kicked out of this university with a minimum of abrasion. My father will get Charlie and me sprung on some technicality like he usually does, or at the very least get up the dough for our bail, and Dora will probably be certified nuts and too incompetent to stand trial, so that if the wheels of justice grind on anyone, it's going to be you . . ."

"Not graduate . . . ?" Aldrich was stricken. He was his mother's pride. The only one of his family ever to have gone to college, let alone get within grasping distance of a graduate degree in architecture. "What will my mother say?"

"Oh. Oh. Mama's boy, huh?" She was pulling on her jeans. Aldrich's erection had withered to flaccid noodle: He held it up, wondering dimly where its power had gone. "Well, maybe your mother will be proud of your stand against the U. S. War Machine. You'll be a hero to some people, you know, after all this is over."

"Not to my mother. She hates war protesters, gooks and Communist expansion to name a few categories she considers worth inveighing against. Where do you think the name Dwight David came from?"

"One of those families, huh? Figures. Are you all the hope there is? I mean for the future of those ranches and packing houses you've got?"

"I'm afraid so, since I'm all there is," he told her, feigning weariness at the prospect of such responsibility, astounded that she had believed him about his ersatz background, the first girl who actually counted that he had ever used the lie upon.

"Well, think positively, Dwight old boy. Your about to be thwarted ambition is the monster created by you and your mother. She might die and you'd have a chance to relax, after all."

"Don't say such a thing, Lydia! Don't even think it!"

"Oh wow, you do have it bad. Well, since the die is cast and there's no turning back, I'd stick it out here in the Alamo as long as those cops are willing. As a hero to the counterculture, there should be a good bunch of contacts for you to lay into in certain quarters. You may have need of rich liberals in your passage through life, if only because rich conservatives will probably be setting a price on your head after this . . ."

"All of this is certainly a splendid irony," Aldrich said aloud to no one in particular, banging his head back on the floor with a painful clunk! sound, wishing it were the worst punishment he might incur from all this.

"If anything it should teach you for the future to be true to thine own self, friend Aldrich. You got into this little protest gig of ours quite a bit deeper than you'd intended, didn't you there, my right-wing fellow traveler?"

"Yes," Aldrich acknowledged miserably, wondering for real now what his local chapter of the Young Americans for Freedom would do to Aldrich the Traitor. For her part, Lydia Welsh only laughed softly and Aldrich supposed she was laughing at his naïveté about eastern ways, about the absurd vulnerability of the position he had unwittingly gotten himself into. He felt stung and emasculated, and searched about for a means of consolation.

She was a frivolous, spoiled rich girl, protected and unpunishable in many ways, Aldrich thought to himself during the onset of a moment of lucidity before sleeping. A causist butterfly who had already done Civil Rights, who would doubtless clamber up to take the reins of the winged chariot of Environmental Beneficence, then ditch that when the horses grew tired for Banning Nuclear Reactors, Women's Liberation, Black African Nationalism or whatever was hot and current in seasons to come. He saw it all now, the frenetic pace, her feet never quite touching ground, an endless line of men endlessly fluttered at and seduced between the mock-penitential treks back to the poetic bedrock of her husband

Hodges, to her father's evidently massive indulgence, to her platonic relationship with Charlie that seemed to Aldrich as platonically safe as setting forth on a sea of molten lava in a wooden rowboat . . .

Aldrich, acknowledging the perverse, chauvinist place in himself, determined fiercely to save her from all that and change her into Mrs. D. D. Aldrich of Inglenook, Vermont, whom her husband would beat black and blue if she ever dared try fluttering at that endless line of men: What this lady needed was a good old-fashioned Kansas woodshed strapping to get her into line.

He got upon one elbow and leaned over to tell her determinedly: "Lydia, I'm going to marry you to save you from yourself!"

She was already asleep and snoring (disquieting to Aldrich that this paragon of absolute beauty should snore at all, and worse, to the identical same ragged rhythm as his dead father sleeping off one of his monumental benders) and did not hear him evidently. Between the log sawing of her snores, an occasional little trill of giggle erupted, and Aldrich, paranoiacally awake, hoped she was not having a very funny dream at his expense.

But for the time being, that was all: Theirs was a one-night stand. For the seven further days that the sit-in lasted she would not even sleep in the same room with the suitor Aldrich.

CHAPTER 19

Enter Danton Welsh

The end, at last, hove into view, in one sense a not unpleasant prospect for Aldrich, who was supplementing his two-cookies-per-day ration with between-meal chewings on his leather belt.

Dora Pffiefenberger gave up on the tenth day. Or rather was given up for fear she meant simply to languish and die, thus conveniently passing into conservative Nebraska history as the sad, innocent victim of radical guerrilla savagery when in fact she had done an almost totally unprompted job of radicalizing herself.

About the middle of the eighth day, she abruptly ceased the manic, enraged pacing of the hallway and sat down against a wall to stare fixedly at the face of a filing cabinet, became a catatonic blob of suddenly sagging parts like a wax-works dummy placed too near heat that no amount of pinchings and entreaties could break through to.

Dutifully, Aldrich and Charlie Wishing Ten Fingers, both frankly acknowledging the hunger-spawned weakness of their own limbs, hauled her to her feet, slung her between them and set off for the front door of the building to hand her over to the State Police and a woman relative of hers, all of whom were kindly and solicitous and keenly grateful that the poor lady still lived until Dora's seething volcano suddenly erupted again and she lashed out kicking and punching at the rifle-toting cops and exhorted the unindictable student horde beyond the line of National Guard to near-killer frenzy with a torrent of radical cant and activist pieties she had learned inside the Records Office during what she continually assured the world were the ten most meaningful days of her life.

"What have you done to her?" Dora's relative tearfully beseeched Aldrich and Charlie as the police, visibly shaken at the possibility of a student charge at them right through the National Guard lines, wrestled Dora to a stretcher on the ground and strapped her down while a medic gave her a knockout injection.

"Dora's not Dora anymore. Dora won a first prize for her strudel at the State Fair six years ago. Dora's a member of Eastern Star. Dora's needlepoint is the most beautiful in the country. Her barnyards and sunsets sell for more than five hundred dollars apiece in Omaha . . ."

"From now on her needlepoint will doubtless be less pastoral and more revolutionary in theme," Charlie said drily.

Aldrich thought that was funny: His starved light-headedness saw Dora's future Grandma Moses scenarios bristling with pitchfork-wielding farmers charging out of Grange Halls at the police. The cozy mottoes below the scene would change from "In God We Trust" to "Off the Pigs! Power to the People!" He became positively convulsed with laughter, barely able to stand. He looked down at Dora on her stretcher and saw that the drug had not yet taken effect, that she too was laughing hysterically, her body shuddering beneath the leather bands that strapped her down.

The captain of State Police with whom Aldrich had shaken hands and categorically assured everything would be all right in the end, spun him roughly around: "What are you laughin' at, Aldrich? I know who you are. I had you researched. Are you one of these anarchist radicals now? If you are, you're in for some real trouble with those Young Americans for Freedom boys."

"I suppose," Aldrich agreed, suddenly sobered.

"He is," Charlie assured the lawman. "He's one of us radical anarchist bastards right to his marrow by now."

"I can't let you boys go back in there this time," the cop told them. "You boys need a bath. You both stink somethin' awful. You're under arrest."

"Lydia! Lydia!" Dora began shrieking up from her confinement. "Lydia, get set to push the plunger and blow the goddam place to bits! The pigs won't let Charlie and Dwight back in!"

"She'd do that?" the captain demanded incredulously. "She'd push the plunger 'n bring the whole place down on top of her?"

"One life is a small price to pay for the cause of peace," Charlie avowed solemnly straight into the lens of the portable TV camera that zoomed in closer upon them.

"Even such a beautiful life as our darling Lydia's," Aldrich heard himself say, staring with identical seriousness at the camera.

"Damn! That's all we need! A goddam martyr on our hands!" The State Policeman stomped an angry footfall in the grass, looked like he was about to throw down his hat for good measure. "All right, boys, go back in. But when you come out, bring Ms. Lydia Welsh and your dynamite with you. Don't think for one minute about settin' a delayed time charge to take out this buildin'. Nebraska law's got all it needs to bury you right now without making it worse for yourselves."

They went in again to the rousing cheers of the unindictable horde, praising the splendid ingenuity of Dora Pffiefenberger, whose admonition to push the nonexistent plunger Lydia had not even heard. They came out two days later about noon to give themselves up, deciding there was no point in staying longer when the university president refused bluntly for the seventh time to negotiate with them, and when Lydia fainted dead outright from lack of food only minutes after rising that morning. Immensely relieved because his hunger had become such that he did not think he would be able to stick out the day himself, Aldrich played at being the last angry man and exhorted the other two to stay longer, then played at glum defeat when they overruled him. Lydia pronounced his radical credentials perfect; Charlie Wishing Ten Fingers pledged his eternal friendship; Aldrich thought of mounds and mounds of mashed potatoes covered with a shining glaze of gravies.

Walking three abreast and holding hands with Lydia in the middle, they went outside to the din of thousands of howling, clapping students to give themselves up to the police. Lydia collapsed into the arms of her father, Danton Welsh, who was in the process of staring down a covey of lawmen who even removed their hats to serve arrest warrants on the three. Danton Welsh patted consolingly on Lydia's back, smiled approvingly over her shoulder at Charlie and Aldrich as the three were read a statement of their rights. Aldrich thought Danton Welsh was the most self-possessed man he had ever encountered.

"Dear, brave Lydia. My darling little girl. Don't worry about anything now but a decent meal. Daddy will take care of everything."

"She was very brave, sir," Aldrich assured him.

"I expect so, Mr. Aldrich. Her grandmother Leila Breckenridge was a legendary famous suffragette in Boston. She once chained herself to the White House fence to demonstrate her zeal for women's voting rights. Lydia takes after her grandmother in many ways."

"Oh, Daddy, they wouldn't negotiate," Lydia sobbed. "It was all for nothing."

Her father kissed at her tear-stained cheeks. "It was hardly for nothing, sweet Lydia. Look at all these cheering students, look at all those signs and banners of support and look at all this TV coverage. Stopping this backwater university from cooperating with the Selective Service is small fish compared to the massive publicity you've gotten for the antiwar movement. We've seen you at home in Boston. This sit-in has been aired on the three national networks. I can't tell you what excitement you've generated back home among our friends. So many have called and pledged donations to the coalition. Why, you were the cause of a standing ovation for me at my club's banquet this week. Even that right-wing, super-capitalist godfather of yours, Charlie Norton, drove over the other day to tell me he hated what you were doing, but he certainly admired the way you were doing it . . ."

"Charlie Norton said that?" It was Charlie Wishing Ten Fingers. He reached over almost as an afterthought to shake hands with Danton Welsh.

"Yes, Charlie, can you believe it? And I've got some good news for you, too. Chief Tom White Stag phoned me to tell me that there's a considerable Mohawk movement afoot to make you a subchieftain."

"These people broke the law," the captain of State Police announced dumbfoundedly. "They broke the law 'n everybody back East is givin' them standin' ovations and subchief-tainships. Have you got different laws back there from us?"

"Let's just say we interpret them differently, Captain," Danton Welsh smiled a tight patrician smile at the lawman, patient the way one would smile at a child. "Or that we give greater latitude to the possibilities for interpretation. Which doesn't seem to be the case out here if the president of this university can be cited as an example. That man is an absolute boneheaded dunce. He wouldn't survive a single night in Boston with his intelligence. Some thoughtful person would murder him from compassion."

"Well, we like him just fine out here, Counselor Welsh," the cop growled at him. "It's a source of considerable pleasure to the honest, taxpaying citizens of Nebraska to know we've got somebody in our grove of academe with a little spine in him instead of one of those permissive intellectuals who give in to this protester riffraff on every demand."

"He sounds like veritable state treasure, Captain," Danton

Welsh told the cop, the tight smile never once flickering on his face. "Do guard him well, I'd suggest. A man with his kind of unyielding righteousness becomes a rather obvious target for the frustrated disenfranchised. Oh, by the way, Mr. Aldrich, it will doubtless please you to hear of an arbitrary decision that the dunce has made known to me concerning yourself. You aren't going to graduate this June. In fact at this very moment you exist in no relationship of any kind to this university. You are in the very words of the good president himself 'to fly your ass off campus at once,' end quote. Your mother has apparently been advised of this decision by telegram."

"Oh no," Aldrich moaned, appalled despite himself at the blunt proof of all the railings against impetuous behavior he had absorbed from teachers, preachers or his mother in a short lifetime: The conquest of Lydia Welsh still but a trembling possibility and already he was paying for his love-struck temerity in spades. No degree, no job, no income, no Lydia: The future a swift-evolving domino theory culminating in a lonely suicide. Reflexively, he turned to face the TV camera, praying it was transmitting live, and threw up his hands in a plaintive gesture to his mother in Abilene, mouthing the words "I'll explain later" straight at the camera eye. Then he smiled reassuringly and blew her a kiss. As he dropped his arm it was shackled into a handcuff before a nationwide audience by a Nebraska State Trooper who muttered somewhat incoherently to himself about the possibility of paying for his lack of caution around a prisoner. . . .

"Danton, that's just plain criminal!" Charlie Wishing Ten Fingers protested. "Aldrich is being made to pay with the price of his career for being courageous enough to profess his beliefs! Except for that crazy Dora who went bananas and didn't have to choose any longer, Aldrich was the only one from this cornhusker diploma mill who stuck it out with us. You've got to go to court on his behalf and get some judge to overrule that dunce president's decision and reinstate him in grad school. . . . He didn't desert us, Danton. I won't desert him."

Danton Welsh had relinquished his daughter to another trooper, who cuffed her to him. He stared a long moment at Aldrich, appraising him almost defiantly, thought Aldrich, who was distressed by his sudden notion that Danton Welsh had become one of the acknowledged warlords of his profession from his special ability to cast an unerring glance into the heart of a man and ferret out the truth. Today he would see there was little truth at all in Aldrich, that his heart was very black indeed.

"Your loyalty is very commendable, Charlie," Danton Welsh pronounced at last, "but we really don't know this person. He elected to participate in this sit-in of his own volition and like anyone else he's got to take his licks for that decision when the time comes. My purpose in coming here was to get you and Lydia sprung and back home to safety in case of any right-wing retaliation. Mr. Aldrich—Dwight, isn't it?—comes from this neck of the woods and knows when to plant and when to harvest, so to speak. His friends and supporters are here. It's they who should get to court and get the dunce's decision overturned. I haven't got time to spare from my practice and probably wouldn't do Dwight here much good anyhow showing up in some sodbuster judge's court with my reputation preceding me."

"But, Danton, he has no friends!" Charlie exclaimed. "He's a converted right-winger with a whole fraternity of instant enemies. He needs our help, Danton!"

"He can make new friends," Lydia said flatly, wounding Aldrich nearly to tears by the finality of her dismissal.

"Lydia . . . !" Charlie upbraided her, shaking his head in disbelief.

"Daddy's right, Charlie. We've got to move on. We can't suspend time from our efforts to stop the war and hang around Nebraska trying to get Dwight reinstated in grad school. Dwight's a big boy. Dwight's got a mother hang-up.

I'm sure Dwight will work tirelessly on his own behalf and do whatever is required to make sure come June that he's here to pick up that diploma preparatory to dropping it into Mumsy's lap. Dwight can get himself cleaned up and put on a Brooks Brothers suit and ask the dunce for an audience. The dunce will not remain everlastingly angry at the sight of repentant Dwight in his Brooks Brothers suit . . ."

Aldrich shook his head to ward off the clanging light-headedness, to dispel the reality of her abrupt betrayal. All around them the cops were sniggering openly except for the captain, who seemed mournful as if he had known about Lydia Welsh all along and told Aldrich pityingly: "See what you get for goin' agin your own kind, Aldrich. See what you get for joinin' up with eastern liberal sharpies."

"I won't be a party to any of this, Danton," Charlie told him coldly. "Charlie Wishing Ten Fingers won't be known as an eastern liberal sharpie when its connotation to these people out here means treachery. This isn't any of Lydia's usual massive indifference to spent playthings. This is pure betrayal. She even invited him to her wedding. So did Stephen."

"Why?" Danton Welsh demanded, knitting his brows in perplexity. "Isn't that going a bit too far, Lydia? You can't be extending invitations to your wedding to every Tom, Dick and Harry you bump into in your work. You've known this person, Dwight, only twelve days by my count."

"The invitation was at Charlie's instigation, Daddy. The invitation is hereby withdrawn. Sorry, Dwight, but there really isn't much point in you looking us up in Vermont this summer, if I make myself clear. I've already tried to explain to you that we're a difficult family to visit with. One of the first prerequisites of making a successful life in New England is learning how to gracefully withdraw when you understand that some people's reaction to you is chill . . ."

"You've slept with me!" Aldrich hurled at her, staring reproachfully at her father, desperate that if this was truly the end, then he meant to silence the sniggering cops. "You begged me to fuck you! You told me I was the best you'd ever had!"

"You bastard clodhopper!" Her hollow-eyed weakened condition made her seem evil incarnate and grotesque in anger. She stumbled toward Aldrich, dragging her startled trooper with her a little way until she was stopped by her father, who took a heavy grip on her shoulder and spun her around to face him.

"I won't even bother to tell you I don't like this business, Lydia! I don't want you ever to be so injudicious as this again in life! You're engaged to marry Stephen Hodges this coming June twenty-sixth!"

"I'm afraid you're going to have to resign yourself to more injudiciousness, Daddy," she told him evenly, her composure remarkably regained in a moment except for a deep harsh breathing. She and her father squared off eye to eye, each staring fiercely at the other, looking for the first blink, and Aldrich understood with an awed certainty, as perhaps did everyone else watching, that for each of them, the one other person in the universe was at hand, that the iron-willed Danton Welsh had finally met his match in his very own daughter. No small amount of parental pride that. Her father smiled the merest conciliatory smile and Lydia deftly shoved her dagger in the chink: "There'll have to be more injudiciousness, Daddy. Since you're Stephen Hodges' chief supporter in the cause of these nuptials, it's only fair to warn you first that he won't be enough. He's lousy in bed, and his poetry won't make up the difference. He's a piddling poet, too."

"Lydia, I won't stand for this!" Danton Welsh growled at her, waving his hand to remind her of the onlookers. "We can't have any scandal! Think what old friends of ours the Hodgeses are. Think how really closely interconnected are all the people we care to know. The business of marriage is to seem married, not to stimulate wagging tongues. Stephen Hodges will be a good and kind husband to you. This has all been arranged for ages. I won't allow you to stand there and tell me to prepare myself for future earthquakes after all the sacrifices I've made for you. You'll marry Stephen on twenty-six June and damn well live happily ever after!"

"Don't try locking me in a gilded cage for life with any sweet-warbling bird of a poet, Father dear, or I may take it upon myself to compromise one very important promise you once asked me to make. I know how to even the score with you, sir."

"You wouldn't, Lydia," her father told her mutely, a sudden sad tiredness in his voice, "because if you did that, it wouldn't matter to me what you did ever after. There would be nothing left between us. I'd renounce your name. I'd drive you from memory."

"If Lydia's promise is anything like the one I had to make, Danton, then I require a favor of you because you can't renounce my name and if you fail me this request it won't matter to me if you do drive me from memory . . ."

Unexpectedly, a bemused smile settled on Danton Welsh's face on hearing Charlie Wishing Ten Fingers' ultimatum. He turned a slow half circle scanning the faces of the Nebraska lawmen who stared perplexedly at the three, hanging intently on the very next word.

"I would imagine the only reason these good gentlemen are not smirking at the intensity of all this silly internecine threatening is that we're certain proof of the axiom that no matter how wild things may be in the streets, it's the family rumble that still provides life's most compelling arena. We three are the stuff of good torrid soap opera. It really doesn't say much for my abilities as a courtroom prima donna to have let this little exchange get as far along as it has, does it?"

"Yes or no, Danton? Do I get my request?" Charlie asked him bluntly. "Can the pyrotechnics."

"Your request, Charlie? Well, the answer is yes, as if I had a choice. Now what's the request, as if I didn't know?"

"I want you to serve as counsel for Dwight Aldrich as well as for Lydia and myself on the trespass charges. I want you to represent him in fighting to have the dunce president's decision overturned. And I want you to reissue the invitation to Lydia and Stephen's wedding that Lydia so ungenerously retracted."

Danton Welsh shrugged: "Agreed, agreed and agreed. Yes, Dwight, by all means do come to the nuptials. Weddings are always such a perfect occasion to catch up on the news with old family friends from Kansas."

"Daddy, I won't have him on that guest list!" Lydia screeched. "Charlie's up to something. He's trying to push someone into our lives who doesn't belong there."

"I couldn't agree with you more, Lydia darling, but your dear old daddy's just been checkmated and your dear old daddy hasn't been a savvy lawyer for such a short time that he doesn't know when to begin benignly smiling as if the whole idea of inviting Dwight here were his all along. Why, Charlie, by the way, are you trying to push Aldrich in on us?"

"It's just that I want to democratize our little society a bit, Danton. The air gets so rarefied along the shores of Champlain. We'll all be positively gasping for breath at lakeside on Lydia's wedding day if someone like Dwight David Aldrich isn't on the guest list."

Danton Welsh smiled broadly at the jibe, clapped an equally broad-smiling Charlie on the back: "What splendid friends we are, Charlie. How we understand each other, you sly old Indian, you. How good of you to care for us the way you do . . ."

"I'm not appeased, Daddy!" Lydia raged. "Aldrich doesn't belong! I'm not appeased one bit!"

"I concede you the option to be an adulteress during your marriage to Stephen Hodges, Lydia," her father told her wearily.

"All right, that's better. Aldrich can come."

"This certainly has been a very unorthodox arrest procedure," the captain of State Police pronounced after a moment while everyone silently digested Danton Welsh's bizarre concession.

"It's been downright surreal," Aldrich heard himself say.

"Surreal . . . Yes, that's a good word for it," the captain affirmed. His voice brought Danton Welsh back from some distant reflection.

"I want to advise you, Captain, that I'll be watching scrupulously for any violation of these prisoners' rights," the lawyer barked at the cop.

"You watch all you want, O magnificent barrister from the fabled East. When I heard whose daughter this princess was, I worked tirelessly at my preparations. It's goin' to be absolutely kid gloves from here to booking to arraignment. You won't get them off on anything that happens in between. Even you're goin' to have to acknowledge the sacredness of the Law."

"Indeed, Captain, the Law is a sacred place." Danton Welsh smiled the tight patrician smile again at him. "But like most sacred places, it's quite murky therein. A good attorney just has to stumble around for a while until he trips over the crack he's been looking for."

"I don't like you, Mr. Danton Welsh," the captain told him levelly. "I'd settle for being called your enemy, in fact."

"I have always wished the pleasures of love even unto my enemies," Danton Welsh assured the lawman as Lydia, Charlie and Aldrich were turned about and led away to the waiting police cars.

Danton Welsh turned toward the cheering mob of students and raised both arms in a V-for-victory salute.

CHAPTER 20

Knight Astride
a Ten-Speed

Danton Welsh won one and lost one.

He lost his suit to have the dunce president's decision overturned and Aldrich reinstated in graduate school, an outcome Aldrich concluded Danton Welsh must have set his sights upon well in advance anyhow, for he was unbelievably haughty and contemptuous in court (causing an embarrassed, wincing client Aldrich to urge him to moderation, please!), and in upholding the dunce president's decision the headshaking, evidently dumbfounded judge assured Danton Welsh that for all the trumpetings of reputation preceding him, his was one of the worst presentations ever heard. Danton Welsh merely shrugged his shoulders in response, indicating his withdrawal from the whole business, and flew home to Boston without as much as a backward glance at his client.

In a grand panic Aldrich solicited the dunce president for an interview. The president admired Aldrich's well-groomed Middle American excellence and told him he might well have rescinded his decision had not Aldrich taken it upon himself to hire that eastern sharpie lawyer and father of the Pacifist Queen of all people, who had pleaded his case with such arrogant disdain for the region and its institutions that he had prejudiced the dunce president irrevocably against Aldrich's case and precluded any possibility of appeal.

Danton Welsh won the one that was important to Danton Welsh.

He got the charges against Lydia, Charlie and, by unavoid-able association, Aldrich quashed at their arraignment on a technicality so simple that a stunned Aldrich could not believe that any code of law anywhere in the universe would allow it to stand after what they had done: The captain of State Police, for all of his assiduous preparations to arrest the daughter of super-lawyer Danton Welsh, had failed to notice the expiration date of their arrest warrants had elapsed by one day: They were off.

Blind the lady Justice indeed, and to Aldrich's curious dismay, bound and gagged into the bargain as well.

At the airport Aldrich bade goodbye to an uncaring Dan-ton Welsh and his equally uncaring daughter Lydia, stiffly ac-knowledged the tight bear hug with feeling of Charlie Wish-ing Ten Fingers, and even blinked back a tear, blaming it on jet blast, confused at the notion that he would miss his radical comrades very much. Before leaving, Charlie provided him with the elaborate directions for reaching Morgan Kingdom Farm at Shelburne, Vermont, where he was expected two days before the June 26 festivities and admonished him to phone well in advance if there were any problems. Aldrich turned about and walked back into the terminal and promptly fell into a spiritual crisis, the first of his life.

He knew what he was culpable of, despite his original amorous motive for joining in the sit-in, and wanted to be punished for it: He had played at radicalism, walked naked with eastern liberals in the Garden of Civil Disobedience, tasted a few berries of the forbidden fruit of the righteousness of the Left, and found the taste not quite as bitter-awful as he had hoped. *Au fond,* the bedrock of his preferred kind of righteousness, the kind that kept his back straight and his head high and insured the hard malice of his gaze when it fell on hippies, protesters or blacks, had become a bit trembly in-side him. Given this, and anxious to restore the old certainty of his prejudices, the notion of getting off scot-free was partic-ularly unsettling, totally unsatisfying to the hunger of the guilt monsters that now bred and multiplied in Aldrich like rabbits, offspring of the parent monsters so willfully introduced to him by his mother in Abilene in defiance of every indulgent, irreligious, indigent and undisciplined principle Aldrich's dead-from-drink father had stood for.

For two days after the Easterners had left, Aldrich slunk around town with head bowed and eyes averted, unnerved at chance meetings with fellow members of the Young Americans for Freedom who smiled an identical polite, myopic and unfathomable smile at him and passed quickly on, not speaking. From loneliness he gravitated to the counterculture, eating in their natural-foods restaurants and drinking in their bars, and on the second night, sodden with beers, he even wept a little when a lithe, bearded young man in whose face Aldrich had once determinedly spit in a counter-demonstration came up to him unprompted, extended his hand and said simply: "I forgive you."

The next morning Aldrich packed his bags and left in his third-hand Volkswagen for Abilene, certain he would get all the flagellation he required there.

She was more than enough, his mother. A shrunken, ascetic woman (she had once been blond and beautiful, the donor of Aldrich's handsomeness), she wept violently among the Bibles and Baptist periodicals in her little clapboard bungalow on the mean, working-class street where blacks had bought up nearly all the houses on the opposite side. Two mournful-eyed Jesus calendars, photos of the Republican saints and Douglas MacArthur stared down from the faded wallpapered walls as she screechingly accused him of a worse betrayal than his father and the drink by getting himself kicked out of the university just short of receiving his master's degree. Steeped in the habit of pessimism, communicant in a punitive religion, she saw no alternative to his future but a life of ruination: Sins of the father come home to roost. Despite his easy shame, his vague recognition that she had always been able to make him jump through flaming hoops from guilt because of the evil set of chromosomes he carried within him from his father, he dared wonder for the first time if it were not because of her that the old man had gone off on his ten-year terminal bender.

Kansas Medea: On his second day home she actually threw one of her beloved Bibles at him in a flash of fury. When it missed and hit the wall instead, breaking the binding and fluttering pages all over the floor, she inveighed against his sinfulness so heinous it caused the dismemberment of the Holy Book. What of her future now, impecunious and miserable on a welfare check whose buying power was being borne ever more swiftly backward on the current of inflation? What of the great house they had planned together in the expensive Wheat Ridge suburb where mother and son would live happily ever after, needing no one else but their servants, on the son's $100,000 per year? Sniffling quietly to herself, she took from a drawer the much-fingered photo of a French *mairie* she had cut from a tabloid newspaper, the building they intended using as the house model, and (near breaking his heart) symbolically tore it to pieces, casting the fragments into a metaphorical wind of doom with the saddest of sad sighs. To underscore the grind of her poverty, she fed him meatless meals of black-eyed peas and rice or okra and rice or potatoes and grits or catfish and macaroni, twice taking up their plates in a sudden, unnamed anger and hurling them to shatter on the floor.

How could she face the neighbors because of what he had done? (The white neighbors, she meant, who could only react with vicious gloating to the sight of Dwight David Aldrich being manacled by the police on nationwide television after all the years of her obsessive mind having no use for any subject but the certain superiority of her own son over any other young man in the neighborhood. The blacks, to whom she never spoke, would not even look at, had come shyly to her front porch, often bearing casserole dishes or plates of barbecued meat and offered her congratulations on

the courage of her fine son who was telling the Government
where to get off. She had accepted the offerings, then contemptuously dumped what she called "the nigger food" into
the garbage after they left.) Aldrich could not answer the
question for her, only made a vague attempt at consolation by
promising her a string of victories in the future that she might
ram down the neighbors' throats, though in fact he had no
idea where to begin the winning streak.

Afternoons, venturing outside for a walk to escape the
cauldron of emotion boiling within the house, he crossed naturally to the black side of the street where his proportions were
heroic, stopping to shake hands and be congratulated by entire families who swarmed out of the houses. On several occasions he was easily enticed inside for a decent meal of spare
ribs and beer or ham stew and wine. On the opposite side of
the street where his mother's neighbors lived, window curtains
twitched slyly at his passing and no one came out to hail him.

When he told his mother in an attempt to placate her
that his participation in the sit-in was a pretense, that he had
done it all for the girl, Lydia Welsh, her reaction was worse
than anything that had come before. Her neighbors, white
and black, came onto their front porches to hear her hair-
curling screams that there was not room enough for the three
of them in her house, that she could not support them and
herself on her welfare check, that he was just like his bastard
father with his lustings after the flesh!

Wasn't his dear old mom the best kind of girl for him?

Aldrich supposed for the first time she was somewhat
mad, could scarce believe that such a volume of sound could
come from such a diminutive vessel, nor that it could contain
such a burning lake of bitterness. When the police came to
the house in response to a complaint (doubtless phoned in by
one of the gloating white neighbors), Aldrich resolved to
leave the very next day and set out into the world to make his
fortune, rekindle his mother's dashed pride in her son whom
all the world now knew carried about a proven bad set of

chromosomes, and restore her to a position of respect among her gloating white neighbors. All this, if for nothing more than it provided a reason to get the hell away from her.

Only for the life of him, he had no idea where to start. . . .

The Young Americans for Freedom were helpful here.

The next morning, when he had more or less decided to drive to Chicago and look for work and was packing his bags again in the face of his mother's pathetic whimperings about being deserted yet another time in life, four of his brother members drove up before the house in a white Oldsmobile convertible with a ten-speed bike affixed to a rack on the back.

"Those are nice, clean-cut-looking young men who I can see come from good families," his mother approved. "At least you've got some decent friends."

"They aren't my friends. Not anymore at least," he told her miserably, thinking it ironic that the single impulsive act of his life had brought the roof of Aldrich's Middle American temple squarely down on top of him, spewing all the pillars in the same fell swoop: He went outside to greet them sheepishly, aware that he was still covered with much dust from the temple's destruction.

"So . . . this is where you live, Aldrich, huh?" one called Morley judged, measuring the size of Aldrich's mother's house scornfully, turning about to eye the watchful blacks seated on their porches across the street, sniggering at the gaudy statue of the Virgin standing in the grotto of an upended bathtub in the front yard of a white Catholic neighbor two houses away.

"Yes," Aldrich answered mutely after a long moment when he decided the question was not rhetorical.

"Kinda thought it would be bigger. I seem to remember you saying something about a ranch or spread . . ."

"Out near the Colorado line. Big fuckin' place. Can't

hardly ride across it on a horse in a day," another named Jensen mimicked the monotone precision of a recording.

"We have no ranch," Aldrich told them stonily.

"No ranch? Hmm. Then that means you drive that old VW because you can't afford anything better, not because it's part of your rich family's plan to teach self-reliance by withholding your money from you until you're thirty. Boy, I must've heard that story from at least ten chicks who went out on beer and popcorn dates with you. And they all believed it! That is the amazing fucking thing!"

"Evidently, Morley, it's not true." He tried to deflate their animosity with a joke: "But then nobody ever said you had to tell chicks the whole truth anyhow. It's better not to. Ha. Ha. Ha."

"How'd your father die, Aldrich?" Edgar Molheimer, with whom Aldrich had once roomed, demanded bluntly, oblivious of the feeble try at humor. "I have encountered not a few ladies who grew misty-eyed on telling me the story of your daddy's horse shying at the rattler and throwing your poor daddy head first into a fence post that didn't move. That tall, proud man. Tsk. Tsk."

"He died of cirrhosis of the liver. He drank himself to death," Aldrich whispered hoarsely, wishing the ground would open up and swallow him and his awful shame in one quick bite.

"It appears, Aldrich, you've been funnin' a lot of people. It seems you've told a lot of people a lot of very different things," Jensen menaced him, advancing toward Aldrich a little. "The truth is you're a poor boy. You're not a rich boy in a holding pattern at all."

"I want you to know I went along with that sit-in because of the girl," the words rushed out of Aldrich desperately. He was afraid they meant to beat him up right on the front lawn of his mother's house. "Lydia Welsh . . . the Pacifist Queen . . . I was going to convert her to conservative principles! That's why I did it!"

They guffawed at him, slapping their knees or each other's shoulders. Aldrich's mother, having sensed the tension perhaps, but thinking it was now defused, chose that moment to open the door: "Dwight David! Would your friends like some Coca-Cola to drink? I could run to the store and get some. Why don't you all come in?"

Aldrich blinked and closed his eyes at the sight of her framed in the doorway. She had put on her best garishly flowered dress from another time when she weighed more, and now it hung shapeless and sack-like over her thin, wasted frame. On her feet were high-heeled, years-old, black patent-leather shoes with ankle straps and clusters of gold sequins at the toes. She had pasted her face with powder and rouge that concealed nothing of her days-long crying, only made her look splotchy and alcoholic, accenting the rheumy boozer's glaze of her eyes, a particularly cruel irony since she had hardly ever touched a drop in her life. Her mouth, the lips curled back in an attempt at a welcoming smile, managed to look somehow lewd instead. Aldrich was stricken: Her description would get back to the university to every person he had ever known.

"Je-sus Christ. Blanche Dubois," came the barely whispered judgment from Molheimer.

Aldrich turned to see there was no guffawing now. The four, members of the apple pie and mother cult, were clearly shocked or embarrassed at the reality of Aldrich's mother. Dim, pitying smiles crept onto their faces, making Aldrich want to weep, his mind a swarming battleground of motion and counter-motion from not knowing whether to defend her or renounce her. All four nodded at her somewhat shyly. Morley opened his mouth to speak.

"Thank you, no, Mrs. Aldrich. We really don't want any Coke. We've just come by for a friendly visit with old Dwight here."

"It's no trouble. It won't take but a minute. You can sit in here and make yourselves comfortable while I'm gone."

"Go inside and close the door, will you?" Aldrich

253

screamed at his mother. "Things are bad enough without you!"

Stung to new tears, certain surely of her notion that he had taken leave of his senses, she stepped inside and gently closed the door behind her, one of her most calculated methods of reproof. A collective sigh of relief issued from the four, who stared fixedly into the lawn as they shifted uneasily from foot to foot.

"What do you guys want?" Aldrich demanded savagely.

"Calm down, Dwight," Jensen advised. "Why don't we all go over and sit down under that shade tree and have a little talk."

When they were seated, Aldrich with his back to the trunk of the elm facing the half circle of his inquisitors, Molheimer got to the point: "Dwight, there've been at least ten various theories advanced among the conservative brotherhood as to why you joined in with those freaks to create pandemonium in the Records Office . . ."

"I told you why I went along with them!"

"That's bullshit. But why you went in doesn't really matter any longer. What matters is that you didn't come out. Not when all those turkeys left the second day to get their scolding from the chickenshit administration. Not when you brought the asthmatic poet-lover boy friend out for a little R and R, and all you had to do was give yourself up to those cops. Not when you brought out the old lady from the Records Office staff who went bats, either. Not until the very last minute did you come out in very obvious communion with Miss Radical Tits herself and that Mohawk Injun Communist. . . . The point is, Dwight old boy, that nobody had a gun on you in there, did they? Nobody was down here in Abilene holding your sweet old mother hostage to force you to stay. Nobody was remunerating you either, though, after today, that would seem like the most logical reason for your treachery against our little organization . . ."

"All of which," Jensen interrupted, taking a grip on

Aldrich's knee and squeezing hard, "I say all of which leads us to the sad conclusion that you were with those people because you wanted to be with those people, that you went temporarily insane, forsaking your conservative ideology, and went off on a radical fling which was unpatriotic, un-American and, worse than anything, unlawful!"

"We YAFs do not break the law! The law is sacred!" shouted Werner Doppenfuller, opening his mouth for the first time and pummeling the grass repeatedly with a fist for emphasis.

"I did it because of the girl!" Aldrich blurted out, pleading at them with his hands. "Because of Lydia! I love her!"

"Her father must have money," Morley judged quietly. The others nodded sagely in assent. Then: "It was just a little fling, wasn't it, Dwight old boy? I mean, a temporary aberration? You are sorry you did it, aren't you? You do want back in our righteous little fraternity, don't you? I mean, it would be a shame to lose the friendship of good men you could know your whole life."

"Yes! Yes, I do!" Aldrich assured them, not feigning his intensity at all: He was lonely out here in an exile where he was welcomed only by blacks whom he did not like, wanted to rejoin the community in whose righteous ideology he felt most secure, notwithstanding the fact that his cover was blown, that it would take an uncomfortably long time before the sneers and jokes about The Big Ranch, A Proud Father's Dying, Blanche Dubois and The Rich Boy in a Holding Pattern would abate.

"It requires a little punishment though, Dwight, I am afraid," Jensen told him in a very measured tone, staring hard at him.

"Punishment? Yes! That's exactly what I'm looking for! Except for being kicked out of school, I've gotten off scot-free! That bastard of a father of Lydia helped us beat the rap at our arraignment and left me with a big dry water hole right in the middle of my conscience!"

He was smiling effusively at them with relief. They regarded him with a collective speculative gaze as if they thought he might be daft after all, or were trying perhaps to envision the water-hole metaphor. Finally Jensen spoke up: "Well, we're going to help you fill that water hole right back up again, Dwight. We've come up with a little plan for reconditioning your mind after all the damage it suffered at the knives of those radical freaks. But it depends on one thing . . . You are going to Vermont soon to collect your inheritance like you've been telling us for the last four or five years, aren't you? I mean, that story isn't part of the big ranch in the sky bullshit, is it?"

"No, that's real. I swear it."

"Good show."

The four rose on a single impulse and walked to the convertible. When they returned, Molheimer was wheeling the ten-speed bike, Morley carried a folded tent and a rain poncho, Doppenfuller had a hiker's backpack out of which protruded a pot handle, and Jensen a manila envelope from which he was unfolding, to Aldrich's growing trepidation, a well-marked road atlas of the U.S. of A.

"This ten-speed, Dwight old boy, is a genuine six-hundred-dollar French whore, just about the best you can buy," Jensen told him. "This is a brand-new two-man pup tent; this is the latest in completely contained camper's backpack equipment; this poncho'll let you keep right on riding through any rain you might encounter; this is a map of the route you're to follow from Abilene to Inglenook, Vermont; in this manila folder are an expense check for five hundred dollars, a copy of the penitential speech accusing yourself of worshipping false gods that you're going to give before brother YAF chapters at the indicated campuses en route, and a list of the chapter representatives who'll be your contact when you reach those campuses. Now, did I forget anything?"

"The sign for the back of old Dwight's bike," Molheimer

reminded Jensen, grinning at the look of stunned disbelief on Aldrich's face.

"Ah yes." Jensen went to the car, opened the trunk and returned with a high-gloss white wooden sign approximately two feet by four feet with the words "America Is Always Right!" in bright orange block letters. There were special brackets for affixing it to the ten-speed.

"Some radical Leftie will run me right off the road when he sees that sign," Aldrich moaned, shaking his head in dismay.

"It promises to be a rough crossing, Dwight," Morley concurred, staring eastward with a vacuous look on his face. "Very penitential, I would say. We called the Vermont State Police and finally found out where Inglenook, which isn't on the map, is. It is exactly 2,736.5 miles from this here Bonanza spread of yours . . ."

"That's too much penance," Aldrich whined. "That isn't the sort of punishment I had in mind at all."

"If you can phone us from Inglenook, Vermont, in fifty days, having fulfilled all your speaking engagements en route, we'll swear to you now that no one else will ever know from us that you weren't all you claimed to be," Jensen promised.

"Only you've got to pedal all the way, Dwight," Molheimer warned him. "No hitching rides with truckers or anybody else. There'll be spotters stationed along the way waiting for you to pass by. A lot of guys are pulling for you, Dwight. I lived with you once. I remember what a neat orderly guy you are. I told the other guys about that. I went to bat for you when some guys were talking about chains and whips and broken arms and shit like that. There's a lot of guys between here and Vermont want to give you a second chance. They'll be watching for you, good buddy. They'll be spying along the road. There's guys who remember you never even looking dazed at a party, let alone drunk. Those guys think something deep inside you exploded for just twenty silly days, and now that you've got it out of your system, you'll be a good war horse for the Right again, once your penance is done. Don't let me down, Dwight! Think of those guys!"

Aldrich bear-hugged with his ex-roommate Molheimer, remembering that Molheimer was a goddam slob, that one of his accepted chores as roommate was to route Molheimer's everywhere discarded and stained jockey shorts into Molheimer's laundry bag.

"I agree to your terms," Aldrich promised huskily. "Remember your pledge. I'll call you from Inglenook, Vermont, in less than fifty days."

"As you ride, Dwight David, think about truth," Jensen advised as the four moved toward the car.

"It's a nice gesture that old Dwight fell in love with the girl, but it's pretty obvious she didn't love him back or otherwise she'd be here with him right now," Doppenfuller said out loud to no one in particular when they were seated in the Oldsmobile.

Aldrich stood at the curb: "Shut up, Doppenfuller. I never liked you anyhow."

"Doppenfuller is a lucky mother," Doppenfuller judged as the car pulled away and headed down the street.

Fifty-six harrowing days later, having finally jettisoned the America Is Always Right! sign outside Manchester, Vermont, after being menaced into a ditch by a girl driving a pickup truck (Aldrich noted the frequency and intensity of abuse accelerated as he drew closer to New England), Aldrich pedaled up to the gates of Morgan Kingdom Farm in Shelburne beside the shimmering blue expanse of Lake Champlain.

Lydia and Stephen Hodges were to be married in three days. Immeasurably depressed at the astounding inhumanity he had encountered in his passage across half the Republic, certain he was powerless now to halt the union of the woman

he loved to the piddling poet that it seemed the whole world
had conspired for her to marry, Aldrich rode glumly onto the
twelve hundred acres of Danton Welsh, nodding to the horses
who eyed him severely over a fence, certain, no doubt, of who
he was and that he was an intruder. Halfway to the house, a
caterer's truck delivering tents and chairs almost ran him
down. A little further on he came upon Stephen Hodges
seated beneath a tree composing a poem.

"Dwight! I'm delighted to see you! So glad you could
make it! I'm composing a poem! These are exciting, heady
days!"

"I suppose," Aldrich half agreed and pedaled onward. In
the near distance where a gently sloping meadow came down
to meet the road, Lydia and Danton Welsh and Charlie Wishing Ten Fingers played a no-rules game of three-man polo
astride tall Morgan horses. Aldrich watched his beloved ride,
dazzled at the easy way she leaned far out of the saddle to
compensate for the shortness of the mallet. Laughing and
shrieking, her hair flying behind her in the wind, she drove
between her father and Charlie, who had collided then separated, and cornered the ball, whacking it downfield toward
Aldrich and the road. She charged after it before either of the
men had gotten their horses around and spied Aldrich about
halfway to the ball's new position: "Hey, look who's here! It's
old shithead Dwight!"

She forsook the ball, rushing right past it toward Aldrich,
a wolfish grin on her face and the mallet raised as if she
meant to clobber him. Aldrich sank to the ground, drawing
the bike on top of him in some witless parody of a defense as
the horse leaped over him and the mallet head whooshed by
inches from his ear. Lydia brought the mount up short behind
him, laughing delightedly as Charlie Wishing Ten Fingers, his
face a mask of concern, reined in his horse and jumped down
to help Aldrich to his feet.

"Dwight! Are you all right?"

"Yes . . . yes, I'm O.K., Charlie," Aldrich said shakily.

"Oh fuck it! I missed!" Lydia mourned.

"You really are getting pretty demonstrative about your antagonisms lately, aren't you, Lydia?" Charlie reproached her. "It doesn't sit well with your famous breeding at all."

"Is Mr. Aldrich all right?" It was Danton Welsh. He sat astride his horse looking down at Aldrich with a level curiosity but no real concern.

"I'm all right, sir, thank you."

"Thank God. Aldrich would really have the goods on us if he were to file suit for damages. Well, I suppose we've got to make Mr. Aldrich feel welcome. He might like a drink after riding all the way from Kansas on a bicycle. We didn't think you were going to make it. Whatever prompted you, by the way, to pedal all that distance out here?"

"It was the best way I could think of for proselytizing the greatest number of people for the Antiwar Movement, sir. I took the back roads and went through all the little towns with a big sign on the back of my bike that said 'End the War in Vietnam Now!' I think a lot of people got the message."

"That's very commendable, Dwight," Charlie congratulated him.

"I think it's dumb," Lydia said. "He could have worked an equivalent number of days and raised the dough to buy a full-page ad in some big paper out there in the boonies that would have reached millions of people."

"I agree with Lydia," her father spoke. "Grass-roots proselytizing can only work in a limited edition, on the statewide level for instance. When you're talking about half a country, it makes about as much an impact as mouse tracks on a snowfield. A waste of time."

Father and daughter had maneuvered their horses side by side and sat relaxed in the saddles, looking for all the world to Dwight David Aldrich of Abilene, Kansas, like the King and Queen of America. It frightened him a little that Danton Welsh, whose regal hauteur had been transferred completely intact to his daughter, disliked him so avidly. In riding boots and jodhpurs and a short-sleeved polo shirt, Danton Welsh had a hard, almost brutal body, very much in condition. The impression of his broad shoulders and thick, fiercely muscled arms was somehow stupefying to Aldrich, considering that Danton Welsh's real forte was the province of the mind.

"I guess I did waste a good amount of time, sir," Aldrich conceded.

"Yes. Good, Come now, let's go to the house and get Dwight that drink."

Charlie led his horse beside Aldrich, who walked his bike the last distance. Danton Welsh and his daughter followed behind. At the house, an old Cape with a wide deck attached to the front of it that overlooked Lake Champlain, Aldrich was introduced to Big Janie, Little Janie and Reverend Dickie.

Big Janie was a sad, wasted alcoholic who reminded Aldrich of his mother, who was not an alcoholic. He liked her and pitied her immediately.

Little Janie was indifferent to Aldrich and perpetually slighted by the fact that her sister Lydia was the sun about which Danton Welsh's universe obviously revolved.

Reverend Dickie was a fool, and less intelligent than Aldrich into the bargain.

"Dwight Aldrich can set up his tent over there in the pine grove," Danton Welsh said after his second bloody mary.

"But, Danton, we have room in the house for Mr. Aldrich," his wife told him.

"No, we don't, dear," Danton Welsh corrected her firmly.

CHAPTER 21

Aldrich's War Canoe

Charlie came to his tent that night to smoke a joint and tell him about the war canoe.

Since childhood, the war canoe was the shared romantic fantasy of Charlie Wishing Ten Fingers and Lydia Alexander Welsh. In the fantasy a great Mohawk chieftain, stark naked but for the wearing of a feathered war bonnet, sails down Lake Champlain standing on the bow of a huge light-man birchbark canoe and interrupts the marriage of Lydia Welsh to a white man in progress on the shore of the lake. The great chieftain extends his arms to Lydia, who immediately leaves the side of her betrothed and wades into the lake, Schiaparelli wedding gown and all, and is lifted into the canoe by the great chieftain with a convincing ease that suggests Lydia is levitating, she's so anxious to leave with the chief.

On shore, among the hundreds of wedding guests, the reactions vary. Some are amused, some genuinely confused, some are shocked at the chief's nakedness, others are impressed with his fabulously well-muscled build. Everybody wants to know if he comes from a good family. As the canoe is being turned about in preparation for returning the chieftain and his bride by fiat up the lake, individual reactions on shore become more demonstrative. The erstwhile groom walks maniacally about begging people to tell him what is happening. The Episcopal prelate, needing to sanctify something, conveniently changes horses and sanctifies the union of Lydia and the chief instead. Lydia's mother is vibrantly happy and applauding. Lydia's sister Little Janie is furious anew at Lydia's continuing ability to steal the show. Lydia's brother Reverend Dickie starts into the water to offer his jacket to the chieftain to cover some of his well-hung nakedness. Lydia's father, Danton Welsh, goes rigid and speechless with accumulated shock. That was the part that Aldrich liked best.

Very stoned, laughing uncontrollably at the notion of the wedding pre-empted, Aldrich rolled about the bed of pine needles in the grove where he had pitched his tent as Charlie sketched in the final scene of the wedding guests singing "Onward, Christian Soldiers" and waving after the canoe disappearing up the lake. The next morning Charlie borrowed Danton Welsh's Mercedes-Benz and drove Aldrich up the lake to St. Albans, where the war canoe was locked in a boathouse on the Mohawk reservation.

"Unfortunately, our people have lost the ancient art of making birchbark canoes," Charlie said sadly. He spoke the truth: The canoe, perhaps thirty feet long, was actually an amalgam of oil drums lashed together and planked over. Birchbark sheathing covered the sides to just below the waterline. An Evinrude outboard was camouflaged in the rear.

"It'll never work." Aldrich paid lip service to the impossible, fascinated by the real possibility that, Lydia being Lydia, it just might.

"Of course it'll work, Dwight David. It's the kind of enlightened caper that's absolutely our girl Lydia's bag. If she knew she was about the creation of a Lydia Welsh legend that would have Boston Brahmins shaking their heads for the next hundred years, she'd be here right now egging you on. Aldrich's war canoe can't miss picking up the right passenger. Guarantee it."

"Why are you doing this for me, Charlie? I've known you less than two months and you've become the best friend I've ever had."

"I told you before, Dwight. Lydia deserves better in life

than Stephen Hodges. It's a goddam shame that she'd end up marrying a nerd like Hodges just because she's been conditioned since childhood to think of him as her husband."

"Who will I get to paddle the canoe, Charlie?"

"I've got your wedding party all assembled, Dwight old boy. Eight fine strapping young Mohawks who realize you don't have time to bring any friends in from Nebraska and are eager to pinch-hit for you. You'll meet them here on the reservation on Friday night. They're throwing a kind of bachelor party for you."

Aldrich's bachelor party was a night-long orgy of war dancing at the end of which an exhausted Aldrich (Charlie had forced him to dance until the last drumbeat) was presented with a great war bonnet of eagle feathers that trailed all the way to the ground. He took the names and addresses of the eight paddlers, intending to send them something of a token gift afterward if the war canoe brought down its prize, and was somewhat astonished to learn that none of them actually lived on the reservation, that they had all come to Vermont at Charlie's behest, one of them from as far away as Seattle.

There was, on the starboard side of the canoe, in first position, Sybaritic Hawk, a cousin of Charlie Wishing Ten Fingers who held a master's degree in linguistics and worked high steel in Manhattan. He had once had a brief, memorable fling with Lydia Welsh, then turned to food for consolation when it was over and now weighed almost three hundred pounds. Behind him, in two position, was Dennis Fleeting Moon, eldest of Chief Aldrich's retainers, who was a used-car dealer in Montreal and married to the sister of a provincial policeman who had testified against his own brother-in-law in the matter of some fuzzy titles. In three position starboard was Malcolm Morris, who was a Seneca, not a Mohawk, and who was a friend of Charlie since they had served together in the Army. In last position was Edgar Drag-a-Leg, who walked with a limp and was bald because his hair had begun falling out in bunches one hot summer afternoon for no appreciable reason at all. He was a government engineer and the father of eight children and was the one who had flown all the way from Seattle.

On the port side in first position was Martin Rice, who called himself Spitting Chipmunk when there were Indians around to appreciate the name, and otherwise was known as Martin Rice when there were not, his name being the same as the line of high-fashion women's wear that he marketed in New York. In two position, port, was John Whistling Crow, who managed the Mohawk Benevolence Society treasury and was apparently a veritable wizard when it came to investment portfolios. Behind him was another John, this one John Lone Stag, who let it be known that he thought the Mohawks were putting themselves out a bit much for Aldrich and that he was only going along as a favor to Charlie. Last on the port side was Raymond Farr, a one-eyed professor of nuclear physics at Rensselaer Polytechnic who was kind and affable and puffed interminably on a very good briar pipe.

All of these Indians had shucked the veneer of civilization along with their clothes and were suitably feathered, war-painted and clad only in loincloths on Saturday morning, June 26th, when Dwight David Aldrich, embarrassingly bare naked except for the wearing of the war bonnet, his body greased and his face painted in a special wedding-day pattern that Charlie had researched at length, settled himself into the great canoe for the run down the lake courtesy of Evinrude to snatch the princess Lydia Welsh from the hands of her betrothed.

The morning was brilliant and clear, the sun reflecting in a thousand fractions off the surface of the deep, cold lake. Pleasure boats spotted their anomaly as it chugged past Burlington toward the farm at Shelburne and by the time they were in position to await the mirror signal from Charlie that the moment was right to charge landward with paddles flailing, they were being trailed by a curious armada of perhaps twenty vessels. In the bow of the canoe Aldrich fondled his penis covertly to make certain it would not look shrunken or affrighted when he stood up to reach out for his beloved.

Charlie flashed the mirror from the middle of the horde of wedding guests barely discerned at the edge of the lake. Raymond Farr opened the Evinrude to full throttle and encouraged the flailing of the paddles. Aldrich stood in the bow, approved of the limp swollen length of his penis, stretched out his arms toward the distant landscape of wedding guests, caterers' tents and the reflection from the burnished flanks of many automobiles, and gave himself up to Charlie Wishing Ten Fingers' fantasy, praying that Lydia Welsh was about to do the same. The armada of trailing pleasure craft came right along behind them, horns sounding in communal support of whatever was afoot.

Lydia was in the water before the war canoe could be completely halted. She extended her arms to be taken, sending a brief bolt of terror through Aldrich when she opened her eyes for the first time to see who was taking her.

"Oh shit, Aldrich! It would be you . . ."

"Isn't that Bernard Richmond from Baltimore?" an old dowager standing right at the shore asked an equally old man who stood beside her.

"No, I don't think so, dear."

"Hmm. It does look like him though. Nice family, those Richmonds."

Aldrich lifted his Lydia into the canoe, nearly falling into the lake from the effort, the quite sodden wedding gown increasing her weight by almost half again. They stood together arm in arm atop the planks that covered the barrels and waved to the wedding guests, who waved reflexively in return, staring at them almost to the very last person with dim myopic smiles except for Big Janie Welsh who jumped up and down clapping her hands, laughing and shrieking delightedly, Little Janie who scowled and stamped an angry footfall into the lawn, Reverend Dickie Welsh who was in the water up to

his neck imploring Aldrich to take his jacket and cover the nakedness of his loins, Danton Welsh who had gone bug-eyed
and rigid from shock and looked as if he were going to keel
over and die, Stephen Hodges who ran about maniacally begging people to tell him what was happening, and Charlie
Wishing Ten Fingers who had engineered the substitution
and wept the most incredible tears that Aldrich could ever
conceive running down the face of a grown man . . .

Raymond Farr put the Evinrude in reverse, backed them
up a bit with a convincing splash of paddles, then headed
them out through the flock of pleasure boats, whose passengers cheered them lustily, wishing them a long life.

In time, beyond the perimeter of the trailing boats,
Aldrich, suddenly feeling light-headed from the effect of all
the tension, sat down, dragging Lydia down beside him. He
felt not a little like crying himself and told her very tenderly:
"It will be wonderful, Lydia. Wait and see. I'll be a very good
husband to you."

But she was too excited for his tenderness, buoyant beyond belief. She slapped his shoulder hard with her fist that
she had been smashing into the open palm of her other hand.

"God Almighty, Dwight! Did you see the fucking look on
Daddy's face! He just about had a heart attack!"

And so they continued on up the lake to the Mohawk reservation at St. Albans and the aforementioned chaos of their
marriage.

PART THREE

Aldrich and Charlie
Wishing Ten Fingers and Danton
Welsh and Angelina Frippi and
Big Janie and Pasquale Mugiani
and, alas, Aunt Zebidiah

–Later, 1975

CHAPTER 22

The Scarlet Pimpernel

Meanwhile, back in North Hollow, in mid-May of 1975, Aldrich approached the final days of his penitential season, savoring the late Vermont spring.

The snows had all melted but for occasional corny patches beneath the rim of north-facing knolls and the white caps of the distant mountains to the south where it still continued to blanket the peaks at night and probably would until the beginning of June. Mud season was still on from the runoff of the final thaw, but it was not so bad this year as the five previous years of Aldrich's Vermont memory, and he had gotten stuck only twice and both times had been able to winch out the pickup on his own.

The geese had already flown north overhead in their great honking wedges making for the lakes of Canada. The scavenging raccoons and skunks were out of hibernation and scattering Aldrich's garbage nightly now. The blue jays and chickadees, sparrows, woodpeckers and grosbeaks chattered and chirped in the birches and evergreens and Aldrich saw with never-failing fascination that they had already begun their custom of strictly segregating themselves by species, the way they always did when the weather warmed and there was a plenitude of food. Their numbers were dwarfed however by a flock of swallows that showed up for the first time and chose to nest in the ruins of the Sangre de Cristo Mountains Recreation Center, which rested upside down and perfectly balanced on the muddy bottom of the dynamited lake—the pitch of its roof a wide wedge of a stabilizing spike—after Aldrich's destroyer, the Scarlet Pimpernel, had borrowed the Vermont Highway Department's Caterpillar yet another time and bulldozed the rec center off its perch on a long steep hill above the lake. It tumbled down to its new site, and, sterling testimony to Aldrich's designer skills, arrived absolutely intact but for the expected shattering of a few windows, though it was upended.

There was nothing left standing now but for the tennis pro shop where he lived. Besides the recreation center, the one other building that still survived at the time of Lydia's assassination was the Tahoe House, but that had gone up the night of April 1 in the biggest explosion Aldrich had ever seen that had driven the blunt end of a two-by-four stud right through the wall of the pro shop and rained burning pieces of debris down on its roof so that, for a minute of touch-and-go, until he could shovel enough snow up on the blazing tar paper, Aldrich almost lost the pro shop as well. Now the beautiful fields of wildflowers, clover and grasses waving in the soft breeze were treacherous underfoot from all the exposed and rusting nails, shattered glass and jagged plumbing pipe the force of the blast had littered everywhere. That night in a neatly typed letter tucked like a parking ticket under the wiper blade of his truck, Aldrich was told he would be meeting the Scarlet Pimpernel in short order.

Somehow he knew that Charlie Wishing Ten Fingers was his destroyer, the Scarlet Pimpernel (well, obviously!), before Charlie rode over the hill into North Hollow on an Appaloosa horse one blue-sky, cloudless day in the third week of May to assure him that it was so.

But then it had to be: In the anarchic context of Aldrich's world where the only constants were his mother's renewed, bitter disappointment in her only son (someone had delivered the Boston *Globe* to her little house in Abilene so that now she knew of Lydia's death, Aldrich's hitherto unacknowledged divorce, the demise of North Hollow, the Vermont Attorney General's investigations, his arrest and extradition to Boston, and much more that made up the awesome litany of Aldrich's abuses, shortchangings and omissions . . .) and Danton Welsh's unstinting malice, it was quite safe for Aldrich to assume that actual reality was the exact opposite of what it seemed that in the case of Dwight David Aldrich his avowed only friend should be the prime candidate for the determined and artful destroyer who styled himself the Scarlet Pimpernel. It made further sense: Love and hatred were invariably intertwined, Aldrich reminded himself, and whoever was having a go at North Hollow bore him no ordinary grudge, was in the grip of an unnatural passion for sure.

With that certainty to go on, that reality was a surefire distortion, that a friend had to be an enemy, and that, somewhat more realistically, he had eliminated the name of every other suspect on a pages-long list, Aldrich confronted Charlie Wishing Ten Fingers with his accusation in late March, more than a month after Lydia's burial. He drove from Vermont to the quarry in Saugus, Massachusetts, where Charlie still lived with Sybaritic Hawk, troubled all the while by the Scarlet Pimpernel's earlier revelation that it was he who had assassinated Lydia. That was the sticking point. For certain Charlie had loved Lydia. For the life of him, Aldrich could not fathom why he would want her dead.

In Saugus, in the foul-smelling tin-sided hut, his accusation cost Aldrich a tooth. Only it was not Charlie who struck him in reactive fury as he had at the time of Lydia's death. This time it was Sybaritic Hawk who lumbered like a rhino in full charge out of a corner where he had been sitting cross-legged and eating and pasted an unwary Aldrich right in the mouth. In another corner, totally unexpected, Charlie had dissolved into tears, shaking his head in disbelief at Aldrich, pleading speechless with his hands to know what prompted such madness. Sybaritic Hawk pushed Aldrich roughly to the floor, kicking him fiercely in the shins for good measure while

Aldrich struggled to keep from swallowing the tooth that dangled from a wisp of skin.

"You pig! You paranoid idiot!" Sybaritic Hawk screamed at him. "Charlie Wishing Ten Fingers is the best friend you ever had! You don't know half the holocausts he's saved you from! Apologize to him on your knees or I'll break your fucking jaw!"

Aldrich apologized on his knees with blood streaming out of his mouth to his one true friend, Charlie Wishing Ten Fingers, who was so stung by the charge that he could only continue shaking his head and uttering spasmodically: "Lydia . . . ? Me kill Lydia? I love . . . I loved Lydia!"

Crushed, convinced of his own madness from too much thoughtful time spent alone, Aldrich kissed Charlie's hand by way of contrition, bloodying it, then went himself weeping into the night, crunching across the gravel of the quarry floor, looking for the path that led up to the rim. Halfway up to the edge he heard the still angry voice of Sybaritic Hawk calling after him: "Hey, asshole, how was Charlie supposed to kill Lydia outside the church when he was a wedding guest inside? Answer that, paranoid dum-dum!"

The next day, gingerly spooning cottage cheese topped with spaghetti sauce into his aching mouth at lunch in an Italian restaurant in Boston's North End with Pasquale Mugiani, he told the cop gravely: "Yesterday I did just about the worst thing I could ever conceive of myself doing. I accused Charlie Wishing Ten Fingers of killing Lydia and destroying North Hollow."

"I could've told you that, asshole, and saved you a tooth. He's clean. He's practically Welsh family. A populist, too. I liked him. You find me another Harvard Law grad throwing around rivets on high steel and I'll turn in my badge. He's a good boy that Charlie . . ."

He was also a marvelous actor, Aldrich considered grimly as he watched the Scarlet Pimpernel ride into the wasteland he had created. Aldrich, who kept to the ridges these days for protection when he moved about his doomed acres and carried his Winchester with him everywhere, had the drop on Charlie. He sat above him, unseen, beside the gnarled trunk of a scrub pine that seemed to grow out of a solid-rock ledge. Below, in the meadow, Charlie's Appaloosa clopped along through knee-high grasses, its hooves sucking audibly at the mud in the low places.

Today, Charlie was dressed like a Plains Indian, a Kiowa or Sioux perhaps, in fringed, embroidered buckskins. Two feathers graced the long black hair hanging to his shoulders. Bright red paint had been applied about his eyes in the approximate pattern of a reveler's mask. He rode the horse bareback and the horse had concentric rings of black painted around its eyes. Charlie cradled a hunting rifle loosely against his stomach as he looked about everywhere for Aldrich. Aldrich thought of blowing his ass off the horse right then and there: The cheek of this Halloween freak who looked today like his fondest wish was to have stopped a cavalryman's bullet in the Indian wars about a hundred years back! The audacity of this silly over-educated Mohawk, this self-styled dispenser of his own warped justice in having so systematically destroyed Aldrich's great commercial venture! In having usurped his ultimate stung ex-husbandly prerogative in wasting Lydia before Aldrich could get properly around to it! Who the fuck did he think he was?

But then what could you expect from a half-breed? Aldrich snorted contemptuously. A rare dichotomous blood flowed in his veins, its parts ever warring, urbane gentility and a penchant for violence having at each other in primal struggle, confusing poor Charlie until look what it begot: A Harvard Law degree in Indian drag on a broken-down horse in the middle of Vermont looking for somebody to kill . . .

From his perch, watching the hunter's slow progress toward the pro shop, Aldrich's anger gave quickly way to ironic sadness: Down there was the man who proposed he was Aldrich's one true friend in life when Aldrich so desperately needed any one friend at all. Better resigned than bitter though: Aldrich had learned much in the six years since he had pedaled east out of Abilene, Kansas: All of existence was something like a melting snow bridge over a bottomless chasm. If it had not quite got to the point of collapse, at least it could be counted on to provide treacherous footing. Well, thought Aldrich, perhaps he ought to slide on down and ask Charlie why he had done all the things he had done to him and was looking to kill him into the bargain. He decided it would be nice to know before he rewarded Charlie for his perfidy.

"Hey, there! Hey, Scarlet Pimpernel!"

Aldrich stood and waved his rifle in the air and flashed Charlie a big wide grin when Charlie turned the horse about to face him. Charlie raised his rifle and pointed it at him in a quick reflexive motion, then dropped it after a long terrible moment when Aldrich thought he had just miscalculated and was going to die, and waved for Aldrich to come on down. Aldrich skidded down the slope to the floor of the meadow and began a cautious walk toward horse and rider. Charlie did not smile at his approach, so there was no joke evidently: Aldrich guessed that in his own mind the Mohawk was finally playing center stage after a thousand rehearsals of his imagination and had really gottten himself up for the Big Avenger from the Manitou role. Only he had miscalculated on the makeup. The red mask about the gray eyes made him look unaccountably sad like Bozo the Clown instead of fierce and glowering, and the black rings on the horse's face made it look cross-eyed. Aldrich began laughing a little and could not conceal it. He supposed yet another time that all his isolation had made him a bit daft.

"You're not playing this right, Dwight, old boy. The script doesn't call for irreverence."

"Sorry, Charlie. It's just that I've become something of an ironic person in the six years since I first bumped into you and Lydia. Why do I have to die?"

"Well, in the first place, Dwight, as a surrogate for Charlie Wishing Ten Fingers, you've obviously outlived your usefulness."

"I guess so. I must confess that it took me almost to this very month six years after the fact to figure out you didn't put me in that war canoe just because you liked me. Why didn't you just climb aboard yourself and break up the party the way I did. It would have made things easier all the way around."

"Wouldn't it have though?" Charlie sighed, looking off into the distance as if he could see an alternative chaos to the one he had engineered for Aldrich. "However, at the onset of puberty, I was required by Danton Welsh to swear literally on a stack of Bibles that I would never become romantically involved with Lydia, even though it seemed like the most natural possibility in the universe. Because Danton wanted that promise so intently and because I worshipped the ground he walked on, I said yes, and Hotchkiss, Darmouth and Harvard Law became the payoff. But I can tell you that little promise precipitated America's most tension-ridden platonic relationship. Nothing like it before or since. I just ached to lay a passionate hand on our girl Lydia. I almost did get into that canoe myself, but I was sure Danton Welsh would get around to shooting me for my trouble once he came out of shock."

"I seem to have heard an identical story of oath taking from another of the principals in our little set sometime back."

"Hmm. Lydia, perchance?"

"Yes, in the very same words, if I remember correctly. She used to have a standard sexual fantasy about you too that did the trick every time," Aldrich told him, the anger rising in him again at the memory. "Right at the moment of climax at home in bed with her husband D. D. Aldrich, she was fantasizing you galloping stark naked across a plain on an Appaloosa horse and swooping her up behind you to save her from some evil white-eyed motherfuckers . . ."

"But that was the same fantasy I had, Dwight," Charlie

said joyously, a look of childlike wonder come into the Bozo
the Clown eyes. He let the hunting rifle drop carelessly to his
side in his excitement and Aldrich saw shrewdly that the
safety was still on. "The exact fantasy! Except that in mine I
was fully clothed and she was naked because she was about to
be raped by the white eyes!"

"Not quite platonic, Charlie!" Aldrich said harshly. "It
seems your relationship was consummated on at least one
level, though neither one knew when the other was making an
advance and physically it was hermaphroditic all the way.
Tough one. But I guess I was brought in from the provinces
to buy you a little time, huh?"

"I'm afraid so, Dwight," Charlie agreed, weariness at the
recall in his voice. The rifle drooped still lower and Aldrich
was on the verge of asking Charlie if he wanted him to hold it
for him while he orated. "I admired your persistence and te-
nacity, all the Middle American bulldog determination. There
are some good things in you. But it was unsophisticated and
wouldn't sit well with the Welshes, who you came to realize
aren't particularly tolerant people, and after a while they'd
end up showing you the door because of that and because of
your predictable blunt assaults upon the Welsh treasury which
begot you the code name Attila the Hun among not a few
of the Welsh friends and acquaintances, who were point-
edly out everytime you phoned to make them a proposition.

"And as we know, all of this came true and bought me
the time I thought I needed, but to no avail, since that nerd
Hodges didn't move on and find himself another woman as I
hoped he would and leave me to rescue a very distraught
Lydia from the rubble of your marriage. Danton just kept
Hodges around on a leash for the interim and championed his
cause all the way.

"It broke my goddam heart to see the way he kept pushing that ineffectual rich fool at her! When I was sure your
marriage was a goner, I went to Danton and begged him for
permission to begin seeing Lydia, but he became furious and

told me I was never to speak of this again, that he was absolutely not having it. He told me what he told you on the day of her funeral: That she was a foolish girl who needed to be married to a rich husband, though he also allowed that her intended was indeed pretty much of a fool himself and that would work as the basis of their compatibility. I was to busy myself with concentrating on my career instead."

A wave of anger swept over Charlie and he smashed the gun butt down hard on the ground so that it jumped a little and he caught it in the air by the barrel, frightening the horse, which rolled its comic crossed eyes and stamped at the earth.

"Why has Danton done this to me?" Charlie pleaded with arms thrown open toward Aldrich, the rifle resting across his hiked-up thighs. "Why did he spend so much time trying to keep Lydia and me apart? How could he knowingly orchestrate the marriage of his daughter to an idiot?"

Aldrich looked at him very closely, saw the broad shoulders and thick arms, the powerful legs that gripped the nag horse's bony flanks, and decided he was absolutely certain now of the reason for the first time, something he had only speculated on in the past. But then what was the point of telling Charlie he had had his own half sister Lydia killed? That Danton Welsh railed against their union because the law simply would not permit it?"

"Who killed Lydia, Charlie?"

"A Mohawk." Charlie smiled enigmatically at him. "Everyone thought the shot came from the belfry of a Catholic church across the street. But it came from a long way off where the guy was working high steel."

"Is it fair to ask why?"

"I wasn't going through all that again, Dwight David. If I couldn't have her, neither could Stephen Hodges. And because after that there wouldn't be another chance. Our Lydia was already settling down a little by then after she combed the snarls out of her hair from you. Hodges would have become a familiar convenience, there'd be children, she'd finally consolidate all those far-flung energies of hers into getting herself elected governor of Vermont, and that would be it happily ever after. . . . Any other questions?"

"Why did you set about destroying North Hollow on me?"

"In small part to avenge the commune's labor you stole. That business of going down to the Big Apple to harass the right-wingers on the World Trade Center construction was pretty deplorable as far as I was concerned, but then the ruthless calculation in you that swept the decks and erased the ledger entries by calling in the feds was worse. Most of all, though, North Hollow offended every aesthetic fiber in me. It was awful, Dwight David. Aggressively ugly. Even in ruins it represents a big burp in Nature's digestion for a century to come. The time has arrived to begin redressing the rape of Vermont. You'll thank me for this destruction in another life."

"I have sinned and I am to die for it," Aldrich pronounced in mock repentance even though he knew damn well it was Charlie who was going to die. "Don't you consider for a moment it's sort of arch of you to set yourself up as executioner?"

"No. I've thought on it for a long while. There are all sorts of precedents and philosophical propositions to cover this, Dwight David. Do you know the writings of Protagoras, the early Sophist? Or of Plato in the *Laws*? No? Well, I didn't really expect so, but let me assure you this forthcoming death of yours is no dumb retribution. Protagoras says it all: 'He who desires to inflict rational punishment does not retaliate for a past wrong which cannot be undone. He has regard to the future, and is desirous that the man who is punished may be deterred from doing wrong again. He punishes for the sake of prevention. . . .' That's it in a nutshell, Dwight old boy. It's for the sins you've yet to commit that you've got to die. I know damn straight you intend to blackmail Danton Welsh because you've found out about Angelina Frippi. I can't allow that to happen. After the mess he's got with Big Janie, he deserves a little something better in life. Look at all the good he's doing for young Angelina. She's become an incredible lady. Danton has seen to everything."

Standing there before the guillotine, Aldrich was not beyond marveling at the way in which an intellectual prepared to take his kill. Protagoras and Plato, an agreeable theory of righteous dispatch, but not an iota of proper instinct or cunning for miles around. If there was any caution it consisted in leaving Kant and Hegel and Thomas Aquinas and other bedfellows of Charlie and Danton Welsh at home for this one. But Aldrich was not having any of it: If Charlie insisted Aldrich needed killing, he was damn well going to come down to Aldrich's level to try it: "You're a dumb asshole, Charlie. A dumb asshole with blinders. Big Janie is in the mess she is today because Danton Welsh put her there. And Danton Welsh ought to be in jail because of Angelina Frippi. She's fifteen years old. He's a pervert."

"I won't listen to this kind of talk, Aldrich. He may have been recalcitrant with me in the matter of Lydia, but Danton Welsh has been like a father to me in every other way . . ."

"He *is* your father, asshole," Aldrich told him quietly as he raised the Winchester and squeezed off a shot that left a neat wide hole right through Charlie's heart. Charlie's shock had no equal in recorded history, Aldrich speculated. The Mohawk toppled from the Appaloosa nag and fell spread-eagle into the crisp Vermont meadow. He was quite conclusively dead.

"I've suffered not a little bit at the hands of you eastern folk," Aldrich spoke out loud to the body as the echo of the gunshot reverberated about the North Hollow hills.

"But then, look which of us Americans is the lone survivor after all . . ."

Then, impulsively, a vestigial remnant perhaps of some homesteading ancestor's blood flowing in his veins, he gave the dead Mohawk body a good swift kick in the ass.

CHAPTER 23

Charlie's War Canoe

Aldrich consigned Charlie to one of the corny snow patches beneath the northward-facing knolls to keep him cool until he could figure out what to do with the body.

After two days he phoned Danton Welsh to persuade him to quit Massachusetts for his farm at Shelburne, Vermont, to bear witness to a fantastic and symbolic event that would occur about a hundred yards offshore just twenty-four hours hence, and knew from the sound of the other's voice that Danton Welsh would not fail to be there, watching. He also phoned Pasquale Mugiani, detective of Boston, to inform him he was about to score on Danton Welsh by way of Angelina Frippi, and resignedly conceded 10 percent for the services of that worthy who would drive up the next day from Boston to North Hollow to collect.

Early next morning, Aldrich dumped Charlie's body into the back of the pickup truck and drove to the Mohawk reservation at St. Albans where the war canoe was still moored in the boathouse. He placed Charlie squarely amidships, face up, crossed his arms over his chest and bound him to the floor planking with heavy wire, then began covering over the body except for the head with lots of free-standing fieldstone he took from the boathouse foundations until the oil-barrel substructure was nearly awash and the birchbark sheathing of the sides had splayed out and floated nearly horizontal on the waters.

Aldrich stole a rowboat with a Johnson outboard and a full tank of gas and started towing the funeral ship out of the boathouse. The day had dawned grudging and perfect for anyone's burial, overcast and drizzling, with blankets of heavy mist rolling right down to the water on the Vermont and New York State shores. Dripping wet and abysmally sad at his task, Aldrich sat in the stern of the rowboat trying to coax a little more speed from the outboard that inched its heavy tow down Lake Champlain past the vague shrouded outline of Burlington toward Danton Welsh's farm at Shelburne.

There were no other boats to be seen, and Aldrich, unconcerned about a collision, spent most of the time staring rearward across Charlie's fieldstone shroud at the Mohawk's face that was uncharacteristically relaxed in death, the normal tautness of its high cheek planes—that had always made Aldrich leery of a barely controlled rage within—dissolved and realigned in peaceful composure just shy of a smile that suggested Charlie had finally arrived at a place he had been looking for all along. Charlie's eyes were wide open because Aldrich had forgotten to close them two days before and rainwater trickled from his forehead and down both sides of the bridge of his nose and coursed out the corners of his eyes like tears that Aldrich preferred to think of as joyful. His skin (certain proof of the truth of Lydia's tauntings) was shades lighter in death than in life as if the emission of body fluids had carried off the color of the dye; the brilliantine black of Charlie's hair was less pronounced also—though not yet enough to tell its original color—and explained to a momentarily mystified Aldrich the black stains about the head in the locker of corn snow when he went to retrieve the body that morning for the trip to the lake. Charlie looked very much like a white man on the day of his final voyage to the Manitou. He looked very much the son of Danton Welsh.

Aldrich wiped tears from his own eyes now. Some tears were self-pitying for sure, because that was a hard habit to break, even if irony had become the stronger habit by far in recent years. For certain though, the little bitch godling that had been throwing the switches on the main line of Dwight David Aldrich's progress through life since his first encounter with Lydia, Charlie and Stephen Hodges had not yet called it a day. See Aldrich now, a Charon from Abilene, a Stygian ferryman putt-putting through the eerie mists down the course of Champlain to consign yet another one to the cold watery depths. Ghastly work. Doubtless, from the shore, from behind the gnarled trunks of fog-blotted trees, the ghosts of the antecedent dead of history or accident who littered the bottom watched the progress of the new arrival. The excellence of the East (and Aldrich still believed in the East's excellence despite its rough handling of him . . .) derived in large measure from all that hallowed past, and Champlain was a veritable treasure trove of it. Charlie buried thus in distant Kansas would be brother to naught but the singing wind for all eternity; here, he would not want for community: Down there were the squabbling dead of Mohawk and Seneca raiding parties, British and French adventurers and soldiers and their respective Algonquin and Iroquois allies, Ethan Allen boys from the Revolution, American sailors from the 1812 War, and more recently drovers whose teams had plunged through the winter ice, inebriated smelt fishermen who had melted their way through, pilots whose Cessnas and Apaches had missed the landing lights at Burlington and Plattsburgh . . . Hordes of the dead there must be down there: Well, move over and make way for my one true friend Charlie Wishing Ten Fingers who is on his way down.

Aldrich's other tears were of course for Charlie. He had loved Charlie after a fashion, he supposed, within the possible limits of the duplicitous world he inhabited, created in part by his own terror and his reaction to Danton Welsh's hard malice. He would even miss him, though he guessed there would not have been much future in their relationship if Charlie had been permitted to live, given the Mohawk's admission of the surrogate use he had put Aldrich to. That smarted, for Aldrich still possessed deep wrinkles of an ancient pride.

Mostly, though, he pitied Charlie. After today, after Charlie was laid to rest and Aldrich was done fleecing Danton Welsh for whatever the trade would bear to preserve the secret of the barrister's enlightened perversion with Angelina Frippi, the curtain would, for Aldrich's purposes, come ringing down on The Fascinating and Capricious Progress of Lydia Alexandra Welsh Through Worshipful Men, some theater of the absurd that had been playing nonstop for about six years to a select Boston audience. Its resolution was rather obvious, Aldrich thought, its characters poignantly identifiable. Danton Welsh, for goddam sure, was the villain of the piece. Lydia Welsh, intended as heroine, had no compelling depth to her, and ended up a burned-out hummingbird whose wings gave up from too much flitting about. Dwight David Aldrich, though about to be the victim, became the protagonist and lone important survivor instead. Tested, strengthened, made wise and cunning in New England ways, he was already preparing to star in a new opening wherein the same protagonist conclusively knocks the world at large on its ass. Charlie Wishing Ten Fingers then was the real victim, a confounding turnabout for many in the audience since he seemed possessed of all the heroic proportions at the onset. A pitiable, pitiable character indeed, well worth Aldrich's tears: To be so naturally intended for the girl as the girl was intended for him, yet neither one allowed to know the secret of the other one's heart: To find out on the instant of his death exactly who and what he was when he had spent an earnest thirty years until that instant convinced he was entirely something else again, whooping it up as an Indian on Life's greatest playground when he had been pretty much one of the cowboys all along: Then, the clincher of all time, to have been sired by Danton Welsh of all possible donors! It positively rent the heart to consider such unfair parceling of the gifts. . . .

Nearing Shelburne, spent with sorrowing, Aldrich left off

gazing upon the dead one and scanned the shore for Danton Welsh, at the same time firing up his hatred of the villain anew in preparation for the shakedown. When he saw Charlie's father standing bareheaded in the drizzle in his favorite shapeless old raincoat before a clump of tall budding birches, Aldrich cut the outboard motor, letting the rowboat drift momentarily until it was brought up short by the near dead-weight of the funeral canoe. On shore Danton Welsh stood defiant from habit, hands to his hips, disdaining to use the binoculars slung about his neck, an unthinkable admission of the very faulty prowess of his eyes. Out on the lake, at that distance, Aldrich knew he had to be a vague blur, barely discerned, so he stood up in the rowboat, cupping his hands, and hollered shoreward: "Better stash the overweening pride today, Danton, and use the binoculars! I wouldn't miss this if I were you!"

Charlie's father raised the binoculars, took a long moment's look, then abruptly staggered backward against one of the birches, groping it with his hand for support: "Aldrich . . . ! Oh my God, Aldrich! What have you done to my Charlie?"

"Put him out of his fucking misery, some folks would say!"

Aldrich drew the rowboat close to the war canoe, stepped off onto the planking of the canoe that was already covered with an inch of water, and then clambered back into the rowboat after he had finished hacking at the war canoe's barrels with an ax and the water was up to his knees and Charlie was decidedly descending. Aldrich waved goodbye to him, forgoing any blessing, catching a last glimpse of the dead one's handsome face beneath the water until the long hair surged up from both sides of the head on the current and covered it over. Danton Welsh had once remarked that the lake was about three hundred feet deep thereabouts.

Aldrich then went quickly ashore to talk business with his ex-father-in-law who was crying softly into the bark of his supporting birch.

"Charlie was my son, you know, Aldrich."

"Yes, I knew. Charlie himself knew for all of about a split second, I guess. He was very surprised to find out about it. Too bad you didn't think to acknowledge him somewhere along the line."

"His mother was a fantastic beauty. Her name was Fledgling Sparrow. My time with her was a moment of profound and unstinting love, passion unequaled in history. She was a chieftain's daughter."

"Well then, at least she came from a good family. What was her head like? Could she pitch a no-hitter against Emily Dickinson?"

"She died some years back, though . . ."

"She died of uremia," Aldrich reminded him, wringing the water from the legs of his jeans. "Precipitated by massive drinking."

"What was one to do?" Danton Welsh shrugged, wiping his eyes, then neatly folding his handkerchief to show his grief was concluded. "Big Janie had—and still has—our money. She can't be displaced. Charlie's mother disappeared along with God knows how many other things into the maelstrom of the monumental lie about my past that became the certainty of my future. I'm a phony, Aldrich. Like yourself I come from the sod out in Kansas. But then, you knew that."

It was Aldrich's turn to shrug: "I knew it, Danton. But in the last analysis, I wonder if anyone really gives a rat's ass about it?"

"They did then. Back in those Harvard days of eating clubs and inherited disdain they did indeed give a rat's ass about it. The need to compete on something of a halfway equal footing with blooded Easterners became an obsession for me. I grew terrified of my lying. I even kept an index-card file of current stories to refresh my memory when I thought I had gotten a bit out of line at cocktail parties. But nothing I ever told rivaled some of those goodies you laid on us when you first pedaled out here on your bicycle, friend Aldrich . . ."

Danton Welsh had gone from crying to laughing in a trice and Aldrich calmly struck back: "I thought you should know, Danton, that it was your son Charlie who killed your daughter Lydia. It wasn't any of those disgruntled freaks from the commune who did it."

"Charlie did? Why? Why did my Charlie kill my Lydia?"

"Just another isolated case of feeling like an outsider. Except that he took some elaborate pains to get even. I won't even mention some of the hell he put me through, including trying to kill me, for which he lies moldering on the bottom out there today. It was a clear-cut case of self-defense, by the way."

The news had found its mark in Danton Welsh's target of last refuge: He was bug-eyed now, convinced of its truth, completely out of character when his normal recourse was to receive the bearer of bad tidings with squinting suspicion. He began crying furiously, the patrician's mien fled and gone, tears roaring down the furrows of his cheeks: "They couldn't marry, Aldrich. It was out of the question. Dear God, I don't know which of them I loved more! What irony! What perfect irony! Talk about the punishment being made to fit the crime! To have the two primal offspring of a life of unscrupulousness and deception such as mine has been end up by canceling each other out . . . Irony did I say? Justice is what I'm sure I mean. A justice I could have conjured up when I was demanding that awed juries give generously of that abstraction and set free some of that murdering, raping scum I specialized in defending because of what the notoriety of getting them sprung would do for my career . . . See how I'm being punished, Aldrich?"

Danton Welsh threw wide his arms, looking tearfully up and down the length of himself, inviting Aldrich to survey the pitiable wreck of a beaten man perhaps. But it was no good: The wreck was still Danton Welsh who looked like a Brahmin prince even if he had been born a Cornhusker. The body was still the wondrously hard and powerful body and the face, even though cosmetized for the moment by tears, did not seem an iota less menacing to Aldrich than any other time he had fallen under that arch gaze.

"Do you believe in God, Aldrich?"

"No. Not since I left Kansas."

"Not at all? Not one little remembrance of the hinterland's Jesus in that cretinous Baptist breast of yours? Wouldn't you kneel with me here in this place to pray for the dearly departed Lydia and Charlie? To pray for the union of their spirits in the Hereafter?"

"No. I wouldn't kneel with you anywhere. It might be a trick. And after all those two did to help fuck up my life I have no intention of praying for the union of their spirits down here, up there or anywhere. You shouldn't either, Danton. You don't realize what you're praying for. If they ever got together in the Hereafter without you around with your checks and balances, you can bet your sweet ass their relationship wouldn't be platonic any longer."

"Jesus, Aldrich, you make a piddling Christian, you do! And you've got a sodbuster's penchant for the precisely literal. What a cheap shot. What I'm asking you to pray for is only a comforting illusion, after all. Religion is comforting at times like this, you know. That's why we keep it about."

The floodgates of Danton Welsh's mourning(?), self-pitying(?) tears opened up again and he dropped like a shot to his knees on the carpet of wet rotting leaves, hands clasped against his binoculars in an attitude of prayer. Aldrich watched fascinated as his body lurched into a rhythmical swaying motion, his head bobbing loosely on the fulcrum of his neck, like someone entering upon a trance state. Words and phrases, a gift of tongues, disjointed and largely unintelligible except for the names of Charlie, Lydia and Jesus came out of him in a rising crescendo until he flung off the binoculars against a tree and advanced to the full-blown theatrics of rolling about full-length on the ground, heaping himself with handfuls of the wet moldering leaves, then rubbing more handfuls of the decaying humus beneath the leaves over his face and even shoving some of it into his mouth, sputtering it back out mixed with ominous rantings about sin, the sinner and damnation: Happily at home again in the earthier clay of prairie fundamentalism, evidently. As Aldrich watched he flipped over on his back and began an uncoordinated rotating of his arms and legs in a mindless parody of an upended turtle. A manic delirium graced the soiled face that in Aldrich's memory had only ever managed the most condescending of tight-lipped smiles. Aldrich did not approve of his enemy thus. He grew frightened that the Commonwealth of Massachusetts' outstanding moral bully had just irreversibly crossed some expanse of ethical salt flats on a horse too lame to return to become an actual moralist, eschewing calculation and avarice, that he had just renounced his liaison with Angelina Frippi and snatched the trump card right out of Aldrich's deck.

Aldrich reached down and flipped him over on his belly, kicking Danton Welsh squarely in the ass as he had done his dead son Charlie two days before. The shock seemed to work: Danton Welsh went rigid again, perhaps with the recall of what he was supposed to be. He shook his head as if to rid it of the Christian hobgoblins that had briefly gotten loose in there. Then he looked up and scowled in the reassuring old way at Aldrich: "Thank you, Aldrich. I needed that."

"You've got to pull yourself together, Danton. You've got a responsibility to a lot of people to continue acting like the archetypal monster you've turned yourself into. Your grief should be stoic. None of this hyphenated American hair tear-see of her."

ing. If she'd been here, Emily Dickinson would have walked out on that scene, and that would've been the last you'd ever

"Shut up, Aldrich. And do forgive me. I don't know what got into me."

Danton Welsh stood up and walked to the edge of the

lake, knelt down and splashed water on his face to wash away the grime, then returned wiping himself dry with the lining of his raincoat. He retrieved the flung-away binoculars, seemed pleased that they were evidently not damaged, then confronted Aldrich head on: "I suppose now is the time you've chosen to play that ace you threatened me with the day we buried Lydia?"

Aldrich touched a hand to his notched ear, remembering the day they buried Lydia, then got down to business. He pulled out his wallet and fished out the photo of young Angelina Frippi that Mugiani the detective had given him and held it up before Danton Welsh.

"I love her, Aldrich," the great civil libertarian lawyer said simply.

"That very nice, Danton. She's quite pretty. Since I'm new to the business of blackmail, I'll just have to ask this question in the crudest of fashion, but what's it worth to you that I don't go to Big Janie with this photo and a couple of others I can produce and give her the wherewithal to get that divorce from you on grounds of adultery and cradle robbing that she hasn't been able to substantiate so far?"

Danton Welsh smiled a tight rueful smile: "How did you come by that photo, Aldrich? Who knows about my Angelina when I was certain no one knew?"

"Pasquale Mugiani. A more or less honest cop."

"Ah me," Danton Welsh sighed. "What crosses we bear. Detective Pasquale Mugiani, recorded history's only inscrutable Italian, and he has to be my enemy. What cursed luck! Well, what are you asking, Aldrich?"

The lawyer in Danton Welsh surfaced and he grew cagey and narrowed his eyes at his adversary and doubtless wondered if Lydia had dropped any specifics about the Breckenridge trust to Aldrich during their dalliance together in marriage: "We aren't talking about as much dough as went to the bottom with the *Titanic,* after all."

"A hundred thousand cash up front right now, and thirty

thou a year tax-free for ten years, and the title to your Mercedes," Aldrich told him.

"I agree to your terms," Danton Welsh said perfunctorily and Aldrich knew sadly he had just underbid. Still, the money and the car could not help but improve his image: He thought of driving home to Kansas and overwhelming his mother, who had last seen him pedaling off on a bicycle. He thought also of his forthcoming meeting with the Abbé Gaston and the two wayfarers at the inn in Manchester on the night of the anniversary of Nixon's resignation when they would formally acknowledge with drinks the end of Aldrich's penitential season. This time, at least, he could afford to buy the drinks.

"This is the last we're going to see of you, isn't it, Aldrich? These six years since you intruded yourself upon our elitist little kingdom in New England have scored themselves somewhat indelibly upon my memory. I must be about the business of repressing and erasing and it would be quite helpful if I never had to lay eyes upon you again. Though I couldn't possibly imagine what further carnage you might precipitate in my life unless you managed to run over Reverend Dickie with your new Mercedes on your way off the place today . . ."

"I don't intend doing you any favors, Danton. If you want Dickie wasted, get some of the criminal scum to do it the next time you get one of them sprung in the face of Mugiani's airtight case."

"Wasted? Is that how it seemed to you? Hmm. I've got to guard against wishful thinking, or its intimation at least, haven't I? But my God, you've got to admit the leavings of the Welsh dynasty aren't exactly what anyone would've planned for it. Let's hope Dickie gets a parish in Samoa or some place like that and never comes back. And Little Janie . . . well, irony compounds itself sometimes, does it not, Aldrich? Despite what you think, I am an avowed civil rights proponent who wants a fair shake for the blacks in America. It's just that I can't stand them socially, and now I'm facing the very real prospect of a black son-in-law and mulatto grandchildren . . . well, at least he's a Harvard man and Janie says the family is pretty decent. . . . I must work very hard to make Angelina perfect. She's really all I've got left."

"She'll leave you someday, Danton."

"I don't doubt it, Aldrich. But it will be later rather than sooner and she'll have given me much pleasure by that time. It will give me even more pleasure afterward to know she's happily married to the right young man."

Danton Welsh's face grew uncharacteristically beatific as he stared out over the lake through the slackening drizzle, thinking certainly of young and beautiful Angelina Frippi whom he loved. Despite himself Aldrich was touched at the notion of such a gentle solicitude in his enemy: "You redeem yourself selectively, Danton. It's too bad you can't go the whole man."

"Proper selectivity is the most important virtue in man, Aldrich. Knowing how much, what for and who. In your case I deplore your existence in its entirety and that suits me fine, but I can isolate parts of your aggregate that I'm even a little fond of. Your incredible tenaciousness and determination, for example. Your survival instincts. Your intelligence. Your native intelligence, I mean, not your esoteric intelligence, since I remember well you couldn't make a spitball fly in either of my two brain-twister parlors. But I do like these things about you, even if they are all so basic. One wonders what I might have done for you if you hadn't incurred my eternal wrath by spiriting my flighty Lydia away in that war canoe and fouling my plan to have her marry Hodges. I would have rewarded you for losing, Aldrich. I intended to. I would have taken you under my wing, veneered you over a bit, introduced you to the right sort of contacts who might appreciate that eclectic obfuscation you specialize in designing . . . who knows but that you'd be able to buy your own Mercedes by now instead of ripping me off for one . . . ?"

"Buying it wouldn't give me half as much satisfaction as

taking it away from you, Danton. It's a symbolic getting even. But then what can you expect from a person with such a proliferation of base qualities as mine?"

"Nothing like a charitable gesture, I suppose. That would be too much." Danton Welsh sighed deeply, then began walking in the direction of the house, Aldrich falling into step beside him. They were silent for a long moment during which Aldrich heard the quickening of his enemy's breathing and knew he was fuming inside and that a pronouncement was on its way: "My God, Aldrich, yours is a fucked-up generation! The worst American generation ever. The least fulfilled. Nothing that came before and nothing likely to come after could so abuse its ability to force changes in this country. Never was there a generation so educated and aware, with so much potential to take the government and make it dance to the people's tune, to put the boots on the military-industrialists, to bring the blacks and Indians and Chicanos and other minorities into the mainstream of American life . . . But, what's the use of talking? Look what happened. All the activists just threw in the towel in defeat when that man Nixon got a second-term headlock on the country and retreated indoors to tend their houseplants or got themselves snuffed out like Lydia and Charlie for having apparently exceeded the limits of personal indulgence . . .

"And behold the surviving triumphant!" Danton Welsh gestured disdainfully at Aldrich. "A closet reactionary who spent the late sixties, early seventies era of turbulence playacting in the company of radical ideologists and utopian zealots and cannily survived the experience with all his old beliefs intact and even prospered because of it, so that to some people it must look like you were right all along. . . . Therein lies your real strength, Aldrich. Your ability to successfully resist change, to withstand being seduced by a new ideal so that you never have to pay the price of growing disillusioned over it. . . . Christ! The Antiwar Coalition, the New Reformers, the SDSers and the McCarthyites . . . Where are they all now, Aldrich?"

"They all grew up and became taxpayers as was intended. That privilege prompts a decidedly less hypothetical view of the nature of government."

"Rubbish. Cowards. They've all settled for macrobiotic foods and wine tasting. Ralph Nader is one of the only ones out there with any balls today."

"I hate Ralph Nader," Aldrich spat.

But Danton Welsh seemed not to hear. They sloshed through the carpet of wet leaves on the long wide avenue of meadow between rows of towering firs that led up to the house. Aldrich's enemy took out a handkerchief and blew his nose, then stopped and turned to gaze another long moment out on the lake: "Charlie and Lydia both dead now. . . . They both seemed somehow larger than life to me. I mean with their handsomeness and intelligence, their vital energy and presence. . . . They had an inordinate share of the gifts, I think! I really must be about publicizing their memory. They might become symbols of their generation's vibrant courage in the way that Janis Joplin is its tragic symbol . . ."

Aldrich stared across the lake to the hazy outline of the Adirondacks and enjoyed an instant vision of vibrant, shining Charlie and Lydia hand in hand stomping along in seven-league boots. Then he remembered and snorted his contempt: "Are you losing your goddam mind in your old age, Danton? They were lousy people! They were elitist snobs who only thought of others in terms of their utility!"

"They were my children." Danton Welsh smiled the tight patrician smile at him. "They were selective people as I had taught them to be selective. And they made you love them until they no longer had any use for your love. The knowledge of that shafting will suffice for my getting even, albeit nonsymbolic, in this affair. Come, Aldrich, let's go make arrangements for your lucre and be off with you."

They went to the house and drew up a contract and the

caretaker and his wife witnessed the signing. When they were gone Aldrich and his ex-father-in-law burned the photo of Angelina Frippi in the fireplace. Then Danton Welsh handed over the title and keys to his lovely gray Mercedes, said he was going outside to think about Charlie who lay on the bottom of the lake, and invited Aldrich to stay and pour himself a congratulatory drink. He did and sat luxuriating in the cushions of a sofa he had not sat upon for six long years. Big Janie, who had overheard a good deal of the agreement through a heating vent that passed into her upstairs bedroom, wobbled in and freshened her drink. Aldrich winced at the awful sight of her.

"What'd you skin him for, Dwight?"

He told her, convulsed by the realization that his deal with Danton Welsh had just died if she knew of the existence of Angelina Frippi.

"Thas good, Dwight. You shoulda got him for more. I like seein' old Danton bleed, 'n he'll bleed 'cause he'll have to pay you outta his own money. He's too smart to go near the trust for this one."

"But now you have the ammunition to divorce him, Big Janie. The deal is still dead for me."

"Don't worry, Dwight, I always like you. We needed your kinda blood in the family, but Danton wanted a Pilgrim, not a sodbuster. I wouldn't queer your deal for you! I know 'bout little Evangelina for more than two years now. I hired detectives to find out 'bout her. But I don't want a divorce anymore. I'm too ruined 'n tired for that. Enjoy your dough, Dwight. You're only collectin' damages anyhow, is all."

He watched as she poured half a glass of straight gin, holding the bottle with two trembling hands.

"Charlie's dead, Big Janie," he told her for no reason he could think of.

"Whish Charlie?"

"Charlie Wishing Ten Fingers."

"Danton know, Dwight?"

"Yes."

"What a harvest for ole Danton. Whew. First his daughter, now his son . . ."

She staggered slightly, grasping the sideboard where the liquor was kept for support, then hiccupped and smiled at him with glazed eyes.

"How long have you known that, Big Janie, that Charlie was his son? I only just found out for sure."

"Charlie's mother tole me years ago when she hit the bottle so bad. Danton deny everything on a stack of Bibles. But then I see him take all this interest in Charlie when Charlie jus' a kid, 'n I know for sure then. Charlie's mother die from drink. All Danton's women take to drink . . ."

Aldrich stood, wanting to flee the object of his immense pity who stared a moment at herself in a wall mirror near the sideboard, then turned disgustedly away from the image.

"I've got to leave now, Big Janie," Aldrich told his ex-mother-in-law, pecking at her cheek on the way out. She grabbed him tightly with one arm to hug him, but he was able to break away.

"Too bad you not a Pilgrim, Dwight," she called after him. "Then you could marry Lydia as a equal, 'n slap some sense into that silly bitch . . ."

But Aldrich had already left the house. He climbed into the Mercedes and drove home to North Hollow, well content.

CHAPTER 24

The Real Victim
of This Piece

Like an augury, to Aldrich's mind, the drizzle quit, the haze
began lifting and the mid-afternoon sun appeared triumphant
toward the west, dazzling his eyes with reflection from the
brilliant waving carpets of wildflowers in the meadows as he
sped jubilantly home to North Hollow in the beautiful prize
he had wrested from Danton Welsh. At North Hollow he
sounded his horn repeatedly on sighting the unobtrusive gray
sedan with Massachusetts plates that must belong to Mugiani
the detective.

He pulled up before the pro hut looking eagerly everywhere for his co-conspirator and was instantly annoyed instead at the sight of his Great-aunt Zebidiah, who sat outside
in the sun at a table, feasting from casserole dishes of pasta
Mugiani had evidently brought with him, and snorting wine
straight from a wickered Chianti bottle.

"Where's the guy that brought all this, Zebidiah? Did he
go for a polite walk because he couldn't stand the sight of you
chowing down like you haven't eaten in a year?"

"He's dead," Zebidiah told him quietly, not missing a
spoonful of the lasagna.

"What do you mean, dead?"

"Look in your little house, Dwight David. Ex-orderly
Stanton can't jilt me one day, then turn around and ply me
with gifts of Eye-talian food the next. I won't stand for it!"

"Oh no," Aldrich moaned, looking in the doorway to the pro hut and seeing Pasquale Mugiani lying there, his eyes bug wide open and a leaking little hole in his forehead that could only have come from Zebidiah's Derringer.

"Zebidiah, you just killed a cop."

"He didn't feel a thing, Dwight David. Promise."

"Oh no. Oh my God, no. Why? Why now when I'm just coming out of the woods?" Aldrich implored the blazing orb of sun. He felt a sudden crushing weariness, defeat actually, and could think of nothing more to do than stretching out on the hood of the Mercedes that was warm from the sun and the heat of the engine. He thought of irony because his mind could no longer manage the comforting proliferation of alternatives it had always spawned in the past at the onset of crisis. There were no alternatives to this last straw: Too much death had bedraggled Aldrich's recent sputtering progress through life. The Boston police would not settle for a loony old spinster great-aunt, certified incompetent to stand trial, in payment for the life of their brother Mugiani. Danton Welsh would accuse him of having murdered Charlie, whose body could be dredged up from the bottom of Champlain. The assassination of Lydia was still unsolved. . . . Aldrich groaned at the forthcoming perfect solution after tireless police work to three distinctly related murders: New England might sleep better now from knowing that Dwight David Aldrich, an outlander from Kansas and accused psychopathic killer, was penned up awaiting trial without bail in a Massachusetts prison. He would not get off, either: Danton Welsh, who liberated actual murderers, would be flogging the chief prosecutor from behind this time, urging him furiously to his task.

Hey, Mother of mine! See your fair-haired only hope of a son right now! Trussed and tied and ready for branding! Oh, how it smote the heart to have survived so many seasons of injustice and malice only to end up more perfectly entrapped by daft consanguinity than any menace Aldrich might have imagined from the outside! Oh, the unlawful predeterminates of heredity! The madness of some people's families that always came round to collect . . . !

Aldrich thought of killing Zebidiah. He banged his heels fiercely on the Mercedes' hood at the notion. But then for what purpose, finally? Even if he caused it to look like an accident, that made four of the dead instead of three orbiting the planet Aldrich. By then an inference of guilt so weighty that no one would bother to differentiate how extra dead came aboard anyhow. And it would do no good to try to dump Mugiani's body somewhere. Some brother police in Boston would doubtless know where the detective had gone; if not, his wife would know, for the four casserole dishes Zebidiah gorged on had to have come from the Mugiani kitchen. Nothing could be properly concealed: The nosy villagers of Inglenook would have seen the cop's car passing through. No matter what he did with car or corpse, the search for the missing detective would begin on the ruined plains of North Hollow. Hordes of policemen would show up, and with them, yarping and drooling, the legendary Vermont bloodhounds that nobody yet had ever conned into a full circle.

"I am heaped upon," Aldrich said out loud to no one in particular, staring west into the first tints of what would be a very red sunset. He considered suicide again for the first time since the year before on the day Richard Nixon resigned the presidency. Then its prospect had seemed a conclusive self-indictment, guaranteed to set the tongues a-clucking. Now it looked like blessed relief: He had no strength left to wage further wars on new fronts. His recent victory (survival) was pyrrhic at best; his first forthcoming adversary (the Law) had no corruptibility that was useful to him. He could not swim away from it, either: Danton Welsh needed five days to produce the up-front money he might use to flee the country beyond extradition; the police would be on him before then. . . .

So: He decided to kill himself. The decision, once taken, produced a surprising euphoria in Aldrich, tinged only by the disquieting realization that, in his case, there really was no one to consider getting even with. Still, relief was relief. . . . Thus close to his mortality he forgave everyone and even turned his largesse on batty Zebidiah whom he had always scorned. He slid off the hood of the Mercedes, walked over and sat down beside her, taking a plate and spooning some of Mugiani's bean salad and antipasto onto it. Zebidiah had not missed a bite.

"I'm sorry about the cop, Dwight David. The blackouts, you know . . ." she said through a mouthful of lasagna.

"It doesn't matter, Zebidiah. I've decided to kill myself. There's nothing much the police can do to a dead man."

"Is that an Aldrich I hear talkin'?" She turned to eye him with a recriminating glance: "You forgotten whose blood's flowin' in your veins, Dwight David? An Aldrich is never happier than when he's lockin' horns with the law . . ."

"This brigand family has got to come to an end somewhere, Zebidiah. It might as well be here in Vermont where it got started."

"That's profound, Dwight David. Very cyclic. You're a chickenshit. I say we take the cop 'n dump him car 'n all down the pond in my front yard 'n let the reign of terror go on. Your mother ain't goin' to like you killin' yourself like that."

"Good!" Aldrich spat, spewing a mouthful of beans across the table, suddenly delighting that he was getting even with someone, after all.

"How you goin' do it, Dwight David? This is good Eye-talian food, ain't it? Are you goin' to crash your shiny new car over a cliff into the ocean like on the telly-vision?"

"I'll use my rifle, I suppose. I'll just blow my brains out, that's all."

Zebidiah spooned herself some of the lobster Fra Diavolo, then as an afterthought put some on Aldrich's plate.

"A rifle's messy. You won't look good in your coffin with the top of your head blown off. They'll have to bury you in a huntin' cap or somethin' . . ."

"There's nothing to worry about, Zebidiah. No one would come to my viewing anyhow," Aldrich mourned. Then he decided to squelch the habit of self-pity for good and all on the last day of his life and go out like a blazing comet: "Fuck it! We've got to look at the bright side of things. It's the state that'll incur the burial costs. Dead or alive it always feels good to get something for nothing."

"Spoken like an Aldrich, Dwight David! You'll make this family proud yet. Here, have some of this good wine to celebrate your goin' to see Jesus. Life on this earth's a misery for sure, but a few happy accidents like fermentation have happened to help it along. Here, drink up!"

The Chianti made Aldrich instantly light-headed: "Hey, Zebidiah, do you want to dance?"

"Dance, Dwight David? You want to dance with your poor old aunt? Lord, how you've changed! You 'n me've missed a lot of fun we coulda had together in the past six years. It's too bad you didn't decide to kill yourself more often. It seems to do somethin' agreeable to your personality."

"I guess I could have done it all differently," Aldrich said, not really knowing what he meant. He stood and walked to the Mercedes and dialed a Burlington FM station on the radio, turning it up to full volume. The languid summer music of Vermont that all the stations played in maddening conspiracy crept sinuously into North Hollow in the midst of a brilliant sunset. Zebidiah bolted a last spoonful of lasagna, then stood up from the table, straightening her Victorian two-piece suit, rearranging the pine cones and ribbons in her hair. Aldrich took her in his arms, determinedly oblivious of her smell, and they waltzed in the old style about the beaten-down circle of meadow before the pro hut, Zebidiah's long skirt swirling in wide graceful arcs. They were a splendidly graceful dancing couple, Aldrich thought as he waltzed along. Anyone seeing them would agree. Unabashed tears of joy roared down Aldrich's face: It was the happiest he had ever been. It would hurt for just one blinding moment when he blew the top of his head off, but then he would cross into a new universe where beleaguerment was unknown. One thing though: He resolved he would not speak to either Lydia or Charlie in Eternity. Not even if they came to him crawling. . . .

They continued dancing through three or four station breaks and the sun continued its descent. Aldrich and Zebidiah danced close and very slowly now, holding each other tightly, until Zebidiah complained of hunger and went back to her place at the table to eat. Aldrich uncorked the other bottle of Chianti and stretched out on the hood of the Mercedes again, watching the last quarter of the orb of sun slip behind the mountains to the west and swigging on the wine. His mind was elaborately clear now. He felt exalted by the realization that for the first time in his life he hated absolutely no one.

In time, when Zebidiah had eaten the lasagna, half the manicotti, all of the bean salad, a good bit of the antipasto and enough lobster Fra Diavolo for four people, to say nothing of a full bottle of Chianti and half a magnum of champagne, she began to burp and stir. She circled the Mercedes a number of times, sweeping its flanks with her swirling Victorian skirts, again arranging her ugly old hair with its festoons of pine cones and ribbons in the side mirror, then got down to the serious business of confronting Aldrich.

"Mr. Stanton, why did you do what you did to me? Jiltin' me like that?"

"I don't know." Aldrich smiled at her. "Probably because I foresaw what an awful old crone you were going to turn into, my sweet old great-aunt lover . . ."

He was not at all surprised or even caring when sh

whipped out the Derringer and plugged him smack in the forehead the way she had done to Pasquale Mugiani.

The lights went out for Dwight David Aldrich and the sun finally set that Vermont day on the sight of crazy Zebidiah circling the Mercedes time and again admiring her spurned beauty in its deeply polished flanks.

S5